Born in Mexico City, Mexico in 1966 and nourished in the bosom of a big loving family, Ricardo Lebrija grew up to become a chemical and sound engineer, prompting a 25-year career in radio and television producing, directing, writing, and performing. As an avid traveller and connoisseur of human relations, Ricardo has had the privilege of discovering the world first-hand, knocking elbows with countless cultures and experiencing the joy of being in places imagined only in dreams.

He lives in Los Angeles, California, where he still searches for that elusive love, that glimpse of heaven, that spark that fills your heart with the fire that makes life worth living.

Ricardo Lebrija

THE LAST EPITAPH

AUSTIN MACAULEY PUBLISHERS™
LONDON • CAMBRIDGE • NEW YORK • SHARJAH

Copyright © Ricardo Lebrija 2023

The right of Ricardo Lebrija to be identified as author of this work has been asserted by the author in accordance with sections 77 and 78 of the Copyright, Designs and Patents Act 1988.

All rights reserved. No part of this publication may be reproduced, stored in a retrieval system, or transmitted in any form or by any means, electronic, mechanical, photocopying, recording, or otherwise, without the prior permission of the publishers.

Any person who commits any unauthorised act in relation to this publication may be liable to criminal prosecution and civil claims for damages.

This is a work of fiction. Names, characters, businesses, places, events, locales, and incidents are either the products of the author's imagination or used in a fictitious manner. Any resemblance to actual persons, living or dead, or actual events is purely coincidental.

A CIP catalogue record for this title is available from the British Library.

ISBN 9781398457928 (Paperback)
ISBN 9781398457935 (Hardback)
ISBN 9781398457959 (ePub e-book)
ISBN 9781398457942 (Audiobook)

www.austinmacauley.com

First Published 2023
Austin Macauley Publishers Ltd®
1 Canada Square
Canary Wharf
London
E14 5AA

Chapter 1
A Prophet's Tale

By the year 2050, half of the population of the world was Muslim and that tendency only grew by the end of 2075. Islam had spread out from the Middle East to almost every corner of the world and even the most religiously traditional countries fell to its temptation. The plagues that devastated the world in the beginning of the 21st Century, had driven people to shelter in the belief of some higher power that controlled their destiny, that was punishing them for their bad deeds. Islam had a lot of answers when other religions, that fell behind with the changing times, couldn't offer.

A new order of things was brewing thru Islam, it was a new type of socialism ingrained in religion, opposing the anti-secular sentiment that socialism was based on, but it did follow the Marxist views on social ownership and absolute government. Basically, the religion controlled all areas of social interaction, government, religion, international affairs, judicial control and even family interaction. It provided a haven for those looking for a new social revolution, a change from the establishment that had ruled for centuries.

Capitalism had reached a pinnacle, the explosion of technological advances had generated a dependency, everyone had to own the latest gadgets to stay on track within the system. This tech craze filled the void people felt as they isolated themselves more and more from other people, they struggled to make ends meet and afford everything they thought they needed to survive. All of these was happening as a very small and select group accumulated all the wealth. This dependency was exploited by the tech and service companies that supplied what was craved, but the great majority couldn't keep up.

The work force became less and less manual and the traditional jobs were replaced by technology related ones, or displaced by robots and machines. Jobs became scarce and unemployment rates skyrocketed. Industries that were the pinnacle of society went bankrupt and new tech companies and start-ups took over. The social divide grew more and more evident as homelessness became an everyday thing. More and more people lost all hope and all possibility to keep up with what the elite considered a standard of living. The gap between social structures raptured into an abyss that couldn't be filled and there was no will to do that by the ones that were lucky enough to control the balance. Two separate realities unfolded, two completely different worlds both happening simultaneously, which opened the door to change, to revolution. The ones that were abandoned were easy targets for Islam and its teachings, its secular divide.

The age of automation was born and with it, society distanced itself more and more from nature, from the reality that surrounded them. Everything became digital, life was lived on the web, inside machines that sucked everything from the users, making humans less unique. Food became more and more expensive, less and less available. Living in a huge metropolis became almost impossible, unattainable, unaffordable. Poverty became more ingrained in every country around the world, homelessness was a mayor social issue as millions of people struggled to get by, to survive, as the social divide grew wider and wider.

People, slowly, started leaving the big cities and moving to farms in rural areas, working the fields, raising their own stock, growing their own crops, looking for means to survive on their own. Moving away from a system that provided everything they wanted, but nothing they needed, detaching themselves from the machine that held them captive, disconnecting from the web, from consumerism, from that endless craving that made humans a client from the system. A race of superficiality that valued possessions and elite status over decency, honor, empathy…human values that lacked substance in their tech world.

Money became meaningless, after a while, crypto currencies soared and flooded the web with so many options that "currency" lost its meaning, consumers went back to trading, the whole system failed when people stopped yearning for all those things that only made their lives more complicated, consumerism dropped, people only cared about feeding their own, about surviving.

Capitalism was sentenced by then, people were tired of trying to catch up, catch up to the ever shrinking number of rich people that ruled their lives, that controlled the governments, that managed every little part of their worlds. They began waking up to the fact that money couldn't overpower their numbers, when the most valuable commodity became something people could actually get on their own: food, and the most valuable asset they could own: each other.

Tables turned on the wealthy, their money couldn't buy them power anymore. A new power structure was birth from the most essential commodity, food. The ones that controlled the supply of it became the new masters. Wealth was measured by the amount of food you could store, the amount of goods you could trade.

At the end of the twentieth century, the Catholic Church had gone thru a crisis of faith and many of its followers were seduced by what Islam had to offer, its power around the globe was diminished by the rising sex scandals and by the middle of the twenty first century, millions of adepts separated from the Catholic faith, feeling disappointed with the hypocrisy and the double standard the church lived by. The largest religion in the world crumbled, aided by the impossibility to justify a wave of viruses that ravished the world, the impossibility to explain why God had allowed this to happen, allowed so many people to die in vain, to warrant the loss of life of so many faithful good Catholics.

Hundreds of new definitions of Christianity arouse, that separated from the Roman Church and formed their own faith. The Pope lost most of its power and credibility, after everything settled, the most powerful figure in history, couldn't do a thing to stop the spread of Islam and counter the logic that the always accommodating teaching of Mohamed brought to a thirsty congregation.

The expansion and reach of Islam was not only limited to religion, its doctrine spread like wild fire across every social structure and seduced everyone eager for social equality and change. It was not only a religious discrepancy that separated communities, families, it was also a cultural struggle that brew after years of conflict, of social unsettle around the world, a lot of it brought over by the cultural disparity and the economic divide, but also by the lack of guidance during a futile time of change.

People were tired and afraid of government control, corruption, greed and demanded a fare system that would give everybody the same opportunities, the same chance. A system that would promise the safety they felt lacked. Islam offered a way to find common ground, a way to end the uncertainty, a way of detaching themselves from material possessions while still retaining control of the lives of everyone around them, well…at least for the men.

Throwing back hundreds of years of social advances in human rights, going back to the system of power thru subjugation. The law of the strongest one. Fear became a powerful tool of control and freedom slowly got crushed under it. Giving room for the substitution of family, for a feudal structure.

Entire families, communities, towns were convinced of that promise and then, got caught up in the frenzy of a system that favored men and gave them the power that intoxicates, the power to control their own little worlds, subjugate the women, the children, the elder in their families, to become tyrants in their own right.

In the Muslim world, governments were replaced by religious authoritarian regimes and sharia law was imposed as a means of social control. Social progress was set back a thousand years: women lost every right they had fought for, for so long; homosexuality was forbidden, punishable by death; private property disappeared and identity was lost in a sea of burqa.

Africa was the first continent to fall to the "Conversion", as they called it. The continent was always tainted by Islam and was the platform and test ground for what was about to come. South East Asia followed and then, one by one the rest of the countries in the world got swarmed by strategic forces that would convince angry, disappointed people that Islam was the way to subjugate their oppressors, the system that had fail them miserably for years.

It was the end of Capitalism and the rise to power for the leaders of Islam. One, above all, became the spiritual leader of the Muslim World: "Almasih al'azraq"/ "The Blue Messiah".

He was considered a deity born in this world. Surely the Blue Messiah became the nemesis of the Free World; his power grew stronger as more and more adepts joined his ranks. The Blue Messiah would become, the way to get to Paradise. His word was not just heard, it was practiced and imposed.

China and India gave the Muslims an advantage over the free world, by then, those two countries, represented half of the world population. After converting the African continent, Islam centered on them. Once they had succeeded, all the other religions were the minority on the planet. Islamic regimes used that advantage to send "infiltrators" to every non-Muslim place around the globe and spread the word, following the same path Catholicism did in the sixteenth century, but this time the spread was unstoppable, faster.

Europe held on for a long time. Democratic governments struggled for years to keep composure and hold on to the way of life they knew, but like an infection that spreads slowly, but surely, Islam took over people's minds and governments fell, one by one, until the whole continent was lost. It started in the weakest countries, the ones that struggled the most: Greece, Spain and the ravished countries of Eastern Europe and slowly took over the rest. It spread thru Syria and Turkey, up the Mediterranean Sea until it reached as north as Finland.

Only a few countries in the world were able to isolate themselves and protect their faith, their beliefs, their culture and the rights of people to live their lives the way they decided to and not under the ever controlling tunics of Islam that made everyone prevalent and that took from women their right to be unique.

The American continent persisted as the largest bastion of freedom and democracy in the world. Millions of people migrated here from all over, escaping, from what they believe to be: the doom of humanity. From subjugation that turned people into pawns.

The few that hanged on to their principles, nurtured for centuries, flee to the Free World, including what was left of the Catholic Church that ended up moving their home to Mexico, that remained faithful till then and harbored refugees from all over the globe, from every corner of the world, from every creed, color or belief. With one common denominator…freedom!

Even the United States of America fell under this pretense. After the great earthquake of 2070, that parted the country in two and killed millions of people, plunging hundreds of cities under the sea and saw millions more perish in the aftermath, everything failed in America. The people held the government responsible for not preparing appropriately for the disaster, for the loss of life caused by it and most of all, for the greed and mismanagement of resources that could have been better applied in preventing such a tragedy, or at lest, foreseeing it. It was foretold by scientists for years, seen by fortune tellers, predicted by gurus, but still, as human nature does, ignored and dismissed by authorities and leaders as something that wasn't an immediate threat, something that would be left for the next administration to deal with.

The constant abuse of Mother Earth was believed to be the main reason, fracking, underground nuclear testing, excessive mine exploration, global warming; they all contributed greatly to the collapse of the San Andreas fault. Ultimately what was left of the country divided into independent states that established their own form of government. Texas finally became an independent country, as it sought to be for centuries and other ones joined in the trend.

Some of these states slowly got tempted by the new world order and opted to join the "Conversion", and became Muslim. Everyone else that didn't agree with those ideas, joined a coalition of other countries in Central and South

America, forming the American Union, or, how people liked to call it: The Free World.

By 2100, the tension between this two opposite sides became unstable, there was no diplomacy between the two. There was no possible agreement, the Muslim side wouldn't concede anything, their position was extreme. Their mission was to convert every living soul to Islam, or see them pay the ultimate price.

The Muslims saw the "Infidels" as opposers of their truth. Two very distinctive sides delimited the world, the Muslim and the Free World. As the separation, between the two, grew stronger, the hatred grew with it. That's when things got out of hand, when the violence between brothers began. The terrorist attacks spawned all over the Free World like wild fire. At first they were condemned and satanized, but eventually, they were answered with the same violence they professed.

Different religions gathered together in harmony in the Free World and tried to convince "The Others" of the righteous path, naming Islam as the opposite side. Those became the two opposing forces in this war, Islam vs the Free World. "The Others" were all the people who had converted to Islam, a religion they weren't born into. These prompted the new inquisition commanded by Pope Gregory X from the Catholic faith, Rebbe Mosses Karo from the Jewish, Guru Gobind from the Sikh and several other leaders from different religions that gathered in the Free World, to try to push back on Islam.

What started out as a good will mission to en-lighten the "Converted", soon became a witch hunt that quickly escalated into violence. It was like the inquisition, all over again, but this time both sides were doing the cleansing.

Brothers killing brothers, humans hunting other humans for their beliefs, on both sides; it became vicious, almost animalistic. There was no morality, no respect for human rights, everything was fare under God's eyes. Both sides believed they were doing God's work, they believed they were righteous and that gave them permission to do horrible things. God was witness as men took his name in vain and justified the evilest actions for his glory, all on his name. An eye for an eye, left everyone blind.

Tensions only grew bitter, over the years, until there was nothing left to talk about and war broke, a global war. At first it was a war of ideology between the two commanding groups that represented each side: The Free World, represented by a Union, of sorts, from every religion in it, on one side and the Islam Coalition, on the other, lead by the Blue Messiah, but this fight quickly became a religious war. The "Great War" as we call it now.

The American Union managed to keep the fight outside of its borders, pushing the Muslims into their occupied territories. Taking the war to their doorstep, attacking the Middle East directly, trying to annihilate the Blue Messiah, but nothing worked. Stories about the death of the Blue Messiah became major news, videos of his mangled body surfaced all over the web, just to be debunked by his live appearances to discredit the claims. People began to believe that he was unkillable, that he was actually a God.

After a few years, the "Great War" had left over a billion people dead, of all creeds and colors. There was no discrimination. As in every war, technological advances were made and new weapons were developed on both sides. Nuclear weapons were eradicated before the war broke up, world leaders, at the time, thought that it would, for ever, free the world from destroying itself, but they were wrong.

Humans, we seem to have this urge for killing, it drives us mad to the point of numbness. To the point of ignoring the most precious gift we can have, life. Mad men will make up any excuse to satisfy their thirst for power, for control, for killing. The one sided craze that leaves you blind to the empathy needed to concede, to see things through your brothers eyes.

After the disarmament, it was too expensive to go back to nuclear technology, so the machinery figured out different ways to kill large number of people at once. New chemical weapons were developed: nerve agents, blister agents, choking agents, blood agents…until they found a way to develop bacteria, fungi, parasites and viruses, genetically modified to achieve the unthinkable. Flesh eating bacteria, paralyzing fungi, nano imploding parasites and finally molecular targeted viruses, or MTV's. They were the perfect weapon, silent, undetectable and deadly.

MTV's were used all over the world to subjugate the enemy. They were first developed in the Free World as secret projects. They weren't sanctioned by their leaders, they were the love child of bitter minds that sought to annihilate the evil they saw spreading all around, without considering the consequences, without realizing the wickedness of their ways, the doom they were inciting.

Like it happens every time in warfare, MTV's were copied by the other side and used on them. The killing was massive, the loss of life unreal. The weapons had done its dead, but the creations then turned on their creators, they took a life of their own, mutated and transformed so rapidly, they couldn't be contained and the outbreak began.

Massive graves were used to dump the bodies that pilled as high as the sky. The stench of death became something normal, it dominated the senses, everyone became accustomed to it. Graveyards were everywhere, the earth was poisoned and food was scarce. Disease spread quickly, there was too much blood and decomposing flesh for nature to follow its normal path, microorganisms fed freely on this perfect breading ground, the monstrosities created evolved faster than our technology could and aggressive flesh eating viruses consumed everything in their path. Not only dead tissue, but alive too.

It was as if nature was trying to get rid of humans, cash in all the wrongdoings committed against her. Natural selection targeting us for extinction. Mutated viruses attacked the essence of the human spirit, they targeted the reproduction system and humans gradually lost the ability to reproduce. Births were fewer and fewer and the ones that occurred gave life to infertile babies, a whole generation of sterile children plagued the earth and after a while it became a grim place. Children disappeared from the picture, laughter with them and everything became sad and stern.

Bacteria spread everywhere too, people infected died within a couple of days from first signs of infection, too soon for scientist to figure out how to stop it. The only thing that helped was isolation and the only thing that seem to hold the spread was fire. Hughe bonfires were seen all over the world, controlled flames that burned the bodies infected with disease. Smoke clouded the skies that mellowed with distain, sunrises and sunsets mutated into on/off switches that gave room to day and night with the sparks contrasting the skies from the fires that burned tirelessly.

The outbreak started in the front lines, somewhere in the Middle East, and before a year had passed it took over Europe, Africa, Oceania and Asia. America was the only continent that was able to contain the spread. So the American Union became our fortress and our prison from the rest of the world that was slowly dying, right in front of our eyes, despite every effort done to save it.

The greatest threat was infection, so to protect the humans left inside, in the so called: "Safety Zone", we isolated ourselves inside a wall of fire that separated us from the rest of the world, the dying world, "The Wasteland" as it was deemed. The firewall, that kept us safe, spread over three thousand miles to the north, from coast to coast and reached the heavens incinerating everything that came in touch with it: people, animals, vehicles. The firewall used oxy-hydrogen technology and it burned at over six thousand degrees Fahrenheit.

Flames shooting up into the sky, spawning a rainbow of colors, as it burned the atmosphere in its path, ever changing, oscillating rhythmically like the waves on the ocean. It was a beautiful sight. It was one of the deadliest things ever conceived, but in its grain you could find beauty. The blueish colored flames that shot into the sky were met by the dark void outside our atmosphere and the ever changing nature of the flames made the wall seem like a living being that guarded the lucky ones inside from the dangers on the outside.

It emitted a hypnotizing buzzing sound, that was actually intoxicating. Except when something tried to cross its threshold, whatever it was, got instantly incinerated making a large explosion, like an electric discharge. From the distance it sounded like one of those electric bug zappers, but there was no trace of whoever, or whatever tried to cross.

There was constant surveillance over the seas that surrounded us, a sophisticated radar network would detect any vessel approaching our coasts and it was dealt with swiftly and definitely. It was a perfect system and kept us safe from infection for decades.

Slowly threats subsided and movement outside the wall and over the seas ceased. We all assumed that everyone, beyond our borders, had perished. It was a grim thought, but somehow comforted us, made us feel better. Empathy was restricted to the ones we knew, the ones that were close. The people left outside of the "Safety Zone" were stricken out of the vocabulary and rarely mentioned ever. As if their mention would, somehow, made them appear out of nowhere.

By then, religion had been replaced by this sense of self, we felt abandoned by our God, any God that claimed to care or love us, any God that had allowed this to happen, any God that wouldn't show mercy to anyone who worshiped him and ended up dying a terrible death.

Faith was placed on humanity and our part in the Universe, we were alone, as we have always been and the only real thing we had, was each other. So we worshiped each other, we held the ones we loved close, lived our lives in harmony, embracing the gifts we had every day and giving thanks to life every morning when our eyes opened, when we realised that we had one more day to go on…

We cherished peace, most of all, that thing we lacked for so many years. Human interaction became the backbone of our society. Complacency became the only form of flattering, everyone was valuable and served a function in society. It seemed that our programming had changed by a hard reset and bad thoughts were erased from the hard drive in our brains.

Scientists tried for decades to reverse the damage done to our genes, tried to give back the gift of life to humanity. There were a few trials that succeeded, but we were too few to count. I was one of them, one of those miracle babies conceived in a lab by cheating nature, by modifying chromosomes and genetically engineering DNA.

My name is Patrick Jarborn and I was conceived in a test tube, hence my last name "Jar-born", the only father I knew were the scientists that concocted me and the only mother, the nurse that adopted me as his own and cared for me, the few years she was allowed to live, her name was Gloria.

All the other miracles that came before me and after, died young and me? I was sentenced to death since birth. Every scientist agreed that I would be dead by three…by five…by eight…by twelve, but I was still growing, like a normal child would have. Scientist were baffled and experimented on me almost every day. I was conceived to be an experiment, and as such, I was treated as one. Except for Gloria, she was as close as you could get to a real mother. From her I learned to care, to love, empathy and grace. I loved her back, as much as she did. She was my human connection, the scientists that experimented on me were distant, to say the least, they had to. I don't blame them for that, I understood what their job was, what they were trying to achieve and generating a bond between us would have resulted in failure of their purpose.

My life was spent inside the confinement of four walls and the few glimpses of light I caught every time they allowed me to wonder around in the library, that was next to my room. It was a beautiful hall with millions of books, a sort of homage to the history of humanity. It had a huge dome on top of it where I could get natural light, feel the sun rays plunging down on me, slightly burning my face with its tingling healing power. I could see the clouds up above and the blue void that coloured my otherwise grey environment. That was where I learned about the history of the world before me, where I was allowed to experience the way people lived before "The Great War", before humanity was marked for extinction.

My brain was active, same as of any child, thirsty to learn everything. I read and that mitigated the absence of a life, like the ones I read in books. Books that filled the library from floor to ceiling and knowledge from dusk till dawn. They were the essence of my life, they gave me reason and hope. Every time I immersed myself into their pages, I was transported to another place, in another time, surrounded by characters that played the part of my friends, my mentors, my family.

I was happy there, amongst the pages that gave me life, hope beyond my prison that inspired me to dream about every little detail I captured in those books. Places that I longed to see and be in: about forests filled with trees that painted the fields with a beautiful array of colours, that oxygenated the air and perfumed it with a thousand different smells; about mountains that towered high reaching the clouds above, that extended for miles, as far as the eye could see; about waterfalls that saturated the air with mist that dripped down your cheeks, water that fell freely from hundreds of feet above exploding into a thunderous constant scream; about rivers and lakes from which nature spawned, from which life aroused uncontained; about the sea that limited everything, that blended with the horizon making it never-ending; about the sand that trickles between your toes, that sticks to every part of your body, hugging it close; about animals that roamed the earth, that flew suspended in the sky, that swam underwater. Dreams of a world far beyond my reach, my imagination, that was limited to what I had been shown, beyond the grey scale I lived in.

Places that only lived between those pages, in images, photographs that, to me, were windows to a magical world which took form in my imagination, that kept prancing around, seducing me, enticing me, filling my heart with excitement. Places that now lived in the history books I loved to read, memories of civilisations long gone, of cities that had disappeared from the face of the earth, devastated during the war: temples brought down by ignorance, by hate, skyscrapers destroyed by greed, entire cities decimated by envy.

I used to close my eyes and imagine I was there: Sailing the Nile in Egypt, approaching Giza, with its majestic Pyramids and effigies, Luxor, with its incredible temples and "The Valley of the Kings" that defined the power of one of the greatest ancient civilisations; Sail down the coast of Greece, visit "The Parthenon" and stood where Aristotle preached; Stand in the middle of the "Colosseum", in Rome, cradle of "The Roman Empire" that spawned the world as they knew it then, visit "The Vatican" and experience the marvellous age of renaissance, that its faith brought, "The Sixteenth Chappell" and the "St Peter's Basilica", watch a game of "Calcio", a sport that later invaded the whole world and was known as "Football"; Roam the French Riviera, along the

Mediterranean Sea, wander around the amazing castles that lined the Loire River, go to Paris, "The City of Lights" and dine in some of the most famous restaurants ever conceived by human ingenuity, wander through the halls of "The Louvre" and its vast collection of art that reflected through all the photographs I watched over and over again; Visit London and its gorgeous skyline, mix of old and new buildings, "The London Bridge", "The Tower of London" and party in "Piccadilly", eat some fish and chips, with a Guinness in one of the pubs there; Travel to New York City, walk down "Fifth Avenue" and along "Central Park", catch a play in Broadway and eat some pretzels from the vendors out on the street and so many other magical places with millions of people filling them up, alive with energy, lights buzzing endlessly night and day.

Most of those places were destroyed during the war; devastated, buildings levelled, museums burnt, memories erased from history. Some of the art was saved, stolen and brought here, to the Free World, to be kept as a legacy for humanity. Muslims didn't have respect for others peoples beliefs, their mission was to erase every trace of the others faiths, every memory of another god, that wasn't Ala. So they destroyed temples of faith that stood for thousands of years and replaced them with mosques that stood on top of the rubble. They destroyed most of the historic buildings, or used them up for housing or official service, vanishing every trace of what was there before. That was the cleansing that took over, not just the physical killing, but the decimation of the mind. Destroying every trace of culture, of history that were the back bone of western civilisation.

The command of "The Blue Messiah" was to extinguish every trace of the infidel. To destroy its substance and every trace of their existence. So, there was no room for museums, statues, monuments or anything that would remind people of the past. We wanted to erase every trace of history, except their own. His empire grew from the Middle East and its culture appropriated the world, where ever Islam was practiced and preached.

Gloria used to tell me stories about her life on the outside, about her family growing up, about her childhood spent on a farm, raising cattle and harvesting the food her own mother brought to the table every day. About the love of her life, that was my favourite one. She must have told me that story a thousand times, nine hundred and ninety nine, requested by me. It made her happy every time and so, I was happy to hear it, happy to see her eyes filled up with tears, as the images flooded her memory. She use to hold me and cry when she was finished and I would cry with her, sharing that sentiment that squeezed my heart. It was enough to share, enough sentiment to convey this sorrow that invaded me.

I didn't know what love was, at least, not the way that she fathomed in her stories. I loved her, she was my mother, I cared for her and felt a deep connection to her, but I didn't feel all those things she expressed so vividly in her tales. She talked about love as if it were air that you breath, that you need to survive, that enters your body and fills it up with life, that roams your every nook and entices it, that makes your body crawl with excitement, your skin yearn to be touched, that arouses desires. I could only imagine what it would be like.

Every time I read about it in a book, I pictured what Gloria talked about, her experiences that she shared with me. Something came over me when I read about it, about love. I yearned to feel that excitement, that arousal that was mentioned so much when two bodies entangle, when they are so close.

For me, that world she talked about, the same world I learned about on all those books that nurtured me, was gone. It was just a reminder of what used to be, the past. A past long gone after everything that had happened. It was a world that I visited, every time I went into the library. I, somehow, kept it alive by reading about it. There were many who fought and gave their lives to preserve the legacy, to keep history untarnished. They hoarded books, paintings, sculptures, photographs, files, everything they could get their hands on and brought it to the "Free World". Hid it out of the reach of the "Blue Messiah" for as long as they could. Still a lot was destroyed, but the memories of it remained. I had bathe in that sea all my life, in the sea of knowledge that was kept in that library.

I ate the food I was given three times a day, a gooey mixture of proteins and carbohydrates that kept me nourished, I got used to the taste, I didn't have anything to compare it too, but every time I had a bite I wondered about the different types of foods I saw on those pages I visited. Dishes that broadened my senses and enticed my taste, my thirst to learn more all the time, to experiment. The taste, that had to be different from the one this "food" they gave me had. I couldn't find all those comfort feelings described on every book I read, when people ate and simply marvelled at what they were tasting. The fruits and vegetables portrayed on those images, the meats, the fancy plates explained inside the cook books, concocted with hundreds of spices and ingredients I dreamed of tasting. Like "bacon" that seemed to jump out of those pages, my mouth just watered at the idea, at the notion of experiencing the feeling the writers tried to explain so vividly.

In my mind, it was all a dream, everything that was written in those books I loved to read. The images I reviewed over and over again, learning every little detail of them. It was all in my head, like a memory that you don't really remember, like a ghost that lingers inside your head. It only became real when I heard it from Gloria's lips, her stories made it real. Every time she sat down and started to open up about her life, it gave my dreams substance and my memories form.

"Come Patrick, sit next to me. Bring that book you love so much" Gloria said, while her hand padded softly next to her on the couch.

I smiled, grabbed the book from the shelf and walked to where she was. I stood in front of her, handed her the book and said: "But you have to read it to me this time, I like it better that way."

"Only if you promise to not fall asleep until I finish reading it," she said.

I smiled and nodded. She smiled back, grabbed the book from my hands and I sat next to her.

She started reading…

I loved to hear her voice, she turned anything she read into reality. Images just appeared in front of my eyes as she described every word, which made my imagination fly, go wild picturing everything 'till the last detail.

She would spend a few hours with me every day, that was as much as she was aloud too, she used to fantasise about taking me out for a walk, out there, in the world. See the sun and the sky, and everything I yearned to see, but somehow we both knew it was just a fantasy. They didn't want me to turn into a normal child, they wanted me to stay an experiment.

So the days went on and my life went on too. They kept experimenting on me, taking pieces of my body for testing, connecting me to machines that would scan my brain, my organs, my body functions. Extracting blood and fluids from me, every day, expecting changes to happen, expecting something to develop differently.

Gloria finished reading the book, placed it down on the table next to the couch and said: "Well, I hope you enjoyed that."

"I always do, somehow it seems different every time. Would you read me another one?" I asked.

She smiled tenderly and answered: "I would love too, Patrick, but you know the rules."

"I know, I just wanted to see if maybe…" I said sadly.

Gloria got close and embraced me tenderly. I could feel her heartbeat kissing my ears, hugging me, loving me.

"Oh Patrick! One day, I promise!" she said, as she walked out of the room, not before looking back and smiling at me.

We both stayed there, for a moment, staring at each other. I wanted to remember her, remember this feeling that she aroused in me, this yearning I had for her touch, for her coddle. She looked at me, the same way she always did, as if it were the last time she ever did. It was a mixture of love and sadness, I knew that she wanted a different faith for me, but she was bound by her work, by her masters that controlled our interaction and saw and analysed every single second of our encounters.

I knew where she was coming from, what she was bound to, what she was forced to feel, but I didn't felt that way, I was alive and I just couldn't see myself as a casualty. I was aware that I could die at any moment, during any of those experiments they subjected me to, but I just couldn't accept that as my faith either, I knew that she didn't. Maybe she did, at the beginning, but not now.

Life was a gift I got to experience every single day. That was the only way to see it, when every day could be your last, when your life is subject to a whim, when your life expectancy is so short, that darkness becomes a prelude to the end and your eyelids fall, only forced by fatigue, like the curtain falls at the end of a show, marking the final chapter of an announced death.

The door closed behind her, as she left the room and the lights started dimming, which meant that it was time for me to fall asleep, but I was just too excited to close my eyes, as I was every night. So, I pretended, the reality is that I was always fantasising and didn't really wanted to stop. I didn't wanted it to end, my life. So I struggled to stay awake as much as I could, make the day, the moment last as long as I could, until my eyelids couldn't hold any longer.

I used to spend hours awake, with my eyes opened, dreaming of being in faraway lands, meeting people, like Gloria, that would make me feel included, welcomed, loved. My mind was always going, it was always on, even in dreams, when I finally fell asleep. All those stories I read, the ones that Gloria fed me and the ones my mind created out of them or in spite of them. I had dreams of my own. Dreams of being in love, of experiencing the world as I read it in those books, as my mind interpreted them. Until the lights went up again, signalling the beginning of another chance.

And so, the days went by. I wasn't sure how old I was, Gloria use to celebrate my birthdays and, according to her, I had just turned sixteen. By then, I had already consumed a big part of that library, like locust feeding on page after page, book after book.

My body started going through normal changes for a boy my age, the books were the source where all my questions were answered and when there was something I didn't find in their pages, I always turned to Gloria for knowledge. At that point I started wondering about girls, I started to have this urges, when I saw photographs of girls in magazines that laid between all those books.

All those stories of love, that Gloria used to tell me, started to make sense. I haven't noticed women before, at least not the way I started to. I began to consume poetry as If I needed it to survive. I use to read to Gloria poems from Pablo Neruda, from Maya Angelou, from Emily Dickinson…

I became obsessed with love, but I only told Gloria about my frenzy, I knew that it would create a conflict with the scientists that studied me. They knew about the changes my body was going through, that was the focus of their investigation but, as far as I knew, the results weren't what they expected. My sperm was sterile, the DNA strains were not complete. Which meant that their experiments weren't working the way they expected them to. They couldn't explain how I was still alive, growing and developing, but they were hopeful that time would turn everything around.

The scientist were baffled, they were sure it would work. Dr Franklin, the head of the team, was the most concerned about the results. He had headed the research team since way before I was conceived. There had been numerous failures in the past and the fact that I had survived this long was a sign of things shifting. He couldn't understand why the result kept being negative.

I use to listen to the discussions they had between them, while I was lying in recovery, after each procedure.

"I can't understand why we are getting these results! Everything was perfect this time. There is no infection and the subject is healthy," Dr Franklin said, visibly frustrated.

"Maybe it's a matter of time, he's going through puberty, maybe the hormones would do the trick," Dr Garcia said.

Dr Franklin thought about it for a second, he scratched his head as he turned and looked at where I was. He nodded his head and said.

"We're running out of time, we can't wait forever."

"Just a little bit longer, I'm sure there will be a shift," Dr Homestead said.

Dr Franklin looked around at each one of the scientists on his team, then lowered his head and said.

"Unfortunately it's not up to us. If these doesn't work, we have to move in a different direction. Those are the guidelines."

An electric discharge roamed up and down my spine. I knew that was not good for me, If I wasn't useful to them, I might get discarded. They couldn't afford to set me free, allow me to just roam out there. I wasn't considered a person, I didn't have an identity or any bio whatsoever.

For the first time, I felt my life directly threatened, but I didn't show it. They couldn't know I was aware of the risk I was in. So I just acted normal, as if I wasn't aware, but this fear began to grow inside, a fear I didn't understand and couldn't control.

This terrible feeling that you are not wanted anymore, that you are just hindering. Maybe it was the fact that I was reaching maturity and began to have a deeper sense of awareness about subtle things like that. I wasn't sure, but it kept me on the edge.

They took me to my room and I laid there for a few hours wondering about what would happen next. The next day, Gloria visited me. I couldn't wait to tell her about it, poke her brain. I needed to know more. I trusted her, I knew she would be honest with me.

"Hi Patrick, how are you feeling today?" she said, as she walked into my room.

She was holding an open box with a few games we used to play with from time to time. Puzzles, board games, things like that.

I looked at the box and then I lifted up my eyes to look at her, she knew immediately there was something on my mind, so she asked: "What is it? What's wrong, Patrick?"

I opened up my eyes wide and moved them to the side, like pointing out of the room.

She smiled and touched my hand, while she said: "Don't worry about it, its fine, you can tell me anything. Nobodies listening."

I looked around the room, I had this paranoia I've never felt before, like I was being watched. It's funny how knowledge changes your perspective, the way you see life, the way you see people or places, the way you behave. I read somewhere: "Ignorance is bliss". Sometimes not knowing, is the best thing to know.

She saw my doubt, sat next to me and asked: "What is it? It's ok, you can tell me anything, you know that."

I did trust her, but I knew that there were things that were beyond her control, it wasn't just that I didn't want them to know I had heard their conversations, it was that telling her would put her at risk. So I thought about it for a second and lied.

"It's just that this time, the procedure hurt more than other times, I'm just a little bit scared."

Gloria smiled tenderly and began to rub my back as she said: "Do you want me to take a look? Does it still hurt? Maybe I can do something to mitigate the pain!"

I smiled and nodded, laid my head on her lap as she pulled my shirt up to look at the site where they had performed the biopsy.

"I see what you mean, it's still swollen! I'm going to clean it up and change the bandage. That will make you feel a lot better," she said.

"Could you scratch it a little bit? It's really itchy!" I said.

She looked at it closely and replied: "I don't think that's a good idea, Patrick, you'll irritate it more and it would only get worse."

She saw the disappointment in my face, smiled and said, while she caressed my face: "I can massage your shoulders! That always makes you feel better!"

I smiled and nodded. She stood up and brought some supplies to clean the wound. I laid flat on my back while she removed the bandages, it was a little bit painful, because they had ingrown and she had to pull them off; she cleaned it up, that burned a little, but it actually felt soothing; when she was finished, she placed a new bandage on top and rubbed my shoulders until I fell asleep.

She was the only person in this world that gave me peace, that cared for me. Sleep time was my own personal time. I use to dream a lot, I usually remembered my dreams when I woke up. Dreams of all the things I read on those books, things I experienced through the pages I read, they were so vivid in my head, that It actually felt like an experience more than a dream, but this time I experienced something I'd never experienced before.

Later I realised it had been a nightmare, for the first time I felt trapped inside my dream. Chased by someone or something I didn't knew. I experienced anguish, fear, desperation, sadness, feelings that clouded my head:

I was in the operation room and I could see doctors, I didn't recognised, operating on me, but this time my whole chest was wide open. I could see them pulling out organs, I could feel them pulling and pulling from the inside. As if I had lost air and breathing became harder each time they pulled something out, until It became almost impossible to breath, I was chocking, unable to gasp air.

They finally pulled my heart out from my chest…it was still beating as they severed the arteries that kept it hooked on to me and I felt my life slip away as I heard a loud steady beep announcing my demise. I felt my body plunging into an abyss and as I was about to fall into a dark hole, I saw her…looking at me from the next room, her eyes fixated on me, her whole expression was filled with sadness, with sorrow, tears were bursting out of her eyes, rolling down her cheeks, but even with her eyes swollen by her sadness, her face was enlightened by her beauty, her long black hair covered her shoulders and kept swerving down her arms and her chest until it vanished. As I was falling down, her hand opened waving goodbye as she disappeared into the dark…and then I woke up!

I was drenched in sweat, all alone in my room and all I could hear was the air flowing from the vent above my bed and everything was as it used to be. My heart was racing and my breath was faltering, gasping air as if it were my last breath. I realised what had happened and I started to calm down. My heart rate went back down and my breathing lull.

I realised that I had just experienced my first nightmare, I never had one before, I guess I wasn't aware of that side of life, of the darkness you can plunge into. I just lived this very steady life, until now, things were changing and I could feel it inside me. My subconscious was warning me of the dangers that lied ahead for me. Giving me a glimpse of what was to come. Warning me of the reality of my situation. There was nothing I could actually do about it because I didn't know exactly what they expected from me, what they were hoping to get and no way for me to force the result they wanted.

I calmed down until I felt my heartbeat and my breathing go back to normal. I kept my eyes closed, like pretending I was still sleeping, I didn't want anyone to notice what I've been through.

Routine kicked in and the day went by, as It normally did. Gloria visited me, in the afternoon. She read me a couple of stories and she made sure I had put on my jammies and was in bed before she left. I wasn't sure I wanted to close my eyes, I was a little bit afraid of going back to sleep, but I was tired and my eyelids had a mind of their own.

I was lying alone in the darkness of my room, only a very tenuous light illuminated the walls and the ceiling. It was my same room, the one I had lived in throughout my whole life, nothing had changed, except this anguish that invaded me, my brain that didn't want to give up.

I had this feeling, this kind of premonition, that something bad was about to happen. It was just a feeling, but it affected me enough to spook my sleep beyond my comprehension. My body was tired and wanted to rest, but my mind was running around thinking. Thinking about anything other than that, so to keep attention away from the nightmare, but her face kept appearing, between thoughts, the face of that girl that looked at me tenderly as I fell into oblivion. Her eyes fixated on mine, her smile grabbing my wit, tempting it, making me forget for a second, all that was happening, like a life vest you grab onto just before drowning, that thing that will save you.

I couldn't get her out of my mind, she kept me sane and away from the bad thoughts that wanted to consume me. It was a safe space that aroused from looking into her eyes, those beautiful blue eyes that seemed like glowing sticks between so much darkness. The light they shot gave me warmth and filtered all the bad thoughts that clouded my head.

The night went by and I hardly slept, just a few flashes her and there. The next morning started with an usual silence, I was surprised to see the hours go by without anyone coming to get me, the usual routine had me in the lab by then, but I couldn't hear anything beyond my door, not a peep for hours. Not even my usual breakfast, or lunch.

I tried to keep my mind busy, reading. I didn't want to think bad thoughts, but I just couldn't help it. It was very unusual, this had never happened before, so I didn't know what to think. Was I still sleeping? Was this another nightmare?

I kept getting up and walking to the door, placing my ear against it trying to get some clues as to what was going on out there. There was no handle on my side of the door, so I couldn't even try to open it up. For the first time, I felt trapped inside my own room, the room that had been my home for so many years, my solace, now it felt like a prison. This little tiny space was my world, where

I've spent all my life. The only thing I knew and I had learned to feel safe inside of it. It was the space where I spent my happy time, where I spent time with Gloria and the stories that formed my whole existence, but for the first time I actually felt trapped.

I kept reading trying to get my mind off what was happening, it was a couple of hours after that, when I heard the door opening up from the outside. I jumped off the bed and stood at the other side of the door, I didn't knew what to expect, It was uncertainty that kept me alert.

Chapter 2
The Escape

The door opened…Gloria was on the other side. She opened the door slowly and as soon as I could see her, she put her finger over her lips, asking me to keep silent. She tiptoed into the room and pulled me to the side, next to the door, against the wall. She got close and whispered: "Patrick, I can't explain now, but you have to come with me!"

I looked at her baffled, I didn't understand what she was asking of me. She looked into my eyes, she could see the confusion in my head. The uncertainty tainting my thoughts. I wasn't used to going off script, my life had never changed in all the years I have been in here. To my recollection, this was the first time ever that my schedule had changed in any way.

"You trust me, don't you?" she whispered.

I nodded and looked into her eyes, I could see fear in them, but also something I had never seen before…

"Grab my hand, don't let go, no matter what you see!" she asked, trembling.

I stood there for a moment, doubting. She grabbed my face with her hand and asked again: "You trust me, don't you?"

I nodded and she grabbed my hand, she squeezed hard and I held on to hers.

We walked outside my room, through the corridors that led to it, until we got to the main lobby outside. There was a loud, intermittent noise and lights flashing everywhere. She signalled me to get down and so I did, we stood there for a moment as she looked around the place making sure that there was nobody around. She looked back at me and whispered: "We have to move quickly, we can't be seen. Stay as close to me as you can."

I looked at her, wondering what was happening. I trusted her, but this was completely out of context. She looked back at me, she knew this was freaking me out. She smiled and tilted her head, placed her hand on my cheek and said: "I need you to be strong! Can you do that for me?"

I still didn't knew what was happening, I didn't even knew what she meant. Strong? I was confused by the notion of it, but there was no time to ask about her meaning so, I just nodded, agreeing to her request.

She grabbed my hand, looked down the hall way and gave the go. We started moving fast towards an area that I had never been in. There were other doors, just like mine, scattered along the wall and the hall seemed to go on forever. Lights overhead were flashing intermittently, like sparks from a star. She stopped next to one of the doors, kneeled in front of it and I followed, grabbed the door handle and looked to both sides before opening it up. She pulled me in and stepped into the room after me.

The room looked almost identical to mine, the lights were dimmed, it seemed empty. Gloria looked around the room, scouting it with her eyes and called, whispering: "Sarah? Sarah?"

She looked around again, like expecting someone to answer her call, but I couldn't see anyone there.

From the darkness a sweet, faint voice asked: "Who is he?"

Gloria grabbed me by my shoulders, we were both looking straight at the darkness, to where the voice emanated. Gloria squeezed me with her hands, trying to give me comfort and answered: "This is Patrick…come out! It's ok!"

Slowly, a figure came out from the darkness and into the light, where we were. As soon as I was able to see her face, I recognised it, I had seen it before…It was her…the girl in my nightmare, the one that looked straight at me while I was plunging into oblivion.

She was real, she was standing right there, in front of me. Her eyes as blue as they were in my dreams, her hair black as night and she was dressed just like me, with the same clothes I always wore. I didn't understand what was happening, my whole world was shattering in front of my eyes. These new experiences that I had never knew existed, this feeling that was making my heart rush, that was pushing it to beat so fast and so hard. I felt it jumping inside, felt it almost jump out of my chest.

I grabbed Gloria's hand and squeezed it, I didn't know what else to do, I was paralysed. My eyes fixated on the girl's, blue as the sky, deep and revealing, that made my whole body tremble without control.

The girl roved me from head to toe, she could feel my frailty slipping out through my pores, my trembling, oscillating with uncertainty, my doubt, filled with excitement and my heart bursting with candour as I stumbled with the most beautiful thing I had ever seen. Her dark hair falling softly over her shoulders, flattering her face while it dripped from the top of her head, her mouth, flickering through the darkness with the bursts of light that reflected on the moisture her tongue provided, as she nervously caressed her lips and then softly bit them.

I was mute, in mobile, overtaken by her presence, filled with feelings I've never had, with emotions that confused my brain, my heart, my soul. Unable to react to so much beauty, overtaken by her grace. I could tell she was also confused, excited, perplexed to see me. To realise, same as me, that her world had changed forever.

She walked up to me, extended her hand, smiled and said: "Hi, I'm Sarah!"

I stood there, unable to react, confined to the astonishment that her smile induced in me. Flattered, beyond response, by this small gesture that flowed from her face into my soul.

Gloria sensed my surprise, the utter enchantment taking over and saw fit to awaken me from the slumber I had fallen into. She shook me and said: "Patrick, it's not polite to stare! Say hi to Sarah."

My hand made the leap and travelled to meet hers, but when I felt her touch, my brain crashed and my reaction was unexpected: A smile showed up on my face, unannounced, instinctively I tried to talk, but I stuttered, stumbling the words that were spitting out of my mouth randomly. I couldn't think straight, my head was possessed, mystified with her spell that hoarded every inch of my being: "Hey, wahesss up?"

She giggled as I shook her hand, without stopping, for over a minute.

Gloria had to intervene, time was of the essence. We needed to get out of there: "Ok, we need to go. You will have time to get to know each other later."

She pushed us towards the door, but before she could open it, Sarah stopped and asked: "Wait, where are we going, what's the rush?"

Gloria looked at her, placed her hands on her shoulders and replied: "We came to get you, I can't explain, but we have to go. I promise I will explain everything later. You have to trust me. Ok?"

Sarah looked into Gloria's eyes, then turned and looked at mine, thought about it for a second and nodded while she said: "Ok, ok!"

Gloria opened the door slowly, picked outside and said: "Ok, it looks clear. I need you to stay close, don't get distracted or pay attention to anything you see."

Sarah seemed disconcerted, but she had just promised to trust Gloria, so she looked at me and we both agreed: "Ok!"

She took Sarah's hand and pulled her out of the room, she, in turn, grabbed mine as she was walking out and I followed. We went through strange looking hallways I had never been in before. Closed doors in a maze of halls, that turned capriciously to either side. Gloria kept pulling us, she knew the way. Lights were flickering, faltering as we walked by. We couldn't see anyone, all doors were closed and there was no signs of life anywhere, just this deafening noise, that was driving me crazy. This loud buzzing that drilled into your ears, hurting them.

After running for a few minutes, Gloria finally stopped and signalled us to stay down and quiet. We were all with our backs against a wall, just before the next corner. Gloria peeped at the other side of the bend, turned her head towards the opposite side and then turned to where we were and whispered: "I think it's clear, we have to go through those doors at the end of the hallway. My vehicle is on the other side...."

She paused for a second and looked at both of us, with so much tenderness, so much hope in her eyes that it made me understand how dire the situation was.

"I'm going to take you home!"

Sarah smiled excited as she turned to look at me and I answered the same way. We would leave this place, for the first time, at least for me. I was so exhilarated, my heart was jumping out of my chest, which was augmented by the fact that I haven't let go of Sarah's hand thorough out the whole ordeal.

Finally, I would get to see that world proclaimed so eloquently on the pages of all those books. I would get to see the sun, with my own eyes and feel that tingling burn my skin, bronze it. Smell the air flowing free, whispering chimes I've only dreamed of. See the mountains surround me, trees shelter me, grass pamper my feet as I walked outside...

The fear and uncertainty I felt a few minutes ago, had turned into excitement propelled by the notion of going outside. Questions kept popping into my mind: Is there an actual world out there? Is the world outside as all those books showed, as all those photos I cherished displayed? What would it fell like to stand out there?

We both nodded, happily. She turned to look at the hallway one more time, before getting up and pulling us with her. We stood up, turned the bend and headed towards the doors, just a few feet away from us. As we were just about to reach it, a voice stopped Gloria, it was the voice of a man yelling: "Gloria! What are you doing?"

Excitement turned into fear, uncertainty. We were caught!

She turned around, pushed us behind her, trying to hide us from whoever that was. The man stared at Gloria and tilted his head to see us, he frowned and said: "You can't take them! They won't survive out there, besides, if they find out, they will kill you all, you know that!"

"I won't leave them behind!" Gloria replied categorically, as she hid us behind her.

We were both clinched to Gloria's dress, using her as a shield against whoever he was and whatever he could do to us. She was our protector, like she had always been.

"Have you gone mad?" The man asked.

"They are my children, I have to protect them. You know this, Juan," Gloria answered, as she looked straight at him.

The man seemed disconcerted, he kept thinking and making faces, closing his eyes shut, looking up, rolling his eyes and mumbling in another language I couldn't understand: "Carajo, carajo…hay manita!"

He finally took a deep breath and said: "Ok, ok, let's go!"

He pointed towards the door, inviting us to go through it. Gloria stared at him not knowing what to do, she was confused. The man looked at her and said: "We have to hurry, we don't have much time," he said, as he held the door open.

Gloria started walking towards the door and we went after her. On the other side, there was a long hallway, that led to an underground parking garage. There was just a few vehicles at the end of it. We ran across, following the man to his. As soon as he got close, the vehicle unlocked and a door opened, he then shouted a command: "Open all doors!"

As soon as he did, all the other doors opened, as we were getting close. Gloria got in front and Sarah and I got in the back. The vehicle started, the doors closed and we were on our way. The man said: "Home!"

Then he turned to look at Gloria for a moment, looked back at us and said: "I think it's better if you guys lay on the floor, just until we are out of danger."

Gloria looked back at us, nodded and said: "He's right, get down on the ground! You will be safer there. That way no one can see you!"

So, we did. The vehicle kept driving, until we exited the parking garage. Suddenly everything got drenched with light. It was too bright for my eyes, the brightness was burning my pupils, it hurt, so I closed them. I could hear Sarah going through the same. Gloria turned around and saw what was happening to us.

"Oh! Here, put this on!" she said, as she handed us a pair of dark glasses to each.

I couldn't open up my eyes, but I reached out with my hand and grabbed the glasses and placed them on my eyes. I opened up my eyes slowly, it was still bright but the light didn't hurt anymore, it was bearable. I saw that Sarah was struggling to grab Gloria's hand, so I helped her, grabbed the other pair and placed them over Sarah's eyes.

She opened up her eyes slowly too and was able to see, like I was. We looked at each other, we had never had the need for glasses, so we stared at each other for a bit. It just looked strange, the whole world seemed a different colour.

I could tell that we had gone through a couple of gates and that we were driving at a steady pace. So I asked: "Are we in the clear, can we get up now?'

The man looked at Gloria, like consulting with her. Gloria nodded and the man said: "Yes, you can come up now, but keep low."

Sarah was looking at me, afraid of what would happen if we did get up. So I took the initiative, sat on the seat and looked outside. I wasn't prepared to see what I saw, to see what was outside of our confinement. I was so used to looking at images on books, photographs, pictures on a single plain. Looking at the trees outside the window, in three dimensional space was mind boggling. I could have never imagined what it would look like, what it would make me feel. The clouds up above, fluffy as If I could almost touch them, suspended over a blue sky that seemed to embrace everything and the movement. I had never been in a vehicle before, I had seen them in books, the transformation they had gone through over the years, but this feeling of moving while you are still, felt so new. I almost fell dizzy.

I extended my hands in the air, trying to get perspective, trying to get my bearings. I looked up at Sarah and she was doing the same, she was sharing this strange feeling we were dealing with. It was almost like floating. I closed my eyes, thinking that it could be a trick of the mind, looking at everything outside move at a fast pace while we were static inside the vehicle, but I could still feel the movement in my body. The traction of the wheels spinning over the floor, the air flowing around us, the light movement of particles, I could fell everything. I opened up my eyes and Sarah was mimicking me, her eyes were closed and this amazing smile was decorating her face. It was a wonderful feeling.

I was content looking at her, when something distracted me, the thought that clouded my head: "There was a girl sitting next to me!".

Everything happened so fast that it didn't hit me until then. I wasn't the only one, I wasn't alone, she was a miracle, just like me. I had seen her in my dreams, which somehow connected us in a way that I couldn't understand right then, but she was real. I had touched her hand, felt her blood warming up her skin, her heartbeat beating through her fingers, inciting my own, the frailty we shared at this moment, not knowing what our destinies would be.

So looked at her, she was staring out the window, marvelled, as I was, of what we were experiencing. The world, for the first time. She was fixated, taking in everything. She didn't turn to see me, but she felt me staring, so without turning her head, she extended her hand to me, open, inviting me to grab it. I looked at it and grabbed it with mine.

With her hand between mine and her presence giving me strength, I turned and looked out the window, at our new home.

Suddenly I felt her hand clinch and tighten mine as she said: "Look, look at that!"

I got close to her window to see what she was pointing at. There were animals running on the fields, alongside the vehicle, jumping while they were running, in a beautiful motion. They seemed to be playing with us, showing off what they could do. They were beautiful creatures, with four slim legs that moved in patterns while pushing them forward.

"I think they are deer," Sarah said.

I looked closely and remember they looked like the ones on a book, I have never seen them in motion, but I agreed.

"Yes, they are. Look at that one!" I said while a big male joined the pack.

He had huge antlers, taller than his whole body. He was running alongside all the rest, carrying this complex figure over his head. Antlers forming whimsical turns. I have never seen anything more beautiful. It was like a dance choreographed by nature. Eventually they ran away from our path and we lost sight of them. Sarah and I just looked at each other, marvelling, and smiled.

The vehicle kept going down the road and we went back to our respective windows, there was so much to see. From time to time we would ask for each other attention to showcase something on our side of the vehicle. Something new, we had never seen before.

We still didn't know what was going on, why Gloria got us out of there, so abruptly, with so much secrecy, how come we were allowed to leave and where were all those people, scientists that experimented on me for so many years, that guarded us so jealously? Why didn't I knew about Sarah before, how come I knew her face if I have never seen her before….or had I?

There were too many questions that roamed inside my head, but I was to overtaken by the beauty of the world outside my window. It wasn't a vision, or an image in my head. It was real and I could smell it, feel it in my skin, sense it with every pore, with every heartbeat.

We drove down a road for a few minutes until we saw some people gathered at the side of the road, they were signalling us to stop. Juan, the man in charge of the vehicle, slowed down as he said: "Do not open the windows, for anyone, for any reason. Do you understand?"

He turned around to see us, he was very serious. I looked at Sarah, a little bit confused, she was too, but we both answered: "Yes, I understand!"

Then he turned around, facing forward and started to speed up, he was not going to stop. The people there started to waive their arms, signalling us to stop, faster and faster, as we got closer. Juan wasn't slowing down. Most of the people in front of us, moved to the sides, to avoid getting hit, but there was one that stood his ground. He just wouldn't move, as if he was willing to stop the vehicle, at any cost.

Juan just floored it and yelled: "Close your eyes! Close your eyes!"

The vehicle hit the man and sent him flying in the air. I closed my eyes, as Juan requested, but I could still felt the man hit the vehicle, a scream and ultimately a big bang as we swept through. I opened up my eyes to look behind us and saw the man, plunged to the ground, distorted, inert, lifeless. All the rest of them waving their arms in disapproval while they rushed to where the body laid.

Juan just kept on driving, Gloria was hysterical, she was shouting in Spanish and covering up her eyes with her hands, swinging back and forth. Sarah had her eyes closed and had tighten her grip on my hand, as hard as she could. I was just perplexed, astonished of what had just happened, but mostly, curious as to why

Juan had done that, he just drove through that crowd, instead of stopping and finding out what those people wanted and what had happened to that man, he just ran over.

I felt, something I have never felt before, this mix of rage and sadness, of loss and disconcert. I was about to say something, to ask why, when Gloria turned around with a horrified expression on her face. When she looked at me, fixated in my eyes, she calmed down and smiled at me. Her eyes were still sad, but her smile denoted resignation. She somehow wanted to convey that, what we just experienced, wasn't a bad thing.

I didn't even know what to ask, or what to feel. I just took the calm her smile gave me and nodded my head. I knew that she would explain everything when the time came. So we drove for a while longer in silence, nobody wanted to talk about it. Sarah was looking at the floor, her mind was rewinding what we saw, I could feel her frailty, because she never let go of my hand. She was holding on to it, like you would a lifesaver in the middle of the ocean. I held on to her hand too, it felt safe holding on to her.

We pulled over and stopped, after a while, in a gated complex. Juan pulled over to the entrance, the system scanned his face and the gate opened. He looked to both sides before going in, making sure nobody was around. As soon as he pulled in the gates closed again, behind us. He parked on the side of the first house, turned off the vehicle and stepped out of it. He walked a few steps away from it, wobbling, until he felt down on his knees and began to spill his guts on the floor.

We all saw him as he did, I turned and looked at Gloria. Her eyes were filled with tears as she looked at Juan, who couldn't take it anymore. She felt me staring and calmly said: "He is a good man, he's always been a good man!"

He kept looking at him, as tears ran down her face. Juan stayed down on the ground sobbing, spitting all the guilt that was clouding him, that had overtaken his sanity. I was still confused about what had happened and I wanted to understand, so I looked back at Gloria and asked: "What's going on Gloria, what is happening?"

She looked at me, Sarah was quiet but alert, she was also looking at Gloria, waiting to hear the answer to the question, that was also on her mind. Gloria turned and looked at her, then back at me and finally her eyes dropped to the ground ashamed. She took a deep breath and said: "About a month ago, our north firewall defence faltered and "the impure" marched in. As soon as they did, everyone in contact became infected. It happened so fast, they closed the firewall as soon as the glitch was detected, but it was too late. Thousands had infiltrated and in hours, thousands were already infected and it took just a few weeks for the spread to get here. A lot of the lab workers got infected and died, and all the rest were being evacuated. It was what we always feared would happen. We felt so safe, for so long, but the fact is that the fear was always present. We don't know who is infected, we couldn't risk it. That is why Juan couldn't stop."

She looked at us, tenderly, with love that we could feel through her tears. She paused, trying not to choke, and said: "You were going to be discarded…I couldn't let that happen. I had to get you out!"

Sarah and I, looked at each other. It was difficult to grasp, the concept of us being something that you discard, like a Petri dish.

I stood there, for a moment, thinking…or trying too. It was just too much information, but the image of that guy being struck by the car, his body flying through the air, contorting, until it fell to the ground, where he stood…lifeless, took over everything else. I raised my eyes to see Gloria and asked: "What about that man, on the road, those people?"

Gloria lowered her eyes, ashamed, even though she wasn't the one driving. She shared the guilt with Juan. I could feel the sadness in her eyes, in her body, that was shivering, like a little girl.

"Those people on the road…we had to assume that they were infected too…we just can't risk it. That's why we couldn't stop. Not even for that man, it was him, or all of us."

I bowed my head, I understood what she meant. I had never seen anything like that, but I still had hope, that he was ok.

Gloria wiped her tears, shook her head, turned around to see us and said: "Ok, we have to go inside. We can't stay outside for long, it's not safe."

She opened up her door and opened Sarah's from the outside, Sarah stepped out of the vehicle without letting go of my hand, so I followed.

The air outside was dense, so breathing was harder, our lungs had to work more to process the air. It was a strange feeling that we both shared, Sarah and I. Gloria saw us struggling, looking at each other. She grabbed us from our shoulders, made us look into her eyes and said: "I know it's a lot to process, but we have no options, this is the only way. If we stick together, we'll be fine. You have to get used to a lot of things. Life is gonna change so much, things will be very different from now on."

We both nodded and looked at each other. Gloria could feel everything Sarah and I were sharing, we both had the same questions and concerns.

"Come on, we can talk inside. I'll explain everything," Gloria said, as she invited us in.

We walked into the house, we were both curious, looking at everything there. We had never seen a place like this one. It was filled with photographs, figurines, sculptures of strange looking animals, books…so much to see. It was one of those "Museums" I remember reading about so much in the library. We were perplexed looking at everything.

"Come! Sit down! Come on!" Gloria said, pointing at a sofa on the side of the room.

Sarah and I walked to the sofa and sat down next to each other, we were still holding hands. It was, as if, we both wanted to feel safe, connected to what we knew, until then; connected to something familiar and even though, we didn't knew each other from before, we came from the same place, we lived the same experiences and that made us familiar.

We were both still taken by everything we were looking at, silent, mute, unable to speak about anything. We were aliens in a strange world.

Gloria began talking, asking and answering our own questions: "I'm sure you are curious as to why you didn't knew about each other? Well, that was part of my job, keeping the secret from each other. They didn't want you to know about each other's existence. I tried to tell you, so many times, but I was told it would be harmful to you…and I believed it! I'm sorry about that! I really am! I was following the advice of "experts" and, even though, It wasn't in my nature, I had to follow protocol, I had to do what they told me. There were so many things I didn't agree with, but I was just an au pair. Tasked to look after you and made you feel human. For all the scientists there, you were just an experiment they were conducting. There were others like you, throughout the years. You were the only two left, the only two that survived so long. I believe there is a reason for that. That is why I had to get you out."

I turned to look at Sarah, she was looking straight at Gloria, in mobile, her hair was dangling around her face, covering most of it, I could only see her nose and her left eye when the hair would bounce off, moved by a slight breeze that ran through the room. She was beautiful, she was perfect. She felt me staring and she turned slowly to see me. She looked straight at me as I did the same. We were both analysing every little detail, every new facet, every angle, every crevice, every nook of our faces. Sarah tilted her head, her lips opened as she asked me: "How old are you?"

I doubted, I wasn't even sure. So I turned to Gloria and asked: "Gloria?"

She quickly responded: "You are sixteen…and Sarah is eighteen!"

When she said that, Sarah turned to look at Gloria disapproving. She wasn't happy about it and said: "Gloriaaa!"

"What? That was going to be his next question, so I just answered it before he made it. So, you're welcome."

Gloria said while she went into the kitchen. We both stayed there, thinking, looking at each other, until it began to feel awkward and we both broke the spell we had on each other, looked somewhere else and mumbled, not knowing what to say, until Gloria asked: "Are you kids hungry? I'm making something to eat."

We both answered at the same time: "We are starving!"

Sarah turned to look at me, wondering if I was mimicking her, maybe making fun of her. I just shrugged. She went on: "What's for dinner? Can we have some of the food that you make?"

I joined her when I heard that. A warm feeling invaded me, I've been wanting to try that food all my life, wondering what it tasted like. All I knew were the meals I was served, so I said: "Yes, can we? I would love to try anything."

Gloria was moving things around in the kitchen, pots and pans, dishes and utensils. She was busy in there, so she took a moment to answer. We both looked at each other, wondering if maybe she hadn't heard what we said.

"I'm cooking something light, I'll give you some when I'm done. Hang on!"

We looked at each other excited, I guess that Sarah was as curious as I was to taste real food, not the gooey stuff they use to serve us.

We were lost in our thoughts when Juan came in, he saw us sitting in the living room, he lowered his head ashamed and walked into the kitchen. Gloria and him started talking in Spanish, well…yelling actually! Gloria finally convinced him to calm down and help her with the cooking.

Sarah and I were just looking at each other, I wanted to talk to her, but I didn't really know what to say and I guess that she felt the exact same way, but there was a lot of curiosity, a lot of things we wanted to know, so I broke the ice and asked: "So, I guess they experimented on you too?"

Her whole expression went south, I guess that she felt bad for me, knowing that I went through the same torture that she did. She stayed silent for a moment, then her face lighted up and she asked back: "Hey, did you visit the library?"

My face lighted up to, my mind started running around in my head. Of course, if she had the same routine I did, she would have gone to the library too, maybe even read the same books I had.

"Yes, that was my favourite thing to do."

"Mine too!" she said.

It was magical to think that she had experienced the same things I had, in the pages of those books. I was wondering if she had read the exact same books I had, when she asked: "Were you the one bending the pages on the top, as you read along?"

I was astonished, I never thought there was someone who noticed, who knew I was reading the books and followed the path I was on. I nodded with my head and her smile showed up…it was a beautiful sight to see.

"I never knew you existed, I never thought someone was noticing that. I always thought I was the only one going through all those books, reading about the world, looking through all those photographs…" I said.

She looked into my eyes and replied: "I did, I thought I was the only one too, but finding those folds gave me hope that there was someone else. I used to search the whole library looking for them, eager to read what they pointed to, like a sign. At the beginning, when I first saw them, I thought they were teasing me, the scientists, making me think I was crazy, waiting for me to react to it, but when they never asked me about that, I just kept it to myself and hoped there was someone else out there. I was right!"

I couldn't help it, I was smiling from ear to ear.

"But, you never unfold them, I never knew you noticed!" I said curious.

"I thought about it, many times, about unfolding the pages. Sending, whoever was doing that, a message back, but I was afraid that if I did, they would lose their place, they would get mad and the signs would disappear. I didn't want that, so I didn't," Sarah replied.

I was ashamed of not noticing her before, of somehow dismissing the fact she was there and mad that we were denied the chance to know each other before. I didn't blame Gloria, I knew she was forced to keep the secret, but the scientists who decided it had to be that way…they were to blame. We could had shared so much, we were already connected, somehow.

"I wish I could had known about you before. I would have left you messages, we could have talked."

Sarah smiled and grabbed my hands, she tilted her head and asked: "I guess it was meant to be this way, but I could feel you somehow...didn't you? Feel me too?"

I thought about it for a moment, searched back in my memory and the images of that girl in my dreams, the one that always showed up. Now I knew it was her, it was always her...

I looked up to see her face, she was waiting for me to say...

"Yes, I did. You were there with me, I don't know how, but you were there."

She smiled and we hugged, it felt so right. It was a new feeling that filled me up inside. This warmth rising in intensity, filling up every corner of my body. Making my skin react to her touch, my mouth salivate, she was my fantasy.

Gloria interrupted when she shouted from the kitchen: "Dinner is ready, come sit down kids!"

We were both smiling uncontrollably, happy as can be, it was the perfect moment. Sarah rolled her eyes and said: "I'm starving!"

"Yeah, me too!" I said.

We both got up from the couch and walked into the kitchen. There was a small table on the side and two chairs. Gloria saw us walking in and said: "Well? Sit down, it'll be there in a minute."

So, we did, we sat down and waited for it. She first brought some soup, she placed the bowls on the table, one in front of each. It was hot and bounty full, I could smell the goodness in it. A combination of new smells that enticed my senses, it was intoxicating. I opened up my eyes and saw Sarah lost in it too. Gloria was standing next to the table, she looked at us both and said: "First you have to wash your hands!"

We stood there looking at her, waiting for her to direct us. Gloria turned around and saw us doubting. She pointed out to the left of the room and said: "The bathroom is back that way, second door on the left. Wash thoroughly!"

So we headed out the way she pointed at, went into the second door on the left and stepped into the bathroom. Saw the sink, placed our hands under the soap dispenser and then under the sink while the water flowed. We both scrubbed our hands together and cleaned them up. Dried them up under the air dryer, as we giggled at everything we did, and headed back into the kitchen. Sat down by the table and looked at what was in front of us. Two bowls, steaming. Gloria saw us staring at them and said: "Well? Dig in!"

We looked at her, picked up the spoons, dipped them into the soup and just as we were about to bring them up to our mouths, she turned around and said: "Watch out, it's very hot! Don't burn yourselves."

We both smiled and started blowing into the spoons, the broth would drip off from the spoon into the bowl, as we did, the smell increased and I felt my mouth craving to taste it. I couldn't believe my senses, the small bursts of joy that the simple smell of it brought up, the amazing colours that flowed inside the bowl, the mixture of textures moving inside.

I brought the spoon up to my mouth and took a bit, it was still hot, but my mouth was focused on something else: the explosion of flavours that I had never tasted before, the texture of the soup and whatever was in there. I didn't recognised any of it, but my tastebuds were tantalising my brain with all this new information, so I was a little bit overwhelmed and the only thing that came out of my mouth was: "Wow!"

Sarah turned and looked at me, she was in exactly the same place I was. She was experiencing all this for the first time too, she nodded with her head and said: "Right?"

We kept on eating, rejoicing on this marvel, we had just encountered: Real food!

Gloria was giggling, entertained, watching us eat her food. She could only imagine what it would be for us, this amazing experience. For her, it was just a soup, a simple concoction that she had made hundreds of times herself and had eaten even more as prepared by her mother and her mother before her.

We both finished our bowls in record time and raised them, asking for more, at the same time. Gloria just laughed and nodded her head. She grabbed them as she said: "Take it easy! You might get a tummy ache after this. Your system is not used to it. I'll give you another bowl, but that's it! I don't want you complaining later…or god forbid, get diarrhoea!"

Diarrhoea? I've read about that somewhere. It sounded like a horrible condition and I got scared. Gloria could see the confusion on my face. She laughed and said: "Don't worry, I don't think that's going to happen. Just take it easy, and don't eat that fast. Enjoy it, savour it, let it simmer for a little inside your mouth before you swallow."

She took the bowl away, one by one, and served us more. She handed us the bowl back. We grabbed it and looked at each other. Sarah was as confused as I was. So I smiled at her, she smiled back and we took the spoon and kept on eating. This time, we did it slowly, doing as Gloria had suggested. Taking it slow, trying to control our urges.

It was a lot better, the experience became richer. My brain had time to process the information my mouth was sending. I could even differentiate the flavours of different elements in the soup. We were a costumed to eating just to feed ourselves, but this...this was a whole new experience. We were actually, enjoying food and it was an overwhelming one, one of those, you have to close your eyes for.

The different flavours bounced inside my mouth, seducing my taste buds that then sent messages to my brain, than in return commanded my salivary glands to produce more saliva, that filled my mouth with anticipation for more of that taste that was driving me insane. That was making me lose all sense of control and reason, over what I was eating, over what I was doing. It just started happening as means to satisfy my cravings for more, rejoicing each and every sip, every bite...

And then it hit me, I remembered something Gloria used to tell me about this, about the feeling that arouses unintended, natural, like when I saw Sarah for the first time, when she took my hand in hers. So I stopped for a moment and looked at Gloria. She looked back at me trying to figure out what was running through my mind and I asked: "Is this love? What I'm feeling?"

Gloria stood still for a moment, thinking. A big smile showed up on her face, her eyes filled up with tears while she looked at me. Sarah stopped eating too and looked at me too, wondering if this was it. If we had finally found love...

I was waiting for an answer, Gloria looked up and said: "Well, you can call it love! There are different kinds of love, but you can definitely be in love with food, but be careful, because love always requires commitment and food is no different. You have to respect it, be faithful and never abuse it."

I turned to look at Sarah as she looked at me, we were both trying to grasp what Gloria had said. I could see doubt in Sarah's face, her brain was struggling with the thought of it, she wanted to clear something out and so she asked: "What happens if you don't?"

Gloria looked at us seriously for a second and then burst into laughter and said: "You get fat like me!"

We all laughed at her comment, even Juan that was eating his bowl of soup, by himself, on one side of the kitchen. It had been a surreal day for everyone, but mostly for both of us, Sarah and I, a whole new world had open up for us. A world we only dreamed of, a world we weren't even sure existed. A world formed by the simplest of things, by the details that make up every passing second. Things that we never appreciated before, those little instances that happen unplanned, that catch you unprepared and become surprises that fill you up with the thrill of discovery. Sort of like the way I felt with books inside that library, every time I turned a page and kept on reading, but this was tangible, it was real and was happening right in front of our eyes, of our hands, of our nose and our taste buds.

After eating, our bodies started shutting down, we haven't eaten this much in…never, actually. So together with all the excitement, the nerves and our bodies getting used to digesting, we were extremely tired and our eyes were shutting down.

Gloria gave us a place to sleep for the night, some blankets, to cover ourselves with, and a couple of pillows. It wasn't a bed, per say, but it didn't matter. I was too excited to notice, besides I was going to spend the night next to Sarah and that was enough to keep my mind entertained, not thinking of the fact that we were actually sleeping on the floor.

Before she said goodnight, Gloria looked at us tenderly and said: "I'm so sorry that it took me so long to get you out of there, I wanted to, so many times, almost since you were babies, but I just couldn't. Security was very tight and I was being watched all the time. As soon as I saw an opportunity I took it, but we are going to have to leave this place tomorrow. We can't stay here any longer. I don't know if they will be looking for us and I'm not even sure it's safe anymore to stay here."

She paused for a second and asked: "You know about the out brake, right? You read the history books"

Sarah and I looked at each other and I asked: "The one that killed so many people? Was that actually real?"

Gloria bowed her head and I could tell that sadness filled her heart as she said: "Yes, it was real and now it's here. For many years we were protected, isolated inside this bubble, but somehow it breached our defences and people inside "The Safety Zone" started getting infected and dying. Everyone left, headed south, away from the infection. That's why I was able to get you out. The lab was nearly abandoned, so there was no more security to hold me back from setting you free, but we are in danger, we have to go south too."

Sarah and I looked at each other with disbelief and as I was looking at her, it hit me.

"So, they had left us there to die?"

Gloria's eyes dropped to the ground, ashamed and said.

"Yes, the scientists ran to save their lives and their families and just left you there to face your own faith, but I couldn't let that happen. That is why I got you out."

Sarah and I both smiled and felt our chests collapse and our eyes fill with tears. We both knew that we owed our lives to Gloria. So we both grabbed Gloria's hands and just looked at her for a moment. We didn't know how else to thank her for saving our lives, for risking everything to get us out. We just stood there looking at her as she looked back at us and suddenly it occurred to me.

"So, this is what love is!"

Gloria broke down and laughed as she squeezed my hand tighter. She agreed, nodding with her head. Sarah was nodding back at her while she held her other hand tight. She had been a Mother to us for a long time, the only one who really cared for us and now she had shown us what true love is by risking her own life to get us out and save us.

I felt lucky, even thought I was born inside a lab, born to be an experiment and not a person, I got to have, what a lot of people just dream of ever having, a mother that cared for me and loved me. So, as you do when you have no words, no way of conveying what you feel and no understanding of how to express it. When that feeling just takes over and overflows your body. We embraced, and cried, the three of us. Sarah shared the same feeling that I did, so it was just natural.

Juan was sitting at the other side of the room, looking at us, observing from a far, but the feeling was so overwhelming that it infected him too. He stood up, got close and joined us.

We stood there for a while, enjoying this amazing feeling that swept us whole. Something that we had never experienced before, I mean, I always felt something for Gloria. I waited every day for her to come and see me and enjoyed every single moment we had together, but it was never this real. Sometimes you need to be shaken to realise what you have. Eventually the feeling subsided and we calmed down a bit, were able to think about something else. We all went back to thinking of the fact that there was a threat still very much real out there.

"How do you know if someone has been infected?" Sarah asked.

"At first, there is no way to know, but it progresses rapidly. The first signs are horrible rashes that look like open wounds, but the worst happens inside the body. Organs start shutting down until they are no longer functional and you die!"

Sarah and I were shocked, afraid that we could get infected too.

"How fast is it?" Sarah asked.

"Within a couple of days, that's why we were never able to figure out how to stop it. The body consumes itself in less than a week."

Gloria saw the concern in our faces and tried to cheer us up.

"But that's not going to happen to us. We will be alright. The virus is more resilient up north. It doesn't seem to like it down south, where we're headed."

"What do you mean, it doesn't like it?" I asked, curious.

Gloria shrugged, she didn't really know the answer to that.

"I guess, the virus doesn't like the hot weather. There are a lot less cases reported there, it's always been a safe haven of sorts," she said.

"Why didn't everyone move there before?" Sarah asked.

Gloria thought about it for a second and responded: "I don't know, people wanted to stay home and felt safe for many years. The wall was supposed to be fool proof. I guess they didn't have to move, so they didn't. This was their home!"

"Why didn't you and Juan did?' I asked.

Gloria turned and looked at Juan, who was still sitting down in the kitchen, listening to our conversation. She smiled and said: "Our families live there still, that's where we are headed, down to Mexico. I met Juan down there, we both came up looking for work and we stayed for love. We found each other and found a new life over here. We thought about leaving many times. About going back home, but I couldn't leave you."

Sarah grabbed Gloria's hand that was trembling and said: "Thank you, for everything!"

Gloria turned and looked at me and said: "I'm sorry I didn't tell you about each other, I couldn't and I thought I was protecting you. If you knew, you would have done anything to be together. I always knew you were meant to be like this, with each other."

I smiled at her and said: "It's ok, we understand. The important thing is that: we are together now."

Sarah nodded, agreeing with what I've said. Gloria caressed our faces and smiled, I understood everything she had to go through to keep the secret, to keep us safe. I've always felt loved by her, but now I understood how much she did.

"Get some rest, we have a long day tomorrow!" she said as she pulled our covers and kissed us goodnight.

We snuggled in our beds. I wasn't sure I was going to be able to sleep with everything that had happened this day. My head was spinning, I couldn't stop thinking about the possibilities that lied ahead. The dangers that were lurking and the risks that we were about to take.

I could feel Sarah going through the same thing I was, but then, I felt her hand reaching out and touching mine. She grabbed mine between hers and I felt her fingers twine with mine. I looked at her, her eyes were closed but her smile wouldn't quit and then I felt this peace invade my whole being. Like a warm blanket that embraces you on a cold night. Before I could make sense of it, I was asleep.

Chapter 3
The Long Road

I was back in the lab, strapped to a gurney ready for another procedure. Doctors were preparing the equipment and getting everything ready, but there was something unsettling about it. Something I've never felt before. I was afraid!

Out of nowhere, the doctors started laughing while they turned and looked at me. I couldn't see their faces, they had their masks on, but I could hear them laughing, making fun of me. One of them was staring at me, with this intense look, he was the only one without a mask on. He was cleaning a long metal object, something I don't remember seeing before. It was a long metal rod with a pointy end and a handle connected to console by wires. He kept cleaning it as he looked at me. His expression was dull.

His eyes were fixated on me, but there was something weird about them. I couldn't tell what it was from the other side of the room, where I was, strapped to the gurney. I looked back at him, wondering what was he thinking. What had him so struck by me, he didn't falter, kept staring at me, which made me unsettled.

The fear turned into desperation, his staring at me made me very uncomfortable and as I concentrated on his eyes, I could see that they were blood shot, veins were protruding out of his eyes, as if they were going to explode and as he centred on me his eyes seemed to jump out of his sockets. His mouth was open all the time, drooling, dripping everywhere, his neck seemed tense, his ligaments sticking out and veins pulsating strongly. The more I looked at him, the weirder he looked, the more cunning details were revealed.

I just couldn't look at him anymore, so I turned away, looked to the opposite side, but I could still fell him staring at me, my skin was burning inflamed by it and every pore in my body was reacting to it. I didn't want to, but curiosity got the best of me and I turned again, to look at him…when I did, he was standing right next to my gurney, with that same stare…I jumped out of my gurney, but I was still held in it by the straps that kept me tied down.

I was freaking out! I could feel the warmth of his breath down on me, the stench was unbearable. He was decomposing in front of my eyes, flesh falling off his face, his neck, melting away like an ice cube and the terrible scream that denoted his pain that slowly decreased as he vanished away on top of me. I just closed my eyes as tight as I could and screamed in desperation…

"Patrick, Patrick! Wake up, wake up!" Sarah was screaming, as she shook me from my shoulders.

I woke up still freaking out, thinking that the thing was the one shaking me, but when I opened up my eyes I saw her face surrounded by a halo that embraced her. She seemed like an angel looking down at me and my heart stopped beating for a second, it actually skipped a beat, so that it could go into a different pace, one that grew stronger and steady with her presence, with her beautiful eyes looking at me, worried for me.

"Are you ok? You were screaming like crazy. What were you dreaming of?" Sarah asked, concerned.

It took me a moment to grasp what I just experienced, I've never had a nightmare before, I was never afraid or concerned for anything in my life. Those stories I used to read, there were no more than that…stories. This, that I just experienced, seemed so real.

I looked around the room, hoping to set myself in the place I was in, figuring out if that was in my head, or was it real?

I finally centred on Sarah and her beautiful eyes, that calmed me down, enough to talk: "It was a nightmare, I was back at the lab, but there was this horrible creature…"

I couldn't go on, as soon as that image came into my mind, my heart started racing again. Sarah noticed I was distressed, held my hand and said: "Don't worry, you are safe here. Nobody is going to take you back to the lab…I promise!"

The sound of her voice saying that and the warmth of her hand was all I needed to relax and concentrate. I laid my head against her shoulder, she was kneeling next to me. She grabbed my head with her hand and embraced it tightly. She was worried about me. She later told me that my screams woke her up, that the screams were so intense that she thought the ceiling was falling down and when she woke up she realised it was me, she tried to wake me up for a while, but that I just kept on screaming...I just wouldn't stop.

"I'm sorry if I scared you, It wasn't my intention!" I said while I was resting in her arms.

"It's ok, it doesn't matter. The important thing is that you snapped out of it, that you are well. I was really worried there for a moment," Sarah said, while I felt her hands tremble.

I lifted up my head and looked at her, her face was looking down, ashamed. So I lifted her chin up, so she would look at me and said: "Hey, thank you for worrying about me, but I'm fine. It was just a nightmare!"

She looked into my eyes and calmed down. We were looking at each other, when Gloria walked into the room and said: "Good morning! Are you awake?"

She was smiling, but when she looked at us, she knew there was something wrong.

"What, what is it? What happened?" she said, she could feel my frailty and sense something bad had happened.

"Nothing, I had a nightmare!" I replied.

"A nightmare? I knew I shouldn't have told you everything at once" she said.

"I'm ok, I just never had one before," I replied.

"Well, you better get used to it!" Juan said, as he came into the room.

Gloria turned and looked at him, with a disapproving look, he looked back at her and just said: "We need to get going! It's getting late. I told you, we shouldn't have stayed the night," he said visibly upset.

Gloria rolled her eyes and then, smiled at us while she said: "Don't mind him, he's not a morning person."

We both looked at him and smiled, Juan saw us smiling at him, he frowned and asked, kind of mad: "What? What?"

The three of us just giggled, although he tried to put this tough image, you could tell just by looking at him, that he was like a teddy bear...soft inside.

He looked at us and nodded his head, disapproving our gesture, blew us off with his hand and said: "Come on! We have to go!"

Gloria stood up and agreed with him as she said: "Come on kids. Get your stuff and lets move out. Juan is right, we need to get going."

We got up and gathered our stuff, which wasn't much, rolled up our beds and placed everything inside the trunk. Gloria was roaming up and down the house as if she was looking for something but couldn't find it. She kept staring at things, picking them up and putting them back down again, then she moved to another part of the house and did the same again and again.

"Come on Gloria! We need to leave!" Juan shouted from outside the house.

Gloria stopped and turned around and looked around her house. She looked at us and began walking out as she pushed us towards the entrance.

"Let's go," she said.

We all got inside the vehicle and we were off.

As the vehicle was moving away, Gloria, that was sitting in the passenger's seat, turned around to look at the place she called home, one last time. I could see sadness in her eyes, that filled up with tears as we rolled away. She turned around, as soon as it was out of sight, and there was silence for a while. We could only hear her weeping softly.

Juan turned to look at her, grabbed her hand and said: "Don't worry dear, I'll get you a new one when we get there. I promise!"

Gloria placed her other hand on top of Juan's and smiled, she nodded, agreeing with him and said tenderly: "I know you will baby!"

Sarah and I looked at each other, she smiled at me. We didn't understand fully what this connection was, this thing that poets wrote about, that Shakespeare referenced in his books, that Neruda talks about over and over again, this feeling that is present in so many songs, this pressure I felt in my chest when Sarah touched my hand, but looking at Gloria and Juan, I was beginning to understand its complexity, its might, its condition.

I smiled back at her and she grabbed my hand as she turned and looked outside the window. I felt the same chill roam up and down my spine, the one she provoked with just her touch, this warmth that gave me peace but enticed my senses and aroused this desire to be next to her, to never let go.

I looked outside the window too, curious, wondering what would our future be like, in this new world we had been thrown into. Where would this path lead us? I knew it was uncertain, but somehow her hand gave me anchor, bonded me to something bigger than myself, like the roots that hold a tree bounded to the ground, safe from the wind and the rain.

I was not alone, I would never be alone!

We drove for a few hours through fields and valleys, up mountains, alongside lakes and rivers…it was beautiful! Just like the books described. The air was clear and clean, I could feel it filling up my lungs that were breathing deeply, taking in as much as they could with every breath I took. Sarah and I, were holding hands along the way and every time there was something relevant, that we wanted to show each other, we just squeezed harder and we would both look out to enjoy what we wanted to share. The marvel it was to experience the world for the first time, to look at the sky filled with clouds floating around, like suspended in the blue void that covered us from one side to the other, as far as our eyes could see.

We even saw a couple of deer, prancing around a field, in the distance. She saw them first and squeezed my hand so I would turn to look her way.

"Are they real?" Sarah asked me as we both admired the sight.

I smiled, because I was thinking the exact same thing, but I answered back: "Sure they are, look at them! Running free through the fields, together."

She smiled with me as we watched them run into the woods, on the opposite side of the field. They were almost about to disappear between the trees, when one of them stopped and stared at us. It was the biggest one of them, the one with the longest antlers. It just stood there staring at the vehicle passing by, but we felt like it could see us and was actually looking straight at us. We looked at each other for a few seconds and untimely he turned around and jumped into the woods and disappeared.

For us, everything was special, it is that way: when it's the first time you have seen it. Our brains were still getting used to so much information at once, that our whole bodies demanded rest. After a while we were both asleep. Our brains needed to reboot, they needed to stop receiving new information and rest for a moment, besides this slow, pacing movement of the vehicle cruising down the road had a strange numbing effect on both of us. It felt the same as those stories that Gloria use to read us to put us to sleep. It had the same effect on us. It brought me way back to when I was a baby, suddenly the image of Gloria's hand pushing my crib, rocking me to sleep showed up in my head, unintended but sparked by the same feeling I had.

A change in pace, woke us up, Juan had slowed down on the side of the road and the vehicle was standing still. I opened up my eyes and asked: "What's wrong?"

Gloria shushed me and turned around, as she placed her finger on her lips and said: "Don't do any noise, stay quiet!"

Then she turned and pointed up ahead. I could see a group of people and vehicles blocking the road. Juan was static, grabbing the wheel with both hands, squeezing nervously. Gloria looked at him and asked: "What are you thinking?"

"They've already seen us, I don't think we can just pass them," he replied.

They were both thinking and there was this awkward silence that was starting to get on our nerves, invading us with desperation. Sarah looked at me and I could see it in her eyes too, she was trembling, uncertain of what will happen next.

I looked back at her and felt the need to ease her stress, so I just asked: "Can we tell if they are infected…somehow?"

Juan and Gloria turned to look at each other and then turned to look to the front again. Juan shrugged and said: "The sensors are not picking anything up, I guess we will have to find out!"

He let go of the brake and the vehicle started advancing slowly towards the blockade, as we got closer, we were able to define better what we were looking at from a far. The closer we got, the clearer it became that we were being deceived. The amount of people we first saw, started thinning out, gradually, as we got closer, the vehicles blocking the road started to disappear as we moved forward, closer to them, but so did the fields around us, behind us. The trees and mountains in the background began to disappear from sight, as if we were moving away instead of towards them.

The sky above began to lose its colour and a blanket of white surrounded us, until the only thing we could see was a single person standing right in front. Juan stopped the vehicle just shy of it. We were all baffled, trying to process what was happening, speechless. I remembering wondering if that was all a dream, If I was actually asleep and everything happening was a fig of my imagination. Everything became clearer when Sarah grabbed my hand and squeezed it, I knew it wasn't a dream.

I turned to look at her, she needed to hang on to me to make sure that what we were experiencing was real, that we were actually there, I could sense that she was afraid, but calm, next to me she felt safe, as I did next to her; as long as we were together, we would be ok. We turned to look at Gloria and Juan, who were stunned at what was happening.

We all looked at this figure in front of us, wearing a mask and covered from head to toe. He wasn't threatening, even though we couldn't see its face, but there was something calming about it. Even inviting about its demeanour. It was just looking at us until silence was broken and it spoke with a booming voice that seemed to come from every direction: "Don't worry your safe. Step out of the vehicle please, slowly!"

Out? To where? There was nothing around us, just a white blank. We couldn't see the floor, or anything, by that matter. We all looked at each other, wondering if any of us had an answer to all the questions that were popping into our heads, but we were all as confused as the next.

"It's ok, your safe! You are not in any danger," It said.

I opened up my door and as I was about to step out when Sarah pulled my hand. Her face said it all, she was afraid something bad would happen to me. I smiled at her, trying to reassure her and ventured into the unknown. Juan and Gloria were looking at me, waiting to see what would happen once I was out there.

I placed my foot outside and slowly reached down, hoping to find some kind of ground under us. My foot reached the ground just beside the car, it was solid, so I pulled myself up and stepped out of the vehicle. I looked around: everything was white! I couldn't tell if we were inside of something, or suspended in mid-air. There were no walls, or ceiling, or floor. I could feel the ground beneath me, but couldn't see it. I couldn't see where it began, or ended.

"It's ok, you're in a virtual reality bubble! You're safe in here," It said.

By the tone of his voice I could tell it was a he, or at least it appear to be that way. I looked at him, it seemed as though he was suspended, floating. His feet were not down on the ground.

"You can tell your friends to come out now!" He said.

I extended my hand to Sarah and nodded my head to Gloria, that was waiting for me to say something. Sarah grabbed my hand, scoot over and stepped out of the vehicle as she held tight. She stood next to me, without letting go. Juan and Gloria opened up their doors and stepped out too. They were both looking around, perplexed of what was happening.

"Step over this way, please!" He said as he pointed towards him.

I started walking to where he was, Sarah walked beside me but Juan and Gloria were sceptical, they were still unsure of what to do, so I looked at them and nodded with my head, assuring them, it was alright,

We all walked, until we were right in front of the man. I looked behind for a second and the vehicle was gone, only whiteness surrounded us. It was a strange feeling, but I wasn't afraid. It was more of a sense of adventure that fuelled my uncertainty. Somehow I trusted him, I didn't feel afraid.

"I'm sorry, but we have to make sure that you are clean. Your bodies are being scanned right now," The man said.

As he did I felt something roaming my body, started on my feet and climbed up through my legs, up my chest and out my head. I didn't hurt, It just felt like a light touch, as if it were caressing me. I could tell that Sarah was experiencing the same because she tighten her grip without letting go of my hand.

When the scan was finished, the man said: "You are clean! Welcome to the Oasis!"

He pointed with his hand towards a light, that looked like a door, glowing in the middle of the white space we were in, inviting us to step inside. We all turned to look at each other, trying to find some reassurance that, what we were about to do, was the right thing, but none of us were sure of anything at that point. We were just running on expectations, hope and an unfounded sense of trust, in something we had no knowledge of, propelled only by curiosity.

So we started walking towards the light that surrounded us, as we went through the threshold that it provided. Our eyes were struggling to adapt to the light beyond the portal and the colours that formed the place into which we were transported to.

When my eyes finally focused, I could see a beautiful surrounding, nature at its most distinguished. Trees of a thousand different colours around us, flowers everywhere, mountains in the distance crowned with a thin white flake and right in front of us a majestic waterfall, a hundred feet high. Crystalline water falling gracefully, hundreds of birds chirping excited around it, flying in and out of tree tops. I could even feel the breeze, from the water that splashed down on the rocks below, damping my face, moistening the air that smelled clean and pure. The sky was a beautiful tint of light blue and a few capricious clouds travelled slowly through the void. It was like a dream, a beautiful piece of heaven on earth.

The strange man was standing beside us, as we all marvelled at what we had been shown, I frowned as I thought and asked: "Is all this real?"

He looked back at me, tilted his head and asked: "What do you mean…real?"

I turned to look at this wonder, all around us and asked: "Yeah, I mean, are we still inside of the Virtual Bubble?"

The man tilted his head again and replied: "Yes, but what is real? Isn't real whatever your senses perceive and your brain process?"

The man turned to look at the ground under us, reached down, grabbed a flower, pulled it out and offered it to me. I grabbed the flower in my hand and pulled it close to my nose to smell it.

"You can see its colours, feel its soft consistency, smell its fragrance and even taste its bitterness, if you want. Isn't that real?" He said.

He was right, the flower smelled wonderful, a soft but enticing fragrance filled my nostrils, my brain reacted and this sense of well-being invaded my body. The calm that brings a pleasant smell. I looked at it up close, the detail was amazing, it looked as real as anything I have ever seen.

I turned to see Sarah, that was standing right next to me, I handed her over the flower; she took it and smelled it, as I had done, and her face lighted up with a beautiful smile. I saw her smile, her eyes poignant with the colours of the petals that adorned it, gleaming bright from inside her soul. I grabbed her other hand and my pores opened up to hers, connecting in another level, not just physical, it was something deeper, stronger. It wasn't something that was just defined by the senses, I could feel my whole being connecting with her, yearning hers, yearning her presence, a sparkle that exploded every time I saw her smile. At that moment I realised what this meant for me, the love I felt for her might explain what real was. So I turned to look at the man and said: "Real, is not only what your senses tell you it is, what you can touch, or smell, feel, hear or see. Real is what your heart tells you it is. Real are the things you can see with your soul!"

The man looked at me confused, I could tell he was struggling to answer, trying to make sense of what I just said. His eyes kept wondering around, as if he was reading from a page, looking for the answer between the lines. After a few minutes everything around us started to fade away, the vehicle materialised behind us, exactly where we left it, the ground appeared under us and everything went back to normal. The only thing that remained from everything we experienced, was him.

I looked at him confused and asked: "Who are you?"

"What's your name?" Sarah asked.

He looked at each one and said, this time in a normal voice: "I'm a cyber being, designed by my creator to provide everything he had lost, to create beauty, to reproduce everything in his memories, but I don't have records of what you said, there is no data to support your claims."

I looked at him and sensed sadness, something I didn't expect from someone without a heart or a soul.

"Where's your creator?" I asked.

He bowed his head and said in a sad tone: "He died years ago!"

"You miss him, don't you?" I asked.

He lifted his head up to look at me. At that moment his face mask disappeared and we could see his face. He was young, maybe the same age Sarah and I were. His eyes were filled up with tears, you could tell he was in pain. He just nodded as he looked at me.

"I'm sorry about your loss," Sarah said.

He looked at her and said: "Thank you!"

"But, he must have called you something?" Sarah asked, insisting.

The man looked at Sarah with a tender glance, we could tell he was glad for her concern.

"He called me "Bit", that's what he creator called me anyway," he answered.

Then he turned to look at Juan and Gloria as he pointed to them, his expression changed, a smile captured it as he asked: "Are those your parents?"

"Gloria has always been like a mother to us, he raised us since we were babies," I said.

Gloria smiled at me, she was proud of what I had said and Sarah affirmed it by extending her arm and offering her hand. Gloria grabbed it and walked closer to us. Juan stayed put, he was speechless.

Bit turned to look at him and asked: "What about him?"

The three of us looked at Juan, who was there, waiting for what we would say about him: "Juan is my husband and the love of my life," Gloria said, as she extended her hand to him.

Juan grabbed Gloria's hand and got closer to us.

"Well, you are welcome to stay here with us!" Bit said, which prompted the obvious question: "Us?" I asked.

"People like you, that passed through here and decided to stay and enjoy the beauty I can offer them, whatever it is that they desire, any place they wish to be, anyone they wish they were. I can give you that."

We looked at each other, wondering about it.

"Where is this place? You must have an actual place where these people are, right?" Sarah asked.

"Yes, of course. They are at my creator's house, just over the mountain," he replied.

We looked at each other still wondering what to do. I knew that Gloria and Juan wanted to go home, with their families, where they knew it was safe, but curiosity had the best of us and we wanted to see this place. See what it was he offered, what this people were doing there, what would life be in this place he sold so eloquently.

"I'll take you there if you want!" He offered.

Gloria and Juan looked at each other and nodded, Juan turned to see him and said: "Ok, we would love to see it."

"Great! Let's get going!" He said, as he pointed to the vehicle.

We all got in, he sat in the back next to Sarah and I.

"Just drive straight, over the hill and you'll see a fork on the road. Take the road on the right and follow it until we reach an iron gate."

Juan listened at what Bit said and he drove following his directions. As we were driving down the road, our curiosity grew, we couldn't take our eyes off him, he was so close. Sarah and I had never seen a being like him, up close.

The likeness with us was undeniable, although there was something almost magical about him, he was perfect. There wasn't a single flaw on him, not a wrinkle, or a mole, or a hair out of place, not a vein sticking out, not a spot or a rash, no moles or freckles, no scratches or burns, no scars at all. He looked…new!

Sarah was amazed, looking at him, admiring the uncompromised perfection of his body, wondering how could it be possible. We were both astonished.

He knew we were looking at him, but he didn't feel intimidated by it, probably because he was used to it. After a few minutes of noticing that Sarah and I were wondering about his constitution, he turned to look at us and said: "You can touch, if you want!"

Sarah and I looked at each other, excited and slowly she reached out and touched his arm. She tilted her head as she caressed his skin.

"You are warm!" she said, surprised.

"It feels so natural, like ours," she went on.

"I was designed to mimic humans as close as possible, but what you see now, in front of you, is just my physical vessel," he replied.

"Your physical vessel?" she asked perplexed.

"Yes, my memory and all my vital functions are kept in a safe room on the main house. This is just a projection, a vessel that my mind creates to interact with humans at their own level. Meant to make you feel comfortable."

"A projection? Like a hologram?" I asked confused.

"I'm more of a stereogram" he answered.

Sarah looked at me, hoping for an explanation, she was still confused about him. So I tried to explain, what I thought could define his condition.

"It's like a 3D puzzle!"

Sarah thought about it for a moment and then nodded her head.

"3D puzzles are made up of 3D geometrical figures that attach to each other, to form a bigger, more complex figure. Now, if you could do that at a molecular level, figures so small that they would be the size of cells, then you could build whatever you wanted," I said, as I pointed at him and smiled.

Sarah looked at him and, still confused, asked: "So, he's a geometrical figure?"

I laughed at her commentary and said: "Yes, in a sense, he's just made up of billions and billions of tiny ones."

Sarah looked at him, extended her hand, reached out and touched his arm.

She caressed her forearm with her fingers and felt his skin, his flesh. We could even see his hairs reacting to Sarah's touch.

"But it seems so real, I can feel his pores, even his hairs, sticking out, it's even warm!"

I nodded and said: "Yes, you can build anything!"

I doubted for a second when I thought about the warmth Sarah was feeling in his skin. There couldn't be any actual bodily functions, or could there be?

He saw my doubt and knew exactly what I was thinking, so he smiled and said: "It's vibration, the heat from the friction of particles clashing against each other. That's what mimics the warmth you feel."

"But, do you have a pulse?" I asked.

"I can maybe mimic that too, if I needed to, but there is no blood flowing through my veins, or veins, for that matter or a heart to pump it," he answered.

Sarah's eyes opened wide, as she asked, with the innocence of a child, who just discovered something for the first time: "Can you change into anything?" she asked excited.

He looked at Sarah and slowly answered: "I'm programmed to mimic humans, but I guess I could mimic some other life form if I could find the correct patterns."

"But, can you change into a woman?" Sarah asked.

As soon as she was finished Bit's skin started to vibrate, transforming, morphing into something else, you could actually see the cells that formed its body, move. His hair grew longer, his nails too, his face expression softened and his body changed form. He turned into a beautiful woman with long blonde hair, deep blue eyes and a kind expression.

We were speechless, looking at this happen, right in front of our eyes. Sarah couldn't contain her excitement: "That is awesome! Can you change into anything you want? Anybody? Can you copy me?"

Bit looked at Sarah, roaming her up and down, scanning her in detail and then its body started vibrating again, morphing, changing until he became a perfect image of Sarah.

It was as though she was looking at a mirror, he mimic her movements, her face expressions. It was a little bit freaky for me, seeing this happen. A terrible thought invaded my brain, what if we were that, what if we were built as a compilation of cells after somebodies will, I've always thought of myself as a human being, but what if we were not…

I got scared and shouted: "No, go back!"

Sarah, that was laughing excited, stopped, looked at me confused and asked: "What's wrong Patrick, don't you like looking at me?"

"I like looking at you, not at that! I don't want you to be a machine, something without a soul," I answered.

She looked at me tenderly, she knew exactly what I meant. I wanted her for what she was, I wanted her to be present, like I was. To make my world real, tangible, my future bright. She caressed my face with her hand and smiled.

Bit morphed again, back into the man we met first. He didn't understood what had upset me, how could he? It wasn't a logical thing.

Bit directed Juan to turn right up ahead, there was a big metal gate that started to open, as soon as we approached it and then closed as we drove in.

"Just go to the end of the driveway, next to the main house," he said.

Juan complied and the vehicle stopped on the side of the house. It was a huge mansion, English eighteen century style, it seemed almost like a castle. I had seen it before, in one of those books I loved so much to look at, but I just couldn't place it.

Bit opened up his door and stepped out of the vehicle, we followed and stood outside, admiring the house.

"It's this way!" He said, as he pointed towards a door on the side.

We all walked in as the door opened up. Inside there was this huge hall, beautifully decorated with old classic furniture, paintings on the walls and huge tapestries, rugs that decorated the floor and fresh flowers on a vase, in the centre of the room, that stood in top of a majestic wood table.

We walked through the hall admiring it, every single inch of that place had something amazing to see. It was like a museum, those places I read about so much inside the books that filled the library I grew up in.

Gloria was amazed, as we all were, she had never seen so many beautiful things in one place. So much history. She stopped to look at one particular painting, or better to say, piece of a wall with a painting on it. She fixated on it and we all stopped to wait for her, she raised her hand pointing at it and asked: "This can't be! Is this a Siqueiros?"

Bit got close to it, next to Gloria, that was still breathless and said: "Yes, yes it is! My creator was a collector of human history, he collected as much art as he could during his life, with the idea of preserving it for the future. This particular one, was brought in pieces and put together here, after the building it was in, collapsed many years ago. This way, please!"

Bit pointed to the other side of the hall and we all followed, still admiring all the pieces we saw along the way.

It was an amazing collection, I recognised several items from the books I had read and looked at for years. It was overwhelming to see them up close and realised they were real and they were there. Most of them were considered lost, burned up in the wars, crushed, destroyed, but here they were, like nothing ever happened.

We walked through a very long hallway that led, through the gardens, to a separate building on the back. As we were walking, Bit got close to Sarah and me and asked: "How old are you two? I can't determine your age. I don't think I've encountered someone like you before."

Sarah and I looked at each other, we realised then, that we were even more unique than we could know. This was a dying world, at least for humans, there were no children around, but the world was big and vast, there was a lot of it to see. Maybe we would find a place where children existed, where the future of humanity was not doomed, where hope was still alive. We knew that we were not the answer to that, we had been tested for years, bred to be the solution to this death sentence, but science had failed and the seed was not fertile. So, the only hope was that some other scientists, in some other part of the world, had actually succeeded and had found a way to reverse this damage and allow humans to breed again.

I wasn't sure of our age, only Gloria knew for sure, she had told us many times what our age was, so I looked at her, hoping she will answer, hoping that she would not falter, not back down from what she had told us before.

She looked at us, smiled, walked to where we were and embraced us both, she kissed us in the forehead and said: "These are my kids, Patrick is 16 and Sarah is 18. I've taken care of them since they were babies, watched them grow, nurtured them and watch them become teenagers."

He looked closely at us, his head kept moving sideways, like beating, in a continuous movement. He was trying to compute what he just heard, but there was no match for that information. He finally gave up and said: "I guess it's true. You do learn something new every day!"

Sarah looked around and asked: "So where is everyone?"

Bit pointed to a door at the end of the hall and answered: "Beyond those doors are the living quarters. Everyone is in there."

He invited us to follow him and as we approached, the doors opened wide. There were people in there alright, most of them were on beds, connected to machines with tubes going in and out of their bodies. The rest of them were on wheelchairs, with masks on their faces or lines hanging over them.

They watched as we walked in, their expressions said it all. They were amazed to see people like us, young, healthy. A couple of them, that were able to stand, walked to where we were and touched us, trying to figure if we were the product of a hallucination, or the same system Bit was product of.

They were interested in Sarah and I, I guess they haven't seen someone this young for a while.

"Are you real?" A sweet old lady asked.

"Where do you come from?" An older gentleman asked.

Sarah and I looked at each other, we didn't know what to answer. We didn't actually knew, we were almost certain that we were real, but we didn't know where the lab, where we were conceived, was. The only thing we knew for sure, was that it was far away. We had driven for a couple of days and drove through a lot of terrain to get here. So, we did what we use to do in this cases, we turned to Gloria for answers.

We turned to her and as soon as we did, so did everyone else. Gloria looked back at everyone watching her, waiting for her to say something.

"We come from up north."

"Beyond the barrier?" The old man asked amazed.

"No, we lived in Forestown, near Houston," Gloria replied.

"Are others like them over there?" The old lady asked as she pointed at us.

Gloria paused for a second and said: "No, they are the only ones."

"How come you are not infected? Everyone else over there is. We hear the news you know?" Another older man shouted from his bed, while he pointed at a screen in front of his bed.

I got curious of what it was and walked to his bed side and looked at the screen. There were images rambling on it, changing. Like looking through a window. They seemed so real that I couldn't resist and tried to touch them.

"Hey, leave my TV alone! You'll mess it up," The old man on the bed said, while he pushed my hand off from the screen.

I kept staring at it, amazed. I had never seen a TV before. Only the screens in the operating room inside the lab, where they performed procedures on us.

"We escaped before it spread to where we were. Everyone else took off too. We are heading down south. Just passing by," Gloria said, trying to calm them down.

"You can stay here with us!" The old lady said.

"That's right! You can stay here with us. There is plenty of space. You would have everything you might want," Bit said, agreeing with the lady.

Gloria and Juan, who were silently standing in the corner of the room, looked at each other. Juan looked straight at her, for a moment, and then, his eyes dropped to the ground.

Gloria turned to Bit and said: "We appreciate your offer, this is a beautiful place, but we have to get going. Our families are waiting for us."

Sarah jumped in, visibly upset and said: "What if we want to stay? This seems like a good place, we could have everything we want!"

She grabbed my hand, expecting that I would agree with her. She looked at me and nodded her head, waiting for me to support her.

My head was spinning, it was an amazing place. There was a lot I wanted to learn from in here, from Bit, that had a lot of information, but we would be confined to one place, just as we had been all our lives.

So I turned to look at Sarah, grabbed her hands and said: "I thought we wanted to be free, must of all, be together, out there."

Sarah thought about what I just said, her head was running around the memories she had of her time inside the lab, the freedom she felt when we left that place to realise that everything we dreamed of, we read in the pages of those books was real. That there was a world out there, that we needed to explore.

She squeezed my hand and asked: "But, what if there is nothing more? What if there is no paradise. Maybe this is it!"

"Well, we won't know, unless we search for it, unless we venture, right?" I asked back.

She placed her other hand on top of ours and nodded as she said: "You're right, as long as we are together."

"Are you sure? The world is dying out there, here you would have a chance," Bit said.

"We will take our chances out there! Thank you!" Juan replied.

"I think we should go!" Gloria said as she raised her eyebrows.

"It's your choice, you are free to go, but consider what you are about to do. In here you can be safe, spend the rest of your lives enjoying happiness, being whoever you want to be, going wherever you want to go. Make your own fantasy. Out there you will die, sooner than later, infection is spreading as we speak," Bit said, with this grim tone.

We looked at each other without saying a word, Gloria, Juan, Sarah and I, we were on the same page. I walked to where Bit was, I placed my hand on his shoulder and said: "Our happiness is somewhere else, I hope you can understand that."

He bowed his head, his eyes started blinking fast. After a few seconds he raised his head again and looked at me. I could tell he was trying to understand our reasons, but logic was not on our side.

"I respect your decision, although I just can't understand why," Bit said.

I could sense sadness and confusion in his tone, he was a machine without a heart, a soul, but he could still appreciate human feelings, he was programmed to care, most likely. So I thought I would share our feelings with him, so that he could record it: "Happiness is different for each one of us, it's not embedded in things, or places, or possessions. It's in the love we share, it's in the hope we have, it's in the freedom we crave."

So we said our goodbyes and Bit walked us back to our vehicle. As we walked through the halls, again, I tried to capture an image of each and every one of the pieces of art preserved there. I don't know if I would ever see this place again, if I would see these paintings, these sculptures, these traces of humanity that lied there, in front of our eyes.

As we got to the vehicle, Bit stood in front of Sarah and I, staring, as if he wanted to record every little detail. He took a moment, shook our hands and said: "I've never encountered beings like you, there is something special about you two, something I can't place yet, but I will. I hope you find what you are searching for. I'm sure that you will find happiness…together. Good luck! If there is such a thing."

We both nodded our heads and smiled.

"Good luck to you to Bit," I said, as we got into the vehicle.

We pulled out of the compound and as we were driving away, Sarah and I looked back at it. The gate that delimited the place closed behind us and blurred with the background, disappearing as if it was never there.

Sarah and I looked at each other, I sensed a little bit of regret on her glance. A part of her had liked that place, it was tempting, it was a beautiful one and the promise of having everything you could want was overwhelming. I wasn't sure what was, that Sarah wanted, we haven't talked about it yet. There had to be something she wanted so bad, that the idea of maybe getting it, made her think about staying there.

After a while, my curiosity grew and I couldn't stay silent anymore. So I asked her: "What is it that you wanted to have so bad, that you thought about staying there?"

Sarah looked at me and thought about it for a moment.

"I don't know! Nothing in particular. I just remembered all the things I read about, that I would want to have and the places I always wanted to be in, the people I would want to meet. It was just the idea of being able to achieve everything I've always wanted to do, to have."

I looked at her as she said all that, but her response seemed vague.

"I don't understand!" I asked.

"Well, it was tempting for a moment, but you were right. This is what I really want, to be with you and Gloria, to feel the way I feel right now. To be out here, free, like we are. When you said that, I looked at the room and saw a lot of people, stuck in a room, glued to their beds, to their screens and it felt wrong. I flashed back to the lab and my room and it hit me. That is not what I want!" she replied.

I smiled at her and she smiled back. I kept staring at her face as she was staring at mine. I don't know if it was the happiness she made me feel or the certainty of her presence, the security of her touch or the goose bumps I got every time I felt her next to me, but I couldn't stop staring at her. My life had become this urge to be around her all the time and I couldn't see it any other way.

Chapter 4
The Dream

We kept driving south, headed to Gloria and Juan's town in coastal Mexico. That is where we were hoping to find peace and a place to live, quietly, far away from danger. Apparently the hot climate had a positive effect on the contagion, the virus didn't respond well to heat.

The barrier, that held the spread for decades, had proven so and now, hot weather, was the only hope that humans had for a safe place. I had studied history throughout my life, Inside all those books that became my school. I knew that viruses and bacteria tend to adapt to their environment and there was a possibility that the virus had done so there, but I couldn't tell Gloria, Juan and Sarah that, it would have been cruel and insensitive. It wouldn't have any real purpose, but to scare them and give them uncertainty.

Gloria and Juan's family lived there, in a town known as "Coatzacoalcos". They were hoping to find their loved ones healthy, as they were when they left many years ago, to look for a better life for them and their families. They kept in touch regularly, but for the last few months, that communication broke down, as people fled from the north and communication systems remained unchecked. Panic overtook everything and everyone when the possibility of them dying too, like the rest of humanity, creeped under their skin.

Gloria was becoming increasingly worried about that, she kept trying to find signal on her mobile device, trying to find some kind of message from them, just to know that they were fine. Gloria kept playing over and over again, this message she got a few months back, from her cousin. It was a simple hello, a hologram of her dancing, happy as can be. She kept pushing Juan to hurry up. Juan tried to calm her down as we moved closer to our destination, but we still had hundreds of miles to go and, for a while, we didn't see any sign of people anywhere.

It seemed that we were past the border into Mexico, at some point. The rough terrain suggested we were somewhere in the Chihuahua dessert. Everything became a sea of sand on both sides of the highway and the vegetation changed into a sombre collection of short and stockier plants spaced out in groups along the valleys. It was hot outside, you could tell by the way the ground oozed, as if it were sweating as the sun plunged upon it.

We were in a cocoon inside the vehicle that kept our temperature stable, but the simple touch of my hand on the window was enough to notice the difference with the outside. We couldn't spot any animals during our time through the dessert, but that is the nature of it, life breaths under the surface, looking for shelter from the harsh rays of the sun.

After a while the landscape changed gradually and the temperature subsided. We were advancing into a friendlier climate.

Sarah and I were engaged in marvel, looking at all the places we drove by. Abandoned towns at the edge of the highway, beautiful landscapes that turned from leafy forests into desolated deserts, rugged mountains into endless plains. We saw nature taking over everywhere, wild animals roaming the fields, packing the tree tops, filling up the sky, land and water. Overtaking the planet that was theirs, before it became ours. It was a wonderful sight to see.

It was nature imposing its will. Virus and bacteria didn't seem to affect them: the animals and plants. It was targeted at humans. Like the immune system in our bodies, singles out the disease, but, in this case, we were it, we were the disease and like viruses that attack everything in their path, even themselves, we have brought this upon us. It seemed to be our fault, humans, we created these abominations, in a lab somewhere…

Then I thought: "Sarah and I were created in a lab, by scientists."

I turned and looked at her and thought: "It cannot be, she could never be an abomination, she is the opposite. She is the most beautiful and innocent creature I had ever seen."

They were trying to build a cure for what they had done before. That was our purpose, not to create a weapon or a means to conquer their little worlds; that was our downfall. We were the hope that kept the dream alive, the dream of survival of the human race. The dream of bringing the best in us, getting back the gift that was given to us, the gift that we lost and now were trying to find again. The gift of life.

Our faith was sealed by us, humans, by our wrongdoings, our greed, our sense of superiority, that drove people mad. Thinking they could manipulate the very essence from which we were spawned, and now it was teaching us a lesson…"some things are beyond your control".

After a few hours of driving down this endless roads, that seemed to go forever, we started to lose the battle with consciousness. Sarah gave up first, she got close to me and laid her head on my shoulder. It felt so good to have her face touching me, her body leaning against mine, feeling her warmth possessing me. It was the best feeling I've ever had. The thought that she wanted to be close to me too, that she needed my closeness to feel safe, that she needed my shoulder to lay on. It made my whole world tremble, it made me feel important and proud that I could be there for her. Such a simple thing, that meant so much to me, that gave structure to my life.

I wanted to enjoy this moment, with Sarah by my side while I watched the world unfurl in front of my eyes.

I tried to stay awake, I wanted to see everything out there, I couldn't lose a single moment of this grandeur, but I also fell victim to this numbness. My eyes couldn't sustain the weight of it and my whole body gave up.

I was in a dark room, I couldn't see anything, but as my eyes got used to the darkness, I realised it was just a bedroom, the shades were pulled down shut and I was lying in bed; so I looked around, but I couldn't recognise the room. There were white walls all around, plain, only delimited by huge windows, in front of the bed, covered by thick curtains that blocked the light that was trying to sneak in through the crevices, where it bickered with the darkness that stood its ground.

I noticed there was someone lying next to me, plunged deep inside the covers. All I could see was her hair entangled with the sheets and her nose sticking out, like a periscope, searching for some breathable air outside. She was breathing shallow, and the sheets that covered her body, responded to her chest moving, to the pace that her breathing traced.

I was quite sure it was Sarah, the hair and that pointy nose gave her away, but I couldn't see her face, lost underneath all that interference, so I got close and, slowly, started removing the covers from her, hoping to see her face light up when she saw me, when her eyes opened and she would see me lying next to her, but instead, as I raised the covers, everything started to pulverise. The sheets started turning into dust as I pulled them up and her body began to melt with everything else, began to turn into tiny granules that fell through my fingers. I tried to hold her, tried to pull her out of it, grabbed her arm, but as I did it turned into sand that just trickled through my hand and everything around me disappeared as an intense light blinded me. All that was left was sand around me.

I was in the middle of a dessert, there was nothing around, but sand and the scorching sun that ploughed upon me, like I've never felt before. My skin began to burn as I realised my shirt was gone, only my skin protected me from the rays that plough on me. It was so bright that my sight was diminished, I couldn't see beyond its white halo, so I placed my hand on top of my eyes to block its brightness.

When my eyes were able to see further away, I spotted a glimpse of a skyline in the distance, marked against the brightness of a wall of light, shooting up at the sky. Could this be the wall I read about in the history books? The one that kept us alive all those years?

I pinched my eyes, that were struggling to focus with this intense brightness all around me, they just weren't able to see clearly. I had to get closer to determine where I was. So I stood up and began walking towards the city I could spot in the distance. The heat was stifling, suffocating me more and more with every step I took. I was sweating profusely from the heat, I could feel the water evaporating from my body through every pore, dripping down my face, cascading off my eyebrows and then evaporating off my cheeks, before even reaching my mouth.

I felt my consciousness slipping away as my sight lost focus, but my feet kept moving, pushed by sheer will. I needed to get to the city!

When I came to, I was walking down a boulevard, with skyscrapers on both sides, the heat was bearable, but I was still thirsty as hell. My mouth was crackling from dryness, my lips unable to seal and my tongue struggling to find a wet spot to rest on. As I turned my head, scanning the surroundings, I spotted a fountain down the street to my right. My eyes opened up wide, doubting what they were looking at, but my mind asserted what they had found. So I walked towards it, pulling my legs, that resisted to move anymore, until I reached the edge of the fountain and my whole body plunged inside, like a prisoner set loose, plunges into freedom.

I stayed underwater for a little bit, I needed to feel my body healing, hydrating with the comfort that water brought. Even my brain felt the rush of relief. I began to experience happy thoughts, beautiful images in my head of Sarah's face, Gloria's smile and moments that filled my memory with joy: like every time Gloria sneaked in a cake on my birthday, or the first time I saw Sarah, that feeling I would never forget, that only grew stronger with every moment we spent together, like the first time I touched her hand, felt her warmth tingling my flesh, feeling every cell in my body responding to her.

It was a nice place to be, surrounded by the healing powers of water and the weightlessness it provides. My eyes were wide open, admiring the refraction of the light that pierced through the water, struggling to penetrate its virtues.

I could have stayed longer, but I needed some air, so I surfaced. I was marvelled to see water surrounding me, embracing me like a true friend that knows your needs and is willing to give himself up for your happiness, your wellbeing. There were drops of water bouncing off the surface, falling from the sky and echoing with the water under it, baptizing me with a sense of joy I had never experienced. I looked up at the sky, I could see the drops fall from hundreds of feet up in the air, all the way from the dark clouds that carried them and I thought: "So this is what rain looks like!".

It was magical, I was overtaken by the beauty of it all, looking at raindrops falling from the sky, freely, with nothing holding their fall, until they finally hit the ground, and around me, bounced off the surface of the water just before melting with it, creating a symbiosis only liquids can achieve. The smell when they fell and hit the ground and soaked the dust that covered everything was intoxicating. It spread all around and whisked through everything, perfuming it all.

I opened up my mouth and stuck my tongue out, hoping to fill my gal with whatever this small pieces of heaven were carrying. The feeling was orgasmic, I could sense each and every drop that soaked my tongue and melted away, enticing my taste buds with their tasteless seasoning, running down my throat until they forced me to swallow them down, feeling them flow slowly inside my body, fusing with my being.

I was enjoying that, but there were more pressing matters in my head: "Where was I?" What was this place?"

So, I snapped out of it and stepped out of the fountain to try to get my bearings. The sun was covered by the clouds, I couldn't tell North from South, East from West. I was in the middle of an intersection, a roundabout that the fountain defined. Surrounded by skyscrapers half destroyed, most of them were missing the top and rubble laid all over the streets. Some of the taller buildings got lost in the thick clouds overcasting the sky. The water falling washed away the dust that covered everything and cleaned the big pieces left of, what used to be, the skyline up above.

I figured I would walk…somewhere, I just couldn't stay still, so I started walking straight ahead, through a clearing on the street. I could still see the wall of light in the background, flashing up into the sky, even with the thick clouds covering everything and the rain falling down. So I headed that way, attracted by the bright light, like a bug, without really thinking why that was. You could hear the constant buzzing of the light in the wall, tantalising, hypnotising me to come near, to join whatever it offered, blinded and mesmerised by its power.

There was all kind of debris on the ground, old vehicles smashed to pieces, crushed under huge pieces of cement and steel that pulverised them into nothing. Abandoned belongings that stood there as clues to what had happened: suitcases, supermarket cars, clothes…all kinds of reminders of a normal life, of what things used to be before the "Great War", of the numbness that habit entitles.

What was this place? I couldn't figure it out. It was hard to determine what city it was with so much destruction around, I couldn't see any defining structures that would give me a hint. It seemed as if time had stopped right after destruction halted. There was no proof of life anywhere around me, only the rubble remained as proof there ever was. If this was one of the cities destroyed during the war then: "What was the wall doing here, so close?"

According to the books I've read, the wall was built up north, far away from cities and towns, so that no one could come close and get incinerated by accident. It was a dangerous perimeter and it was kept protected as such.

I kept walking, making my way closer and closer to the wall. The place was deserted, I couldn't see any sign of movement or life around this wasteland. I was all alone. I got to the top of a hill, almost at the outskirts of the city, from where I could see the wall in the distance. The rain was falling down hard and that made it difficult to see clearly far away, but in the short glimpses, between drops, I thought I saw swarms of people close to the wall.

"That can't be!" I said out loud.

What were they doing there, so close to the wall? I tried to focus better by placing my hand on top of my eyes, trying to avoid the rain that blocked my view. At that distance, they looked like ants all headed to the same destination, gathering at their nest, moving like waves in the sea; thousands of heads asserting the same motion.

I had to get closer, my curiosity was driving me there, my feet were moving without me commanding them, they were moving of their own free will. Attracted by a force beyond my comprehension.

I got close enough to see them better and as I did, the rain suddenly stopped, as if someone had turned off the water, the heavens just opened up enough to allow a few rays of sunshine to melt through the darkness. I stood on the top of a mount, to my right, just over the valley where everyone was gathered. The wall of light was just in front and you could clearly hear the humming noise it made, while the light beams shoot up into the sky. It was almost haunting, it seemed that everyone gathered there was possessed by its beauty, its power, its overwhelming spell. They were all staring at it, like dormant, advancing towards it.

I could see them tip toeing closer and as I looked further down, to the front of the group, a few hundred feet away, I saw people walking into it, without hesitation. Just stepping onto death! The moment their bodies crossed the threshold, they were pulverised. Turned into dust. A loud buzzing sound, accompanied the bright flash of light that marked the end. I couldn't believe my eyes! They were all committing suicide! They were so many, that the events seemed like one huge explosion.

I could see their bodies disappear, turned into particles, separated by the incredible power of the light that dismembered every single cell in their entities and as I looked up, following the beam that rose up into the sky, I could see their souls traveling with it, like ghosts flying towards the light.

My whole body was trembling, seizing in desperation. So many lives were ending, thrown into omission by so much pain and sorrow. Trying to find a way out of this hell, but I knew there was hope, I could feel it in my bones.

As soon as I realised what they were doing, I started screaming, trying to get their attention, something inside me was directing me to stop them: "Hey, hey! Stop! What are you doing? Stop!"

But it was futile, no one was listening. They wouldn't even acknowledge my presence there, I was invisible. I ran into the crowd, hysterical, yelling at the top of my lungs, grabbing them, shaking them, hoping they would come back to, but they were numb to my intent to save them. Their eyes were blank, staring into nowhere, so I started pushing them aside, trying to get to the front: "Hey! Stop! Hey!"

I had to do something to stop them, to make them realise what they were doing, but every effort was useless.

I pushed them, screamed at them and they would just ignore me, like I wasn't there. They would go back to their walk, to their slow commitment with death. It seemed that they wanted that, that they were hoping for it.

As much as I tried to get to the front, it was impossible, they were too many, too close. It was like trying to get through an impregnable barrier. After a while of trying, my body couldn't take it anymore, there was no more strength left in me and I fell to the ground, desperate. I cried out of frustration and grief for so many deaths, so many souls being set free for no other reason: than surrender.

I could understand their motives, their offset with life: so many years of looking death in the eye, so many hopes crushed, vanished, yearning for redemption, for some kind of freedom from so much pain, so much suffering, so much death. They had given up, accepted the fact that death by their own hand, was better than the misery they've had to endure for so long.

My crying wouldn't wash away any of it, my sorrow wouldn't help them anymore. It was done, this was the end. I sat there, looking at them walk into their faith, to the only freedom they would be granted…death!

Their expressions said it all, their ravished bodies told the story of their lives. The lack of food, nourishment, had taken a toll, disease had snatched every ounce of health they could've had, every trace of happiness they could've mustered, and turned them into decaying shells. Feelings had long been vanished, together with their humanity…they were dead long ago, they just wanted to speed up the process and they didn't care about anybody else, about anyone beside them. It was a common wish, they were a flock, just following everyone else.

I couldn't look at them anymore, I was horrified at their condition, at their lack of empathy, but they were everywhere, all around me. Thousands of them, women, men, hoping for one thing…the end.

I was about to close my eyes, in shame, feeling a ton of guilt oppressing my chest, hoping that, when I opened them up, I would be somewhere else, far away from here…but when I was about to close them I saw something in the distance that caught my eye, between the bodies dragging past me. Something that didn't fit in the picture. It was a figure that stood still, a shorter version of the ones walking by. As my eyes centred on it, filtering away all the noise that blocked my view, I saw a child looking back at me, curious, his head was tilted sideways.

He was clean, healthy, his hair was short, blonde, dressed in a tee shirt and jeans, holding a teddy bear in his hand.

I could see his image flashing between the bodies that moved past my field of view, he was still, looking back at me. We were…around fifty feet from each other. I raised my hand, to say hello, and he did the same, but he added something…his face lighted up with the most beautiful smile I had ever seen, his innocence belated all the pain that surrounded us and made it diffuse in the background, making me forget for a second what was happening all around us and I smiled back.

A smile, that represented all the hope that had been lost and the perseverance we lacked.

The boy kept smiling as everything around me started disappearing, everything faded to black and as darkness took over, I began hearing Sarah's voice, calling my name, pulling me out of the emptiness I was in…and so I opened up my eyes!

Sarah was shaking me and repeating over and over again: "Patrick, Patrick wake up!"

I could feel her worry as she did, wondering if I would ever wake up. Apparently I had been asleep for a long time, moving constantly from side to side, making noises and talking in my sleep, until finally she couldn't contain herself anymore and committed to waking me up.

As soon as I saw her face, vanishing all the darkness I had been through, I smiled and launched myself at her, attracted by her lips that called on me, from beyond my dream, from the hereafter that defined my hopes in the future, from the love I felt for her…and so, I kissed her.

She was stunned, but delighted, as I was, to finally surrender to the feeling that besieged us, that started consuming us since before we met for the first time; when she lived in my dreams. She kissed me back, looking for the same thing I was, the thing that I found in her lips, that overtook my senses, the love I yearned for so long.

We were trapped in that moment when Gloria turned around and saw us kissing, her first reaction was surprise and embarrassment: "Kids! What are you doing?" she asked.

We stopped, just enough, to see her looking at us, but her expression changed. She was smiling, which actually meant that she was glad to see us love each other, but she didn't know how to act on it. So she turned around, facing away from us.

We weren't going to stop now, now that we had found heaven in each other's arms. So we looked at each other and, like magnet and steel, that can't stop attracting one and other, we kissed some more. It was the most innocent thing I had ever done, to love without prejudice, to care without interest, to let your heart guide your every move, your every yearning.

Gloria and Juan, pretended not to notice what we were doing in the backseat. The explosion of passion that drenched every inch of space, scented by so many hormones bursting out of our bodies. It was just normal that we felt this way, we were teenagers still. Gloria and Juan had memories, of the time they shared together, when they were young, so they were happy to see us feeling the same.

We had discovered what our mouths could do, besides eating and drinking, and this was way more fun. We were learning a new language, a new way of communicating beyond words. It felt as if every part of my body vibrated with her and exploded in my mouth, with the touch of her lips.

I wanted to venture with my hands and touch every part of her body, but I was cautious, maybe a little bit afraid that it would be too much. That she would consider that rude, invasive. After all, we had just met a few days ago.

I had read so many books about love, in the library, but nothing compared to the feeling that besieged me when she was close, when her lips were entangled with mine. This had to be love. It mimicked every description I had read before, every aspect was revealed as she gave herself up to the same feeling I was. Everything else just blurred in the background, we were closing in on the end of the world and all I could think of, was her…

I guess that is the point, we live in this huge, complex place where millions of other humans coexist with us, but at the end of the day, the only world that matters is our own. Our own little world, the one that surrounds us and the part of that bigger one that we let in. We have a responsibility with the commonality as a part of it, as an individual, but it all starts with yourself. In this dire times, it was about surviving and counting that it would then contribute to the whole.

She had become my world now, she was the most important part of my small sphere, the one that defined me and the one thing I wanted to live for.

Nothing could separate us now. We were beating with one heart, breathing at the same pace. We couldn't stay away from each other.

And so, the journey went on. We had been driving for eight hours straight that day, Gloria and Juan were in charge of the vehicle and setting up directions, but most of the time, they were answering questions that we had. Sarah and I marvelled at the scenery and each other. We were enjoying every moment.

It was beautiful out here and looking at it first hand was mind boggling. Sometimes it still felt like I was looking at one of those books in the library but the depth made it so real, I could actually reach out my hand and touch it. Like I could reach out and touch Sarah, she was real and she was sitting next to me.

I was still trying this on for size, this new feeling, this whole world that invaded my senses, so, instinctively, I reached out and touched Sarah's hand. I just gently placed my hand over hers. The first thing I noticed was the warmth that radiated from her, this tender sensation that merge into my hand when I did.

I looked up and Sarah was looking back at me, smiling. I felt ashamed and pulled my hand off hers, as If I had done something wrong. She just giggled a bit.

We were running low on food and supplies and we had to stop for a technical run, again…you know, we needed to go to the bathroom, desperately.

"I'm serious, we need to stop soon or I'm going to burst right here!" I said, clinching my legs.

Gloria turned around to see me as she frowned and said: "You should have gone on the last stop, I told you!"

"Well, I'm sorry but I wasn't ready then, I'm ready now thought," I said, with urgency.

Juan looked at me on the rear view mirror, he looked around us and pointed out to a city, just beyond the horizon. Gloria turned and looked at it too, you could see some of the skyscrapers in the distance.

"What is that, where are we?" Gloria asked.

Juan shrugged and said: "It can be Zacatecas, or some other city south of that. I haven't seen any signs for a while."

Gloria looked back at Juan and asked: "Do you think it's safe? We could just pull over on the side of the road. It's just number one right?"

I was thinking of my dream, the city looked somewhat like the city in my dreams, so I didn't pay attention to what Gloria had just said.

"Patrick!" she called my name, upset.

I snapped out of it and turned to look at her, I was completely lost on the subject.

"It's just number one?"

I nodded as Juan started saying: "I think we need to stop there, we might be able to find some supplies. We are running really low and I'm not sure how far away we are. Maybe we will be able to get directions."

Gloria looked at him, like he was crazy and he said: "There is no one there, we haven't seen a soul for days."

Gloria didn't look convinced, I noticed her voice shivering when she turned around and said: "Don't talk to anyone, don't get close to anyone. We don't know how things are over here. There could still be infected!"

Sarah and I nodded, but that wasn't enough.

"Are you listening to me? This is very serious."

"Yes, we understand. Don't worry, we'll be fine!" I replied while Sarah just nodded.

We were aware of the dangers we were facing, but somehow, looking at all this beautiful places we have driven by, made it less urgent. It's this weird thing, you relate something bad with darkness and ugliness. You never expect to find danger in beauty, surrounded by light, inside of calm and something familiar.

Chapter 5
The Glimpse

We drove to the city, that seemed bigger as we drove closer. It was just over a valley and as we began our descent, we could see it was massive. It spread for miles on both sides.

We approached from the north on a huge highway that seemed to be the main entrance. All signs were in Spanish and as we were trying to figure out where we were Juan said, while he pointed at a sign on the side of the road: "San Luis! We are so close."

Gloria got excited at first but then, as she looked around the city, her eyes open wide and she said to Juan: "This can't be San Luis, this is one of the biggest cities I've ever seen. San Luis was just a small town."

"That was over 30 years ago Baby, a lot of people moved down south getting away from danger."

Gloria thought about it as she looked at the buildings around us. The city looked deserted, abandoned houses and stores. Cars on the side of the road, belongings long forgotten. The buildings looked intact, this wasn't like the city in my dreams. There was no destruction, only emptiness. I was trying to spot some people, but I couldn't see any. It seemed to be a ghost town. Time stood still, as if every inhabitant had been snatched from their lives in a whim. It was the afternoon and the sun was going down on the horizon, there was plenty of light still and we could see for miles ahead of us.

"Where is everybody?" Sarah asked as she looked outside the window.

Juan and Gloria stayed quiet, they didn't knew the answer to that question. It was the same one on their minds, repeating itself, like an omen, curiosity turned into concern and concern into fear. It was chilling to watch. We kept driving down the main highway, miles and miles into the city and still not a soul.

Juan and Gloria looked at each other, I could see that they were thinking the same bad thoughts. They couldn't know what had happened here, but they were afraid it would be the one thing that they dreaded the most. That everyone had died, that the spread of the virus had reached down south.

The hope of finding their families alive and well was disappearing by the minute. We were close to our destination and the fact that, this city was deserted, wasn't a good sign.

"I'm getting off the highway, we need to take a look up close."

We all remained silent, we trusted Juan by now, he had gotten us this far, but still, part of us doubted that this was a good idea.

We drove through the streets, between the high rises that seem to go on forever, each one was taller than the other one, but still, the one thing we wanted to see was not there.

"Wait! Stop!" Sarah shouted while she pointed at something down the street.

Juan stopped the vehicle and backed up a little, to see the place where Sarah was pointing to.

At first we couldn't see what Sarah had seen, it just looked like rubble, furniture laid on the floor, garbage taking over the streets, but as we all looked closer, we could see something moving on the background, slowly. It was all shades of grey, everything was covered with a monochromatic light.

Juan turned towards the movement, slowly got closer until we could define what we were looking at.

There were people moving between the rubble, searching for things they could use. They were concentrated on it, so much so, that they didn't even noticed us approaching them.

Juan found a place where he could park the vehicle on the right and pulled over. As soon as he did, Gloria said, I could tell she was upset: "What are you doing? We can't stop! What if they see us?"

Juan turned to look at her and tried to calm her down: "It's ok, we need to know what's going on."

"But what if they are infected, we can all die right here!" Gloria said, getting to the point of breaking down.

Juan signalled with his eyes, he was worried about what we might think of that, but he didn't wanted to say it out loud. He grabbed Gloria's hand and caressed it. Gloria calmed down a bit.

"It's ok, I have the scanner. If we detect anything, we will leave, but we need to find food and supplies," he said.

Gloria turned around, looking at the empty streets, the rubble and said: "Look at this place, do you think we will find anything in here!"

"We have to try! What other options do we have?" Juan responded.

"Yes, we have to try Gloria, It will be ok!" I said, trying to reassure her.

She looked at me and smiled, she took Sarah's hand, that was on the side of Glorias seat and said: "Ok, but we have to stick together, promise me that!"

We all agreed, nodding our heads. We opened up the doors and stepped out of the vehicle, grabbed a few bags and followed Juan down the street to where those people were.

Juan was looking at the scanner, to make sure they were free from infection. Tensions grew as we got closer to where we had seen movement. Gloria turned to look at Juan, he raised his eyes and nodded, he wasn't getting any indication of infection. We were in the clear…for the time being.

We kept walking down the street, hoping to see a market, or someplace where we could find some supplies, but all we could see: were closed doors and shattered windows covered with wood panels, abandoned cars and empty buildings surrounding everything.

We finally found something that seemed to be a market, the doors were wide open, almost torn out. We walked in, hoping to find some left overs, but there were just empty shelfs, broken up fridges and trash all over the place.

The market had been abandoned a long time ago, emptied and sacked by people, looking for the same thing we were. Gloria realised it would be almost impossible for us to find any supplies and got worried, she felt responsible for all of us.

"Don't worry Gloria, we will find something!" Sarah said, trying to comfort her.

Gloria reached out, caressed Sarah's face and just smiled, she didn't knew what to say.

We all walked out of the market and stood on the street. We were just wondering what to do. There didn't seem to be any options. We were all lost in the midst of the devastation we were witnesses of.

A few people picking anything they could find, between the rubble, the trash. They seemed lifeless, like zombies; their eyes were lost, wondering in another place. They didn't even noticed us walking amongst them. It just felt as if they were disconnected from this world, they were in survival mode, just looking for something to eat.

"We shouldn't get that far from the vehicle," Juan said as he slowed down and stopped.

"We need to find supplies, if it's not here, where?" Gloria asked.

Juan looked around in silence, he didn't seem to have an answer for that.

We were all overtaken by sadness and despair. I could feel it in the air, all around us, it was contagious and it was infecting us too. I turned to see the expression on each one, I looked at Sarah first, it was like looking at a ghost. Her expression was lost in the void, it was fixed straight ahead, looking at nothing and for the first time, since we met, she wasn't looking back at me as I looked at her.

"Sarah! Sarah!" I called her, but it was as if she couldn't hear me.

I turned to look at Gloria, she was in the same trance Sarah was. Juan was as well. I knew that we needed to snap out of this, before it took me too and then we would all be under.

"No, no. Sarah!" I shouted again, but this time I took her arms and shook her as hard as I could.

She finally looked at me and asked confused: "What happened?"

She looked around and saw Gloria and Juan in a trance and asked again: "What's happening to us?"

I forced her to focus on me.

"Look at me! Sarah, look at me!" I said.

She looked into my eyes and calmed down.

"We need to get out of here!" I said.

She nodded and I asked: "Help me wake up Gloria, we need to move!"

Sarah grabbed Gloria's shoulders and shook her as hard as she could while she screamed: "Gloria! Gloria!"

I did the same with Juan, until we were able to wake them up from the state they were in.

"What happened, where are we?" Gloria asked confused.

"We need to get out of here. I think it's a pathogen," I said.

"A pathogen?" Juan asked. As he regained consciousness.

"Yes, we have to get out of here. I'll tell you all about it later," I said, prompting them to move.

We all rushed to the vehicle, got in and drove from that place. While we were driving, Gloria asked: "What do you mean a pathogen? Like an infection?"

"No, I read about it in the library. Germans and Americans started experimenting with behavioural science back in Second World War and it got finally perfected during the Vietnam War. That same science was used indiscriminately in the Great War. The military experimented with different drugs, drugs that would allowed them to control people's behaviour. Made their enemies more prone to defeat. They even used it in their own soldiers, to incite aggression and eliminate remorse," I explained.

"What are you saying? We didn't eat or drink anything," Sarah asked.

"We wouldn't have to, the book said that they had found a way to make it airborne. They only needed to release it in the air," I answered.

"So, if we move far away, we would be ok?" Gloria asked.

"I think so, it would dissipate. Besides, we were exposed for just a little bit, those drugs take time to change you," I answered.

"How can we know if we're safe?" Juan asked.

"Oh! We would know. You should have seen yourselves, you were also acting like zombies!" I said.

Gloria and Juan looked at each other.

"Right!" He answered, as he looked at Gloria from top to bottom. She seemed normal.

"Why are you looking at me like that?" Gloria said upset at the way Juan was looking at her.

Juan just shrugged and kept on driving.

"You were all zombie like too! Mira este!" Gloria said. Sarah and I couldn't avoid laughing.

Juan interrupted our fun and said: "We still need to find supplies!"

I looked around, we were still inside the city but I couldn't see any more zombies roaming the streets.

"I think it's safe!" I said.

Gloria and Sarah looked out the window and agreed.

"It looks ok!" Sarah said.

"Well let's stop around here and look for some!" Gloria said to Juan, he nodded and pulled over to the right. Parked on the side of the street and slowly opened up his door.

He took a big whiff and paused for a few seconds, we were all looking at him, waiting for something to happen, or not. He turned around, his eyes were open wide and his expression seemed lost.

Gloria was worried, she was looking straight at him and I could tell she was starting to panic.

"Juan?" she asked as Juan started to mumble and growl.

Gloria's face turned pale, she started to pull away from him, pushing her body against the door. Her hands were clawing down on the seat, frightened.

Sarah and I looked at each other wondering what to do, we were speechless, paralysed.

Juan was still acting up, Sarah and I looked at each other and I felt this thunderbolt roam down my spine. Gloria was still freaking out, looking at him, imagining the worst.

We were looking at him in silence, he was still mumbling and growling...but the growling turned into laughter. He started laughing so hard while looking at Gloria, he was just mocking her, making fun of her face, of the way she freaked out.

We realised that, he was trying to be funny. Gloria didn't think so, she got pissed and started hitting him while he laughed and laughed. It was contagious, we couldn't help it and we started laughing too. Everyone, except Gloria. She was pissed!

"You're an idiot! I can't believe it!" she kept yelling.

Juan couldn't stop laughing, he got out of the vehicle and said: "You should have seen your face! It was priceless!"

Gloria got angrier and stepped out of the vehicle too. She kept cursing at Juan: "Asshole! You think that's funny? I almost had a heart attack!"

"I'm sorry, I just couldn't help it. I knew you would freak out," Juan responded.

"And how is that funny? Fuck you!" Gloria went on.

Juan's eyes opened wide, he turned to look at us and said: "Hey! Language!"

I've never imagined that Gloria could get that mad, she just extended her hand and gave Juan the finger.

Sarah and I got out of the vehicle and tried to change the subject: "We need to look for supplies," Sarah said.

"Yeah, we need to hurry, before it gets dark," I added.

Juan nodded, Gloria was still angry and couldn't focus. So Juan took the initiative and said: "Lets walk that way, there seems to be a commercial area over there!"

Juan started walking and we followed, only Gloria stayed behind. After a few paces, I turned around and saw her standing there, unwilling to follow Juan. So I turned around, walked to her and said: "Come on Gloria, It was a little bit funny!"

She looked at me and shrugged as she gave me the eye.

"No, it wasn't! It was mean and insensible!" she replied.

I smiled a little, because I knew deep down inside she acknowledge, it was funny!

She looked at me and couldn't help but smiling a little too, so I placed my arm over her shoulders and pulled her our way. We started walking behind Juan and Sarah.

As we got to the end of the block, we could see Juan looking down the street to his left and Sarah standing right beside him. They were looking at something we couldn't see yet, hiding behind the buildings lining the street we were walking on.

"What? What is it now? This better not be another one of your pranks Juan!" Gloria said upset.

We kept walking until we reached the corner and looked down the street, at the intersection, the one they were looking down on. Gloria's face lighted up!

Right there, in front of us, we could see a building with the logo of the company they worked at, the one that kept us captive for so many years. I felt a chill that overtook my body as I felt Sarah's hand grab mine. That same chill had already taken her and now we were both standing there, looking at this sign, holding our breath.

Gloria saw us, frightened like kittens, looking at it. She approached and placed her hands on our shoulders, looked into our eyes, so that we would focus on hers, and said: "Don't worry, I would never let them do that to you again. This is a good thing for us!"

I looked into Gloria's eyes, wondering what she meant. Puzzled as to why this would be a good thing.

"I'm sure we can find some supplies in there," she said, as she looked into my eyes.

"You can stay in the vehicle while we go in!" Juan said, while he got close to us.

He turned to look at the building and the surroundings and said: "It looks deserted anyway. I don't think there is anyone in there."

"It's your choice, I won't make you go in there, if you don't want to," Gloria said.

Sarah and I looked at each other, I felt her hand tighten her grip. She was waiting for me to decide for both of us. She felt safe with me, when we were together, and that was enough assurance. She wanted me to decide.

I turned and looked at Juan and Gloria and said: "We will go with you, you'll need our help."

Sarah just nodded, while she grabbed my arm with her other hand. We all walked towards the building. Every step we took, raised my heart rate a little bit more and by the time we got to the entrance, my heart was jumping out of my chest, but I couldn't show it. I had to be strong for Sarah, she was hanging on to me, as if she was falling and I was the only thing she could grab on to.

We approached the building and walked in, the doors were wide open. It seemed to be abandoned. We walked to the stairs. Juan stopped just before, he was looking at the map of the building. Gloria got close and asked: "What are you looking for?"

"I don't see a supply storage, or anything like that, but there should be some supplies in this level," he said as he pointed to an area on the map.

Gloria looked at it, frowned and said: "That's underground! Are you sure?"

"Yeah! It's just offices on the upper levels, but this area looks like labs. The supplies would be there. Besides if we find anything at all, it would be better to find it under there. They would be better preserved."

Gloria agreed and we kept on walking towards the stairs. There was no power, so when we reached the stair case and looked down, the only thing you could see was blackness.

"Are we going down there?" Sarah asked. Her voice was trembling.

"Don't worry, we'll be ok!" Juan said, as he opened up his hand and a little drone took off and raised above our heads. It lighted up, illuminating everything around us.

"Come on, let's go!" Juan said, as he started walking down the steps.

The little drone followed him. We were still standing still, not really sure about what we were going to do.

Juan paused, looked at where we were and said: "If you stay there, you'll end up in the dark. The drone follows me, everywhere I go, so we have to stick together."

We didn't want to be left alone in the dark, so we stepped it up and followed Juan. We went down a few levels, which seemed like a lot more. We could only see the area we were walking on, the area the drone was illuminating. Everything else was pitch black.

There were scratching noises all around us, as if the building was moving and a distant dripping sound, continuous, rhythmic, almost haunting, it was driving me mad.

"How much longer?" I asked.

"It's the next level, level SUB5," Juan answered, as we kept on walking down.

I could see the marking on the walls, we were passing level "SUB4".

"It's only been four floors?" I asked confused.

"Yeah! The darkness makes it seem like a lot more. Almost there!" Juan answered.

We were walking slowly, holding hands to avoid getting lost or someone tripping. Sarah was holding my hand and I was holding Gloria's. She was right behind Juan.

"This is it?" Juan said, as we reached level "SUB5".

He pulled the door opened and a vacuum sound deafened us. It sounded like a fridge being opened, but amplified a thousand times. We walked inside, it was cold and dark.

It was a long hallway filled with metal doors. Juan stopped in front of one of them and pulled it open. He held it opened as we walked inside.

"Where are we?" Gloria asked.

"This is where they kept the supplies," he said as he pulled out a flashlight and pointed it at some shelves in front of us.

They were filled with cans and boxes, organised and labelled.

"Oh my god! I can't believe this!" Gloria said excited, almost screaming, when she saw all that.

Sarah and I were still confused, we didn't know exactly what that was. You see, Juan worked in the kitchen that prepared our food and everyone else's, apparently, so he knew exactly where to find the supplies and knew what they looked like.

Gloria was the one that served us, she wasn't part of the kitchen staff, like Juan was, but she use to see the cans and boxes we were looking at, all the time.

Gloria and Juan were happy, embracing each other and jumping up and down, which made the light flicker on and off all around us. It was making Sarah and me dizzy.

"Stop, stop!" I said, while I grabbed their hands.

They stopped jumping and looked at us, they were still smiling.

"It's like you found a treasure. So, Is this what we were looking for?" Sarah asked.

"It is a treasure!" Juan responded.

"Yes, we hit the jackpot!" Gloria said.

"We could feed a hole village with this much food," Juan insisted as he pointed at it with the light.

I looked down, to where the beam of light was aiming. Everything looked untouched, aligned and very neatly organised.

"But, how long have this food been in here. Is it still good?" I asked.

"It's packed and processed specifically so that it lasts for years. I'm sure its fine. Even though there is no power, it's freezing down here," Juan responded.

Gloria was reading the labels of the boxes closest to us, she was looking for the expiration date.

"It's fine, the expiration date is not for another few years," she said.

"But, how are we going to get everything upstairs? There is no light!" Sarah asked.

Juan and Gloria looked at each other and ponder the problem for a moment.

"I guess that we are going to have to do a lot of trips. Somebody will have to light the way, while the rest of us carry the stuff," Juan said.

Then he turned around and opened up a cabinet based him. There was some equipment inside. He grabbed some flashlights.

He handed over a flashlight to Sarah, she looked down on it, doubting. We were all looking at her, so she took it and looked at me. I smiled and nodded.

Juan, Gloria and I grabbed some boxes, as much as we could carry and began the task. Sarah was walking behind us, lighting the way up so that we could see where we were stepping on and wherever Juan went, the small drone helped light up the way too. We made it to the top of the stairs, pushed the door opened and walked across the main lobby. Before we made it to the glass doors, Juan said: "Wait, let's put them down here, next to the door. We have to first bring as much as we can up here. When we have enough, I'll bring the vehicle around and we'll transfer them there."

We all agreed and began piling them up on the side of the door, where they couldn't be seen and went back down again for more.

We must have done a hundred trips, my legs were killing me, but time was not on our side. We knew we had to finish before somebody outside realised what we were doing. We hadn't seen anybody around, but that didn't mean that there was no one.

"Ok! I think that's enough. I don't even know if we can fit this much in the vehicle. I'll bring it to the front and get as close as I can to the door. We have to do this fast!" Juan said as we all struggled to catch our breath, we sat down on the floor and laid against the boxes.

"Wait! We have to rest, besides its not completely dark out, if we start doing this now, someone will see us!" Gloria said.

Juan looked outside, then looked at his watch and said: "You are right! We need to wait a little bit, until it is completely dark. We'll rest for a while."

"I don't think I've ever been so tired in my life!" I said.

"My legs are killing me and I didn't even carry all of this up the stairs. You guys must be exhausted!" Sarah said as she massaged her legs.

Juan was still standing, looking at us. He was pumped up, still excited about our discovery.

"Try to sleep for a little bit, get your strength back. I'll keep an eye out," he said.

Gloria had closed her eyes already, Sarah snuggled against my arm and laid her head on my shoulder as she closed her eyes. I kissed her forehead as she gave up and fell asleep. I loved feeling her beside me, completing me. Her warmth was all I could ever need to feel fine.

"Aren't you tired?" I asked Juan.

He nodded and said: "I am, but someone has to be alert and watch over. I'll take the first watch. I'll wake you up in a while, so you can relieve me."

I agreed and closed my eyes, just before I could even think about it. I was sleeping.

It was a comforting feeling, to have Sarah close, being so tired, even my brain was refusing to spawn the classic nightmares I was used to. I don't remember what I dreamed, I just remember what woke me up: "Patrick, Patrick!" Juan said, over and over, while he shook me.

I opened up my eyes, he was kneeled next to me, waiting for me to wake up. I could tell that he was worried, something had spooked him.

As soon as he saw I was awake, he placed his finger over his mouth.

"Shhh, don't make a sound!" He said.

"What's going on?" I asked.

"Shhh!" He repeated as he placed his finger over his mouth again.

He then moved his head, pointing at the door.

"Don't wake them up!" He whispered as I got up.

I made sure Sarah was comfortable, leaning against the boxes. I placed my jacket on her and followed Juan to the edge of the door.

He pointed out to the side of the plaza where the building was. I could see some movement, but it was difficult to pin point. It was pitch black out there, so I whispered: "What is it? What did you see?"

Juan placed his finger on his mouth again and then pointed to the right of the glass door, just a few feet away.

I focused on what Juan was trying to show me. It was so dark, all you could see were different shades of grey, blue and black.

My eyes began to get a costumed to the darkness and that was when I was able to see silhouettes moving on the side of the building, at the beginning, they were just undefined silhouettes, moving erratically, slowly, but as they came closer I could see that they were people moving around, almost dragging their feet.

They were getting closer to the door and as they approached, their condition revealed. Their faces, their hands, their whole bodies were ravaged by disease, malnourishment and God knows what else. You could feel their pain, even through the darkness that coveted them from the sun, from the light that made their condition worse.

They were "nightwalkers", I had read about them in the library. On the briefs that still came in, that spread out the news of what was going on out in the world. I always consider them fiction, they read like a comic book to me. I was inside this secluded place then, cut out from the world outside, from its wonders, but also from its terrible flaws, from the sins that had destroyed it. So, to me, they were just a legend.

The "nightwalkers", according to the briefs, were pseudo-humans that survived the Great War, but came out of it changed, morphed into a different species. Still human looking, but had adapted to withstand the worst abuse a human could endure. Adapted to survive the damage all the viruses and bacteria had left behind, the diseases that destroyed most of their integrity, of their human condition, but by doing so their bodies had to protect themselves against nature, against the exposure to sunlight. So they only came out at night, when the sun wouldn't expose their fatal failures. Hence the name "Nightwalkers".

According to the briefs, they were a dying breed, subject to extinction in just a few short years. Unable to reproduce, they were just prolonging their agony in this world. Extending their inevitable demise until not even their ability to mutate could keep them alive.

Still, they needed to feed. So, they would come out at night and look for food, anything they could get their hands on, even human flesh. It became sort of like an urban legend, like the ones told for centuries in books and passed from generation to generation. "The Bogeyman", "El Coco", "Babau" and so many others that coloured ancient cultures and were centred on scaring children into venturing outside their comfort zones and as a deterrent from misbehaving.

I remember my skin crawling when I read those stories, they were meant to woke you up to the real dangers that lurk out there; like when I first read about the "Nightwalkers", but now that I was looking at them, up close, I couldn't help but feel sorry for them. Seeing them, struggling to move, thinking about the pain they were feeling and heartbreak they must have gone through, the horrible ordeal that transformed them into a parallel species, forced to hide underground and survive through this cataclysm, knowing that their faith was sealed, long ago, and that they were just dead men walking.

Even if my first instinct was to help them, we couldn't risk being seen. They were a lot of them and we had no idea how they would react to us. To me, they still looked human, their essence, at least on the outside, was human like, but we had no idea of how their brains had been modified and if they were even capable of interaction with us. They acted more like a pack of wolves than a human society. They were just following their instinct to survive, to find something to feed on and then, go back to their hole, from where they arose from, before the first light of day.

These supplies, we had found, were coveted commodities out there and whoever found out that we had them, would do anything to get their hands on them. We had to lay low.

Juan and I stayed quite, observing them closely, to make sure they wouldn't find a way to get inside and find us and the supplies. They were just circling the entrance to the building, like mad dogs circling its prey.

We were hoping they would get bored, or find something else that would keep them away from there, but the hours went by and nothing really changed. They were just doing their thing, the same thing they did every day and until their last day.

Gloria and Sarah were still sleeping, Juan and I took turns closing our eyes for a bit, trying to gain some strength, but we couldn't really rest without being disturbed by the thought of them finding us, making their way inside the building and feasting, not only on our supplies, but on us too.

We couldn't let that happen. We were so close to getting out of here with our supplies. We knew that we would have to wait until the sun scared them away. Until the light of day would force them underground, to their hideout.

So, we waited! I could hear the growling noises they made, the screeching sound their feet emitted as they dragged on the concrete, moving relentlessly; they couldn't stand still. I was tired and as much as I wanted to stay awake, those sounds became hypnotic, bewitching my will to stay focused, to stay awake.

I finally subjugated to their enchantments, I closed my eyes for a moment but got awaken suddenly by a viscous sound coming from the glass doors at the entrance to the building. The nightwalkers were trying to pry them open. Pulling and pushing them violently while they became more agitated and mad when the doors wouldn't give in.

More of them piled up and pushed the doors that seemed to give in to the pressure. There was just so much the doors could withstand and something motivated them to break through. Maybe they had caught our scent somehow, because they seemed to be determined to get inside the building. As if something was pulling them to do so.

Gloria, Sarah and Juan woke up, disturbed by the loud sound and fearfully observed as the nightwalkers finally broke the locks on the doors and broke into the building. One of the doors hinges gave up and the huge glass door came crashing down and exploded into a million pieces that scattered all over the marble floor. The sound was terrifying, as well as the thought of what would come next.

We got up and ran to the back of the hall we were in, heading towards the door to the stairs we had walked up and down a hundred times, but before we could reach the door, we were spotted by some of them and like hunters after their prey the locked on us.

We ran desperately towards the door, went in and just as they were about to cross in, Juan pulled the door shut and held it closed from the inside.

"Quick, get out of here! Go down to the basement and lock yourselves up in one of the rooms. You will be safe there!" Juan screamed.

Gloria terrified looked at him and asked: "What are you going to do?"

"I'll stay here and hold the door!" Juan answered.

"Are you crazy? Come on! let's go!" I yelled back.

Juan looked at us, he was holding the door with all his strength. The nightwalkers were pulling it from the outside and the door kept slamming back, pulled by Juan, but it was giving up, there were too many of them. There was no way that he would be able to hold it closed for much longer.

"Hurry, go!" Juan yelled.

We were confused on what to do, we knew that going downstairs into one of those rooms was probably our only chance to survive, but we didn't want to leave Juan there, abandon him to his faith.

Gloria looked back at Juan and then turned to see us. She was caught between her love and her duty, she didn't want to leave Juan there, but knew that she had to take care of us.

"Come on kids, let's go!" she said, as she pulled us away from the door.

As we began to go down the stairs, she kept her eyes fixated on Juan, asking his forgiveness, saying goodbye, hoping to see him again. We kept going downstairs as fast as we could. We only had one flashlight and the batteries seemed to be running low, the light was dim and fragile as we reached level three.

We could still hear Juan struggling to keep the door closed and the growling of the nightwalkers pulling the door open, until we finally heard a large bang! And the terrifying screams of Juan as the nightwalkers made its way inside the stairwell.

We stood there for a moment, Gloria was shivering, crying uncontrollably, powerless to do anything to help the love of her life. It was fast, the screams stop within a few seconds and only the growling noises remained, accompanied by terrifying sounds I've never heard before.

Sarah was embraced around my chest and I was holding her tight, we were both shivering in silence, tears were running down our cheeks propitiated by the image of what was going on up there. It was unimaginable and yet we had to accept that Juan was gone and move on.

Gloria was frozen, traumatised by what was happening.

"Come on Gloria, we have to move!" I said, while I pulled her from her arms.

She looked at me with a look I'll never forget. She was devastated, had surrendered her reason to live and her will to go on was gone.

"Gloria, come on!" I said again, while I yanked her arms trying to get her to snap out of it, but she wouldn't move. She just looked at me and Sarah, and said: "You go, I'll hold them here, as long as I can!"

"What? No, let's go! We can lose them down there," Sarah said, her voice was trembling, scared out of her mind.

Gloria looked back at me and nodded, there was the trace of a smile on her face. Maybe hoping that I would understand her logic.

Sarah was still yelling at her, desperately: "Gloria! Gloria, come on! Move! Let's go!"

I reached out and grabbed Sarah's arms and pulled her close, she stopped for a moment, enough to look into my eyes. She was confused when she saw me so calmed.

"Let her be! It's ok!" I said with a clam voice, that contrasted with all the growling we heard coming from a few feet away and getting closer.

Sarah's eyes couldn't contain everything she was feeling inside, they just folded. I embraced her as I pulled her towards the stairs.

"Come on, let's go!" I said, as we began descending into the dark.

I turned to see her as we left her behind. Gloria was smiling as we lost sight of her. She was hoping that her sacrifice would save us, that her sacrifice would have a purpose, that her end would come fast and that she will be with Juan soon.

As we went down the stairs, we could hear the nightwalkers as they reached the level where Gloria was, waiting for them. There were no screams, no signs of her resisting, no indication that she was fighting them off, just the horrible sound of the nightwalkers feasting on her flesh, tearing her body out, piece by piece and the growling that entice them all to do the unthinkable.

Sarah couldn't take it and she stopped suddenly! She tried to go back up but I was able to grab her from her arm as I said: "Are you crazy? We can't go back there!"

"It's Gloria! God knows what they are doing to her!" she said upset, visibly disturbed by what was happening. Her eyes were filled with tears. She was trembling!

"I know, but she gave herself up so that we could have a chance. A chance to escape, we can't go back!" I said in a calm voice, trying to comfort her.

She looked into my eyes, calmed down and nodded.

I took her hand and we began going down stairs, we went passed the fifth level and kept going down until we reached the end of the stairs. We were ten levels underground. There was a door at the end, we didn't knew what was behind it, but we needed to go in, so I tried to open it. The light was almost off, the batteries were giving their last effort to keep the bulb on.

"Come on! What's going on?" Sarah asked me.

"it's locked!" I said as I turned to look at her.

I tried to force it open, I pushed it and eventually started hitting it with my shoulder as hard as I could but it wouldn't give up. Sarah joined in and, between the both of us, tried, as hard as we could, to force it open but it didn't give up.

We both knew what that meant: we were trapped and the only way out was up the stairs, through them...we would never survive. Sarah looked at me, her eyes spoke to me as words could never do, I could see her heart, her soul, gleaming through her pupils, shinning like stars, telling me the story of our love, of what I meant to her. I guess she was looking back at mine, talking back to her, telling her of what I felt for her.

At that moment, close to the end, we both wanted to die in each other's arms and I needed her to know how I felt, we had both surrendered, but suddenly I just rejected the idea of that happening, of our deaths, of reaching the end in this cold and dark corner, so many feet underground, like trapped in our own grave.

Frustration began taking control of me, combined with desperation and anger. This couldn't be the end of us, this couldn't be the way it went. I began to hit the door with everything I had. Sarah was calmed, she just looked at me tenderly, understanding what I was going through, but accepting our faith.

We could hear the growling in the distance and their steps, coming down.

We had to try something else, try to survive. I grabbed her hand and pulled her with me as I went upstairs to the level above us. She just followed me, holding my hand. She would stay with me, no matter what, that is all she wanted, to die by my side. We went upstairs and tried the first door in that level. It was locked, so I tried to force it open and couldn't.

I grabbed her hand and moved to the next door and tried the same, without success, and then the next door, and the next and the next. With every door I tried, my frustration grew and grew. By the time we reached the last door on that corridor, we could hear the nightwalkers approaching down the hall. They were already behind us, in the same level we were in. Sarah was stuck to me, keeping me as close as she could, clinching her hands anywhere she could. Her eyes were filled with the fear that made her whole body tremble. Fear that aroused from the images that kept invading our heads, of suffering the same faith that Juan and Gloria had.

Suddenly, she looked at me, she was calm and composed, as if everything around us had past. At that precise moment everything stopped, the noises ceased and the fear was gone. She closed her eyes slowly while she repeated, over and over again: "A sunny beach with beautiful white sands and blue waters, a soft breeze blowing through the palm trees, swaying in the wind and you by my side."

I could feel the peace that took over her senses, her will to live...I knew what she was doing, giving herself up, casting the fear away, so that her last thoughts were happy thoughts and that would take her to a better place.

I got tainted by it for a moment, I didn't knew what to do, I just embraced her as tight as I could trying to protect her from the harm I knew would come to her...to us.

We stayed like that for eternity...that was basically a few seconds outside our bubble. I couldn't give up, I couldn't let it happen like this. Something came over me, an uncontrollable force that pushed me to survive and save her.

I got loose from our embrace and lashed at the door with my foot up and kicked it as hard as I could. The door latch broke and it opened. I grabbed Sarah's hand and I pulled her in, we both went in the room, hoping it was a way out.

We ran through the room, roaming everywhere, moving as fast as we could, without really looking at things, we needed to find another door, a way out of that room, a way to safety. We were both desperately looking for it, but all we could see were shelves filled with boxes and equipment. Until we reached a wall at the end, where the light ceased to exist. We turned around and walked frantically the other way, I was moving the flashlight from side to side, trying to cover as much space as possible, but there were only walls and shelves, and boxes.

We got back to the entrance door, that was wide open, I looked down the hall outside of the room, I could see the nightwalkers moving in the distance, barely lighted by the beam coming from the flashlight, that dimmed together with our hope, they weren't stopping, they were coming towards us. I closed the door and began to pile boxes and things behind it, so that they couldn't open it. Sarah helped me to pile up everything we could get our hands on, until we had covered the entrance up to the ceiling.

When we were done, I took her hand and we ran to the end of the room, sat down against the wall and pointed the flashlight directly towards the door…we sat there and waited, waited for it to happen. We were clinched to each other, hoping that we could give comfort to one and other. Hoping that this closeness could ease our fears, that it will give us the courage we lacked to face our end. Hoping the love we felt for each other would be enough.

We knew, in our minds, what was going to happen next, but hope has a way of giving you a false sense of reality. It will lead you to ignore the obvious and foresee another outcome that will sit better with your idea of happiness.

We both took it in, we were together and, at that moment, nothing else mattered. So I put the flashlight down and grabbed the side of her head with my hand, I pulled her head up so that she could see mine. There was enough light bouncing off the floor to light up her face. There were tears running down her cheeks, she was trembling, her eyes were sad, but her beauty transcended it all. The light that shined through her eyes was brighter than anything I had ever seen before.

So I pulled her close and kissed her, and she kissed me back. For a moment we forgot about what was happening outside that door that separated us, from our faith. Nothing mattered, but the love we shared, the infinite seconds that made our bond strong, endless.

We could hear, in the background, the loud noises the nightwalkers made, while pushing the door open, hitting it over and over, and over again, forcing the boxes and things, we had piled up, off on their way. Growling mad while they did.

Sarah couldn't contain herself, her fear regained control for a moment and she tried to look that way, but I held her head in place and kept on kissing her lips, trying to dismiss the threat. Wishing that our love would protect us from harm.

The nightwalkers broke through the door; they creeped to the end of the room, attracted by the light, until they reached the wall we were leaned against.

They first pulled Sarah away from me. She was screaming, trying to hang on, I tried to hang on to her, as hard as I could, but they pulled her away from me.

"Patrick! Patrick!"

"No! Let me go! No!" she kept yelling desperately.

"Sarah! Sarah! Let her go! Let her go!" I yelled, over and over again, although I knew it was useless.

I never lost contact with her eyes and she never stopped looking into mine as they started pulling and sticking their teeth into her flesh and mine. I kept looking into her eyes!

They kept tearing her body and mine, piece by piece until I saw her life slip away from her eyes, until I saw her light dim. I closed my eyes, hoping the pain would subside. As I closed them I began hearing Sarah's voice calling my name: "Patrick! Patrick!"

It became louder and louder: "Patrick! Patrick!"

It dominated the darkness that I could see, the pain went away and I was in peace.

Until a force shook me out of my dream.

"Patrick! Patrick, wake up!"

I opened up my eyes and the first thing I saw, was her smile!

"You're awake!" she said, as she smiled.

"Yeah!" I answered confused.

I looked around, roaming the room, trying to figure out where we were, placed the time line in the right order.

"So, that was all a dream?" I asked her.

She frowned, wondering what was I referring to.

"Did you have a nightmare? You were moving violently while you were sleeping, I got worried," she asked.

I tried to recall what the nightmare was about, flashes of it came back, they were still lurking in my mind, haunting me.

"Yeah! It was a bad nightmare, but everything is fine right?" I asked.

"Of course Baby, everything is fine!" she answered, trying to reassure me.

I could see Juan and Gloria in the background, they were facing the other way. Looking down a hallway right in front of them, and then I started hearing it again…the growling, rising above the silence that surrounded us.

"Do you hear that?" I asked, almost freaking out.

"Hear what?" she asked back.

"That! The growling?" I asked.

Sarah seemed disconcerted, she kept silent as she moved her head trying to hear what I was hearing.

The growling grew slowly, until it was impossible not to notice it.

"You don't hear that?" I asked.

Sarah turned around and looked at me curious.

"I don't hear anything," she answered.

Maybe I was going crazy, maybe I was still affected by that crazy nightmare I had been in. This horrible experience I had just awoken from.

Sarah got up, extended her hand and said: "Come on, let's get out of here!"

As I was about to grab her hand, Juan and Gloria turned around and I could see their faces…they were not the ones I remembered, their faces were ravaged, their skin was melted, fused with their flesh that was exposed, you could see the bones peeking through it, their eyes were clouded white, lost and dead, their mouths open, just a few teeth were left and the ones that still stood were dripping with blood and pieces of flesh still hanging from them. They raised their hands at us, as a group of nightwalkers joined them and grabbed Sarah, that was freaking out, screaming at the top of her lungs: "Patrick! Patrick! Save me!"

I tried to get up, but by then the Nightwalkers were all over me too. I could feel their hands grabbing me, their claws ripping my skin. Their teeth stabbing me, biting off my flesh down to the bone. The pain was unbearable! I closed my eyes, I couldn't stand looking at my impotence commanding me, there were too many of them. I felt this rage invading my whole body, exploding in my throat, concentrating all my anger, my fear, my pain and desperation into one loud scream: "Noooo!"

As I opened up my eyes, all I could see was Sarah's face. She was looking at me, worried.

"Patrick! Patrick! Wake up!" she said, as she shook me, to wake me up.

It took a moment for me, to realise what had happened, all that pain and frustration vanished when I felt her presence and realised that all of that, was just a dream, a nightmare that my mind had created.

"Are you ok? You were shouting at the top of your lungs, something I couldn't understand and I couldn't wake you up," she said concerned.

My breath was still agitated and I was sweating profusely, as if I had ran a thousand miles.

"I'm fine, it was just a bad dream! A horrible, terrible bad dream!" I said, while I was still seeing flash backs of the horror in my mind.

Juan and Gloria came to me in one of those images and that made me react.

"Juan, Gloria? Are they here?" I asked, while I looked around, trying to see them.

Sarah placed her hands on my face and made me concentrate on her.

"They are fine, they went to make sure everything is clear and we can get to the vehicle. We're all safe," she said.

I fixated on her eyes, those beautiful portals, that transported me to heaven, every time I looked into their depth. Into the calm that invaded me, each time I fell for their charm. I needed that, more than ever. She was the one reason I had, to go on, the only reason that kept me sane.

I just nodded and grabbed her hands, that were caressing my face, the softness they had was intoxicating, it was like touching tranquillity, like caressing eternity, while it cleansed my worry that was pouring out of my body, through my fingertips.

My whole body eased with her next to me, I was able to catch my breath and my heartbeat, dominated by her presence, went back to normal.

We both got up and went looking for Juan and Gloria, we saw them outside admiring the dawn out in the distance, it was a sight to see. The concentration of gases in the atmosphere, product of the war, made the heavens light up in an abundance of colours that painted everything below. The phenomenon, known as the "Helios Plasma" was probably the only good thing that came from the war. The beauty that remained after all the destruction.

It was impossible not to admire such grandeur, it was a reminder of our significance in this world and of how, even though, we were responsible for the desecration of our race, the world would still be a beautiful place, without us, in spite of us and even, because of us.

We joined Juan and Gloria outside. I was still worried about the nightwalkers, about the horror I had dreamed.

"Where are the nightwalkers?" I asked concerned, searching all over for signs of them.

Juan turned and looked at me, he placed his hand on my shoulder and said: "They are long gone, as soon as the light started to break through. Relax, they won't come out again until dark."

I nodded and tried to relax. It had all been a nightmare.

The sun was up in the horizon and it was time for us to move.

"I'll bring the vehicle to the entrance and we can load up, as much as we can," Juan said.

The three of us nodded and he went on his way. Gloria, Sarah and I went inside and began to push the boxes closer to the glass doors. Juan pulled right next to them and we began to load the vehicle. Gloria was in charge of placing each box, so that we could use all the space inside, while Sarah and I brought the boxes from inside.

We were almost done. At that point Gloria was having trouble fitting all the boxes left. We couldn't use our seats and there seemed to be a few boxes that wouldn't fit.

"We're going to have to leave those," Juan said.

"What are they?" Sarah asked.

Gloria looked at the labels, outside of the box and said: "It's mostly preserves and canned goods, but we have plenty of those already. I think we can do without these."

As we were discussing, I noticed something in the distance. Between the debris that lined the street in front of the building. It was hard to see, I tried to focus by pinching my eyes. The sun was already high in the sky and the glare was blocking my view.

Sarah saw me and got close: "What are you looking at?" she asked.

I pointed out and replied: "Over there, there is something moving. Can you see it?"

Sarah placed her hand over her eyes and tried to see what I was pointing at.

"I don't' see anything moving. Are you sure it's not the glare playing tricks on your eyes?" she asked.

"No, I saw something moving. I'm sure. I'm going to check it out!" I said.

Sarah turned to look at me, looked me straight into my eyes and said concerned: "No, are you crazy? I don't want you to go. What if…?"

"Don't worry, the nightwalkers only come out at night. This is something else," I interrupted her.

"I don't understand. Why do you have to go see what it is? We should just leave," she said, while she pointed at the vehicle.

"We can't let that food go to waste. What if there's people who can use it, we can't just leave it here," I replied.

Juan was close enough to hear, he got close and asked: "What's going on? What are you kids plotting?"

"Patrick says that he saw something moving over there, somewhere, and wants to go and check it out!" Sarah replied.

"Where?" Juan asked.

"Over there, by that glass building, next to the tall pole," I answered.

Juan focused there, placed his hand over his eyes and said: "I don't see anything, are you sure?" He asked, as he pinched his eyes, trying to see.

"Of course I'm sure, maybe somebody that could use the leftover food," I said.

Juan looked at me and thought about it for a moment.

"If you are sure you saw somebody, I can go with you," Juan said.

Sarah wasn't happy about it, she was worried that something bad would happen. Her eyes turned sad, when she saw that Juan was supporting my idea. She was visibly concerned about us going and investigating, so I placed my hand on her cheek and said: "Don't worry, we'll be alright. You will be able to see us from here."

She grabbed my hand with hers and held it there for a moment, she wanted to feel my hand caressing her face, she wanted to feel me close. That chemistry we had, was undeniable, when your whole world is shaken, gets moved by a simple touch…magic happens.

I smiled, as I always did when I saw her face. I felt the exact same way for her.

"Come on! If we are going to go, now it's the time," Juan said.

I turned to see him and nodded. As I was taking my hand of Sarah's face, we heard Gloria yell: "What's going on? Where are you two going?"

"We're going to give this left overs to someone who can use it," Juan yelled back.

"Hurry up, we have to get going," she replied.

Juan signalled with her head and we began walking.

We got to the street and crossed over to where I had seen movement, at first there was nothing resembling life, but as we got closer to the opposite corner, we saw an old couple searching through the rubble, pushing a beat up grocery store cart filled with their possessions.

As soon as they saw us, the old man raised a bat over his head and began threatening us with it, yelling at the top of his lungs.

"Stay back! Stay back!"

"We are not here to do you any harm!" Juan yelled back.

"Stay back! We don't have any food. Leave us be!" The old man yelled.

"We don't want anything from you. The opposite, we want to give you something," I yelled at the man.

It was obvious, that they weren't used to defending themselves from people and he was afraid we would do something bad to them. There was a reason why they had survived this long. Thousands of scenarios rushed through my head, vignettes of what they could have lived through in their lifetime. These were survivors of the war and the aftermath that was inherited from it, but they had survived by the will of god, and their own.

The old lady stayed behind the man, seeking his protection, but, right away, she focused her attention on me and as her husband was yelling, threatening us, she walked towards him, placed her hand on his shoulder and prompted him to lower the bat and calmed down. As he did, she walked past him, straight to where I was; never, not even for a second, talking her eyes off me, until she was inches away.

"What's your name boy?" she asked.

"Patrick" I answered.

She smiled and grabbed my hand, placed it on top of hers and covered it with her other hand, she closed her eyes and a beautiful smile, took over her rugged face. Her hair was a mess, mostly hidden under a turban that stretched down to her waist. Her body was covered in wrappings that made her clothing, her feet were naked, you could read the story of their journey through the calluses that covered every inch of them. Her hands felt like scrolls, their ridges were deep and pronounced, but there was a softness about them: in the way they gently communicated with mine.

"You're a new soul!" she said with a soft, deep voice, as she opened up her eyes.

I was surprised, I've never seen eyes like hers. They were almost white, covered with a thick veil that made the surface seem dead, but behind that film, you could see a light shining through, you could tell that life was flowing through them. I couldn't stop staring!

The old lady raised her hand and slowly placed it on my face. It felt warm and soft, she roamed every little part of it, as if she was trying to learn its contours. While she was doing that, I was analysing her, surprised at everything she made me feel just by looking at her. It was like reading one of those books I loved so much. The ridges, the scars, the wrinkles that formed her face were like lines on a page. I could read between them, learn about her ups and downs, about the sorrow and pain she had endured and also about the happiness and love she had shared, the one that had kept her alive.

"I haven't felt youthfulness in a long time, I thought death was the only thing that survived. I had lost faith!" she said, as she lowered her hand.

I couldn't help but to look into her eyes, they were captivating.

"Are you blind?" I asked intrigued.

"I lost my sight many years ago, but I'm not blind! I can see you as clear as day!" she responded.

I felt ashamed, thinking about all that she had been through in her life. The survival that she wore, like a badge of honour on her face and in every inch of her being. I realised at that moment: She was the lucky one!

In that instant it became clear to me: we all suffer in our lives, we all go through things that might seem unfair, moments that we wish we could erase, events that overshadow everything else that define us and in those moments, we only see the bad; we only feel pain and sadness, and depression takes a hold of us; but life goes on and those things become part of who we are, they become part of the past. They make us stronger, wiser, more human. Humanity is not define by heritage; by the chromosomes that form us that give content to our essence. Humanity is define by our actions, by those things that happen to us…to each one of us. It's the path we follow and the story that registers in our eyes, in our hearts, in our soul, those are the things that make us human.

"How can this be? Where do you come from?" The old lady asked.

Juan was standing next to me, I could tell that he was as moved as I was. These were good people, survivors, innocent victims of this doom that surrounded us.

"Life always finds a way!" Juan said.

The old lady lowered her head and thought about it for a second.

"Yes, it does!" she said.

"We are on our way out of here, but we wanted to share what we have with you," Juan said.

The old man looked at his wife, got close and placed his arms around her. He looked at us and asked: "What is it that you want to share with us?"

"We have food, enough to last you a year," Juan responded.

I saw their faces light up with hope for a second, but then doubt took over and the man asked visibly upset: "Is this a trick? Why are you taking advantage of us?"

I was confused at first, Juan and I looked at each other in disbelief. Why were they doubting us, thinking we would hurt them, take advantage of their despair? But then, I realised that this was what they were used to. This was exactly what they would run away from. Faith in humanity, in good will, was the first thing that was lost during the war. It became about survival and in that mode, everything else is discarded and the only thing that matters is you.

"It's not a trick. We found a warehouse filled with supplies. We have what we need, but we can't fit it all in our vehicle. We just thought you might want it," I said, hoping they would trust us.

The old lady grabbed the old man's hand and paused for a second. They didn't speak, their connection was beyond that. The old man looked into her eyes and I saw a smile growing on his face.

He turned around to look at us and asked: "Ok, where is this food that you talk about?"

Juan and I smiled, it was the only way that we could repay their trust.

"It's next to our vehicle, over there!" Juan said as he pointed towards the building.

"It's on a cart, you can take it with you," I said, inviting them to follow us.

They did and as we got close to where the vehicle was, we were received by Gloria and Sarah, that were waiting for us to get back. They saw the old couple and bowed their heads and smiled, saying hello.

"These are Gloria and Sarah!" I said, introducing them.

The old couple said hello. Juan was standing next to the supplies.

"These are the supplies, they're all yours!" He said.

The old man got close and looked at the boxes. You could see the excitement on his face, he couldn't believe what he was looking at. For them: these supplies were a miracle, something out of a sci fi novel. It had been years since they had fresh food. Surviving on whatever scraps they could get their hands on, eating, maybe once a day, maggot infested, rotten food they could find on the dumpsters, or between the rubble.

For them, this was a treasure, something beyond what they would have dreamed of. First thing he did, was to share his happiness with her. He pulled her close to the boxes and held her hands, they embraced and tears ran down their cheeks.

We couldn't ignore their happiness, it was contagious, that spontaneous joy you feel, when it sneaks up on you; the natural well-being, that it gives to your heart, to your soul. For us, these boxes were the left overs, things we couldn't fit in our vehicle, they meant space. For them: this was the greatest single act of kindness anyone had ever done for them.

I couldn't help thinking of what I use to read on those books, the stories of incredible treasures, about pirates that sailed the seven seas, looking for mountains of gold and precious gems; about thieves riding the dunes in the desert, searching for richness in secret caves.

I always imagined being on the taking side, I pictured myself as the pirate, or one of the thieves, but here, we were on the giving side. The side that possessed the richness and the will to give it away. The measure of a treasure, depends on what is precious to you. We didn't have gold, or precious gems, but we had something even more valuable to them. Survival!

The old couple were static, they embraced us, kissed us and thanked us a hundred times. We just returned the gesture and hoped that this small token, would last them a long time. We couldn't take them with us, although the thought crossed my mind. Our paths had crossed, but we weren't heading in the same direction.

We said good bye and went on our way. They stood, looking at us leave, Sarah and I looked back as they disappeared in the horizon and the sun went down behind them. I was sad to part from them and Sarah could feel my sadness. She held me close and that was exactly what I needed, to feel her heart beating with mine, sharing my pain, making it disappear with her tenderness.

Chapter 6
Sad Release

We travelled for a few days South East; long stretches of road surrounded by emptiness. We didn't see anybody walking, or driving. There were no signs of life along the highway. Gloria kept pointing at landmarks she remembered from her past. Mountains, rivers, lakes, even a small town in the distance, to the side of the highway, where she said she had been in the past.

"That's San Miguel de Allende, it's one of the most famous cities in Mexico. It was declared World Heritage before the war. The Cathedral still stands, but I don't know if it's safe to go now," she said.

Sarah and I looked at it from the distance.

"It looks deserted!" Sarah said.

"Yeah, I can't see any movement, anywhere," Juan went on.

"We can't stop anyway, we have to keep moving. We don't want anyone to see what we are carrying. We are so close," Gloria said.

We didn't knew at the time, but the towns that surrounded us had been deserted for a while. An outbreak of cholera, that resurged after almost two hundred years of being eradicated, had wiped out most of the population and forced, the ones that survived, out of that area. The pathogens released on the atmosphere during the war, had spread far and wide all over the world, reviving long lost enemies that humanity had conquered, but this time they had a boost of evil sprung on them, that common medicine couldn't cure.

The sight, from far away, was beautiful. The colonial buildings that formed the city still stood tall, reaching the sky, and the crosses that crowned every single peak in the distance, contrasted with the light blue sky that sheltered them up above. Birds seemed to have taken over the city and flew constantly around it, like guarding it, while they waited for their masters to show.

Sarah and I spent most of our time inside the vehicle, cuddled to each other. Nurturing the love that had grown bigger and bigger, with the passing of the days. Our connection grew stronger with every moment and kissing became our pastime. Her lips were made to fit mine, as perfect moulded pieces do. We felt this undeniable attraction, this force that pulled us together, a force we couldn't explain, a force we couldn't ignore.

"Hey, you kids need to get a room!" Gloria said one day, while we were cuddling and kissing.

She was sitting in front, next to Juan that was usually the designated navigator. They were usually watching videos, old movies that reminded them of how things used to be, but Gloria would always be interested in what we were doing, like a Mother gets drawn to their kids, she was drawn to us.

We were surprised by what she had said, we didn't really understand.

"Get a room?" I asked, intrigued.

Sarah and I looked at each other, wondering what she meant. Gloria and Juan just laughed, we wanted to join on the fun, but we didn't get the joke.

"It's an expression we used when two lovers were getting to excited. When it got to intense," Gloria explained.

Sarah and I were still puzzled, to us, this was just visceral, a natural thing that aroused from the love we shared, from the attraction we couldn't contain. We were not ashamed of it, but for one moment we felt judged.

"Why? Is this wrong?" Sarah asked.

"No! Not at all. It's a beautiful thing. I'm happy that you kids feel that way about each other. I couldn't have wished for anything else," Gloria answered.

Sarah looked at me, confused, not knowing what to think of it. Gloria sensed it, and said: "Love is the one thing that we have, the one thing that no one can take away from us, not even the chaos that we have lived through. It is the one thing that bonds us together, that makes our hearts beat. It is the one thing that will last, even after we are gone," she said.

She was looking at us with the tenderness she always did. We were her kids and nothing would change that.

"I want you to love each other. I want you to never hold back. No matter what happens, life would have been worth it," she went on.

Sarah looked at me, the same way she did the first time we met. It was the will to discover something new, something amazing, some life changing moment that sets off a feeling which sparks a fire within. The fire that fuelled our lives, the fire that tingled our skin: whenever we touched; whenever we looked at each other.

We weren't taught much about love, there was no specific rules outlined in the books that actually mentioned it. It was more of a description of how it happens. Of how two people reacted when they were together, motivated by it.

"I think it's time that we tell you the story about the birds and the bees," Gloria said.

"The birds and the bees?" Sarah asked intrigued.

Juan turned and looked at Gloria and they both giggled.

"What? What is it?" I asked.

"Well, it's a very old story that our grandfathers used to tell our fathers, it was told for generations to young kids that began to explore their sexuality. It's been lost lately, there was no need for it anymore," Gloria said.

Sarah and I looked at each other, puzzled. Sarah looked at Gloria and shook her head.

"Well it's a way of explaining to a kid, sexual inter course," Gloria went on.

"You mean sex?" Sarah asked.

Gloria and Juan broke laughing, as they looked at each other.

"What? Why are you laughing?" Sarah asked them.

"I read about it on a book. A man and a woman lay in top of each other and it happens. They have sex. Right?" Sarah went on.

I looked at her as she said that, I couldn't help but feel closer to her. I just thought she was the best.

"Yeah, well, there's a little bit more than that," Gloria said.

Sarah looked at me and then turned to see Gloria. She waited for a few seconds for Gloria to say something, after a few seconds of silence, she said: "Well? Come on Gloria, spill the beans!"

Juan and I just laughed at the joke, but Sarah was dead serious, so she looked at me wondering why I was laughing.

"Sorry, sorry, it was funny!" I said, trying not to laugh.

Juan was still laughing, so I looked at him and said: "Juan, it's not a joke!" I said.

Juan realised that neither Sarah or Gloria were laughing and stopped.

"Sorry! I'll try to contain myself," Juan said to all.

Sarah turned to look at Gloria and asked, very seriously: "So?"

Gloria began to tell the story of "The birds and the Bees" as she remembered it. It tried to explain, in layman's terms, what the sexual act is and how two people achieve reproduction. At the end of the day, we were two kids brought up in complete isolation. We only knew about each other when Gloria introduced us a few months ago, and the fire burning between us, was something we couldn't contain.

Inside the lab we were used for experimentation, to find out if science could turn back time and erase what humanity had done to itself. If we could procreate and repair that missing part that had our future condemned. It didn't work the way they had planned. Sarah and I hadn't really talked about it, about what they did to her and what they did to me.

In fact, I hadn't spoken to anyone about it. Not even Gloria, although I was sure that she knew, that is why she was compelled to get us out of that place, but the idea of talking about it was unthinkable. I wouldn't even know where to begin, or how to explain it without breaking up and crying my eyes off from shame and regret; and I didn't even dare to ask Sarah about what she went through.

They never made us interact with each other, they just harvested my sperm and used that for their projects, their trials, as they called them. That was all I knew, when I was old enough to produce sperm, they began to do it, but even though It was a simple medical procedure, It felt wrong, I felt violated, raped.

They would connect a suction cup to my penis and then connect electrodes to my scrotum, shocking them, to produce ejaculation. It was a painful process, but they led me to believe that it was my purpose. That this was what I was meant to do, who I was meant to be. I only found out later, between the lines of the books I read, that there was a natural order to my body, that didn't involve this abuse. The magical act of love making. Or I could have just masturbated, if they asked.

When Gloria was finished telling the story, Sarah and I looked at each other. We already knew about our differences from the books we use to read, you know? Men and Women, but this time it was different. Now, we knew where this passion could lead and we were excited to try it.

Gloria peeled her eyes, when she saw us. She had seen that look before.

"Don't worry, we will give you some privacy so you can…do your thing! Eventually," she said, nervously.

We would have to wait, even though our hormones were telling us otherwise.

We drove for a few minutes and finally Juan and Gloria began to get excited while recognising places they had been in before, places that reminded them of home.

"Look Juan! That's where my family used to take our vacations. There were thermal waters where we used to dip, they said that those waters had magical healing powers."

"I think I went there once with my family!" Juan replied.

I knew we were close to our destination, the excitement kept building and stories kept being told, but as we got closer, something unexpected happened as well. Juan and Gloria began to notice that there was no one around.

"People must be gathered somewhere, for safety reasons," Gloria said, a little bit worried.

"I don't see anything showing on our scanners. The air is clean," Juan added, hoping to calm Gloria down.

Sarah and I were looking everywhere, trying to spot someone in the distance and reassure them, but there was no one around. It look as deserted as everywhere we had been in the last few days.

We finally reached the town of Coatzacoalcos in the state of Veracruz, part of what was left of Mexico. The city where they were from, the city where they met many years ago. The country had been absorbed by the "Free World", Mexico persisted in its people who preserved their customs, their way of life, that survived the invasion of millions of refugees that fled the rest of the world during "The Great War". Each one bringing their own beliefs and traditions, that blended with the Mexican ones and spawned a whole new one. Catholicism still persisted as the base of their tradition, although the Catholic Church was no longer represented as before. After "The Great War" religion lost ground to a new sense of Spirituality based on knowledge and science. Religion was blamed for the debacle and so, churches were closed or destroyed. In Mexico, most of them were kept as museums, places or remembrance of another time.

As we rolled through the streets of the town, confusion took over our minds and a chill rolled down all of our spines. The place was deserted, there was no one around. It seemed as if time had stopped and people had just vanished.

We wondered around the streets in silence, there was nothing said while we witnessed the desolation in front of us. Juan navigated the town almost by mere instinct, until we reached Gloria's family home. It was a humble house, nested at the end of a long avenue that stretched to the boardwalk, overlooking the sea.

He parked the vehicle on the side of the house and we all got out, fearful, but still hopeful that what we were looking at, was a mirage, an illusion prompted by fatigue. Gloria was the first to step inside, hailing her family, shouting their names, over and over again: "Susy! Manolo! Javier! Adonde están? (Where are you?)"

Juan went after her, he was more aware of what was happening. He appeared to have feared the worst, but didn't share it, hoping that it wouldn't become real and now that everything was materialising in front of him, all that was left was her.

Gloria, on the other hand, had never pictured this. In her mind there was no scenario where this was possible. She was running around the house, slamming every door open, screaming at the top of her lungs while the sad truth, slowly creeped up on her. Her family was gone, they were nowhere to be found.

Juan chased after her, trying his best to slow her down, embrace her, ease the pain she felt, the desperation she was in, but there was no holding her back. She just ran all over the house, she searched every room, every corner, every nick, until there was no place left to look in, until her voice cracked and her eyes were overflowed by grief. She dropped to the ground and sobbed in Juan's arms. Sarah and I were standing, in the same place we had been standing for the last hour, watching her unravel, unable to do anything but watch.

Now that she was done, we got down and embraced them both. We could feel her pain diminish by our love. That was the only thing we could do, be there for her, to let her know she wasn't alone.

"Maybe they left, maybe they are somewhere else, safe," Gloria said, hoping to get our support.

"Maybe! They have to be somewhere," Juan replied.

"Yes, maybe they left to a safer place," Sarah said.

I wanted to say something encouraging, something that will make her feel good, but a bad premonition kept me from saying anything. I didn't want to be the one to say it, although I knew that we all thought the same thing. We had seen this before, we knew, exactly, what this desolation meant, but hope and love blinds us to the obvious and I just couldn't take the blindfold off.

Juan knew the truth, but he was as compelled to hold back as I was. He could feel the desperation that commanded what Gloria was doing and didn't have the nerve to say it out loud.

Gloria kept searching in her mind, for possible explanations, for alternate realities than the one bluntly in front of her. Mumbling between thoughts, pacing around the living room, holding pictures of the family, smiling as she looked at them in the photographs, remembering times long past.

Finally, she found a photograph of her family, it was an image of her, as a young girl, her two brothers and her parents. She must have been five or six years old. She was holding a doll on her hand and her mother's hand in the other, while her father had his arms around his two brothers. They were all smiling. Gloria smiled at it, sat down on the floor and leaned against a wall, crawled up in a ball and began to cry, while she looked at it.

Sarah, Juan and I just looked at each other. There was nothing we could say to ease her pain, all we could do was sit with her and share it, so we did. We sat there for a while, embracing her so she wouldn't feel alone. We were her family know.

After a while, we all fell asleep, one by one, starting with Gloria, she was drained of strength, tired of suffering this much, of having her world crumble in front of her eyes. All that hope she had for her, for us, for the future, had been taken away in a second, so her body shut down, it needed to reboot and try to see things in a different perspective. We all did, so, when the night fell, we were all embraced in one hug and life, for a moment, stopped moving and slowed down to watch us rest.

It could have been hours, or days, we lost track of time. It was, as though, we had been powered off. The end of a long journey, that even though, didn't have the ending we had hoped for, it had reached its conclusion.

I was still out of it, when I felt something moving around me, sniffing and stepping all over. I was afraid to open up my eyes, my mind was sending me signals of survival, putting thoughts in my mind, explanations of what it could be; that's how fear creeps up on you: your mind swivels around terrible thoughts of the unknown, scenarios of how things could go sideways, but something in me was also curious, even playful about it. So, when I felt it come close to my face, I opened my eyes slowly, it was right in front of my face, it looked at me, tilted its head and started licking my face, making warm noises, as if it was happy to see me, to realise I was awake, I was alive.

It was a dog, I recognised it from the books, from what I have learned through so many tales of man's best friend. It began barking, like trying to tell me something, that's when Sarah woke up, startled. She grabbed a hold of my arm and protected herself behind me.

The dog stayed put, tilted his head again, looking at Sarah, got close and sniffed her arm. Sarah pulled it closer to me and tighten her grip on mine. The dog got closer and licked her hand. Sarah tighten her grip even more while she made a funny sound, I've never heard her do before: "Arghh!"

The dog licked her hand again and she reacted: "No, don't do that!"

The dog stopped and looked at her, it got closer and placed her nose under her hand and pulled it out of my arm, hoping she would pet hit. Sarah paused and then lifted her hand and placed it on its head, she pet the dog as she smiled.

It was an instant connection, I extended my hand and pet the dog too. Gloria woke up and looked back at us, she focused on the dog and out of nowhere, she asked: "Charlie?"

The dog lifted its head, looking straight at Gloria. It's ears up, reacting to her saying his name.

"Charlie?" she said again, while she opened up her arms.

The dog went straight at her, wagging his tail, licking her, he was happy to see someone familiar.

Gloria was so happy to see him, she was trying to embrace him, but it was hard with all this emotion, he wouldn't stay still, he was hopping, and barking, and licking everyone, he was so excited to see us.

"Juan, es Charlie, si te acuerdas no (It's Charlie, you remember him?)?" Gloria said to Juan in Spanish.

"Of course I remember him, he was Susana's dog," Juan responded.

"Yes, de Susana!"

"Who's Susana?" Sarah asked.

"She is my nice, she must be 18," Gloria replied, while she was still petting Charlie, trying to calm him down.

"Where is Susana?" Gloria asked Charlie.

Charlie raised his ears and tilted his head.

"Yes, Susana! Where is Susana? A donde esta?" she asked intrigued.

Charlie tilted his head again and barked once. He turned to look at Sarah and me and took off.

"Wait! Charlie!" Gloria yelled as she got up and went after him.

We all followed, we ran out of the house and chased after Gloria, who was chasing Charlie across the street. He went into an alley and then through a field that was behind the building in front of the house. Gloria kept yelling: "Charlie wait! Charlie!"

Charlie kept running until he got to the end of the field, there was a cemetery at the side of it. It went down a hill, you could see the crosses, over the tombstones, dominating the horizon, adorning the cliff, before the hill took over. We saw Charlie go down the hill, but Gloria stopped, just at the edge, she was halted by what she saw. We catch up to her and got paralysed by the same image she had been confronted with. The cemetery was huge, it covered the whole hill and beyond the opposite field. There was thousands and thousands of graves, marked by tombstones of different heights and forms. there were mausoleums scattered all over, breaking up the perfect symmetry of tombstones lining along the hill.

Looking at so many graves, knowing what that meant, made my body shiver. Sarah and Gloria were taken by the same feeling of lost. Paralysed by the same impotence I felt.

Juan finally caught up, he had lost his breath, running after us.

"Hey, what's going on?" He asked before he got to the ridge.

As soon as he saw what was lying beyond the field, his question was answered. We all stood there for a few minutes, in silence, there were no words to describe it, nothing we could say.

Charlie was a few yards away from us, sitting next to some graves, waiting for us to catch up. He began barking, calling us to go where he was.

"Look, there's Charlie! I think he wants us to go there," Juan said.

We all saw him, barking in the distance. Sarah and I began walking towards him, Gloria and Juan followed.

The sun was high up in the sky, it was a beautiful day, the wind was blowing softly across the hill. The trees that limited the cemetery were swaying to the rhythm of the gusts that blew constant. There was a soft fragrance that filled the air, a smell of flowers that contrasted with the sight of so much death. The fragrance gave the illusion of something new, something fresh blowing in the wind. It kept reminding me of life on this planet, earth, the place that had become our grave, but somehow found a way to make it about renewal for the rest of nature. It was as if this, was our time to fade away and give course to a new order of things.

As we approached where Charlie was, we could see a group of graves lined up perfectly, with the same type of tombstone placed at the head of each. The tombstones were made out of grey marble with names and dates carved on each one. Charlie was sitting next to one of the last graves. Gloria got close and began to read the names on the tombstones and as she did reality began to take shape, her eyes filled up with tears and her breathing became erratic, her sobbing peaked every time she moved on to the next grave, by the second one, she was down on her knees. Juan was holding her hand, trying to help her crawl to the next grave. Sharing her grief, her tears, that became his own. All of those graves were the final resting place of her whole family, the ones they were hoping to see, to embrace, to kiss. All those hopes had become sorrow, and the tears were their last goodbye.

Sarah and I just stood there, we couldn't contain the flow of emotions that overtook our senses. We didn't knew any of them, but we shared what Gloria and Juan were feeling. We felt for them, we felt their pain striking our hearts. It was a sense of powerlessness as I saw Gloria inconsolable, heartbroken, and there was nothing I could do to ease her pain.

Charlie was sitting still, in front of the same grave he had been since we followed him here. The last one in that line, he had put together a bed with pieces of foam and dry leaves, by the foot of the grave. Sarah and I got close to meet him, he was waiting for us to come near and as we did, he shrugged, as if he was ashamed of what he had done. As if it weren't allowed for him to be there.

I read the name on the grave: "Susana Sanchez Suarez", "2110-2125". As soon as he heard me say the name, he turned to look at me. He recognised it, it was the name of his friend, his master.

Charlie stood next to her, living beside her grave, missing her, since the day she was put in there. He wanted us to do something, maybe, bring her back.

Sarah and I were looking at Charlie, not knowing what to do, how to ease his need to be with her, when Gloria got close and said: "Susana! I was here when she was born. It feels like yesterday, I remember it so vividly."

She got close to the grave and patted Charlie on the head and said to him: "I don't remember you though, back then, but you remember her, don't you?"

Charlie barked once, it almost seemed like he was answering her question. Gloria wasn't crying anymore, there were no more tears to cry.

"What are we going to do now?" Sarah asked.

Gloria placed her arms around us and said: "Survive! We have to keep living, for as long as we can."

"We have to find out where the rest are," Juan yelled from behind us.

I turned around to look at him and asked: "The rest?"

"There are some family members, friends, that are not here. They could be in a different area of the cemetery, or maybe…" Juan replied, doubting a little about the last part.

Gloria wasn't ready to hope again, she interrupted Juan and said: "Let's go back to the house and rest there. We all need it, tomorrow will be a new day. We can talk about it then."

"That sounds like a good plan. I would love to eat a hot meal, for a change," Sarah said.

We all nodded and smiled, we all agreed with that. We began walking back, but a few feet away, I noticed that Charlie wasn't with us, so I turned to look at where we last left him. He was still sitting next to Susana's grave.

"Come Charlie! Come here boy!" I shouted, but he stood there with his ears up, listening to what I was saying, so I called him again: "Come here Charlie! Come with us!"

Charlie tilted his head, turned to see the grave for a moment, maybe asking permission to leave. So I insisted: "Charlie! Como here boy!" I said, while I tapped my legs with my hands.

Charlie finally caved, he ran to where we were and followed us home, not without looking back, again and again until we reached the top of the hill. We went over it and the cemetery was left behind.

We got back to the house, everything in it was perfectly set up, as if there were people still living there.

We looked around the house marvelling at everything we saw. Gloria sighted at every turn, as she re lived memories of her youth.

Juan asked us to help unload a few of the boxes down from the vehicle and we placed them in the kitchen. Gloria would open the boxes and organise them as she took what she needed out of them.

Juan started a fire in the living room and fired up the stove in the kitchen; Gloria cooked a delicious soup with some of the supplies we had and, as we enjoyed her cooking, Juan and Gloria, spend hours telling us stories about their family, how she learned to cook from her mother, how she played with her brothers, sisters and cousins when she was young. We heard the story of how they met: "Juan grew up a few blocks from here, we use to attend the same elementary school. He was a couple of years older than I was. He actually, used to ignore me when we were kids," Gloria said.

"When I was younger, we didn't really look at girls that were younger than us. We were focused on older girls. It was exciting!" Juan replied.

"And we didn't look at boys our age, they were very immature for us," Gloria said, while she looked straight at Sarah.

She laughed with Gloria, and I couldn't help but smile at that. Looking at Gloria laughing after all the pain she had to endure, realising all her family was gone, just like that; all that hope shattered, all those images she forged in her head, gone in an instant.

I guess that, by this point, she got, somehow, used to the loss. Life was something brittle, something fleeting, at least, more than so. Life is always been fragile, it has way fewer possibilities of persisting than it has of ending. So many things can go wrong; but life is meant to be. Even though it is conceived with an expiration date attached to it, it's meant to be celebrated every day, as if opening up your eyes would mean: being born again. Life has a way of breaking through.

After the Great War, death was a commonality, it became normal, maybe to normal. Before the war, before everything went south for the human race, people were used to seeing life through the eyes of the young, babies represented the blooming of life, it was what gave balance to the world, knowing that there would be a new generation to replace the one decaying, always provided a sense of renewal. But now there was only death. It made everything grim, life had lost its spark. Days went by like days in a calendar that just wash away, counting down towards the end. So, even though it hurt, the death of her family settled faster than it should have on her. It was…expected, somehow, even though there had always been hope, hope that she would reunite with them. Her mind played tricks on her, showed her that one option, never giving place to the opposing one, the one that she was confronted with, the one that took her down this path she was in and now the only important thing was: surviving…moving on!

"We have to figure out what we're going to do next," Juan said.

"We can stay here, I think it will be safe. There doesn't seem to be a threat," Gloria replied.

Juan bowed his head, he was ashamed of what he would say next.

"Honey, look around you. Something happened here, and we don't know what it was, but it killed everybody we knew. It may look safe, but I wouldn't be so sure," Juan replied.

We all looked at each other, our heads filled up with terrible thoughts. There were a million things that could have gone wrong in this place that we didn't knew about.

"You're right! We need to find out what it was that killed everyone here," Gloria said.

"How are we going to find out? There is no one here to ask," Sarah interrupted.

There was silence for a moment, I needed to say what was on my mind: "There must be clues. We know that the air is clean. The sensors would have detected something."

Juan nodded and said: "It's true, we are safe, for now, but we need to be vigilant."

"Maybe one of us can stay awake, while the others rest," Sarah said.

"That's a good idea!" Gloria replied.

"I'll set up a perimeter on the computer, it should sense if anything is moving. I'll take the first watch, you guys need to rest," Juan said as he was getting up.

"Do you think it's safe to go outside?" Gloria asked.

"I'll be ok, I'm just going to the vehicle to set it up. We need to get some stuff out of it anyway," Juan replied as he looked at me and asked: "Can you give me a hand?"

"Sure!" I replied as I got up.

As I was walking towards the door, Sarah grabbed my hand and stopped me.

"Be careful ok?" she said to me.

I smiled and said: "We'll be fine, don't worry!"

I squeezed her hand and let go of it, as I walked towards the door. Charlie was laying down next to Sarah and got up when he saw us walk to the door.

"No, stay!" I said to him as I raised my hand and showed him my open palm.

He looked at me, sat back down and moaned softly in disapproval.

Juan and I walked out.

It was so quiet and peaceful outside, night had fallen and you could hear birds chirping on the top of the palms that swayed with the wind that blew softly. It was so hard to think of something wrong happening in a place like this, but then I remembered something I read in a book: "Everything is the quietest, just before the storm."

We had to be alert and expect the worst, that was the only way to survive.

Juan and I brought some supplies inside, he set up the computer in the vehicle to sense movement in a 200 foot radius and alert us if it sensed anything suspicious. We went back in the house. We placed the supplies on the kitchen floor and went back into the living room. Gloria and Sarah were waiting for us.

"I'll stay down here and keep an eye on things. You guys go up and take a bed, get some rest," Juan said.

Gloria, Sarah and I went upstairs.

"You guys take that bedroom, it has a big bed. I'll take my old room, I always slept peaceful there," Gloria said while she pointed at the master bedroom, down the hall.

Sarah and I walked over and opened up the door. There was a huge bed in the middle of the room, crowned with a canopy that surrounded it.

"I've never seen a bed like this!" Sarah said, amazed of its complexity.

There were different colour veils covering the outside, surrounding the bed. Sarah pushed them a side, one after the other one, layers and layers of colours revealing a clearer view of the inside as they were pushed out of the way. After pushing all of them out of the way, she was able to get in and giggled as she threw herself on top of the bed. The bed was topped by pillows and cushions of different size and forms. Sarah began playing with them as she moved from side to side.

I could see her through the veils, the image of her body moving, entangled with the pillows that flew all over her, pushed by her silhouette that swished around inside this cocoon of colours. My heart was pounding, dancing to the rhythm of her movements, enticed by her smell that came to me like waves every time she twisted and turned inside.

"Patrick, get in here! This is the most amazing bed I have ever seen," Sarah yelled from inside.

I was standing at the edge of it, just admiring her being her. Her movements were like art to me, the way her hands swayed, the way they frisked the air with their motion. The way her head played tricks on her neck, tilting softly in obtuse angles while she looked at me. The way her lips would never close, obstructed by her teeth that picked through, tempting my thoughts.

I finally decided to join her inside and made my way through the sea of veils that surrounded it until I was in. Sarah was waiting for me. I could tell her heart was racing with excitement, just like mine was. Excitement of discovering the unknown, of giving ourselves to this desire that spawned unconsciously, that flowed through every cell in our bodies. She got close and gently placed her arms over my shoulders and slowly got close. Our lips began the journey and our bodies quickly became the vessels of the love we felt. The urge to consume every inch of hers with my mouth, with my hands, with my legs and she did the same. Nobody had showed us how, but somehow it was already programmed in ourselves. We ripped off our clothes and felt our bodies naked, embrace one another. Pealing layers, uncovering new ways of enticing each other, allowing our minds to play and our bodies to feel every instance of passion we had for each other. We discovered what love really is, between those sheets, covered by those veils that reacted to our every move, that flaunted our every breath.

It was sealed, this fortune that defined us since we were conceived in that laboratory years ago. Even though they tried to keep us apart, tried to conceal the obvious, we were like Adam and Eve. Conceived from the same essence, spawned from the same fabric. We were one in the same, attracted to each other, like atoms to its core.

We made love until our bodies shut down and couldn't take any more excitement, until our minds were filled with every thought we had leading up to this, this heavenly place we had encountered in each other.

We slept, like we've never slept in our lives. We had found what we were looking for, without even knowing that we were and that gave us peace. A peace that scared away every nightmare we ever had and gave way to beautiful dreams. Dreams of a future that we could only have in our minds, a future far brighter than we could have imagined.

We wanted to stay there for as long as we could, stay in our dream world, inside our duality that shared one heart that beat in synchrony. This was the perfect place to be.

The smell woke me up, the intoxicating smell of magic being cooked in the kitchen. Our bodies needed to feed and our senses reacted by instinct, pushed our eyes to open and our mouths to long for the taste of whatever was invading our smell.

I turned and saw the face of an angel beside me, resting on top of my arm that nestled her lightness. Her hair decorating the beauty underneath, barely allowing the sunlight, that sneaked through the sea of murmurs that surrounded us, to cuddle her cheeks that glowed between the strands of hair over them. I pushed them aside gently with my fingers, so that I could see her face as it came alive, reacting to my touch. Her eyes opened slowly and her breathing mustered a loud lull that filled her lungs with the musk left between our bodies. She smiled when she looked at me, idling over her, admiring her beauty.

"What are you up to?" she asked tenderly.

"I'm looking at beauty, waking up!" I said.

She grabbed me by the neck and pulled me closer until my lips and hers met. We kissed, that felt like the first time we did. This explosion of warmth that roamed my body, the sweetness of her lips while they fondled mine and the crudity of her tongue that invaded my head with reminders of last night. We were on our way back there when she pulled away as her nose guided her on a different path. She pointed her nose up as she focused on the same smell that had awoken me before.

"That smells delicious. I'm starving!" she said while her eyes opened mischievously.

I just smiled and nodded, inviting her to go down and discover what we craved. We both got out of bed, looked for our clothes and dressed up as quickly as we could. Stepped out of the room and ran downstairs into the kitchen.

Gloria was there, hard at work, making breakfast for all.

"Oh! Good, you are up. I was just about to go up and knock on your door," she said, but something caught her attention.

"Why are you guys smiling like that?" she asked, that prompted us to look at each other and giggle.

Gloria smiled when she realised what had happened the night before. It wasn't something she needed explained, so she just said.

"Here, grab some plates and I'll feed you. How's that?"

We did so, she served us and we sat down on the table to eat.

"Be careful, it's hot," she said.

Just in time, because Sarah and I were just about to take our first bite without even noticing. We were still haunted with each other, re living what had just happened last night in our minds, over and over again. Looking at each other while everything else blurred in the background.

Juan walked into the kitchen, chasing after the smell Gloria's cooking was emanating through the whole house.

"What's for breakfast?" He asked.

"Sit down, I have your plate ready," Gloria answered.

Juan sat down in front of us and as soon as he did, he noticed something was off.

"What's with you two? Why are you acting so strange?" He asked while he was looking straight at us.

I just nodded, looked at Sarah again and we both giggled. It was inevitable, we were in love.

"That's weird!" Juan said sarcastically as Gloria was putting down the plate of food in front of him.

Gloria and Juan looked at each other and smiled.

Juan began eating and Gloria sat on the table with her own plate and we all ate in silence for a while. Only sporadic glances between the four of us happened, there was a lot of thinking and wondering going on.

After breakfast we all sat down in the living room to discuss what we would do next. Charly was wondering curiously around the house, always following one of us, trying to find his place. He sat down on the floor next to Sarah and me and cradled on my leg so I would pet him.

"So, we have to figure out our next move," Gloria said.

"We have to ponder our options, take in account the things that we all want, what we think we have to do," Juan followed.

Sarah and I just looked at each other and nodded.

"We all have to participate, this decision affects us all, so you have to speak your mind," Gloria insisted.

"I just want to stay with my family, wherever we go, if we stay here or if we decide to go. The only thing I want is that we stay together," I said.

Sarah agreed with me, nodding.

"Yes, me too," she said.

"Of course, that is the best thing we can do. I don't think that any of us thought otherwise," Gloria said while she looked at Juan who nodded.

"Definitely, we stick together! But we have to figure out if its best to stay here or keep driving south," Juan said.

"What's wrong with staying here?" Sarah asked.

Juan and Gloria looked at each other.

"Well, we can try to set up here. It's a great place and its ours now, but we are not sure it's safe. Something happened here and we can't be sure that the same thing won't happen again," Gloria said.

"Whatever happened here, happened some time ago. We should scout the town for survivors. There might still be someone around that we haven't seen.

Maybe they know exactly what happened. I mean, Charlie is still here!" Juan said.

Charlie stood up as soon as he heard his name being called. I pet him and he went down again.

" So, maybe that is the first thing we do. Walk around town. Search for any survivors and find clues as to what happened here," I said.

We all nodded agreeing with it.

That day we grabbed some gear and went out to walk around town. The town looked deserted, but it didn't look like the cities we had gone through. There was no trash on the streets, no debris laying around and no signs of vandalism. It just seemed that time had stopped and people had vanished. Charlie was with us but he seemed scared, he was as close to us as he could.

Juan wanted to go visit the house where he grew up, where his family lived, or at least did, many years ago. He wasn't even sure they lived there anymore. He had lost contact with them when he decided to go up north looking for a better life. His family didn't agreed with his decision and they cut ties with him back then.

We walked through several blocks, following Juan, that seemed to doubt where he was going. Things looked different from when they live there. We finally got to a street he recognised and Juan pointed at a house, down the street.

"That is the one," he said.

He pointed at a big house down the street, it was a colonial type building, surrounded by a fence six feet high that, by that point, was already overtaken by weeds that claimed up the metal bars that formed it and made them their home.

We were all walking steady down the street, heading towards the house, but looking all around, trying to spot someone moving, maybe some curious eyes looking at us through a window, another dog or cat wondering the streets, a place that was fortified where people might be hiding in groups, anything that would seem out of place, but nothing so far. Only the same emptiness we had seen for miles.

Juan pushed the gate outside that was wrapped up in weeds, until he pushed it open. He stepped up to the door, it was closed and Juan stood in front of it doubting. He first looked through the windows on the side of it, looked around the entrance before finally turning the knob and pushing the door open. The door screeched as it showed us the inside of the house. It was dark and humid, the drapes were closed and light wasn't getting in. Juan walked inside and we followed. The house seemed empty. Gloria got close to one of the windows and pulled the drapes open. Light began to show us what was inside. At first, the only thing we could see was dust suspended, covering everything around us, but Gloria kept pulling the drapes open, one by one and we could finally see clearly. Everything seemed to be in its place, there was nothing on the ground, nothing on the table in the dining room, nothing on the sofas in the living room, nothing on the stove in the kitchen, nothing but dust covering everything.

"It seems that nobody is been here in a while!" Sarah said while she graced her finger on top of a table, removing the dust that covered it.

Juan was busy looking around the living room, walking towards the kitchen, trying to find something but the truth is that he didn't even knew what to look for. I guess some signs of life, like we all were. He hadn't been close to his family in years, so he wasn't expecting them to be there, didn't even knew what they looked like, or how many of them were, it was just hope that drove him. Hope that we could find someone that would fill in the blanks, that would tell him the story of his family since he left, the story of that town and what had happened there.

Juan finally went upstairs, looking for any signs. We stayed downstairs, waiting for him to come down, hoping for some good news. Charlie kept sniffing around the house, trying to catch some familiar smells. Juan took a while and we could hear him walking around the rooms. He finally came down and we all knew, just by his expression, that there was nothing to be found.

"It's like time stood still, while everyone disappeared," Juan said while he looked at us, shivering.

Gloria got close and embraced him, he needed to feel loved, cared for, protected somehow. They embraced for a moment, the shivering stopped and slowly turned into sobbing. It was amazing to watch. Sarah and I were just stunned, looking at them.

It was something that we didn't knew how to relate to, something that we didn't read about in all those books we devoured growing up, something, I guess, you had to read between the lines, something you had to experience for yourself. This powerful force that binds us, this miracle that flows between our bodies when they touch, the warmth that tingles in your fingertips, flows through your skin enticing it, the connection that another human being can have with you, just by being close, just by caring.

It was wonderful to watch and I couldn't help it, even if I wanted to, to relate and feel empathy. It wasn't sadness, or sorrow that prompted tears out of my eyes. It was the connection that spread around them, that scattered uncontrollably.

I felt Sarah grabbing my arm, getting close to me, sharing what I was feeling too. It was something we had never experienced before. There was so much we had to learn about us, about ourselves.

"Let's go, there's nothing here. Let's go back home," Juan said while he looked into Gloria's eyes.

Gloria nodded and smiled as they both walked to the door. We followed and we all stepped out of the house. There was not much said, on our way back home. I guess that Juan and Gloria were going through all the memories they had in their heads, from when they were young, from when their families were around. Sarah and I just respected their silence. We just walked behind them, holding hands.

When we got back home, Charlie was the first one to run to the house. He was excited to be back to something familiar. He stood at the entrance and looked back at us, prompting us to get there and open the door. We all felt that way, even though it wasn't our home, per say, we had adopted it as such. I once read: "Home is where you hang your hat." Which seemed appropriate to describe the feeling, home is where you want it to be, where you feel safe, where you can gather yourself and be with the ones and the things that you feel yours. I have never really felt I had a home, until now. The lab never felt like this, it was not a place I felt safe in, never really felt any connection to it, except when Gloria was around, she made her feel like home with her presence; but now it was about Sarah, and Gloria, and Juan, and Charlie and this place that adopted us.

We spent a while there, we had no plans of going anywhere and no reason to. So we stayed and enjoyed the comforts of having a space to call our own. Sarah and I spent a lot of time together inside our veil surrounded piece of heaven, enjoying each other. I couldn't ask for anything more. I felt whole every time she was around, she filled every ounce of my being with hers and I couldn't get enough. I knew she felt the same way I did. The scattered moments we were apart, I was thinking of her every single one and I knew I was also on her mind.

Gloria and Juan made their mission to show us how to survive out here, how to grow crops, how to hunt and fish, how to surround ourselves with the essential, so that food was never an issue. There was plenty of it out there. The earth had found a way to thrive by itself, animals were roaming freely, reproducing and taking over what was always theirs. Vegetation overtook the landscape, growing all around, covering the cities that were once dark, grey areas, with green tapestries and coloured sparks throughout. It was wonderful to see.

In their mind, they were responsible for our lives. They took the role of parents seriously. They wanted to make sure that we survived, even if it was without them taking care of us. Sarah and I were eager to learn, so it was a symbiotic thing, they taught us everything they knew and we assimilated and repeated everything we learned.

It was perfect because Juan and Gloria had grown up here, living out of the bounty of nature around them. Fishing in the sea, hunting in the woods and growing crops. It was a generous land, everything grew around here with ease. Mangos, bananas, pineapples, avocado, everything grew wild and you just had to extend your hand and grab it.

There was peace and quiet for a while. We enjoyed the time that was given to us. The chance to enjoy each other's company and the opportunity to be amazed every day for everything that surrounded us, but nature, in its wisdom, had adapted to the changes that were sprung upon her by humans. Life always finds a way to change, to master the opposition and embrace the new condition given and so new life forms appeared. Mutated versions of the ones that roamed the earth for thousands of years, morphed into this new, improved versions. Resilient to the threats that were out there, adapted to survive in this hostile environment.

There was no literature on them, no way of knowing exactly what their skills were and for us, what threats they represented. The laws of men were no longer present and now it was just nature laws that prevailed. We were forced to be vigilant and protect ourselves every time we went outside. We had stunt guns in hand and were always mindful of our surroundings.

Juan and Gloria would note everything that they saw that was different from what they knew, new plants and fruits that seemed to bloom in this new environment. New species of animals that were everywhere, new versions of the ones they knew and completely new species that had emigrated here and adapted or just transformed incited by the new conditions they lived in.

Inside the house, life went on as normal as could be. Sarah and I had bonded far beyond what I ever imagined we could. We were inseparable and enjoyed each other's company, she is an amazing person and the more I got to know her, the more I fell in love with the woman she was. We spent our days doing chores around the house, Gloria was in charge of the kitchen and Sarah helped her out while learning, at the same time, the art of cooking, while Juan and I were in charge of cleaning and fixing things around, finding whatever was needed and scouting the surroundings.

We still didn't know what had happened here. It was obvious that, without children, the population was doomed to disappear. Even if it was old age that took the majority of people in this town, there were a lot of younger people buried in that cemetery, without explanation as to why they were there. Sometimes I sat with Charlie, he would just look at me, like trying to speak to me, trying to tell me something, trying to convey what he had seen happened in this place.

Juan was obsessed with finding out, he was worried that the same thing would happen to us. He kept saying: "The worst enemies are the ones you can't see."

He kept close attention to the sensors, the ones that measured the air quality, that alerted us to the presence of viruses and bacteria in the air all around us. He knew that could be the reason why so many died here, but we couldn't be sure. There were no signs, no note found warning people about any danger. It was as if something would have swept all those lives in a moment, without a trace, but the question remained: "Who had dug up all those graves, placed the bodies inside and marked them one by one?"

Somebody had to. Even if it was one person, at the end, that gave burial to the last one there, there had to be someone that survived. So, Juan and I went scouting every day, for a while, going to different directions each time. Hoping to find someone alive, but weeks had passed and places began to seem familiar.

"I think we have been here before," I said to Juan one day while we were scouting.

Juan looked around and nodded.

"Everything looks the same to me, I think we have been all over, at least twice," he replied.

"So, what do you think we should do?" I asked.

Juan looked at me and shrugged.

"Your guess is as good as mine. I was hoping we would find some clues by know, but it is as if people just disappeared in thin air," he said.

"Well, I remembered something I read that said: "Doing the same thing over and over again, expecting different results is the definition of…"

"Insanity. I know!" Juan interrupted.

"Maybe we are going in sane, maybe that is the worst part of it…" he said as he paused and thought for a moment.

"…or maybe, dismissing it all and settling is what did it," he went on.

"What do you mean, that people died of boredom?" I asked.

"No, not boredom, 'complacency'," he said.

I looked even more confused, I wasn't getting what he meant. Juan waited to see if I would finally get it, but I just stood there.

"Yes, you let your guard down! You think that everything is fine and you let your guard down. You stop being aware and that is when it happens," Juan said.

"I think you are over reacting Juan, we've been here for almost a year. We've gone out every single day to scout around town and we've seen no signs of anything bad, actually, anything at all," I said.

Juan looked at me while his mind was going on, finally he lowered his head and nodded.

"You're right, let's go home!" He said.

I asserted and we began walking back home. I was amazed looking at everything around us as we walked by, everything was in its place, nothing like the other cities we had gone through. War didn't reach this down south and the town looked like a postcard. The only thing that was different was that nature had overtaken the place and there was foliage growing all over. On the walls, on the ground, on the rooftops. It was a sight to see.

When we got back home, the first one to greet us was Charlie, he ran outside, followed closely by Sarah who threw herself in my arms and kissed me. I loved her so much, she made every single moment seemed like an epic one, as if I had been gone for months, as if I was a hero of war coming back home. Her happiness was contagious, although it didn't needed to be, because I felt the same way she did. I was excited to see her after only a few hours.

Juan just stood there watching us, smiling. He turned towards the entrance to the house, hoping that maybe Gloria would do the same, but she was inside preparing our food. The smell coming out of the kitchen was intoxicating. So we went inside and Juan went directly into the kitchen and there she was by the stove cooking. Sarah and I followed as Juan embraced Gloria from behind. She got startled and jumped.

"What are you doing? I almost knocked down the pot! She said upset.

Juan let go and opened up his arms.

"I missed you honey!" He said.

"Stop goofing around and wash your hands, dinner is almost ready!" she said.

Juan looked back at us and made this weird face, trying to make fun of the fact that their relationship was a lot different than ours. They were so comfortable with each other that this fleeting sparks of drama that Sarah and I had were long gone.

Sarah and I sat down at the table.

"So, did you find something? Is anyone out there?" Sarah asked.

"No, the same emptiness we have seen for weeks. Some animals running around, but no one else. It's like they all disappeared," I replied.

Gloria stopped stirring the pot and turned around for a moment to look at me. Her eyes dropped at the thought of it. There was no one left but us. I could tell a shiver went down her spine, it was sort of normal, at that point, to know that we were singular. That hope we all had, but mostly Juan and Gloria, of finding people to be with, was slipping away day by day.

I got up and got close to her, looked her in the eye.

"It'll be ok Gloria, we have each other, we will be alright," I said.

She smiled and embraced me. It was hard to accept, but she knew I was right.

Juan walked back into the room.

"So, let's eat! I'm starving!" He said as he sat on the table.

Gloria pulled away and looked at me.

"Go wash your hands, food is ready!" she said as she kissed me.

I smiled and did so, sat on the table and we all had dinner. It was nice to feel like a family, after everything we've been through, after all that we've seen, we still craved this unity. We all needed to feel as part of a clan, even if we were only four, or two, we needed the company. The thought of us being the last ones, being part of a dying race was scary, but we found comfort in each other.

Knowing that when we woke up, there would be someone by your side. We are, as humans, contained in our own space. We are a unit, one body, one mind, one heart that makes the unit work independently from others, but still we crave company, we gather in groups to feel safe, to feel warm, feel loved and cored for. We were spawned as a unity, but not meant to be alone. Yes, the body could survive on its own but the mind would crumble, if only with the thought of it. That is why, throughout the ages, the worst punishment that could be inflicted in someone was always isolation.

At night when everything was quiet and everyone was asleep, I use to wonder about it. How alone in the world I was, how fragile my relationship with this place was, with life. I wanted to be with Sarah, I wanted to spent the rest of my life with her but I couldn't be sure of how long would that be. If I could ever protect her against harm, make sure that she would be beside me and I would be there for her. It was, probably, a selfish thought, thinking of hanging on to her.

Sometimes I felt like I was falling, without anything to hang on to, just falling down, no end to it and this sense of emptiness took over. Like I wasn't contained in my body, as if the minuscule pieces that form me were breaking apart, just scattering out in the atmosphere. I guess that must feel like when you die. We all are part of this cosmos, we are a combination of matter and energy that, when the time comes, will fuse with other parts to conform a different entity. So, we never actually disappear, we only transform, but this life, this hope that I had of being with her, of loving her would never be and that scared me to my bones, it actually hurt, whenever I thought about it. I just opened up my eyes and watch her sleeping peacefully next to me. This amazingly beautiful being that, for some reason, loved me back, that shivered with me when we touched, that shared my desire to become one.

I didn't wanted to fall asleep, I just wanted to remain like that, next to her, watching her, making sure that we would not disappear into nowhere, but my eyes couldn't stay open, my eyelids grew heavy and my mind settled.

That became a normalcy, spending the days with my family, with Sarah, Gloria, Charlie and Juan and the nights with my fear of darkness, of the emptiness I so much dreaded.

So many wrong turns along the way, humans were at the brink of extinction. With all the gifts that we were graced with and we still allowed our instincts to command us, to drive us to the end. This had been the story of this world, millions of years in the making. This planet that had seen hundreds of eras swish by, begin, blossom, decay and die just to give way to another one. It was the way it had been for a long time, but we thought we were different, we thought we were unique, we considered ourselves gods, owners of our own destiny when we were just like candles that get blown away as easily.

All the things we learned in history, all the advances we uncovered and at the end, we realised it was always meant to be this way. This world will keep spinning, the sun will still rise every day, the night will fall and life will go on, just without us. The only thing left was hanging on to what we had until it was taken away.

We even searched for answers among the stars, we tried to jump out of this planet, away from our home, to conquer new places where we could spread. We got to the moon, to Mars and even to the far reaches of our solar system but we couldn't make it work. It was a futile attempt to find a way to leave this planet and claim another one. There were many attempts to do so, but we were never able to find the conditions in which we could properly thrive. Adapting to them was not in the cards.

Besides, we were too busy dealing with our own prejudice. Science was losing ground to religion and the magical explanations for everything and all that we experienced. It was an easier way to explain it all and it overtook the simple minds and gave them a peaceful resolution to the dilemma. "It was god will!" And that was the end of it. So, people got complacent with that explanation and left it all to the will of a higher power that doomed everyone to a fatal flaw.

We were all sinners one way or another, we were all to blame for whatever was happening, because we were human, imperfect beings that defied the will of god. There wasn't that much we could do about it. The end was the only way out, so people searched for it, walked blindly to it as if it was salvation, but for the lucky ones that hanged on to life, that had found a reason to go on, it was all we had.

So we lived, each day, as if it was the last. We held on to each other, we kissed and laughed. We sat down by the fire and listened to stories that Juan and Gloria told about their lives, Sarah and I shared fantastic tales from all those books we've read. We sang songs we remembered and when the night was darkest, when our bodies needed the rest, Sarah and I went to bed. Made love and embraced until our bodies shut down.

Chapter 7
The Struggle with Life

It wasn't a bad life, we filled our hearts with each other's company and filled our days with each other's presence, but Juan was right when he said that it was maybe complacency that took the lives of all those people in the village and we were starting to fall on their footsteps.

Charlie had gotten used to being around us, he had forgotten the past and didn't have the will to go back to the cemetery and lay next to "Susana's grave", but even though he was loved and cared for I still sensed fear in him. He would react to every single noise heard outside, even if we didn't hear it, he would sometimes just react to something he'd heard. At night he slept close to us and wasn't too keen on leaving the house when we went out as if he were afraid of going out.

It created concern on everyone, but we just thought that he could have been a rescue, back in the day, and went through some abuse that he never actually got over. So we dismissed it and got used to him acting up sometimes.

That is what I mean when I talk about "complacency", we just assumed that this was the way things were and settled on our everyday life, as you do when it feels comfortable. You dismiss the subtle details that point to something outside your purview. Little things that seem out of place, that change so slightly that you discard them as nothing, but Charlie knew, he had lived through it before and now feared them coming back, so he was always alert to the things we weren't.

We had no idea of the things he had seen, he couldn't tell the story of his life and the why he had survived, it was just a fact. We were something he never expected but surely appreciated, just like we did him. We had found each other and that was enough.

Days went by and life began to feel like a routine, even though it was just us four and Charlie, we felt like a community somehow. We each had our chores to do every day, we enjoyed meals together and took walks outside if we felt like it. We had the freedom to do so and no restrictions. We enjoyed the dawns and the sunsets, marvelling at nature and its gifts, I was in love with Sarah every day just a little more; so life wasn't bad at all, but after a while something strange started happening, Juan began to get agitated for no reason, began lashing out at Gloria or me, even with Sarah, for whatever reason.

At first it was at things that would be understandable, like one day we were dinning together and I reached out across the table to get a plate and knocked down the water pitcher, I made a mess and even got Juan pants and shirt all wet. He went ballistic, lashing and swearing in Spanish at me. His eyes were on fire and I really felt threatened by him. He got up from the table and went outside. Gloria was perplexed, she didn't understand what had set him off so much. She kept apologising for him over and over again, as if she was the one that was to blame, but there was no explanation for his behaviour. We all make mistakes and this could have happened to anyone, it wasn't intentional and there was no real damage done.

Gloria went after him and they stayed outside for a while. We could hear them arguing outside, mostly Gloria would tell him her mind and he would just listen. Sarah and I cleaned up the table and sat down to finish our meal. When we were done, Gloria and Juan came back in. Juan seemed ashamed, his eyes were looking everywhere except at us, he couldn't even do that. Gloria just shrugged, as a sort of apology. There was no explanation given by Juan, who just sat on the table and finished eating. Sarah and I felt uncomfortable and since we had already finished, excused ourselves and went upstairs.

Things like that began happening more and more, he lashed out at smaller and smaller things. It was obvious that his temper was not in control, but there was no real reason for his attitude. At times he even began to have this feuds with himself, getting mad at whatever he was doing. Calling himself names and eventually began self-punishing. Hitting his legs, his arms, his face. It began to be very noticeable. He began isolating from us, preferred to be outside by himself, looking for food or supplies, or just out for long walks. One day when he returned and rushed through the living room, like he usually did, we noticed he was bleeding and Gloria immediately jumped up and went after him.

We could hear the screams coming out of the kitchen. Gloria was trying to help him, clean him up and fix whatever had happened to him. Apparently he had broken his nose and was bleeding profusely from it, but he wouldn't let Gloria close. After a while he calmed down and Gloria was able to clean him and patch him up. Sarah and I were concerned and thought about going into the kitchen and helping Gloria, but we decided it was better left to them to deal with it as a couple.

As the days went by things only got worst. His temper tantrums just got more intense as well as his self-punishment tactics. He had begun cutting himself on his arms and legs, but it became unbearable one day when he actually hit Gloria. He had just walked in from one of his usual tantrum walks, was bleeding from his arm and Gloria tried to grab his arm and clean his wound. He just pulled his arm back violently from Gloria's hands and slapped her across her face. Gloria fell to the ground. I just couldn't take it anymore and got up from the couch and pushed him from the back. He fell on top of the dining table, that was already set up for dinner, and knocked down everything on top of it. He got up, turned around and looked at me with this devilish look on his face. I thought he was going to kill me, but Gloria jumped in between us holding a huge pan in her hand, threatening him.

"Don't even dare touch him!" Gloria shouted at him.

That just made him angrier, he was foaming at the mouth, enraged like a wild animal. You could see his veins pumping blood to his head that looked like it was about to explode.

"Quítate de en medio Puta! (Move away, you whore!)" He shouted in Spanish.

Gloria was heartbroken, she couldn't believe that this was the same man she loved, the same man that stood by her during the worst times in her life. She couldn't believe that he had changed so much in such a little time, out of the blue.

"Juan, qué pasa? Que tienes? Somos tu familia! (Juan, what's going on? What's wrong with you? We are your family!)" Gloria said.

By then Sarah and I could pretty much understand what they said every time. Some of the first things you learn in another language are bad words and I knew what "Puta" meant. It was so out of character for Juan to be shouting those words at Gloria, the love of his life and without reason. "Puta" means "Whore" in Spanish and there was no justification for him to call her that.

Sarah got up from the couch and walked to where I was, right behind Gloria that was still holding the pan on her hand. The three of us stood there looking at Juan and he was looking back at us with his blood shot eyes, still foaming from the mouth, but we stood our ground, together in silence, waiting for him to do his move. His eyes fixated on ours, they just jumped from one to the next, over and over as he slowly found solace and calmed down. His expression changed from rage into shame and despair. His eyes filled up with tears as he fell down on his knees and began wailing uncontrollably.

"I'm sorry, I'm sorry" he went on and on.

"I don't know what is happening to me. I can't control myself. I'm so sorry!"

Gloria dropped the pan and embraced him, Sarah and I were still a little bit cautious about it. It had been a while since he started shifting into this other person we didn't recognise and it had only escalated dramatically, so we didn't feel like taking any chances right then, but Gloria, that knew him way better than we did, was all in. She didn't even blinked, she held him close and consoled him.

"I'm so sorry, so sorry!" Juan kept repeating over and over.

Gloria wouldn't let go of him, she was feeling the same hurt that he was, sharing every second of his pain, hoping that it would go away and he would go back to being the same Juan she was in love with. I wasn't sure that would happen. It had been a steep decline into this person he had transformed into.

Finally Gloria pulled away and looked him in the eyes, she smiled at him and grabbed his face tenderly. She was crying too, sharing the guilt with him, guilt she had no part in, she had done nothing wrong. She removed his shirt that was soaked in blood and threw it on the floor. She took a cloth and wiped his wounds and soaked his tears.

I saw the shirt laying on the ground and instinctively went to pick it up, I don't know why I turned, as I was picking it up, and looked at Juan's back. It was filled with little red dots that looked like dimples, small round spots, all over his back, covering every inch of it. It almost looked like a rash, but it seemed to have symmetry, as if it was done on purpose, systematically in a certain pattern.

Gloria lifted her eyes and saw me staring at Juan's back, her expression changed, she was concerned when she looked at me, at my face, my expression that was completely bewildered with what I was looking at.

"What? What is it?" Gloria asked.

I just looked back at her and pointed at Juan's back. She pulled him forward and peeked at his back.

"What is that?" she asked scared.

She moved to Juan's side to see better.

"What is that?" she asked again.

She was about to touch one of the dimples.

"No, don't touch them!" I said.

"Why, what are they?" Gloria asked.

"I don't know, but don't touch them!" I replied.

Sarah walked behind me to look at Juan's back and stood there in silence, her expression said it all.

"What's on my back? It's very itchy," Juan said as his hand was about to scratch his back.

"No, don't touch it!" Gloria said as she pulled his hand from it.

"Why, what's back there? What's wrong?" Juan asked concerned.

Gloria looked at me and Sarah, like looking for an answer to his question.

"There is something on your back. Some kind of rash" Gloria replied.

"Rash? Is it bad?" Juan said as he got up and walked towards a mirror that stood at the side of the entrance.

He looked at it and instinctively try to touch it.

"Don't touch it!" Gloria yelled.

"It's itchy! I need to scratch it!" Juan yelled back.

"No, don't. Just hang on!" I said.

Juan stopped but kept staring at it disgusted.

"What is that? I can't see it clearly," he said.

"Come lie on the couch face down," Gloria asked him.

Juan walked to the couch and laid face down. We all walked cautiously towards him. Gloria grabbed a lamp that was next to the couch and pointed it at Juan's back. Once we were close and the light was shining on it, we could see that the rash was actually perfectly round pulps. Hundreds of them forming a pattern that looked like something else; it looked like a scab, as if he had fallen on his back and got a big scratch that later began healing and a crust had formed.

I got close to it, trying to determine what it was. I extended my finger to touch one of them and Gloria reacted.

"No, don't. Here, use this," she said as she handed me a chopstick.

I pocked one of the pulps with it, lightly, I didn't want it to burst. I just wanted to see how it would react, what the consistency was. As soon as I did, I saw something move inside and I jumped back away from it.

It was small, but I could still see it moving inside, reacting to the poke and the light that was hitting it directly.

"What? What did you see?" Sarah asked, she was standing right behind me and I almost knocked her down.

I turned to look at her, I must have been scared because she got worried. I just remember my head going around and around thinking of different scenarios.

"What did you see?" Sarah insisted.

I just nodded, I didn't have an answer.

I turned back to look at his back, Juan was just lying there almost unconscious.

"Juan!" I called him, but he didn't answer.

Gloria, that was standing behind us, walked closer to the couch to look closely at Juan.

"He's out!" she said as she looked at him.

"Is he breathing?" Sarah asked.

Gloria turned and looked at Sarah, almost mad at her question.

"Of course he is breathing, he is snoring!" she said.

Sarah and I just looked at each other.

"Here, let me see," Gloria said as she grabbed the chopstick from my hand.

She got close to the pulps and did the same thing I had. She pocked one up, but she did it harder and the pulp burst and as it did, something jumped out of it. It looked like a larvae, a really small worm that reacted violently to the light and moved quickly to another area of Juan's back and somehow drilled its way inside before Gloria could react. She just jumped back scared.

"Madre mía! (Holly Shit!) What the hell was that?" she said while she turned and looked at us.

"I don't know, it looked like a worm," I replied.

"Where did it go?" Sarah asked.

"It went back into Juan's back," I said.

Sarah's eyes opened wide as she looked at me and then at Gloria that was concerned for Juan. Her mind was rushing, thinking of what to do and trying to remember if what she just saw was something in her recollection, but I could tell she was completely baffled.

She turned and looked at me for answers, she needed someone to comfort her, to tell her everything was going to be alright, but I just couldn't tell her that. I wasn't sure myself. I had never seen anything like it and I didn't remember reading anything about it in any of the books I saw in the library. So I just lowered my eyes.

"What do you think it is? We have to clean it or something," Gloria said.

"I don't think we can just clean it Gloria, there is something hatching in there. That is probably why he is been acting so weird lately. It has to be," I said.

Gloria faltered when she heard me say that, it was also on her mind, but she was dismissing it. She didn't want to face the fact that Juan could be infected with something we didn't knew about. Something that was affecting him in such a way, transforming him into this other person. Her world just crumbled, she fixated on me as she vanished into desperation. I could feel her frailty and before she fainted I embraced her and she passed out in my arms.

"Gloria! Gloria!" Sarah yelled worried about her.

I slowly brought her down and laid her on the other sofa in the living room. Sarah grabbed a pillow and placed it under her head.

"Is she alright?" she asked.

"She's fine, she just fainted," I replied.

Sarah sat next to her and caressed her head.

"But she's going to be alright, right?" she asked shivering.

"She will be, she just needs to rest."

"How about Juan? Is he going to be alright?" she asked, scared.

I turned and looked at him, laying there on the couch, passed out, his back exposed. The light was still hitting him and the tinny pulps on his back were still reacting to it. So I walked over and turned off the light.

"I don't know," I said.

"Do you think that is contagious. Could we get it too?" Sarah asked concerned.

I thought about it for a moment, I had the same concern she did, but I didn't knew the answer to that question, not with certainty. I finally turned and looked at Sarah.

"I don't know. It could be infectious, but we don't have any symptoms, so it's unlikely," I said, trying to calm her down.

"I haven't seen anything like that on your back, have you seen something on mine?" she asked insisting, while she touched he'd back and tried to look at it, as she lifted up her shirt.

I looked at her back and ran my hand on it from top to bottom.

"No, nothing. You are fine, don't even think that way," I said.

"What are we going to do with Juan, what if he wakes up mad or worst?" she asked.

"I guess we will deal with it when it happens."

"Shouldn't we lock him up or something?" Sarah asked.

I turned to look at her surprised.

"Lock him up? It's Juan," I replied.

"Yes, but he is not the same Juan we know, and what about those things. Aren't you concerned about getting infected?"

She was right, she was being objective and I was being short sided about what could happen with Juan. We had already seen what this thing was doing to him and it was down spiralling fast. We had to protect ourselves from whatever could happen. It was a grim thought, having to protect ourselves from the only people that were our family, the only people we knew.

"You are right, we can't take that chance," I said with a heavy heart.

"Maybe we can put him in the room downstairs and lock the door," Sarah suggested.

"Yeah, but he could get out through one of the windows. It has to be a room he can't get out of easily. What's the point if he can get out, he would just get mad and escape. Who knows what he could do next," I replied.

"What about the bathroom upstairs, the one at the end of the hall?" Sarah proposed.

"It still has a window. He could get out through there," I said.

"How about that little closet in the garage, the one with all the lawn stuff?" Sarah asked.

I thought about it for a moment, there was no other place where he would be isolated.

"We would have to get everything out of there and put in a mattress or something for him to lay on."

"Yes, let's do that," Sarah said while she nodded.

So we did, we cleared out all the stuff from that room and placed it outside the house. Then we brought a mattress from one of the rooms upstairs and placed it on the floor.

As we were doing that, I noticed something on the rooms walls of the little shed. There was writing on them, images carved into the sides of the room. Messages that put together, ricked of desperation. "Auxilio!(Help!), "Porque a mi? (Why me?)", "Ayúdenme!(Help me!)", "Me duele! (I'm in pain.!)", "Me tienen encerrada! (I've been locked up!)", "Que día es hoy? (What day it is?)". They went on and on, all slashed by a thousand random cuts, without sense. Proof that someone had been locked up in here before, proof that, what was happening to Juan, was not an isolated incident.

I also noticed that, the door to that room, had been reinforced. It was not like all the other doors inside the house. This door was a steel door, made to withstand a constant attack. To keep something precious in there safe, or to keep something or someone, from coming out. The door had been kicked and struck constantly from the inside and it was scratched all over and then painted over and over. There were coats and coats of paint, one on top of the other one. This room had been a prison for a while. It had been used for the exact same purpose we were going to use it now.

Sarah was just standing there, looking at me, in silence. She was with me when I was looking at the carvings and then the door, getting to the same conclusion I was. She just looked at me with the same uncertainty I had in my eyes, with all those terrible thoughts going around in our heads.

"Come on, let's just get him in here, before he wakes up!" I said.

Sarah just nodded, agreeing with me.

Carrying Juan to that room, was going to be the difficult part. We would have to cover him with something and we were afraid that he would wake up in the middle of it and react violently to what we were trying to do to him. We had to do it as quickly as possible, before he woke up. It had already been a while since he dozed off, so we were not sure that we could do this.

When we got to the living room, they were both still out.

"I'll grab him by his hands and you grab his feet. I don't think we can carry him, we will have to drag him there," I said.

"He's gonna wake up!" Sarah said shivering.

I just looked at her and shrugged.

As soon as we were about to push him off the couch on to the ground, It came to me.

"Wait!" I asked Sarah.

"What? Let's just do this!" she said.

"Wait!" I insisted.

I walked to the kitchen and grabbed one of those large trash bags and brought it to the living room, I placed it on the floor.

"Let's put him on top, it will be easier to drag him over this," I said.

Sarah nodded and we slowly pushed him from the sofa and on to the plastic bag on the floor. It wasn't pretty, he was very heavy and in an awkward position, so he fell hard, hitting the floor as we did. We were sure he was going to wake up. We waited for a moment, looking at each other, ready to jump at any sudden movement he did.

We just waited in silence, just to make sure he was still out. After a few moments, I looked at Sarah and nodded.

"Ok, I'll grab his feet and you grab his hands. Make sure you wrap them in the plastic bag as you do."

Sarah just nodded at me, she didn't understand what I meant.

I showed her how to do it in my own end with his feet. I grabbed the plastic bag and with it on my hand, grabbed his feet so I would be pulling his body wrapped in the plastic and not just on it.

Sarah grabbed the plastic bag with one hand and then grabbed Juan's hand and did the same with the other one and we began dragging him to the garage.

"Slowly, we don't want to wake him up!" Sarah said as I was beginning to pull him towards me.

It took us a while, but we got him to the small room, placed him inside on the mattress and walked outside. We were standing at the door, looking at him, still doubting this was the right thing to do. We didn't want to do this to Juan, but we knew that it was the safest thing to do.

I finally grabbed the handle and closed the door. I locked it from the outside, made sure it was locked and we both walked into the living room with our tails between our legs.

Sarah went into the kitchen and washed her hands on the sink. I stood there and looked at her rub her hands relentlessly over and over again. She would rinse them and then start all over, poured hand soap and rub them as hard as she could, then rinse and start again. She was not only trying to get rid of whatever was on Juan's back that could have transferred into her hands as we touched him, but also get rid of her guilt for doing what we had done to him.

I stood there for a moment, looking at her freaking out and going on and on until I had to do something. I walked to her, stood right next to her and placed my hands inside the sink. I poured some soap on them and rubbed them against Sarah's.

As soon as she felt my hands between hers, she calmed down. I rubbed her hands with mine and then pulled them under the water flowing down from the faucet, cleaning our hands. Once our hands were clean and the soap had receded, I turned off the water, grabbed a towel and placed it over Sarah's hands, dried them up, dried mine and grabbed her hands.

Sarah looked at me and I knew exactly what she was going through. We shared that same feeling of blame even thought, we knew it was the only thing that was logical. We still felt like shit.

I just grinned, trying to make her feel better. She smiled back.

Sarah went to check on Gloria who was still out, sat down and placed Gloria's head on her lap.

I sat down and closed my eyes for a second. I was tired, exhausted physically and emotionally, my body needed to rest.

Sarah was going through the same and so we both dozed off.

A faint, distant constant sobbing woke me up. It was getting dark outside, I must have been asleep for a few hours and this sobbing wouldn't stop. Sarah and Gloria were still asleep in front of me on the couch, so I tried to figure where the sobbing came from and suddenly it came to me.

"Charlie? Where are you, boy?" I whispered.

I knew it was him, he had been absent through the whole ordeal with Juan. So I stood up and followed the sobbing. He was hiding under a big bookcase on the side of the living room, crawled into a ball, still shivering, scared.

I kneeled down on the floor and lowered my head to look at him.

"Come here Charlie, it's ok, you can come out."

He looked at me, doubting, still scared, so I insisted.

"Come her Charlie, everything is fine."

He raised his ears and began to stretch himself until he came out from under the bookcase and slowly got close. I picked him up, he was still shivering.

"It's ok Charlie, your safe," I said.

I sat on the couch with Charlie and he just laid there with me. We waited a while until Sarah woke up and saw us sitting there.

"Is everything ok?" she asked.

"Yes, Charlie was scared," I answered.

Right then Gloria woke up, you could tell she was confused. She looked at Sarah and then turned and looked at me and Charlie, then looked around the living room.

"Where is Juan?" she asked.

Sarah and I just looked at each other in silence. We didn't know what, or how to say it.

"Where is he" she asked insisting, as she sat up on the couch.

She was still dizzy, she grabbed her head with both her hands.

"My head is killing me. What happened?" she asked.

"You don't remember?" I asked her back.

She thought about it for a second, as she closed her eyes, but her head was pounding.

"I…I don't know," she said as she tried to remember.

Slowly it came to her, her breathing became erratic, her heartbeat rose. We could tell she was in distress.

Sarah got close to her and embraced her.

"Clam down! It's ok."

Gloria calmed down, she had remembered everything that happened a few hours before.

"Oh, my god!" she said.

After a few moments she looked up at me and asked.

"Where is he?"

"He's ok, we put him in a room by himself," I answered.

"You carried him upstairs?" she asked amazed.

"No, he is inside that small room in the garage."

"Small room? You mean the tool closet?" Gloria was visibly upset.

She got up right away and began walking towards the garage. We both stood up and followed her there. We all went into the garage, Gloria was headed directly to the tool closet with the intention of opening up the door so I jumped in between and stopped her.

"What are you doing? He's not staying there, are you crazy?" she said.

I grabbed her shoulders and looked straight into her eyes.

"Gloria, we need to isolate him, you know it's the right thing to do. We don't know what's going on with him. He could infect us or go crazy and hurt us. He almost hurt you, don't you remember?"

Gloria looked at me as if I was the crazy one. She kept pushing forward, towards the door.

"He struck you, remember? He is not well!" I said.

Gloria stayed silent for a moment, going back to what had happened in that living room, thinking about everything that we had gone through in the last few weeks.

"This is Juan we are talking about!" she said as she tried to get to the door.

I just embraced her so she wouldn't be able to reach it; she broke down crying. She knew that it was the right thing to do, but that didn't meant it wasn't destroying her inside. She fell down on her knees weeping. She couldn't take so much pain. Sarah and I embraced her, tried to comfort her, but I think there are times that not even all the love in the world can ease your pain.

We stood there for a while, we wanted to be there for her until that pain subsided. During all that time my mind was running around trying to figure out what to do. Trying to find a solution to this problem, as if there was a formula that could be applied, as if there was a guideline of what to do, but there wasn't.

We sat Gloria down in the living room and Sarah staid with her. I headed to the door.

"Where are you going?" Sarah asked.

"I'm going to the vehicle, I need to find out more about this. Maybe there is something we can do."

"Don't leave me alone!" Sarah said as she signalled with her eyes at Gloria.

"I'll be right outside. I won't be there long," I said trying to comfort her.

Sarah sighted and nodded.

So, I headed outside. It was almost dark. I walked to the vehicle and sat inside.

I had to access the archives, try to find some information about this affliction that was consuming Juan. There had to be something about it, so I went to the vehicle and searched on the computer.

"Ada, find information about contagion."

"I need more information, what type of contagion are you looking for?" she replied.

"Infectious hosts"

"I need more information, is it viral or bacterial?" she asked.

"I don't know, find anything you can about mind control or behavioural manipulation."

"These are some of the known afflictions…"

There were over a hundred different entries on the archives related to that topic, but none of them seem to explain, in detail, what Juan was going through.

None of them dealt with parasites that took over and controlled a host like this ones apparently did, but then I began reading about something that seemed to have some similarities. It was a bio weapon developed during "The Great War". It was a larvae that would latch to the brain stem and ate part of it, making the subject prone to command, eliminated pain and rational behaviour; exactly what you would look for in a perfect soldier, but the larvae eventually died after doing its deed and the subjects would go mad, lose any grip with reality and ended up killing themselves after a while; that is the ones that had survived the War. The project was called "Ares" referring to Ares the Greek God of War. According to the files, the larvae was spawned in laboratories specifically for that purpose and was not known to reproduce or generate. So, it wouldn't follow what I just saw happening on Juan's back, but the file was limited to a few years after the war as the scientists who created it saw the few subjects left commit suicide, the project was cancelled and the remaining materials were burnt and discarded.

Or were they? What if some of the larvae survived and found a way to reproduce. That would explain the pulps on Juan's back and their eating habits, the change in Juan's behaviour. That would also explain what happened here, the absence of markers that would suggest that the war got to this place. That there had been a fight or looting, violence of any kind. The fact that we hadn't seen anyone around, the fact that the cemetery was filled up with graves.

There was no information that would explain what was happening right in front of our eyes, there was no answers as to what we could do about it, no hope that we could cure and save Juan. I'm sure that people in this town had searched for a way to cure this disease, a way to stop this attack on their loved ones. I would only assume that eventually the ones that were left at the end fled this place, hoping to get away from this curse.

There was no cure or treatment stated in the report. The project was just terminated and the subjects burnt together with all the larvae and the files. This was the only information in the data banks. So, we had no way of bringing Juan back, of curing him of this infection. The only outcome specified was death.

Then, as I realised what must had happened here, in this small town in Mexico, a chill ran down my spine. We were in danger, we would have to leave this place if we wanted to survive. We weren't showing any signs of infection, but it was just a matter of time. We would all have to leave. All of us, except Juan.

How was I going to tell Gloria? I thought about it for a long time, while searching every single data base I could find. Even though I knew there would be no answer to any of this.

What if someone would ask me to leave Sarah behind, to give up on the one I loved. There was no way I would do that. My heart was pledged to her as well as my life and I would gladly give it up for her. I was sure that Gloria felt the same way I did, I was just hoping that reason would prevail and she would see things objectively.

So, after a while of searching in the vehicles computer, I went back inside. Gloria and Sarah were in the living room, Gloria had crawled into a ball at the edge of the couch and was rocking back and forth, her eyes were swollen from so much crying, her hair was a mess and it covered most of her face. Sarah was just sitting on the other end of the couch lost in her thoughts, but I could tell that she was scared.

I walked up and sat next to her, lifted her face up so she would see me and smiled at her. She saw my eyes and smiled back. We embraced for a while, we both needed to feel that energy that flows from one body to another, giving you a feeling of well-being. We were still embracing when I got close to her ear.

"We need to talk!" I whispered.

She pulled away and looked into my eyes. She then turned and looked at Gloria.

"I don't want to leave her," she answered.

"It will just be a moment! She will be fine. Come with me outside," I said while I got up and grabbed her hand.

She pulled me back and gave me this look. She was worried about Gloria, I was too, but we needed to make a decision. There was no time to waist.

I nodded and smiled.

"Come on! It's important," I said with a calm voice.

She got up from the couch and followed me outside.

It was getting darker and the sun was set on the horizon, filling the sky with beautiful tones of red and blue, magenta and purple. For a moment we were sucked out of all that was happening around us, all that was going on in the world. It was a beautiful sight in the middle of so much chaos. We both sighted while we looked at it. Sarah grabbed my hand while we did and I put my arm around her. We needed to share this moment, this majestic gesture of peace.

"I think I'm ready now," she said while she turned around to see me.

"I couldn't find anything specific, anything that could actually help Juan. I found some disturbing things about bio weapons that could explain what is happening to him though and what happened to this whole town."

"So, what does that mean? We can't help Juan?" she asked confused.

"No, there is nothing that suggest we can. There is no place that we could take him or magical solution to it. I think that this is what happened to the people here, they got this disease, this parasite, went crazy and died from it. I think that the marks on that room, where Juan is right now, prove that there had been other people locked in there with the same affliction. I think that this whole town was doomed way before we got here and I think that the ones that were not infected, left," I said.

Sarah looked at me, trying to make sense of what I was saying.

"So, you think we should leave too?"

"Definitely, I think we are in danger if we stay here."

"But, what about Juan? Gloria is not going to want to just leave him and go," she said, while she began to wonder in her head what would happen next.

I grabbed her shoulders and looked into her eyes.

"Hey, don't go there, we have to do this step by step. You have to help me to convince her that this is the only thing we can do. There is no going back, we can't fix Juan if we don't know how and we will die the same way, if we stay here. We have to leave!"

Sarah's eyes filled with tears as she thought about it. She knew it would be an impossible task.

"I can't! How can I ask her that? Would you leave me if they asked you to?" she said trembling.

I embraced her and kissed her forehead while she plunged into my body. She clinched on to me so tight that I could feel her hands touching my heart.

"I don't want this to happen to Gloria, or you. I wouldn't be able to take it. I don't want that to happen. We can't stay here another minute!"

Sarah loosened her grip as she looked at me.

"You are right! We can't stay here."

"I'm hoping that we can make her realise it's for the best," I said doubting myself.

Sarah nodded and we both walked back into the house. Gloria was in the same foetal position, sitting at the edge of the sofa, rocking back and forth.

Sarah stopped at the door looking at Gloria, I walked in pass her and stood in front of her. Sarah was frozen, looking at Gloria, powerless. It was as if she had lost her courage as soon as she saw her there, at the edge of the couch. I walked back to where she was standing and grabbed her hand, pulled her with me, as soon as I did she turned to look at me with tears in her eyes and nodded.

"It will be ok!" I said, trying to reassure her.

She unwillingly walked with me until we were right in front of her. I placed my hand on Gloria's shoulder and she stopped rocking the moment she felt my touch. Sarah was standing right behind me, like sheltering herself between me and Gloria.

"Gloria! We have to talk, are you up for it?" I asked.

Gloria lifted her head up and looked at us, standing there, right in front of her. She smiled and offered her hands to us. Sarah approached and grabbed her hand as I did too.

"I'm so grateful that you are here with me," she said, as she smiled and looked at us.

It was one of those smiles that pretend to hide all the pain we knew she had inside. So, we sat with her and cried, hoping that the pain would ease.

We sat there for a while, together, until our biggest fear became true. Until we began to hear the pounding on the door and the voice of Juan in the distance.

"Gloria, get me out of here! Open the door! Gloria!"

The pounding resonated all over the house, it vibrated in the walls, in the furniture, on the floor. It was constant and deafening. Gloria tighten her grip every time, as if he was pounding on her. His screams became louder in our heads, shaming us for keeping him there.

After just a few minutes, Gloria jumped out of the couch and headed for the garage. We stood up and followed her. She was headed directly for the door, but I couldn't allow her to set him free so I jumped in between and stopped her from opening that door.

"No Gloria, we can't let him out!"

Gloria looked at me, as she had never looked at me before, I could see hatred in her eyes. She was determined to open that door. I understood what she was going through, It was Juan in there, begging her to set him free.

"Get out of my way Patrick!"

"You can't open up that door Gloria, you know I'm right."

"It's Juan in there, it's Juan!"

My eyes dropped to the ground, I knew that it was the best thing for all of us, to keep him in there, but I could also relate to what Gloria was feeling, with what she wanted to do.

"You open up that door and you've doomed us all, is that what you want? I care for Juan too, but he is not going to get better and I don't want the same thing to happen to you, or Sarah. Do you?"

Gloria looked into my eyes, she knew I was right. As she was thinking of all the possibilities, of what I just said. The pounding stopped and a soft voice was heard through the metal door that separated us from Juan, that kept the threat contained, that limited the sanity we had left.

"He's right Gloria! I'm sorry! This is the way it has to be," Juan said from the inside of the room.

Gloria heard that as her eyes closed and her head dropped. She slowly crawled to the door and sat next to it.

"Aqui estoy! (I'm here)" she said as she placed her hand on the door.

Sarah was sitting at the other side of the garage looking at everything that was happening, powerless to do anything but stare. She had her hands on her head and her sight was lost somewhere far from here.

I got close and offered her my hand, she took it and I helped her up. Placed my arm around her and we both walked out of the garage. We were both silent, there was a lot that we needed to talk about, but at that precise time, silence was the only thing said.

We went inside the house, Sarah sat on the couch and I went into the kitchen to get us a couple of glasses of water. I did and sat next to her on the couch. Gave her the water, she drank a little bit as we both thought about everything that had happened and everything that could, from now on. It was a lot to process. We knew what we needed to do, in order to survive. We obviously didn't wanted to end up like Juan, infected by some parasite that would drive us crazy, but we were also aware that a lot of people got infected in this town and we had been here for a while.

"Can you please check my back?" Sarah asked me out of the blue.

I looked at her concerned.

"You are not infected!"

"Just, please! I feel my skin crawl and I don't want it to be..." She said while I interrupted.

"Stop it! It's your imagination playing tricks on you," I said.

She began to pull her blouse up to uncover her back.

"Please, just take a look!"

So I did, I placed my hands on her back and looked closely to all of it. I caressed her as gently as I could. There was nothing there but her soft skin and her beautiful back. I could feel her bones sticking out of it, like mountains delimiting a valley. Her skin was so soft and inviting that I had almost dismissed everything that was happening and all I could think of, was her.

I guess I was lost in it for a while, because she suddenly jumped, trying to wake me up.

"So, is there something weird in my back?"

"Sorry, no, nothing weird at all. Everything is fine, you can relax now," I said trying to comfort her.

She stood up and pulled her blouse down, looked at me and threw her arms around my neck and nestled in mine, that embraced her. I could feel her trembling, her whole body vibrating softly, her soul looking for some peace in mine.

I love her so much; everything could be wrong, we were at the end of the world and she was the one thing that I wanted to hold on to, as everything went dark. I knew she felt the same way about me, I gave her the strength she couldn't find in herself, the strength we both needed to go on.

Sometimes I wondered why we did…go on, why were we so kin on surviving, on living. We were at the edge of the abyss and we were still kicking and screaming. Trying to figure out the obstacles in our path, so we could get somewhere, when we didn't even knew where that was or why we needed to get there.

I knew I wanted to be with Sarah, love her, protect her, make her happy. I knew that much. I was sure that my happiness laid with her, so I wanted to do everything I could to keep her safe, to stay by her side.

Gloria was the only Mother I ever knew, she had taken care of me since I was a baby and she was the one that freed us from the destiny we had set, as common lab rats and gave us a reason to live, she showed me happiness in Sarah's arms, she introduced us and gave us to each other. So, I also wanted her to survive, to make it.

I didn't even knew how long we were there, sitting on the couch, cuddling each other. We needed that, we needed to feel loved, feel safe, we needed to get our bearings. Sometimes the best thing you can do, is nothing. Just let your heart settle and your mind slow down, so you can get perspective on what is really important in life.

I was certain of what it was, of what we needed to do and Sarah was too. We just needed to figure out how to do it.

"So, what are we going to do?" Sarah asked.

She was thinking the exact thing that was on my mind. I sighted and kept on caressing her head.

"We need to get away from here, that is for sure. It's not safe."

"I know, but what about Gloria and Juan?" she asked.

"We can't take Juan with us, we have no idea how to cure him, or if there is a cure. We can't risk getting infected or spreading the disease somewhere else."

"But, what if we already have it!" she asked.

"No, I don't think so, we would have already had signs of it. Have I been acting crazy lately?" I asked.

"You mean, more than usual?" she asked back while she cracked up a laugh.

I knew what she was trying to do, break the tension by making a joke…she was adorable!

I laughed to, it was the only thing sane to do.

"Whatever it is that we do, it has to be fast," I said.

Sarah lifted up her head and began to look around for something.

"Hey, where's Charlie?" she asked, concerned.

"I don't know, I haven't seen him for a while."

Sarah got up from the couch and began to look for Charlie, calling his name and looking under every piece of furniture in the house.

"Charlie, Charlie! Where are you boy?"

I got up to help her find him.

"Charlie! Charlie!"

We both looked around the house, we went upstairs and searched every room, but there was no answer. Charlie was nowhere to be found!

"That is so strange, where can he be?" Sarah asked.

"Maybe he ran away to Susana's grave, he use to like it over there."

"He hasn't been there in months. I don't think he would do that," she said.

"Wait! What's that?" I said, when I heard a faint noise coming from Susana's old room.

"What's what?" she asked.

"That noise, you don't hear it?"

Sarah stood there silent for a moment trying to hear the same thing I was supposedly hearing. She stood there making faces.

"What noise? I can't hear anything!" she said a little bit upset.

I asked her to be silent for a moment while we tried to hear the sound.

"There it is! You can't hear that?" I asked.

"You mean that kind of screeching sound? That could be anything. It's very faint."

"But It could be Charlie!" I said excited.

Sarah just rolled her eyes at me. I followed the sound to one of the corners. There was a pile of plush toys, teddy bears and different animals, right on the corner.

"It seemed that the sound is coming from in here," I said, while Sarah looked at me like I was crazy.

I looked at her and pulled her hand so she would get closer. She placed her ear close to the pile and her eyes opened wide.

"I can hear it, it is coming from here," she said as she began to pull, one by one, the plush toys off the way, until there was just a few left. As she pulled one of the last ones away, she could see a familiar ball of hair in between. Sarah figured out where the head would be on that particular hairy beast and pulled out a plush toy revelling what was under it.

"Charlie! There you are," she said as Charlie looked up at her.

He looked scared, we had just discovered his hiding place, where he felt safe from what he was scared of. As soon as he raised his head, his whole body began trembling. Sarah grabbed him and picked him up, embraced him and kissed him in the head.

"It's ok Charlie, everything is going to be ok!" she said as she pet him on the head, trying to calm him down.

Charlie looked up at me, still shivering, so I try to comfort him too.

"I think that he has seen this before. He is afraid that someone else close to him might die," I said.+

"Poor thing, I can't imagine the things he has been through," Sarah said while she pet him.

She picked him up and we all went downstairs to the living room, Sarah sat on the couch with Charlie snuggled at her legs, he needed to feel safe.

"I'm going to check on Gloria, I'll be right back," I said to Sarah, she just smiled and nodded.

I went into the garage and saw Gloria sitting right next to the door, talking with Juan who was sitting on the other side. They seem happy, they were even laughing, telling stories to each other in Spanish. I couldn't understand what they were saying, just a few words here and there, but they were remembering better times, I knew that much.

I got close and Gloria offered me her hand, she pulled me close.

"We were just reminiscing, talking about our lives, when we first met and the journey that brought us here," she said.

I just smiled, I could see serenity in her eyes, a calm that wrestled with all the sorrow and pain she was feeling. A calm that came from accepting the faith that had fell upon her. She knew in her head that Juan was doomed, but she still had him, right there with here, before the end. She could still enjoy the few moments she had beside the love of her life.

I had learned from them about love, about that uncontainable feeling I had for Sarah, but there was so much to learn still. This unwavering faith Gloria felt for him, this unconditional support that she had, even though she knew she could get infected and suffer the same faith as Juan. She was there, by his side, no matter what. That is also love, never turning your back on the people you care for.

"I can see that," I said.

Gloria looked around and asked.

"Where's Sarah?"

She is inside, in the living room, we were looking for Charlie," I answered.

"Did you find him, is he ok?"

"Yes, he is fine, he was hiding in Susana's old room, under a pile of plush toys. I think that he has lived through this before. He's seen the same thing happen many times," I said, while I looked into Gloria's eyes.

She looked back at mine and thought about it for a bit. She sighted, held my hand and padded it softly.

"Well, I guess you are right."

"We have to figure out what we are going to do next Gloria."

She turned to look at the door in front of her. The one that divided the space between her and Juan. The one that kept her from the love of her life.

"I know what I'm going to do next, but you guys should leave. It's not safe for you here," she said.

I was just shocked at what she just said.

"No Gloria, we all need to leave. You are coming with us. We can't stay here."

Gloria looked at me, she grabbed my face with both her hands and smiled.

"You guys are young, strong. You deserve to have a life, but me, I made my choice a long time ago. My life is here, with Juan, no matter what happens. Maybe I will be granted a miracle, or maybe I'll just see the end, but whatever it is, it will be next to him."

She never stopped smiling at me, but I was still in denial.

"You are not serious, we need you too. You can still have a wonderful life with us, the three of us, out there. You don't have to stay here, there is nothing you can do to save him."

I was desperate, thinking that my job was to make her understand and follow my lead.

Gloria tilted her head as she placed her hand on my shoulder.

"I don't have to stay, I want to. This is where I belong, I did what I had to, get you out of that lab and give you a chance at life. I'm so glad that it worked out so well, that you and Sarah love each other. I couldn't have asked for anything better than that. You have each other, you don't need me anymore. This is where I want to be. Wouldn't you do that for Sarah?"

I thought about it, if I was in the same situation she is in, what would I do? Love is selfless, you only care about the needs of your partner, you stop caring about your own because she is looking out for yours. It's a two way street. I couldn't be selfish with Gloria, they meant more to each other than I would ever understand. In my eyes she was committing suicide, staying here, it was stupid and irresponsible and I wasn't about to let it stand. She needed to come with us, but then it hit me. "What is survival without love?"

I've seen the emptiness inside those shells that roamed the world without purpose, just functioning without sense of being, without warmth in their hearts. They were just things without identity, without meaning, without anything to motive them to be better, to enjoy life, to care for someone else, to find happiness and the small instances that make life grand.

I didn't wanted that for Gloria, I couldn't take her away from the one that made her whole, that gave her life purpose and sense. I could snatch her away and save her life but I wouldn't be actually saving her. You can save someone only if they want to be saved.

I looked into her eyes and a rush of emotions hit me.

"I just don't understand. Staying here means you'll die, you know that right? If you come with us you can go on, you can live. There is nothing you can do for Juan, he will get worse and you will be witness to that and there will be nothing you can do about it. When he is gone and you begin to fall on that same road, there will be no one to take care of you. No one to help you along, you will be by yourself…"

Sarah came into the garage and stopped me. She grabbed my shoulders and turned me around. Looked into my eyes, disapproving of what I was doing.

I bowed my head in shame, she was right. Gloria knew all that, she was aware of what would happen, but she had chosen love. It was an easy decision for her and nothing I said would made her change her mind.

To her, this was not even a choice she had to dwell on.

I realised then, that it was me who couldn't let go. I was thinking about me and what I felt for Gloria, what I thought was the best course of action, what would be the best for me, but it wasn't my decision to make. It wasn't about me at all.

All this time Juan had stayed silent, he was sitting inside this tiny room, this solace that had become his cell, listening to everything. I knew that he wanted the best for Gloria, I knew that he would agree with me. He would want to save her, give her the chance that was taken away from him. He wouldn't want Gloria to suffer the same faith he was. Because he loved her and that is what you want for the people you love. So, I was surprised at his silence.

I got close to the door that separated us and placed my ear against it, I thought maybe he was out again but as soon as I placed my ear on the door I could hear him inside, weeping. It was shallow, but constant maudlin that came from impotence.

"Juan?" I asked.

"It's my fault, It's all my fault," he answered between sobs.

"You didn't choose to get infected, it just happened. There was no way for you, or any of us, to know," I replied.

"I should have seen it. I should have known that something bad was lurking, that something killed everyone in this town. That it was a dangerous place to be in. I should have seen it! I should have known!"

I placed my hand on the door and pushed myself back. There was nothing else I could do or say that would change what was going to happen next. All I could do was to look forward and make the best of it for Sarah and me, for us.

"We should go!" I said as I turned and looked at Sarah.

She just nodded and bowed her head.

"You should take the vehicle and all the provisions you can carry," Gloria said.

The three of us walked back into the house and began to grab things we might need. Sarah went upstairs to get our stuff together and me and Gloria went into the pantry to look at the boxes of food we had left.

"Take everything!" Gloria said.

"No, what about you and Juan? You don't know how long this will take. You still need to eat."

"I rather you take it, you will need it more than we will. I have plenty of food prepared already that will last us a long time," she said while she nodded.

I smiled and began to carry the boxes outside and placed them inside the vehicle. Sarah was bringing our stuff from upstairs and she would organise it inside so that everything would fit. It felt as if we were going out on a trip, but we had no destination and it wasn't a happy farewell.

I didn't feel the excitement you crave when you are setting off on a new adventure, that sense of discovery you have when you set your sights on something unknown. This was the opposite, it just felt wrong.

When I was loading the last box inside the vehicle, my hands were shaking and my legs would hardly stand still. I placed the box inside, dropped it actually, because it got consistently heavier as I got closer and closer to the vehicle. My hands were losing their grip and my whole body was absent of strength, of the will to do this. As I pulled up, from dropping the box, I just lost it. The whole thing invaded me and I broke down. I couldn't contain the rush of emotions that poured out like wildfire. I had never experienced something like this; I was completely overtaken by grief, by a terrible sadness that pressured my heart so strongly that It brought me down on my knees. I just couldn't stop crying and sobbing and everything got fuelled by what my head was going through, a slideshow of images of Gloria throughout my life, her smiles, her hugs, her kisses; our liberation from that lab, our journey here and the pain I saw in her when we got to this place and her family was gone. Everything kept repeating in my mind and the sadness wouldn't yield, it just got worst as it flooded uncontained with every feeling in my heart.

After a while the breathing softened and my mind was liberated, while I was still on my knees and my hands were bolting down on the ground, sustaining the weight of my guilt that kept pulling me down. I kept struggling with the act of leaving Gloria here, by herself, abandoning her to a certain faith, but It was not debatable. I knew we had to leave and I couldn't force her to leave with us, but, even though it was not my decision, I still felt guilty for what I was going to do.

I began to breath long breaths, trying to regain my composure. I was thankful that no one had witnessed this moment of weakness from me. I needed to be strong for Sarah and for Gloria too. I couldn't be the one to break down and screw up everything. It was my job to be the pillar, or at least that was the way I wanted them to see me.

"Breath! Long breaths!" I thought to myself.

And I repeated that over and over again, doing what I thought would help me out of this abyss I had fallen into. I was down on my knees, right next to the vehicle. The wind was blowing lightly and the world seemed to be in pause as if taunting me to ease my grief. To soften my sorrow and let calm overtake my affliction.

I finally felt I was ready to go back inside and face Gloria and Sarah. So I did, went inside and found Sarah embracing Gloria next to the kitchen. They were both crying, trying to console each other. Gloria was hoping to make the moment less awkward by being strong and not breaking up in front of us.

I stood there watching them for a moment. Gloria turned to see me standing there and opened up her arm inviting me in. I embraced them and the three of us enjoyed our last hug together. I remember taking a deep breath and drenching myself in her scent, that always reminded me of home, that is what she meant to me, a safe place where I felt secure and cared for.

After a few moments Gloria pulled away and said.

"Ok! Ok! It's time for you to go."

She looked at both of us, she lifted up her hand and wiped away the tears from Sarah's face and smiled at both of us.

"You need to get as far away from here as you can. You need to go south, as far south as you can," she said while she looked at us, as if she was recording everything about us in her mind.

"I love you and I'll always will. You are my children. I want you to live, I want you to love each other and be happy together until the end."

"I love you Gloria. I'll always be thankful for everything," Sarah said.

Gloria smiled and kissed her tightly. Then she turned and looked at me.

"Patrick, I don't want you to feel guilty, I don't want you to carry that burden. It needs to be this way, it's my decision and my decision alone. I would have loved to be with you guys, but you have each other and Juan only has me. I could never leave him," she said.

I just nodded, there was not much I could say. It was decided, it was done. I just kissed her for the last time. I grabbed Sarah's hand and we both began walking towards the vehicle. Sarah turned and looked at Gloria, who was standing at the doorway.

Gloria smiled and raised her hand saying goodbye, Sarah responded the same way. I stood there looking at her as she saw me, the way she always did, with her motherly glance, with her heart on her sleeve. She smiled and nodded. All I could do, was smile back.

"Hey! What about Charlie? Why don't you take Charlie with you?" Gloria yelled from the door.

Sarah and I looked at each other wondering what to do about Charlie. We didn't even had to say anything, we both knew that it would be better for Charlie to stay with Gloria and Juan. That way, at least, she would have somebody to keep her company, no matter what. Charlie had been there for everyone that had gone through this before and he would be for Gloria too.

"He should stay with you! Keep you company. You need that way more than we do," I said.

At that precise moment Charlie came out of the house running towards us. Sarah and I got down on to greet him. We both pet him and Sarah embraced Charlie. He kept licking us, waving his tail as vigorously as ever. He was happiness in a small packet.

After a while Charlie turned to look at Gloria and barked. Gloria smiled as he did. Charlie looked at us and then ran back to where Gloria was. She received him gladly, pet him and Charlie sat next to her. It was as if he knew exactly what was going on.

Sarah and I looked at each other and smiled, we turned to look at them and said our goodbyes.

Sarah got into the vehicle and I caught the last glance of my Mom and Charlie standing in the doorway.

I would keep and cherish that postcard in my head for as long as I lived.

Chapter 8
The Trip Ahead

I got inside the vehicle and it slowly pulled out of the driveway. We began moving away from the house. Sarah was looking back at Gloria, who was standing at the edge of the street, just outside the house, waving goodbye. She was smiling, pretending that all the pain that embodied her was not there. She knew what she was doing, she knew what she traded and that had broken her heart, but she also knew it was the right thing to do. She needed to be with Juan and keep us safe. Her trade had given us a chance at life.

Tears were running down Sarah's face while she looked at Gloria turn smaller and smaller as the vehicle kept its march. I was sitting at the controls, looking at the backward monitor, looking at the same thing Sarah was but trying my best to hold my tears. You see? Goodbyes are usually filled with hope, hope that you will see them again, so it's sad, but hope gives you a sense of calm. This was not that, this felt different, we knew that we wouldn't see her again. We knew this was our last goodbye and it left a hole in my heart that would never be filled with anything else.

We kept going until we lost sight of Gloria and then the house, and the town. Sarah cried for a while and I held her tight because we shared the same feeling. I tried my best to be strong and allowed her to carry our sorrow, but what I was feeling inside was overwhelming. I had lost a Mother, the only person that had loved me since the beginning and would love me in the end. The only thing that comforted me was the love of Sarah, it would do for the rest of my life.

We were moving south along the coast in the Gulf of Mexico, but it became impossible to follow the road after a while. Vegetation had taken over the road and everything around it close to the sea. It was a beautiful sight to see. There were thousands of plants, growing every which way you looked, flowers of a hundred different colours were decorating the scenery and we could spot, from time to time, animals roaming the top of the trees. We were in the middle of a jungle, foliage was just too dense for the vehicle to keep moving forward, so we had to turn back for a few miles and take another road that lead west, away from the sea.

We didn't have a destination in mind, we were just trying to get away from the threat, from our guilt for leaving Gloria to her faith. We didn't knew how far the infection had spread, how safe we would be as we got farther and farther from that place. The computer didn't have information about it, the data banks were incomplete. It had been a while since the computer had connected to the web and downloaded any updates or anything at all, so we were on our own. With only the information we had and it didn't sense the threat back there and it wouldn't sense it going forward, we knew that much, so we were just hoping that we would be safe somewhere far away; that the spread of, whatever it was that overtook Juan, had not reach everywhere.

The fact that we didn't see any signs of humans at all for a few days, wasn't a good sign of that. It meant one of two things, either they were all consumed by the disease, or they had all left looking for a safer place down south. We knew that, as time went by, the population would decrease more each day. This was the last generation on earth, time was running out on humanity, the end was closer than we could even muster. Without new blood, without new births, humanity was doomed.

It felt like standing at the edge of an abyss, without end, only darkness. I had flashes that came back constantly from that nightmare I had, from that horrible dream that had repeated itself so many times, the dream where I watched over humanity, giving themselves up to desolation. Where people were just walking into their deaths, closing in on their demise, moving like zombies into the threshold of the firewall so that their bodies would incinerate, with the hope that their souls would go to a better place, wishing that, wherever they would go next, would be a better place, would give them peace. Tired of hoping, of waiting for the end, worn down by misery and pain. Every sense of self had gone out the window, had vanished and all they could hope for, was to rest. To finally reach the end, as if that was the only option, the only thing in their minds. I could see it in their faces, their expression that reflected all the suffering they had to endure for so long, all the loss they had to bear.

Their dead expression kept popping in my head, invading my dreams, the look of emptiness on their faces was chilling. It was as though they were looking straight through me, as if I didn't existed. Every memory had been wiped out of their heads, every image of joy and happiness, every trace of the love they once had was gone, they were just blank sheets of paper headed for the shredder. That was the way it seemed.

I've never thought of death like that, as a mare transaction. Death always seem to be a catastrophe, a sudden end to a beautiful thing. A blackout that abruptly disrupts everything drenched in light and only leads to darkness, but watching them march into the firewall with purpose made, the deadliest weapon known to man, seem like something good, like a portal. A gateway to another place, better than this one. They were abandoning ship while it went down. Saving themselves from something worse than death.

I use to think that I would lose myself too, like them, if I were to lose her. I would join them in that last stride towards redemption, straight to the end. I empathised with them, I understood their pain, it was so close to my heart that I could even share it and as time went by, the dreams became less frightening, it even became somewhat familiar.

The fact that we all shared the same destiny, made the image somehow bearable, even acceptable. For so long we had stride to be better, to reach a pinnacle, to uncover the secrets of the Universe, to control everything around us. We had succeeded in a lot of it, we were the masters of our own little worlds until, like Icarus, we flew to close to the sun, burnt and fell to our demise. This was it for them, for those lost souls just standing by in life, the only thing pushing them forward was the comfort of the end.

That image kept bouncing in my head though and surfaced every time I felt threatened by the fear, by the uncontrollable terror that awaited us, by the thought of being alone in this world. When I felt weak, when that dread invaded me, her presence was the only thing that calmed me down. She was the reason why I was still here, the only thing that grounded me and kept me going. I couldn't see myself waking up every day without seeing her face, feeling her warmth next to me. I was committed to her, to seeing her safe and happy until the end. Committed to surviving alongside Sarah until life decided it was time.

We drove for a few days, stopping along the way, we were not in a hurry to get anywhere, so we stopped every time we had to go to the bathroom or anytime we saw something beautiful worth exploring. There were a lot of those. Nature was booming around us. We passed several towns that were overtaken by her, shacks and even big buildings that were claimed by a constant growing and unstoppable force that seemed to want to erase every trace of human existence out of this planet. It wasn't personal, it was just the way it was. Our time had come and gone and now, it was time for something else.

What we still didn't see, throughout our journey, were humans. Not a single one, not in the towns we passed along the way, not beside the road we travelled on. For the first time in my life I felt that we were completely alone, it was just Sarah and I in all this vastness.

At night we parked on the side of the road and laid down on an inflatable bed in the middle of the cabin, we would watch the stars through the glass ceiling of the vehicle and marvel at the sight. We would make love under them every night and fall asleep in each other's arms. I wanted to stay like this forever, it was so perfect. There was nothing else I wanted from life, this was the only thing I needed, to be with Sarah, to embrace her, to make love to her, to feel her heart beating with mine, to share my thoughts, my dreams with her.

It had been almost a week since we left Gloria, we were driving down a narrow road, moving slowly through the wilderness that had grown on the side of the highway and almost claimed back the space the it took.

We could tell that no vehicle had been through this place in a long time. Nature had found a way to break, even the asphalt, that formed the road and plants were growing in between the cracks made by tree roots growing un contained.

It became increasingly difficult to navigate through all this, we were reaching the end of the road we could actually drive on, so we pulled to the side where I could see a clearing and a part of the road that remained free. We drove for a few feet as the road narrowed, overtaken by nature that was claiming all that had been taken away from her, until there was no way of getting through. We had reached the end of the road.

The vehicle stopped in front of a wall of brush that had grown between two cliffs that delimited the passing. There was nowhere to go, so we stepped out of the vehicle and looked around us, when we spotted a waterfall in the distance. A majestic drop of water that fell from tens of feet up, from a cliff down to a lake, just a few hundred feet from the road. We could hear the roar of the water falling and hitting the rocks in the bottom, just before melting with the lake, we could even feel the breeze that saturated the air around it and moisten it with life.

You could sense the moisture in the air drenching everything in its path, your nose, your lungs. I opened up my mouth and I could almost swallow the water brought by the breeze. We haven't had a proper shower in a while, so we both looked at each other and knew exactly what we wanted to do.

I took Sarah's hand and we both headed towards the waterfall instinctively, we were automatically drawn to it. We tore our clothes off, as we were walking towards it. Sarah stopped at the border with the intention of dipping her foot first and sense if the temperature of the water was good. I just let go of her hand and jumped into the lake, submerged myself in its crystalline blue waters. Water was cold, but my body needed to be immersed in them. It needed this breakthrough, it needed to wake up to the tingling that the cold water incited in me. It needed to feel alive!

Sarah watched as I jumped in, as my whole body submerged and then came back out.

"It's delicious, jump in!" I said as soon as I came back up.

She saw me and smiled, I smiled back while I was struck by her beauty. She was standing there bare naked at the edge of the lake, with nature as a backdrop and I've never seen anything more beautiful. I was lost in her, possessed by her pulchritude, wondered at how beautiful she was. Humbled to know that she loved me, that every inch of that majesty longed for me.

Sarah felt my weakness and tilted her head.

"What?" she asked.

"You are the most beautiful thing I've ever seen!" I replied.

She just took a step back and jumped into the lake to meet me. Her whole body dipped into the water and her head rose up just next to mine, her wet hair pulled back behind her face that sparkled with a million reflections as the water dripped down her eyelashes, into her eyes that looked straight at mine, and down her nose and her cheeks, into her mouth as she kissed me. It felt as if her candour had melted in her mouth and rushed at once into mine, invaded me with joy an baptized me in her grace.

I wanted to melt with her, become one with her body, with her soul. Our frames were a perfect fit, they were meant for each other's. Without even trying I was in her, as her legs embraced me and her mouth conceded with the passion we both felt. It was this magical place that nurtured the love we shared and had set it free for us to bask in.

The roar of the waterfall behind us was incentive enough to get to the climax we both wanted, this renewed feeling we both cherished so much. It felt like the first time we made love. There was nothing holding us back, so we took advantage of that and allowed every single desire rise out, every single feeling explode.

We needed this, it was the fuel that supplied our will to live. The love we shared was the only thing that kept us sane, alive, that kept us going each day, no matter what, we were there for each other.

For now, we had forgotten everything that happened leading to this, we put aside the horror that surrounded us and we let ourselves be carried by this feeling of lust that defined us. We were surrounded by beauty and harmony, incited to be part of a bigger plan, the future that awaited us.

We pulled ourselves out of the water and lay next to each other on the side of the lake, our hearts slowly paced to a calm as the sounds of nature surrounded us. Birds chirped on the tree tops around the lake, the sound of the waterfall blended with the background and a soothing wind blew our cares away. We closed our eyes and finally got overtaken by calm, the calm that we needed so much, that we craved so.

We had been running away from guilt, from the pain of doing what we knew was necessary to survive and now we could let everything slip away. We were together, we were safe and that was all that mattered. Our bodies needed the rest, needed to find redemption in the midst of so much beauty that was blooming all around us. We slept for a while, it could have been hours or days, time stood still watching us, cradling us in its womb.

When I woke up, Sarah was sitting up next to me. She was there, in silence, just admiring the view of the waterfall.

"Hey!" I said.

Sarah turned to see me.

"Morning sleepyhead!" she said with a smile on her face.

"What are you doing? Why didn't you wake me up?" I asked.

She grinned at my question.

"I was watching you sleep for a while, just looking at you breathing next to me and I didn't have the heart to wake you up from your dreams. You seemed so happy and calm," she answered.

"Don't be silly, I was dreaming about you!" I said, that prompted a big smile on her face.

Sarah got close to me and kissed me.

"How is it that you always know what to say?" she asked.

"I just say whatever thoughts you put in my head. No filter!" I replied.

Sarah laughed and I just marvelled at how beautiful she was.

"How long was I asleep for?" I asked, stretching my arms.

"We were out for a while. I don't know how long," she answered.

"Should we get dressed?" I asked curious.

Sarah looked at me with this playful smile.

"No, I think I'm gonna go naked for the rest of my life."

"That sounds amazing!" I said while I got close to kiss her some more.

We kissed for a while until she bit my lip and sucked on it. So, I pulled away.

"Hey! What was that?" I asked as I touched my lip.

"Sorry, I'm starving and you look pretty yummy to me," she said while she laughed.

"Oh! So your plan all along, has been to eat me?" I asked concerned.

"You got me! But I need to fatten you up a bit," she said while she pinched my belly.

"Hey!" I said as I embraced her and pulled her down next to me.

I could feel her naked body over mine. There was no better feeling in the world, she instigated every single cell of mine that responded to her touch un contained. I kissed her again, hoping that she wouldn't bite. So I kissed her and pulled away nervous and looked at her mouth. She was smiling.

"Are you afraid of me?" she said while she did.

"Are you gonna bite me again?" I asked.

She just laughed.

"I love you!" she said.

"I love you too!"

We kissed again, this time I was not thinking about her biting me anymore. It just felt right.

I pulled away and opened up my eyes, I wanted to see her face smiling, as she always did after we kissed, but this time her face reflected pain, she seemed scared even. I didn't knew what to make of it.

"Are you ok? What's wrong?" I asked concerned.

She just nodded and pointed at whatever was behind me, so unwillingly I turned around to see what she was pointing at, what she was so scared of. I just couldn't believe at what I was looking at. It was the firewall shooting up into the sky just feet away from us and suddenly all I could hear was the buzzing sound of the firewall and all I could see was the light emanating from it, blinding me.

Instinctively I extended my arms trying to shield Sarah from the light, from the danger that the wall represented.

"Close your eyes!" I shouted to her.

I turned around to see if she had complied with what I asked, but she wasn't there. Instead I could see a million souls in front of me walking purposely towards the wall. The same image I had seen before in dreams. I was standing on a dune, above the sea of people walking towards their faith. I could see the front of the line, people throwing themselves into the beam of light, giving themselves up, getting incinerated as soon as they entered the threshold. It was instantaneous, their bodies disappeared into the light, as if they had never existed, as if their lives didn't mattered, only the flickering of a zapping sound that emanated from the firewall as they vanished into oblivion.

I just watched, powerless, just as before, there was nothing I could do for them. Nothing I could say to make them change their minds, no option I could muster for them. I thought about it, my brain was running around trying to figure out what to do, what to say to them, but there was nothing, I was blank. My mind was overwhelmed by what I was witnessing.

It had come to this, we had built our own demise. Death seemed like a fit redemption, a way out from all the pain, all the suffering this souls had to endure for so long. It was imminent, they knew their faith was sealed, they just wanted it to end as soon as possible.

It was then I realised that the firewall was not a weapon, it wasn't evil, it didn't represented something ill. For them, it was the light at the end of the tunnel, it meant salvation, redemption, peace. Everything would stop, everything they've had to endure for so long, the unimaginable pain they had gone through, all the nightmares in their heads, all the trauma from what they've lived through.

They just wanted to be free from the demons that tortured them every day. It had been many years since any of them knew happiness, since they were allowed to enjoy life. They were just hanging on as days went by and they got closer to the end, starving, enduring the pain of their bodies decaying, ravished by disease, loneliness and disdain. This was no way to live, death seemed logical and there was no reasoning strong enough to dispute that.

I couldn't promise them redemption, there was no tale with a happy ending at the end of it, there was nothing I could say or do to give them hope. My mission in life had failed. I was conceived as a means to an end, to save humanity by resurrecting the race, by reproducing again, so we wouldn't end and I had failed.

Even though it wasn't in my hands to fulfil my purpose, I still felt guilty, I still felt like a disappointment.

So, I just watched in silence as they marched steadily, unconsciously towards the end.

They were so many, thousands and thousands. So many stories would end abruptly, as they began. It was the worst of times. I couldn't stand anymore, my legs were weakened by the sorrow I felt for them, by the sense of loss I got from each and every one. So I fell down to the ground and I lowered my head, ashamed to see them. Defeated, because there was nothing I could do. I wept like a baby, without solace, without console. All I could think of, were the hundreds of stories I read, time and time again in those books that filled the library I grew up in. The stories of humanity that lined every page of them. The tale of our race, the human race, the good and the bad, the efforts and failures, the achievements and the losses, the dreams that would never be fulfilled.

It was done, we had destroyed ourselves, imploded in our sins. Evil had won and now the curtain was about to fall for the last time.

A million thoughts rushed through my head in the time I was down, I must have brushed through human history all together. I just couldn't stand idle and watch everything end without remembering what lead us here.

I was calm, after a while, and so I ventured to open up my eyes again. I looked up, straight ahead and everyone was gone. Except for an image I recognised from a previous dream, a child that stood in the middle of the field in front of me, looking back and smiling from ear to ear. He lifted up his hand and waved at me saying hello, I smiled back as I cleaned up my face from all the tears that had rushed down my cheeks.

We stared at each other for a moment, he never stopped smiling at me. His face lighted up by the intermittent flashes from the firewall that oozed constant a few feet away from us. As I was looking back at him I thought about Sarah so I looked away, wondering where she was. When I turned back the boy was gone and the sound of the firewall transformed into the soothing echo of the waterfall. I was back in our paradise. I could feel the breeze moistening my skin, my lips that were longing to get soothe. I opened up my mouth so that I could ease my thirst. I felt the moisture in the air fill my lungs and relief the dryness in my tongue as I heard Sarah's voice calling me.

"Patrick! Patrick"

I turned to look everywhere for her, but she wasn't around me. The waterfall and everything around me had disappeared and only a vast empty land was left. My heart was beating fast inside my chest, the sound of the beating got louder and louder in my head.

I closed my eyes, thinking this was all just a bad dream, I concentrated on the beating of my heart until that is all I could hear, blocking everything else around me. Slowly I opened up my eyes, I was in a dark room, I couldn't see anything around me, not even the floor I was kneeling on, and then the beating stopped. It seemed like an empty space, there was no light, but when I pulled up my hands to see them I could see every little detail of them as if the light was coming out from me. I stood up and looked around, up at the ceiling and down at the ground and saw blackness surrounding me. My head was spinning inside, trying to figure out where I was, what was happening and what that all meant.

I tapped the floor with my feet, I could feel there was something solid under me but still couldn't see anything. I extended my left foot and stepped forward, there was a solid surface to step on so I took a few steps but got nowhere. So I looked up, and then straight ahead, hoping to see something in the distance, but there was only emptiness and darkness.

"Hello!" I said in a loud voice that just died without any echo or resounding flare.

It was the strangest feeling I had ever had, I extended my arms hoping to touch something, thinking I could be inside a casing of some kind but there was nothing.

"Hello!" I tried again, this time louder.

I thought it was odd that there was something to step on but nothing around me so I lifted up my foot and pushed it straight until it stepped on something in front of me. I pulled my other foot in the same direction and now I was standing on the space right in front of me. I walked a few steps on it and then tried the same bit again and now I was standing on the space on top of where I was first standing. I was mystified while this macabre thoughts began to cloud my head.

"Am I dead? Is this the end, emptiness?"

I was afraid this could be it, I was all by myself and there was nothing around me, nothing to show for a lifetime of memories, but they were still there, my memories. I began to think about Sarah. I closed my eyes and pictured the waterfall behind her, her smile adorning everything, the trees swaying in the background, crowning a jungle of green that surrounded it all, the sound of the thundering water falling from up high, crashing onto the rocks at the bottom, the wind blowing softly around us filled with the enticing moisture that gave life and the warmth of the sun shining up above in the bright blue sky. I turned down to look at Sarah, she was smiling at me, she was beautiful. I was in this amazing place with the one I loved, but it was all in my head. I was afraid to open up my eyes and have the memory fade away. I wanted to stay with her forever, in this magical place.

I couldn't understand what this was, where was it that I was. I kept asking myself what could it be? Was this a choice I had to make? But it wasn't even a choice, I had made my choice a long time ago, to be with Sarah for the rest of my life. So, what was this?

My eyes were still shut, I wasn't willing to lose her, I wasn't willing to go back to the emptiness I was in before, but I couldn't keep my eyes closed for much longer.

I kept them shut, waiting for something to happen, for some sign. Slowly my senses began to flourish, the smell of the water in the air filled my lungs, the subtle sent of the millions of flowers and plants around us tickled my brain, the sound of the waterfall in the background surrounded me, the chirping of a thousand birds up on the tree tops and the most beautiful sound I could register brought me back.

"Patrick, Patrick! Wake up!"

The darkness I was in began to dissipate and light took its place, my eyes opened up slowly, letting a rush of colours filled my head and the most beautiful image I could ever imagined appear right in front of my eyes.

"Wake up sleepy head!"

Sarah's face was right in front of me, looking at me, watching me sleep. I grabbed her head with both hands and pulled her close. I kissed her mouth, without closing my eyes and tasted heaven.

"What's going on? Are you ok?" she asked.

"I am now!" I answered.

She looked at me, wondering what I meant, tilted her head while she did and smiled.

"It was just a strange dream I was having. Everything is alright now. You are here and that is all that matters."

Sarah caressed my face as her eyes roamed every detail of it.

"This place is amazing. I wish we could stay here forever," she said.

I sat up and looked at the beauty around us and then I turned and looked at her.

"I don't see why not?"

She looked at me as she tilted her head again, her smile exploded.

"Really? Can we?"

"This is as good as any place, it seems like the perfect one. We have all the drinking water we could ever want and I'm sure that there is food around."

Sarah threw herself at me, embraced me as tight as she could.

"I would love to stay here. This place feels so right," she said.

She was right, this place was perfect.

"Let's do that, we should look for a spot where we can built a home."

She agreed and we scouted around the waterfall for a place where we could settle. We found a big enough flat space just across from the waterfall, overlooking the lake and a few feet over the ravine. It was the perfect spot. We could see the lake and the waterfall in the background. It was a levelled spot where we could built a cottage and the road was just a few steps away, so we could keep the vehicle close.

We still had a few boxes of food left, so we would be able to survive on that for a while. We first set up a tent on the far side of the plane, closer to the vehicle. We just felt safer there, the vehicle had been our shelter for a while and it would be our escape if anything bad happened. Not that we expected it to, but we were always alert to any threat. We had learned as much.

We brought our inflatable bed out of the vehicle and we set up there, inside the tent. We spent our first night awake, admiring everything around us. The sky above was filled with stars and we laid upon each other admiring the view. It was quite there, besides the sounds of birds chirping, the rumble of the waterfall and the sounds of the jungle that surrounded us, that sounded like a lullaby, there was nothing else in our minds but each other.

I just wanted to keep her as close as I could and she felt the same way. We were clinched to each other, it felt safe in her arms, with her body around mine and making love was just as natural as breathing.

Days went by and we kept busy building our dream place. We took whatever we needed from nature around us and used the knowledge, I could remember, from all those books that nurtured us for so many years. It was a good thing that Sarah was obsessed with architecture and dedicated a good portion of her time, learning building techniques. From foundation to interior design, she knew it all.

So, she directed the construction from start to finish. I did most of the work while she just directed my efforts.

We had all the materials we could need, there were some tools in the vehicle that I used to cut and form the wood. It took us a while to build up something, we were not in a hurry and building it kept us busy. We started out with the foundation, which Sarah was very insistent on.

"The foundation is extremely important, as in everything you do in life!" she said.

I agreed but with a little bit of sarcasm. My crooked smile gave it away.

"What? Are you making fun of me?"

"No, not at all. It's just that you sound so serious. It's actually super cute!" I said.

"Hey, we are working now! There'll be time for fun later," she said very seriously.

I saluted her as a good soldier would his superior.

"She smiled and nodded her head."

I picked up a log and placed it down on the perfect spot. She looked at it and said.

"A little bit to the right. Just a few inches," Sarah said while she measured with her thumb.

I looked at her and nodded while I pushed it aside, a few inches.

"Perfect!" she said.

This went on for days, she was in charge of the project and knew exactly what to do, or at least I thought so. I wanted her to be happy and this seemed to do the trick, so I went along with it. Every day that passed the project took form, little by little it became the dream we both had.

We took our time to enjoy the paradise we were in. We swam in the lake, we sat on the lakeside to watch the waterfall, we marvelled at nature and how it covered every little space around us. We would walk around the lake, getting to know our surroundings. We were in the middle of a jungle. Everywhere we walked natured had flourished. It was as if humans had never pass through here, it was untouched, wild and free. It just felt virgin, as if humans never existed.

Every day I went up to the vehicle and checked on the monitor to see if there was any kind of sign from the outside world. The vehicle had a link to the satellites up above, but it had been a while since there was anything flowing through there. Communications had stopped months ago, a sign that the world had gone silent. Power had stopped around the world, all the electric generation had ceased to produce the massive amounts of power needed to light up the globe and that meant that we were isolated from the rest. So, there was no way of knowing if there was anybody out there. Still alive, still hanging on, like we were, until the imminent end.

As time went by, the possibility of finding someone or getting any news had become slim to none. There were nights when I couldn't sleep, my mind just went on and on thinking of the fact that we were all alone in this huge world. That we would eventually die and the human race would disappear from the face of the earth. We were a species in extinction and we were the last ones, or so it seemed. I couldn't believe that would be the case. This world was so big and vast, there had to be pockets of people in different places, there had to be, but without children it was just a matter of time until the human race faded away.

It seemed like punishment for everything that we did as a race, that we were left without the chance to reproduce, to perpetuate the species. We had neglected that task that, for a lot of people, was pointless. To have babies was only by choice and not a means to survive. Some called it selfish, others applauded and practiced the doctrine, but when the time came and the virus made it impossible, the world fell in this era of depression, in this time of darkness. A world without innocence, without laughter, without life.

Still, the sun rose up every morning, and its heat would warm up your skin, the water flowing from that waterfall would still flow and life would go on. It was the way it was supposed to be, life has a beginning and an end and no power in the universe could change that. I was part of that process and that gave me solace. The world was not against us, It wasn't trying to annihilate us. The process was the same for every living creature, but us…humans had played god and tried to control that process, tried to become the masters of the universe and determine how the laws of nature preside over everything and realised, too late, that it was never meant to be that way. That those laws are unbreakable, that we are just a small part of this vast universe and are in no position to change them. Tampering with them had brought on our own demise.

There were a lot of faults that had been committed against nature, against the order of things because we thought we were superior to all of it, because we felt that it was our time to dominate our little tiny space. So much greed, so much self-gloating, so much pride, so much lust, I don't know if it was in our DNA, but it couldn't be contained, controlled, handled. We saw the end and how it would happen, for so many years, and we didn't stop. We just didn't wanted to, or just couldn't. Maybe it was our destiny all along, to rise and fall, to begin and end just as everything in this life does.

I read, thorough out the years, the teachings of the mayor religions that dominated the world. The Greek gods, the Egyptian deities, the Roman, the Phoenician, the Mayans, the Jews, the Christians, the Catholics, the Hindi, the Muslims, the Buddhist and a thousand other ones that rose and fell as times changed, as Humans tried them on for size and adopted their beliefs as they struggled to explain our pettiness in this world. There had to be a reason, an explanation for why we were here, there had to be a higher power that created all, that made us the way we were and with that came guidelines, laws and limits to what we could do, what we could achieve and how high we could climb before we fell back down.

Science and Religion both tried desperately to uncover the truth of how it all came to be. Science by explaining it through reason and Religion through faith. It was always a war of ideology and it ended up imploding, destroying us from the inside.

Since the beginning humans needed to explain the things they saw happening around them, the stars that shined every night and illuminated the void above them, so far away, unreachable; the sun that rose every morning and endowed everything in its path, that gave life to everything it touched; the weather that affected their lives, the water that fell from the sky, the snow that plummeted down and covered it all in whiteness, the periods of dryness; death and every little instance that happened that could not be explained. So, they turned to and looked for a higher power to explain it for them. They conceded those powers to gods, super human beings that would be able to control what they couldn't explain, what they couldn't master.

Gods gave and they also took from them, limiting their lives and governing what they did and how they behaved amongst themselves and with nature. Religion was the guideline in which they interacted with everything around them.

Civilisations rose based on that premise, conquests and wars befell to spread the truth they believed in and humanity was enslaved to that need. To the need to feel protected, managed, directed, controlled.

The truth is that humans have never known what to do with their freedom, with the fear that limits their lives, with the intelligence to dream and achieve whatever those dreams reveal. Throughout civilisation we uncovered the laws of nature and bend them at our will, we have been able to take advantage of our superiority and command nature around us, but hardly ever measuring the consequence of our actions, ignoring one of the basic laws we uncovered: "To every action, there is an opposing reaction" and the world had pushed back.

Sarah and I had been witnesses of it, had survived the extinction, thus far, and were tasked with living out our days in harmony and peace with ourselves, with each other and with nature. We were actual product of this travesty, of man messing with nature. We had been conceived in a lab by scientists and not in a womb through sexual reproduction. We were made with an specific purpose and not as a product of chance, as a labour of love.

Deep inside we knew what our nature was. Gloria had taught us to see ourselves as human, but we were defined as something else. We were an intent to defraud nature, once more, to bend the rules to achieve a purpose, to regain control by other means. To push science over religion, over logic.

The weird thing is that we didn't feel alien, we felt comfortable in our bodies, in our nature. We were as close as you can get to being human. We had everything a human did, we were conceived to imitate humans in every way, made from human material, purposely and genetically perfected to be as human as any.

But, what it is to be human? What defines you as part of this species? Throughout history, human nature has been redefined by those who consider themselves better than others. Some have even tried to purify the species, had tried to limit the characteristics that make us human. Separating us by colour, or shape, or religion, or beliefs. Tracing our origins as far as possible, to determine the root of our beginning. To where it all started, but sometimes beginnings don't start at cero, sometimes beginnings are just what's left from another end. Change is the only constant and certainty, its only flaw.

We were alive, Sarah and I, and we were a product of everything that human history had uncovered, everything that defined humanity. We felt human, so we were human. It wasn't a question of if, but a matter of will. All that history written in words, all the things that had to pass for us to exist. It was a long road.

It had been a painful process, as every birth is, the pain is the proof that there is life. We, as humans, had been through a lot of pain throughout our history in this world, but had also enjoyed intense happiness along the way. We were fortunate enough to understand it, to embrace it, to recreate it, to enjoy it, to build our lives around it. It has been the ultimate drug.

It is happiness that we seek, that we crave; it is what defines us, what separates us from the rest of the Universe. It's a feeling we share with every living creature, but we are the only ones who can purposely benefit from it.

I still felt as small, as we've all had, under the stars. We were a minuscule part of this universe and as petty as our problems were, they represented everything to us. We had made our mark in it, arguably good, but I chose to remember the positive things we did. The expressions of mastery in the arts, the joy they bring to our senses and the beauty of love that had defined our humanity for centuries. Those were the things I would chose to remember, to cherish, to hopefully pass on to whomever or whatever would come next.

I sometimes shared my thoughts, my dreams with Sarah. We would sit on the grass, next to the edge of the cliff, overlooking the waterfall and all its marvel and we would talk about it, about the past and what laid ahead, before the end.

It felt strange when we talked about it, about the end of humanity. Fear took over, the same fear of the unknown that had purposed every explorer to search into the darkness for a new light, but it wasn't a blinding fear, like the one you bend into, defenceless, without reason. This fear was enticing, like the fear that arises from a new adventure that pushes you to move forward, to venture into the obscure.

Life would go on in this planet, a new species would surge and conquer it all again, like it happened before humans. It was exciting to think what that would be like, the future we wouldn't see. The future we wouldn't be able to enjoy in our lifetime, but the one we would plant.

Chapter 9
Life Intrinsic

We were advancing in the construction of our home. Every day was a milestone, a new decision had to be made and my skills with the laser cuter were becoming sharp. I began to dominate the tool and it became easier to fulfil the deadlines that Sarah established, as the head of the project.

We entertained ourselves with this and kept our minds focused on the task at hand, instead of going around our biggest concerns and our greatest fears. The elephant in the room was always present but we lived our life's as if it wasn't there. We stop and ate when we were hungry and we rested when we needed too.

We enjoyed each other's company, most of all, there was always time for that. It kept us sane, alive and hopeful. Knowing that we had each other, waking up to a new chance at love.

One particular day we were sitting by the cliff, having our lunch. I was staring at Sarah, who was busy enjoying her meal and the majestic view we had as a backdrop. The light hit her face on the side and the edges would glow as if the beams of light would be emanating from her face. The perfect lines her nose had that sheltered her lips that opened up and closed as she fed. Her eyes sparkled filtering the light and her hair dangled in the wind as the glow of a thousand shimmers danced on her head. She looked like an angel that sprightly sprung from the pages of one of those fantasy books I loved to read.

"Did you ever thought about having kids?" I asked, the thought just popped out of my mouth, out of nowhere.

Sarah stopped eating and looked at me, surprised at my question. Her eyes wondered around, looking for the answer inside her head.

"All the time! I mean, that was my purpose. It was something that was expected of me and I was frustrated that it never happened. It made me feel like a failure!"

"You were not! It wasn't your fault!" I interrupted, I didn't wanted Sarah to feel bad. It wasn't my intention.

She raised her hand and placed it over mine. She wanted me to know it was ok. She needed to get this off her chest.

"I was conceived for that purpose, but I always felt that there was so much more in me. I felt like a failure, because they made me feel that way, as if I had done something wrong, as if I was to blame, but I knew it was them and the frustration they projected on to me. I thought about the possibility of getting pregnant and having a baby of my own, I actually dreamed of it all the time. How it would feel to have that tiny life inside of me, growing, feeding off me," Sarah went on.

She paused for a moment, thinking about it, caressing her belly with both hands. She had a million different smiles that I had been cataloguing since I met her. She had one for every occurrence that sparked her wit. She had one for every dawn that rose her torpor just to watch her glow. She had one for me every time our eyes met, it was sculpted on her lips like a badge of honour, but this one, the one she had at that precise moment, I had never seen before.

"Sharing everything I do. Beating inside to the rhythm of my own heart. Giving birth to it and seeing it grow. I wondered how it would feel to have it close to me, touch it and hear it grumble. Feel her tiny body moving unequivocally free. Smell its scent taking over everything. It's hands reaching out and its little feet kicking the air around it. It's chubby body enticing me to embrace it. I dreamed about it almost every night before I went to bed," she said as she paused and looked at me ashamed, twitching her shoulders.

I paused for a second, looking at her, I was overtaken by what she just said. Just smiling like an idiot!

"That's amazing!" I finally said.

"I never told anybody, ever, not even Gloria!" she seemed embarrassed as she did,

"It's wonderful that you feel that way, there is nothing wrong with it!"

Sarah looked into my eyes and wondered.

"I was supposed to get pregnant, but I never did. I was afraid of what would happen to my baby. I don't think they would have let me keep it, you know?" she said while she lowered her head.

I reached out and lifted her chin up to see her face, she looked at me.

"Well, you will never have to worry about that ever again. I would never judge you."

Sarah smiled and nodded her head.

"I know."

Then she turned the tables on me and asked.

"Did you ever thought about it, having kids?"

"Yes, of course. I read everything I could find about it in the library. Ever since I knew and understood what my purpose was, I wanted to know, what were they talking about. I even tried to understand what had happen to humans. Why couldn't we conceive," I said excited.

Sarah smiled and sighted when she heard me say that. It wasn't only her that felt that way.

"I was hopeful too, I wanted it to work. I could only imagine how it would feel to hold a baby in your arms, have it close. A tiny person. That must have been incredible," I went on.

Sarah was overtaken by the thought of it, smiling from ear to ear. She was glowing and I understood right then and there that the bond between a Mother and her child is a natural thing, a unique thing, something only women can comprehend and experience.

Suddenly I felt sad, humbled by the thought of it, the pain that women had to endure throughout this whole ordeal, when the possibility of giving birth was gone. Snatched out of them by something we, ourselves created in a lab while we were playing god. For men, it was just the tragedy of not being able to reproduce, to perpetuate the species, but for them, for women all over the world, it was a part of them that was broken, taken away and now they had to go through life incomplete, without that part that defined them.

I raised my head and looked up at the majesty of the sun going down in the horizon, the light morphing into different colours as the day gave up. There was beauty all around us, even though life had taken away that, there was still so much to marvel on, to appreciate. I grabbed Sarah's hand and interlaced my fingers with hers, we looked at each other and smiled, turned to watch over the sunset that was putting up a show for us.

The sun went down that day and we laid on our bed, we made love under the stars that lighted up jealous up above. At that moment, when we were in ecstasy, when we reached climax, we felt one with nature, we felt in complete harmony with everything that surrounded us. It just felt so right to be in her arms, to lock our lips together and feel our bodies merge. There were no words that defined what we felt at that moment while our heartbeats reached their peak, while every single cell was awaken, prompted to react to the heat that flowed through them.

Happiness is fleeting, it is complete for only a very small window of time and then its distracted by all the little things that make up life, because happiness is a state of mind and it is always changing, like a merry go round, you can only see your favourite mount every time it goes around and even then you can get distracted by all the other ones or by something that will caught your attention away from it as it passes by, but when you are able to grab it, to be blessed by it, it defines your life.

We were gifted with each other and that provided all the happiness I could want. It helped me focus in the important things and it scared the bad thoughts that surrounded my head, that lingered in my brain. We had this time, that was precious, and we needed to take advantage and live our lives one day at a time.

The cottage was coming along, every day we achieved a new milestone in the construction and could see our dream becoming a reality. We had found trees around us that provided fresh food, fruits of all sorts and even vegetables. There were tons of animals in the jungle that we could feed from and, even though, Juan had taught me how to hunt and prepare them, I was skeptical about doing so. We still had a lot of food in the vehicle which gave me a chance to postpone that for later.

I just didn't had it in me to sacrifice an animal so we could eat. I knew it will eventually come to that, but I wasn't ready, not yet.

We were all focused in finishing the cottage, that kept our minds occupied and not wondering around thinking about Gloria, Juan and Charlie, and about the future and what it meant for us. We tried to live in the moment and enjoy what we had to live for, each other.

Eventually the cottage was finished and we could move into it and enjoy what we had made. We were so happy the day we moved in and our house was christened. From now on life would be shared under this roof, inside these walls that we had built with our own hands.

I've never had anything that I felt belonged to me, this place felt like an extension of myself. I knew every single corner, every single log, every single patch, every single beam that we use to build this place. It was ours, our creation and we were proud of it. It was a home, where we would feel safe, but, even though, it was everything we wanted, it was not complete. There will always be an emptiness that wouldn't be filled by anything else. That space that was always present in our minds, the love that bonded us with the ones we had lost.

We didn't know how life transpired for the rest of the world, we were living in a bubble, in the middle of a jungle away from the world as everyone else knew it. There could have been a miracle somewhere else, maybe someone had found a way to reverse the curse imposed in humans. Maybe life had found a way. We didn't know and probably we never will.

The facts were laid out many years ago and if that miracle didn't happen, that meant that the human race was reaching its end. Years had passed since we were saved by Gloria, since we were taken out of our miserable existence inside that lab and set free to roam the world, to enjoy our being here and we have, but that also meant that death was taking its toll on humanity.

I still checked, every day, to see if there was any sign of the world outside. The vehicle was still running but I was worried about the batteries eventually running out. Even though they were supposed to last a life time, they were never tested under this extreme circumstances, so I couldn't be sure if they would last through it all. We didn't rely on it to survive, we had found our own means and nature provided much of what we required, so it wouldn't be a life or death thing, if it stopped working, but somehow it still gave me chills to think that we would lose the last piece of technology that kept us pinned to our era.

It was the thought of moving on that scared me, of letting go of the last proof of the world from which we came from. The last clue of the pinnacle we had achieved, as a civilisation, in the development of technology. It was hard to let go, but It will eventually happen. We had gone from total automation, to the Stone Age in a few years' time.

I kept building things for the house, furniture and accents for it, although I think they were more for Sarah than anything else. I wanted to give her everything I could. To make her happy and didn't realise that, as I was, she was happy just to have me with her. Life had taken away everything from me, but had given it back in one soul. She was everything to me and I went to bed with her, dreamed of her and she was the first thing I saw when I woke up every day. My world was built around her, she defined all that I was.

We lived a good life together, we marvelled with the beauty of nature every day. We enjoyed its gift and we cherished each and every one of them, but still there was this tickle that bothered us. I guess that you can call it human intuition, or maybe human paranoia, but it manifested as a kin sense of curiosity. I don't know where it comes from. If it is engraved on ourselves, in our human condition, or if it is our instinct of survival just blushing. Making us feel ashamed of our condition, or just curious of the fact that we could be the last living humans on earth.

It really wasn't a question that we needed answered. We had everything that we could possibly need here, within ourselves, but it kept popping out from time to time. Either me or Sarah would ask it, it was always lingering. It was an itch we couldn't scratch.

Until it happened one day. Sarah and I were looking at the sunset, sitting against an old tree that grew almost at the edge of the reef in front of the waterfall. It was one of our favourite spots. We would sit there for hours every day and just gasped at the beauty of it. It happened every day, but it was different each and every one of them. The colours changed, the clouds made it morph each time we saw it, there was always something unexpected that made it unique. It was the canvas where nature painted a portrait for us every single afternoon.

"So, what do you think is happening out there?" Sarah asked.

I smiled, because she took the words right out of my mouth.

"Your guess is as good as mine," I replied.

"Seriously! What do you think?" she asked.

"Wow! Ok, we are being serious?"

"You know what I mean. It's on your mind a lot, I can tell," she said.

"I mean, we knew for years that the world was ending. That people were dying outside our walls, but still a lot of them were able to sneak in when the firewall failed."

"Yeas, but that was years ago," Sarah interrupted.

"That is right, in whatever condition they were in when they came through. Time would have taken them, eventually."

"So, what do you think is going on right now?"

"I think that by now, most of them are dead, if not all."

Sarah sighed, she knew I was right but didn't want that thought to linger in her head.

"I just can't believe that it will come to that," she said, with a sad tone.

"What do you mean?" I asked.

"That we will end. That the human race will disappear. That will be the last ones."

"Well, that is the way it seems," I said.

"But this world is huge! There must be places where humans could survive, right? Maybe someone, somewhere actually found a cure. Maybe there is children growing right now," she said excited.

"Yes, of course, it's possible. Anything is."

"Don't say that," she said while she tightened her grip on my hand.

"Don't say what?" I asked.

"Anything is possible! It just seems that you are dismissing the whole thing," Sarah said.

"I don't meant it like that. I really believe that. I have hope that we will find a way."

"You mean you hope?"

"Yes, I hope!"

"I've been thinking. What if we take a trip?" she asked.

I was astonished at her question. I've thought about it in the back of my head a thousand times, but have always been afraid of bringing it to the front, much less actually saying it out loud.

"A trip?"

"Yes, exploring around. Maybe for a few days. This is our home, but aren't you curious what's out there?" Sarah asked excited.

She stood up and turned around to look at me, she was curious to see my reaction.

I smiled when I saw her face, she looked like a little girl, all blushed and ablaze.

"I didn't knew you felt like this. I would have said something but didn't wanted to upset you," I replied.

"I felt the same way, but I've been dying to say something."

"I love you so much!" I said, it just popped out.

Sarah got closer and kissed me. We were soul mates.

"So, what do you think?"

"Yeah, we can do that. We can chose a path and walk it for a few days to see what we find and then head back," I said.

She smiled with one of her most beautiful smiles. The one she had every time her emotions were about to burst.

"I would love that, can we?" she asked excited, it was the little girl inside bursting out through every pore in her body.

"Of course, we can do whatever you want," I answered.

"But you want to, right?" she asked.

"Yes, of course. Why would you ask me that?"

"I just want to be sure it's something you want to do to and not just because it is what I want."

I looked at her, smiled and nodded. She was so cute and nice.

"What?" she asked when I did that.

"You are so cute!" I answered.

So, the next day we prepared everything, we got some canned food and all the supplies we thought we would need in a trip like this, put it in our back packs. Made sure everything was secure, we didn't wanted animals roaming into our things and our food, and we headed out.

"Which way shall we go?" Sarah asked, jumping up and down.

I couldn't hold my excitement either and the joy of looking at her. It was overwhelming. We were going to venture into the unknown. We had done it before, but that was out of necessity, running away from the threat that infection represented. This was solely to follow this desire we both had of exploring. There were a lot of questions that needed answers and this was an attempt to find them.

"Well, I believe that we should go south. That is where we were headed since the beginning and it seems to be the safest way."

Sarah smiled and nodded, agreeing with me.

I took out my compass and we began our journey south. It wasn't easy to navigate through the thick jungle ahead of us. There were no paths to follow. We walked for a few minutes as the roaring of the waterfall disappeared with every step we took. We were pushing nature aside, trying to move forward. Sarah was behind me, trying to stay as close to me as she could.

The jungle was thick and vast, the tree tops were filled with birds of beautiful colours, chanting hundreds of different chirps. Monkeys swinging on lianas and jumping from one tree to the other. This place was alive and we were aliens in this world, foreigners passing through.

We made our way down until we reached a road, and old highway that moved through the jungle.

"We should follow this road," I said as soon as we got there.

"That is a good idea, I've got nature in me…literally," Sarah said as she took her blouse off and removed a tinny gecko from within it and through it on the ground, the small gecko made its way back into the jungle.

I laughed at such a wonderful sight. Sarah just looked at me surprised.

"It was driving me crazy!"

All I could do, was laugh and nod.

"We'll see how you react with one of those things running around inside your shirt," she said upset.

I pulled her close and kissed her, she was the perfect girl. I just couldn't stay away. She kissed me back and everything else dissipated, it was just the two of us in that moment. She looked at me smiling.

"I love you so much!" I said.

She roamed me with her eyes and sighted.

"I love you too! I should take off my blouse more often!"

I couldn't help it, I laughed at her comment and embraced her. She embraced me back but then pushed me away.

"It's so hot here, give me your canteen. I need some water," she said.

So, I handed her over the canteen, she opened it up and took a big long gulp and when she was finished she splashed some water on her face and offered it to me.

I took it and did the same thing she did.

"I miss the waterfall already!" she said gasping air.

"Come on, let's keep going!" I said as I pointed down the road.

So we began walking down the highway. It was a two lane paved road that swerved through the jungle. At some points, it was completely gone, overtaken by the foliage that ate it hole. We would have to cut ourselves a path through it just to find the road again on the other side.

"How far away are we from home?" Sarah asked while we were walking down the road.

I looked at my GPS tracker, I had to pinch it a couple of times to see our home.

"We are twenty five miles away. It looks like there is an old town a few miles down the road. It looks like an archaeological site."

" Good, I need to sit down for a while. Maybe a whole day!" she said, snorting.

"Are you tired? We can stop here."

"No, let's get there and then we'll rest," she said.

So, we did, walked a couple of miles down the road until we got to the town. It was hardly visible but we could tell it was a pre-Hispanic settlement. There were pyramids spaced out perfectly in a geometrical form, almost completely covered by brush, so they almost seemed like small mountains that rose in a straight pattern from the ground.

"Let's sit down here!" I said while we stood at the edge of the road, just over the town.

Sarah immediately did, she was tired and thirsty. I noticed and passed the canteen to her. She opened it up and clinched her thirst with what was left in it.

"We need to find more water!" she said as soon as she finished.

I pulled out another canteen I had attached to my belt.

"We still have a full one. Do you want more?" I replied as I offered it to her.

She looked at it and gasped, nodded and smiled.

"No, I'm good for now. You should have some. I haven't seen you drink any water in a while."

I smiled and took a sip of water from it as I sat down next to her. We were both admiring the view from the ledge. The whole town was nestled on a valley just beside the road. There were six big pyramids in the centre and a group of other structures surrounding them, delimiting the borders, but they were all covered in green.

It was a beautiful valley, overlooking a chain of mountains in the background. The sky over it was filled with thousands of birds flying in flocks, chirping on the tree tops. It was a wonderful sight to see, but as I was admiring the view, something else caught my attention. The gorgeous creature sitting right next to me. Sarah was looking at the view, in front of us, as she twitched her head around. Her neck was tired from carrying over all the tension her whole body had.

She was glowing with her own light, that was shooting out of her skin, drenched in her sweat that was more appealing to me than the water inside the canteen. That was the liquid that would quench my thirst. Just the thought of her spice invading my mouth, that salty sweetness exploding in my lips was tantalising enough, but then I saw a drop spawn out from her forehead and began running down her face and I couldn't contain myself. I got close and caught it, with my tongue, before it could reach her chin. That single drop of elixir filled my whole mouth with her taste.

Sarah looked at me sideways, like I was crazy.

"What are you doing?" she asked, giggling.

"I couldn't help it. It was a drop…it was getting away!" I said as I looked at her mouth.

There, above her lips, between her nose and her mouth a tempting group of tiny drops had formed, inviting me, hoping that I would save them from anonymity, from just disappearing without fulfilling their purpose. So, I kissed her and consumed each and every drop of moisture on her lip, I just couldn't get enough.

She kissed me back, but I sensed an unrest about my intentions. So, she pulled back and looked me in the eye.

"Are you kissing me, or drinking me?" she asked.

I just smiled and looked into her eyes.

"Both?"

She just smiled and kissed me some more. She allowed me to kiss her all over her face, taking in all that wonder that rose from her pores, that jumped out of her self to invade me with wonder, to quench my thirst for her.

When I was finished, she just looked at me and nodded as she wiped her face with her hand.

"You're crazy!" she said.

"I am, crazy for you!" I replied, the comment made her frown.

"That sounds like the title of a song I've heard before," she said, intrigued.

"Yeah, that's where I stole it from."

She just nodded and turned to look at the view in front of us while she sighted, which immediately made me smile.

We stood there for a while, admiring the view.

"Should we go down there?" I asked.

"Sure, let's see what we can learn," Sarah answered excited.

We made our way down to the mayor street, right between the pyramids, in the centre of the square. It seemed deserted and it was obvious that it had been like this for a long time. Everything was covered by brush, plants were everywhere. You could still see the structures of the pyramids under the leaves and the stems that grew embracing it.

We went around the biggest one, hoping to find a clearance, something that will give us a clue as to where the people that lived here had gone to. We had almost done a whole turn when Sarah noticed something between the brush.

"Is that a door?" she asked.

I got closer and tried to move some of the plants out of the way.

"It looks like a hallway into the pyramid," I said.

I took out the laser cutter and opened a passage so that we could walk into the hallway. I removed the brush from the entrance and we walked inside.

"Wait! Let me turn on the flashlight."

I did and we could see down the hallway. It went into the pyramid. Sarah looked at me a little bit scared but excited to uncover something new. I smiled and grabbed her hand as we walked inside. We walked a few feet until we reached a room inside. It looked like a chamber of sorts. It must have been twenty or thirty feet wide on each side and the ceiling was about the same. As soon as the light hit the walls we could see they were decorated with paintings. A sort of message or recount of the story of this civilisation.

We didn't really understood everything that was written in a language we couldn't read, but the images told the story the words couldn't. It started out with a primitive culture that worshiped nature and the gods that gave them life and supplied for them. As the story unfolded, it was obvious that men became more aware of their potential, of the power they were endowed with and developed systems and ways to control their surroundings. Conflict arouse between themselves for power, for control until it developed into war.

"Look at this!" Sarah said white she pointed at some paintings ahead.

I moved the flashlight to where she was. The paintings depicted what we already knew, the war that consumed the planet was portrayed there and just after it, the plagues that took over humanity, death and destruction. Their gods punishing them for their indifference, for ignoring their precepts and for their insolence, leading to their annihilation. It was all there, the same story we were still living through. Told in their own images, as a warning to other humans…maybe too late.

Sarah was holding my hand while we were looking at it all, it was a natural thing, we needed to feel connected to each other and that feeling gave us strength. Strength we needed to look at our story painted in those walls. The story of humanity told by a culture we didn't knew but that we, somehow, were a part of.

We finished looking at the paintings, looked at each other and walked out of there invaded by sadness, you couldn't help it but feel empathy for them. Feel their pain, their shame reflected on those walls. They portrayal was honest and heartfelt, they shared the guilt that every human had for our demise. They believed that their gods had taken revenge for our faults and decided to end humanity; we couldn't argue with that logic.

We reach the end of the hallway and it took our eyes a few moments to adapt to the light outside. The sun was high in the sky and its rays were shining down on everything. We could feel the warmth on our skin contrasting with the cold we felt inside, the sadness that lingered. We embraced for a while, we felt the guilt roam our bodies, so we needed the comfort of each other.

"That was tough!" I said, trying to break the ice.

Sarah looked up at me and smiled.

"It was, I didn't expected that. It's easy to dismiss what happened when all you know is happiness," Sarah said.

I looked into her eyes.

"You are happy?" I asked intrigued.

"Of course I am, what is happiness if it's not what you make me feel every day?" she answered.

I was overwhelmed, I felt so lucky. I had everything I could ever want standing right in front of me. Materialising in this beautiful woman that I could make as happy as I was.

"I'm happy too, as long as we are together," I said as I looked into her eyes.

We sat at the steps that led to the top of the pyramid and watched the sunset on the valley. It was a beautiful sight. I pictured how it could have bean, when this place was filled with life. When people roamed the streets, went about their lives and enjoyed the same view we were. Children running around, playing in the plaza right in front of the pyramids. Saying goodbye to another day. It must have been grand.

"We can set up camp here, in the plaza, and spend the night," I said to Sarah.

She looked around and pointed to the edge of it.

"How about, under that tree at the edge. I would feel better there," she said.

It was a huge tree that stood by itself, delimiting one of the corners of the plaza.

"Sure, that seems like a perfect spot," I said.

We grabbed our gear and headed to that spot. The tree looked like it have been there for ages. The trunk was at least thirty feet wide and the span of its shadow covered at least fifty feet all around. It was the tallest tree there. I kept thinking about the stories this tree could tell, if we just understood its language. The things it must have seen pass in front of it.

We set up the tent and laid inside. We embraced, like we always did. It had been an emotional day and we needed the rest.

Chapter 10
The Search for Eternity

That morning, when we woke up, the air was blowing subtlety through the branches above us, the leaves flapping around in the wind made a wonderful sound, that was complemented by the thousands of birds chirping harmoniously, to what seemed to be, a joyful melody. They were all celebrating the dawn of a new day.

We were nestled in each other, enjoying the concert around us. It was the perfect way to wake up, embraced by her, baptized by her transpiration that instigated my senses. She was all I needed to wake up and welcome the morning.

"How did you sleep?" I asked.

She just moaned and purred while she snuggled on my chest, she was still resisting to open up her eyes. Hanging on to the dreams that filled her sleep with wonder.

She was right, it felt so good. Sometimes you wish that everything was just a dream, that you could reset and start over, like the day does. Erase every mistake, everything that has gone wrong in your life and have a clean slate. Enjoy that single moment when you are between fantasy and reality, when you can still hang on to your perfect construct of what life should be, before facing the day.

It just seems like such a better option, to keep dreaming, to keep hoping that, whatever happens, is not real. That knowledge that fills our brain, the occurrence that marks our life, the choice is never an easy one and the consequence is what forges our destiny so, it's a lot better option to dream. The dreams dissipate when the light of the sun hits our face and wakes us up, everything is gone and all we are faced with, is reality.

I mean, don't get me wrong, I wanted to wake up every morning just to see her face. To feel her presence hanging on to me. She was the reason I woke up, my purpose. So, I looked forward to waking up from the dreams I had of her, just to live my reality, but there was a truth that I couldn't ignore. The one that had brought us here, it was a terrible one and it kept unfolding, like a nightmare that slowly punctures your truth and becomes real.

I guess, somehow, we had to accept the fact that we were born into a dying world, at least for our race, but even though we were experiencing the dusk of humanity, we were still human. That would not change. We still felt deeply, loved, rejoiced and represented everything human nature entitled.

"I was dreaming of this place. Before everything happened, when people lived here. It was filled with children, running around, playing in the plaza. It was wonderful!" Sarah said while she sigh.

I caressed her hair with my hand and pushed it out of the way, so I could see her face. She was smiling as her eyes were wondering, looking at an image she had in her head, an image she had seen in her dreams.

I try to imagine what she was seeing. The portraits she had created in her mind of what life use to be in this place. This urge that still resonated in every corner, the way we gathered in groups, the sense of community that always brought us together and the glue that bonded us, the youth that gave everyone a sense of purpose, a glance into the future.

Slowly that image dissipated, the memory was gone.

"Can we go back home?" Sarah asked out of nowhere.

I looked at her face, she was looking back at me.

"I wanna go back home," she insisted.

"Of course! Anything you want. Let's go back home," I said.

She smiled at me, happy that I would agree with her.

So, we got up and gathered our stuff. It wasn't much. As the sun was rising in the horizon, we began our journey back home. We said goodbye to this magical place and we went back into the jungle, tracing our path back the same way we came.

Our GPS pointed the way and our recollection directed us through familiar places. Somehow it felt like going downhill, getting closer to our home. It took us a couple of days, but we made it back on the third day as the sun was going down on our valley. Our house was waiting for us with open arms and the beauty that surrounded it, was blooming with joy for our return.

We stood at the edge of the valley and admire the wonderful place we called home from a distance. I embraced Sarah and we both marvelled at the sight.

"I missed this place!" she said.

"Me too, we are lucky to have found it."

"I'll race you to the waterfall!" Sarah said as she set off running.

"Hey! Wait up!" I yelled as I saw her take the lead.

I ran after her, excited to see her so happy. We got to the edge of the lake, Sarah began dropping her gear way before and when I caught up with her, she had stripped and was plunging into the lake but naked. So, I followed her example and tore my clothes off before jumping into the lake after her.

It was a wonderful feeling, our own personal paradise awaiting our return.

Sarah swam towards the waterfall and I followed, we both got under the drop of water that cleansed our bodies as it pounded them. Sarah embraced me, happy as can be, we both loved this place and it loved us back.

We kissed and made love, as we had done so many times before. It was our favourite spot, we didn't care that our bodies were tired from the long journey, that our minds were filled with images of what we had witnessed, everything just vanished and all that we cared about was each other.

When we were done we laid on the lake side and gave in to our fatigue, closed our eyes and rescinded.

The sound of the waterfall embraced us and whispered its lullaby, the same lullaby that had snuggled us, so many times before. We couldn't resist, we were home.

I woke up a few hours later, when darkness had overtaken the sky and the crickets were serenading our calm. Sarah was still sleeping next to me. She seemed so peaceful and content. I took her in my arms, lifted her up gently, she embraced me unconsciously, hanging on to my neck, between dreams and I brought her over to our bed.

I laid her down and she scattered on the bed, entangled with the sheets and went back to sleep.

I stood there for a long time, watching her sleep, wondering what was going through that beautiful mind of hers. Wondering if I was present in her dreams, I was jealous even of that. She represented so many things to me, looking at her laying there gave me calm, filled my heart with the peace I needed to look into the future with some optimism. At the least, I would get to spend the rest of my life with her beside me.

After a while, I too yielded to tranquillity around us. The night sky was upon the valley and everything was still. I fell asleep on the couch, as my eyelids subsided, tired of holding on while I watched her.

She looked so beautiful, scattered over the bed, her body fluctuating between the sheets, tempting my imagination, reminding me of the small details I've seen, of the gorgeous curves I've conquered, of the hidden treasures I've uncovered.

The light dimmed slowly as I plunged into slumber. My body was tired, we had walked for miles through the jungle, it was hot and humid and I needed the rest. I just dozed off on the couch. I remember wanting to stand up and join Sarah on the bed. It looked so tempting and cosy, but my whole entity just unplugged right where I was.

I just remember darkness all around while the sound faded away as it slowly tuned out, I was in another plane, captured by my sleep.

The silence was interrupted by the sound of paper whistling as it swished by, it moved around from side to side, tantalising me. I slowly opened up my eyes to find myself surrounded by thousands of books, suspended over them while a subtle breeze turned their pages, one by one.

I extended my hand and grabbed the first one that I could, lifted the book up and closed it with my other hand so I could see the paste. It was "War and Peace" by Tolstoy. I held it in my hand as I recalled the passages on it that struck me, those five families struggling to cope through the Napoleonic era in a ravished Russia of the 1800's.

I put it down and picked up the one next to it. Grabbed it with both hands and looked at the cover, "The Iliad" by Homer. The Greek masterpiece that set the birth of war stories for centuries. I put it down and picked up another one, this time, from the other side.

I closed it as I brought it up to my sight. "The Ramayana" by Valmiki, one of the mayor Sanskrit epics of Hindu culture.

Books I grew up with, stories that filled my childhood with wonder and knowledge of humanity, that helped me understand human nature since a very young age. A story filled with contradiction and struggle. Coloured by love and empathy but tainted by greed, envy and pride. A story of survival, of dominance and loss. So many different chapters that defined a species exertion with its own power, its own capacity for change and control.

The story of humanity is a savage one, fuelled by knowledge which is a two edged blade. It can give you a glimpse of a better being, a brighter future, or it can plunge you into desperation, make you vulnerable and weak. The eternal choice between good and bad, that is what troubles humanity, up to this date. It was curious to think about it, to me it was pretty simple, obvious even, what was good and bad. Gloria had taught me a lot about it, but most of it was ingrained already, hot-wired in my brain.

I looked around the space I was in, the books were still suspended in mid-air, we were floating in the vastness of an empty space. We were suspended in time, the books and I, they were thousands surrounding me. Slowly they began to organise, one by one they took their place and gravity took its toll, until we were all down on the floor. The books had taken their place and I was sitting down on the floor of the library I grew up in.

The lights were dimmed, as they were after hours, I was all alone. I looked down and noticed I still had a book in my hand "The Catcher in the Rye", which I remember reading unceasingly for years. I would read it and then pick up another book, read it and then go back and read "The Catcher" again. It was my go to book for a long time.

I put down the book and stood up, wondering why was I back in the lab, inside the library non the less. I had this strange feeling that someone was watching me and as I turned around to see behind me, the lights went out and I was left in darkness. I couldn't hear anything around me or see a single thing, It is the weirdest thing being in a void. Emptiness is a cathartic thing, you have all the options at your disposal, anything you can think of, anything can be. You are the one who decides what route you are going to follow, which emotion you will allow to control you. They are all available and willing to embrace you.

I could have chosen fear an desperation, that is so human like. The utter sense of abandonment that triggers our defence system, our instinct of survival, the uncontrollable need to be accompanied, the false sense that threatens our individuality as a self-sustainable unit. We have everything we need within ourselves, information floods our brain through the senses and attaches to everything around us, making us dependent on anything external. I mean, we need food and water to survive, to generate the energy we need to perform our basic functions, but everything else are attachments. We spend our whole lives searching out instead of folding in.

I didn't feel threatened by this emptiness, I was calm and collected until my heart intervened and messed it all up. I began thinking about Sarah as I closed my eyes. She was right there in front of me, looking at a sunset. The light hitting her face, illuminating every crease on it, revealing the glow that embalmed her skin, igniting her pupils that fired up like light storms and her hair that tangled in the wind, sparkling with nuance between the shadows that they projected on each other as they bounced off.

She represented everything I desired, the only thing I cherished in this world, but with that came uncertainty, the fear of losing her, the utter terror of being without her, of being all alone. It was something that was always lurking around in my head. The thought of not having Sarah was something I willingly blocked from my chain of thought, but like every childhood nightmare, it came to hunt me from time to time.

She vanished from my sight, first it appear to go out of focus, loosing clarity and then, slowly, I could see the particles dissipate in the murk.

I was left all alone with nothing but my heart beat, but I was not going to let despair take over. I could not let those thoughts cloud my world. I concentrated on my heart beat, on the perfect rhythm it signalled. One beat after another, without stopping, without falter. Each beat became an expression of its own, the spaces between them began to fill up with echoes, they were resonating in my head. Filling everything around me.

I needed to block those bad thoughts that could feed the darkness. So I did what my heart commanded, what my soul yearned. I filled those empty spaces with notes, notes that formed a melody that aroused from within and with it the emptiness yielded.

Light began to pierce the darkness and as it took over transformed everything around me into a canvas, light detracted and colour took over, splashing it all with life. My head filled up with images that morphed out of the pallet that was flourishing in front of my eyes. Images of people laughing, children playing, images of happiness long forgotten. Snapshots of what humanity had lost, portraits of the diversity we were blessed with, of our identity being shared through sheer happiness, through love.

It was all there, in my memory, there was proof of it. I was witness from a far, in the pages of all those books gathered as a memoir of what we were before we gave out. It was the legacy we wanted to be remembered by, our achievements, our triumphs, our extraordinary capacity for caring, for empathy, for love.

There was a dark side to us though, an extreme nuance that tilted the balance, the one that had overtaken our final hour, but that didn't define us. Humanity was way more than the faults of a few, that gave in to their most sombre side. Fanatics that clinched to a fixation, to the sense of superiority and power they held on to, the misguided god complex that cost millions of lives throughout human history and doomed us at the end.

We didn't wanted to know how deep this whole was, how rotten our soul had become. They say that humans are the only animals that stumble more than once with the same stone, but I say its hope that leads us to try again and again, failure is prone to success. We are resilient creatures, we don't give up in the face of adversity, we thrive and that was what lead us to greatness, but everything that raises, falls and our fall was steep.

So, the images turned dark. The trail of misery that we struggled with, was laid out in front of me, like a reminder of what we had done to ourselves. I couldn't contain the rush of feelings that took over me, my eyes filled up with tears and my heart with shame. I was part of this world that we created and fed, every day. A world filled with pragmatism, with the avenging words of spineless preachers who raided their flocks into submission, to do their bidding, to fulfil their vision of their own little fucked up worlds.

There was no mercy for us, there was no truce. Our sentence was carried out and our faith sealed. I couldn't take more of this sadness that had taken over me. I wanted it to stop but it kept rolling out, like an endless stream, there was an infinite supply.

I tried closing my eyes, but that didn't work, the images kept pouring in. The memories of terrible things human race had done, the senseless killing, the mass annihilation of humans by humans, it was there to witness since the beginning of time and, as technology progressed, it became a more discrete occurrence. It diluted within the masses. As the population rose, the dead rose too, decease and crime spiked out of control, but in the big picture, the percentages kept levelled.

It was evident, by what I had seen, that humans have always stayed true to their savage side, to the part of them that answered to the animal within. That responds to instinct, that reacts to threat as any other animal will do, with violence.

There I was, bombarded by those images that pierced my heart and incited my brain. I couldn't take more of that, so I tried to focus on something else, something particular, a single face. The face of an old woman who was looking straight at me, without any expression, without intention. The images in the background began residing, slowing down until they disappeared and all that was left was the image of her face. I was concentrated in every detail I could see, the marks imposed by the passing of time, layer after layer of experiences, of moments caught in time, frozen and tattooed on her face reflected as lines that overpassed on each other. Her eyes were dim, they were missing brilliance, the sparkle that once ignited them was almost gone and in its place there was a deep stratus like cloud that swirled in until it disappeared in itself. You could tell there was an endless collection of images imprinted in those ridges that formed her iris. There used to be a bright colour that illuminated them but it faded a long time ago. The veins around her iris had turned dull, opaque and rotten, some of them had burst and were swaged on her sclera, like words on a page, telling the story of their transgression. Her nose rose impetuous from in between her eyes, sticking out from her face, it had grown disproportionately from the rest of her face and it overtook her semblance. It was uneven and rough, blemished by the relentless scorching of the sun. Her lips were cracked beyond repair and the skin that covered them was flacking unevenly, but you could tell there was still flare on them, they still kept the fierceness they enacted through so many passionate kisses that transpired through their veil. Her hair was scarce and thick, it fell freely around her face, waiving endlessly in a shade of pale. She was a sight to see. Her candour transgressed far beyond her image, the lightness of her soul transpired through every pore, with a soothing sent and gloomed in a dimmed eternal glow through her eyes.

She was looking straight into mine, communicating somehow in a non-verbal language, as if she could read my mind. Slowly going through my thoughts, that were open for her to see, to analyse. Her eyes roamed my face as I did hers, mimicking what I had just done until, after a long pause, she smiled softly, just enough for me to know it was alright, enough to make me feel comfortable, accepted. So, I smiled back and as soon as I did beautiful images of a thousand faces began to swarm the background. A multifaceted, multicultural explosion of diversity filled my view. They all joined the old woman, they all smiled at me, filled my heart with hope, with a warmth feeling that invaded my body. I was amongst friends. Their presence grew closer and after a moment I was surrounded and it felt good to be among them.

I was part of them and that gave me solace, I wasn't alone. As long as I was part of them, I wouldn't be. I guess this is what a party must have felt like, friends sharing a space, enjoying each other's company. The energy that generates would have been enough to light up the world. I kept staring at their faces, they were so many, so different but at the same time, all the same. Part of the same race, the human race.

Slowly, one by one, the faces in front of me began to fade away. They nodded, like saying goodbye, before they did. Some of them vowed their head to me and I vowed back. Some of them placed their hands together, in front of their face, before they did. Some of them winked at me and some of them smiled with their eyes. After a while of goodbyes, I was left all alone again in this vast darkness.

I realise then that I was the one left with the responsibility to represent them all, they had all given me their torch to carry and I needed to oblige. I was the chosen one to lead the final stretch of humanity and represent. We both were, Sarah and me. Sarah! My mind was distracted thinking about her. A light appeared in the distance, piercing the darkness that surrounded me. It was so beautiful! It was moving, twirling around, flashes sparkling in my eyes. I could feel the warmth of the rays that landed on my skin, caressing it with heat, with a sense of life.

From the light, right where it began, I could see her image, drenched in the majesty of the glow that emanated from her, from every inch of her being. She was the light that brightened my darkness, she represented everything good in my life and as she approached me, the light transformed everything around me and the darkness was gone.

I could feel my body being renewed, re-energised, it was a marvellous feeling. She was with me, looking into my eyes as she always did, with this confidence in mine. It made me a better version of what I was, she improved me in every sense.

And then I heard her voice calling me.

"Patrick, Patrick my love. Wake up!"

I slowly opened up my eyes and that same light I had dreamed with invaded my iris and pushed it open and as it saturated my view her face appeared, right in front of mine. Her smile crowning my view, adorning the world around me.

"You fell asleep on the couch, why didn't you laid with me on the bed? Come!" she said as she pulled me out of the couch.

We both plunged onto the bed together, her arms and her legs embraced me and her whole body nurtured me.

"I was looking at you sleep, you looked so beautiful, I couldn't stop staring and then my eyes just closed," I said.

Sarah kissed me, with so much tenderness, that it made every inch of my body shiver with excitement, every tinny cell responded to her touch, to the sweetness of her lips as they smeared mine with her dribble. That taste that bewitched my sanity, that fed the liveness in me.

We kissed as if we had just met, for the first time. The heat our bodies generated was seducing the waves of linens that surrounded us, that embraced us hoping to be part of the lush that we were making. It was love being cast between our souls. My eyes were wide open, admiring her beauty unravel in front of them, my ears indulging with the hymn that her chest murmured as it gasped for air, humming with anticipation as her whole body reacted, her skin curled with rapture as we both gave in to desire. It was heaven in our grasp, the world was literally ending outside and it didn't matter.

We laid on the bed on top of each other for a while, I feast my thirst on her, the salty sweet taste of her transpiration was my feeding ground and my fetish. She would caress my hair with her fingers and moaned at my advances. We loved to enjoy each other.

We both conceded to the tranquillity that followed and rested for a while. We always tried to keep ourselves busy, developed this new ideas for things we wanted to have, something we could do together to pass the time and put aside the weary thoughts of what the future would be for us.

We were young and still had that spark of invincibility that leads you to challenge yourself, to duel faith without hesitation. Death wasn't on our radar, it wasn't even a thought that we dwindled on. We were only concerned with being with each other and enjoying every moment we had.

After a while, we decided to take another trip, everything was perfect in our paradise and all we talked about was the faith of the world around us. We speculated, we hoped that there would be people like us, that had found a way to survive and were now enjoying this rebirth of nature, as we were. It was possible, anything is possible and we were naïve enough to think it true.

So, we planned our next adventure. Gather our supplies and got fitted on our travel clothes and set off on a beautiful morning, as the sun was picking out on the horizon. This time we would be headed West, hoping to find what we were looking for.

I found a road on our map, that headed west and began walking on it, following it as faithfully as we could. The road, as many that we had seen before, was interrupted suddenly by the overtaking of nature that temperamentally took over sections of the road and claimed it back as its own. Which got me thinking.

"Do you see this part of the road that has been erased by nature?" I asked Sarah.

"Yeah, it is completely gone, while this part we just went through is untouched," she pointed out.

"What if that happened with everything around us. What if that mountain there, use to be a huge city from an ancient civilisation that lived in this earth thousands of years ago and then got overtaken by nature and it transformed it into the mountain we see today," I said, while I pointed out to a mountain in front of us.

Sarah nodded as she thought about it.

"It could be, or maybe it happened in a split second as a volcano erupted suddenly and ploughed that city with magma, buried it and everything in it, like Pompeii," Sarah said.

I couldn't believe what I was hearing, I was astonished by what she just said. So, when she turned to look at me and saw my expression she said.

"What? Why are you looking at me like that?"

I'm just surprised that you would go there. Destruction and mayhem.

She just shrugged and made a funny noise.

"Maaah, everything is possible!" she said.

I just cracked off laughing, she was amazing. She laughed with me and we began to navigate our way through the brush that covered the road, trying to figure out where it had gone, so that we could follow its path forward.

We found the road a few feet over and kept walking down on it. The road began to swivel on to a mountain as if it was grabbing on to its side, revealing a beautiful view of the valley up ahead.

Sarah and I just stood there, marvelling at the view in front of us.

"I don't honk I've ever seen so many shades of green, all in one place. There is literally no spot on this valley that is not covered in green," Sarah said.

I turned and looked at her, she had this amazing expression on her face, she was actually in love at what she was looking at. Her eyes were lit, her pupil was almost completely closed and her blue iris was reflecting the light off, shining like a beacon thorough the darkness. Her smile was flourishing, bending her lips open allowing her teeth to show under them. Her cheeks were protruding, fancying the redness on them like an honour badge. Her eyebrows were hanging on to her eyes, almost falling on their sides. I was jealous of the beauty in front of us, knowing I could never make her see me like that.

Sarah sensed my stare and turned to look at me.

"What?" she asked as she smiled at me.

"I have all the beauty in the world with me, all the time." Those words just popped out of my mouth.

Sarah roamed me with her eyes.

"Come on! Look at this, isn't it gorgeous?" she said as she turned to look at the valley.

I snapped out of it and looked at it, it was breath-taking, there were no words to describe so much beauty. The wind was softly blowing thorough the valley, swaying the leaves from side to side, it made the whole image seem alive. As if it were strutting itself as we gazed upon it.

Sarah extended her hand and grabbed mine, she interlaced her fingers and we were connected, admiring this portrait as one. We stood there for a while, admiring the view. We were overtaken by it. After a while we began walking down the road and the views kept getting better as we moved forward.

We walked down the road until we were down in the valley, surrounded by all that green we could see from the top of the mountain. It was as dense as it seemed from up there. We were having trouble moving forward, there was just too much undergrowth, every time we thought we would reach a clearing, more of it just showed up.

Finally we reached a small stream that ran through, it gave a little bit of leeway for the sun to shine through the foliage that covered everything. We sat down to rest on a formation of rocks that nestled the stream, we drank from its crystalline waters and we filled up our canteens.

Sarah grabbed some water with her hands and threw it on her face. Took a rag, damped it on the stream and placed it on her neck. She had this talent of making every single trivial detail look sexy.

She took another rag, repeated the same and offered it to me.

"Come, sit here."

So, I did, I sat next to her and she placed the rag on my neck, as she had done in hers. I felt my whole body adapt, react to the moisture on the rag, the coldness of the water, it changed my whole body temperature. It just felt so good.

"Nice, ain't it?" she asked.

"Yes, it feels so good. It is so hot here."

"We should take our shoes off and put our feet inside the stream," Sarah suggested.

I nodded agreeing with her. We both did, we dipped our feet into the stream and as soon as we did we felt relief. Sarah stood up, she was standing on the stream, she bend down and threw water at me with her hands, right at my face.

"Hey! What are you doing?" I asked.

"What? What are you going to do about it?" she replied as she threw more water at me.

I stood up and fired back, but I used both my hands together, so this time it was a lot of water that splashed on her face.

"Ohh! You didn't!" Sarah yelled as she bent down and did the same back.

We kept on throwing water at each other, laughing as we did, we were kids playing in the garden, enjoying the magic of innocence. I just loved to see her smile, her quirky smile as she figured out ways of getting back at me. It just came natural, we didn't enjoyed our time as kids, back in the lab, we didn't get to feel this nonsense of doing something just because it's fun, just because it makes you laugh. It didn't make sense, it wasn't logical, but we still felt good doing it. It was fun, just to get the other one wet and suffer the same faith at their hands. No bad intended, just clean fun.

We both got completely soaked from running around in the stream and throwing water at each other, we embraced and completed the process of it. We were both the same, nobody had won although, I guess, we both did.

We were laughing like we never did before, it was uncontrollable, this joy that invaded us, the wonderful feeling that possessed our youth that was eager to come out and play.

Her laughter made everything grand, it was loud and contagious, honest and frivolous. It arouse from deep inside her soul and bounced around with a wonderful echo that incited more laughter, that then boomed all over and fleeted with the cutest unintentional giggle.

We eventually got tired from running around. We sat down by the side of the stream, still laughing. Slowly the laughing subsided and we began to catch our breath. I looked at her face, that was smothered red but graced with a portentous smile as she looked at me. I extended my hand to touch her, feel her bliss pouring out and I kissed her.

This was a beautiful place, we stayed there for a while enjoying it all. There was nothing prompting us to leave, we were on a quest to discover new things, to know more about the world that had become our home and we were yearning to learn.

"I don't think I've ever laughed so much!" Sarah said.

"Me neither, that was so much fun."

"Did you ever play when you were a kid?"

"No, I was secluded, just like you were. My only pass time was reading books."

"Me too. I use to dream of running around and playing in the dirt."

"Playing in the dirt?"

"Yes, didn't you? I mean, I use to see pictures of a park, children playing on the turf, running around on the mud, climbing trees, it just seemed so entertaining, so much fun. I wanted to do that. I use to wonder how that would feel. To touch the grass, to feel loose dirt in my hands," she said.

"I use to wonder about all those things too. I was just afraid of wanting it, you know?"

"I use to ask Gloria about it. She would tell me stories of when she was young and all the games she would play with her friends. I always wondered how that would be like…having friends." Sarah seemed sad when she said that.

"Yeah, me too, but now we have each other. You are my best friend!"

"I'm your only friend!" she said sarcastically.

I shrieked at her comment, it was a little mean. She looked at me and smiled.

"You don't need more friends do you?" she asked.

"No, I just need you."

"That is such a good answer! Come here, that deserves a price."

So I got close and she kissed me.

We decided to stay there for the night, we set up the tent and snuggled in our bed surrounded by the sounds of a million crickets stridulating around us. It was almost hypnotising. We were tired from the trip, from walking for miles in rough terrain, so we dozed off almost immediately.

Chapter 11
The Edge of Omission

The subtle light of dawn woke us up the next morning, the sun was coming up on the horizon and everything was filled with life. The birds were chirping on the tree tops and the smell of new some invaded the air around us.

Sarah was still nestled in my arms and I could smell the scent of her hair that covered everything around us, I enjoyed that so much that I took a whiff of it to fill my lungs with her musk. I looked down and I could see her body entangled with mine, her skin glowing with the morning light seemed like it went on forever, lost in my purview. I could actually see her pores opening up and the tinny hairs that covered her body stand up, like soldiers, to greet the sun. I extended my hand to caress her skin and as soon as it felt my touch, it crawled responding to my closeness and in unison her whole body reacted and her skin filled with goosebumps.

"Oh! That feels so good," Sarah said, with her eyes still closed.

I smiled because I knew she was aware I was there, playing with her and she liked it.

"You like that ha?"

"Yes, a lot. I love waking up to it, to your provocation," she said.

"I was just…"

"I know exactly what you want," Sarah said as she got close to me, with her eyes still closed and she kissed me.

I couldn't contain my excitement, the sole idea of her body curling next to mine, her willingness to mate with me. I don't know exactly what it is, but in those moments the air changes, it gets filled with a strong musk, it propels my body to yearn her touch, her closeness. The sounds that exude from her chest excite me beyond comprehension, it's a natural reaction to her calling. To her surrender to my passion.

Making love to her is my favourite thing to do, it's the way I exist in the midst of this prophecy that we were cast in. It's the way I can make sense of it all, the joy it brings makes every bad omen disappear. I feel safe in her arms, between her legs that hold on to me and never let go. It's my sacred place.

So we welcomed the morning with ecstasy, we greeted the day the best way we knew how. We then dipped into the stream to wash up, picked up our tent and got ready to continue our journey.

It was a beautiful day, the sky was cast blue, not a single cloud was in sight and the sun was plunging down. We walked in the shadow of all this nature that covered us in green. The brush was so thick that the sun would barely shine through and only the light that bounced off the tree tops and sneaked passed the hundreds of layers of leaves, would brighten our path. The moisture trapped inside this cocoon of green was so dense that it made it hard to breath.

"Here put this on," I said to Sarah as I handed over a scarf.

I placed mine over my nose and mouth and she copied me.

"It will be easier to breathe through the mesh, it will filter some of the moisture."

She tried breathing through it and took a few deep breaths.

"It's a lot better," she said.

We walked under this mantle for a few hours until we made it into a clearing. A huge circle that interrupted the commonality we were covered in. We stopped at the edge, wondering what it was. We looked at each other baffled. It didn't make any sense. It seemed to be a bald spot in the middle of the jungle. There was nothing growing inside of it, as if nature would be afraid of invading its limits.

"What is this place?" Sarah asked intrigued.

"I don't know. I've never seen anything like it."

The ground was covered by some sort of sand like dirt, or at least it seemed like it. As soon as the light marked the limit, nature stopped, all the green that covered everything around us, including the moss that covered the ground, was cut off.

I was curious, so I stepped into it.

"No wait!" Sarah yelled.

"It's ok, I don't think it's anything bad," I replied.

"How do you know?" she asked concerned.

By then, half of my body was inside the light that plunged unchallenged over the clearing. I extended my hand, with my palm open. I felt the sun warming it up, but nothing out of the ordinary happened. I looked at Sarah's expression of uncertainty while I stepped into the light.

I extended my other arm as I walked a few paces into the clearing. I spun around, waiting for something to happen, but nothing did. It was such a bizarre sight, to see the emptiness inside the clearing in contrast to everything that surrounded it. Everywhere you looked, you could see a wall of green delimiting the view.

I completed a turn and there she was, looking at me, still concerned, scared even.

"It's ok! It's just what it looks like, a clearing," I said to her, hoping to ease her concern.

She kept looking around from inside the shade, still doubting.

I was wondering about it too, so I leaned down and grabbed a fist full of the sand on the ground and lifted it up to see it closer. As I did, I noticed that there was a shiny component to the sand dripping off my hand. Most of it wondered off, but I could see a distinctive component on the grains that remained on the palm of my hand. There were some grains that reflected the light of the sun in a unique way. Like mirrors reflecting the light. I touched one of them, but as soon as I did it dissipated into my hand.

"Wow!" I said impressed.

"What? What is it?" Sarah asked.

"I don't know, there is something on the ground, mixed in with the sand."

As I was saying that, I touched another grain with the tip of my finger and it dissipated again.

"So, get out of there! What if it is something bad?" Sarah said almost shivering.

"Don't worry, I don't think it's anything bad. I think there is just a mineral in this clearing that prevents the soil from being fertile, that's all."

"It's creepy, that's what it is," Sarah said.

I giggled at her comment. Sarah didn't like it.

"I'm serious Patrick! What if it's something else?"

"Like what?" I asked.

"I don't know, something bad."

"I don't think so. You have blemishes right?" I asked her.

She looked at me funny, like I was asking something crazy.

"Blemishes?"

"Yes, spots or marks on your skin. Little patches that make it uneven."

"You mean like moles?" she asked.

"Yeah! Like that."

"Yes, of course. We all do, don't we?"

"Well, I think this is something like it. It's just an earth mole."

"Moles can be bad, you know?" Sarah insisted.

"You're just being paranoid!"

"Well, I just think we should go around it either way and you should get out of there."

I smiled, she was so cute.

"Ok, if it makes you feel any better."

I said while I walked back into the shade.

"Is that better?" I asked.

"Yes, I don't trust that clearing."

I nodded my head and grinned.

"I don't know what you mean, it's a clearing!"

"Just trust me, there is something wrong here. Don't you find it strange that suddenly the jungle stops abruptly like that?" she asked me.

I turned to look at the clearing, wondering what she meant. It was kind of strange, it was a phenomenon I have never witnessed, but there could be a hundred explanations that made more sense than the one she was thinking of.

"I mean? Yeah, it's strange, but not evil!"

"I never said it was evil! Just…you know! Could we just go around?"

"Yeah sure, I don't mind."

So we began walking around the clearing, making our way through the jungle and around the bald spot in front of us. It did had a strange vibe to it, but it was, somehow, inviting or maybe challenging would be a better word. Like a mystery that you want to unravel, discover what's hidden underneath that smilingly innocent façade, but I couldn't defy Sarah. She was vigilant, making sure I wasn't tempted to go back in there, so I tried to dismiss the temptation and move on.

We got to the opposite side of it and began to move forward in our same path as before. We were still heading west from where we had started. I turned one last time to see the clearing, that strange and mystical place we were leaving behind as it disappeared between the thick brush.

After a while, I was able to dismiss it. We kept walking through the jungle until we got to the edge of a town in the middle of it all. First, we noticed that the undergrowth had changed. We were in the middle of a completely different type of herbage. It was symmetrical, perfectly defined rows, endless groups of the same type of plant were laid one after another in unison. This was man made.

We made our way through it until we reached a wider space, that seemed more like a road, going along side. So we walked on it for a while until we could see a few houses along the border. Our hearts began beating faster, prompted by excitement and fear. We hadn't seen another human in almost a year, since we last saw Gloria and the thought of finding someone alive was overwhelming, but there was also the danger of infection if we did, so we moved in closer with caution.

When we got to the edge of town, we could tell that people lived there, at some point, because there were still traces of their lives laying around everywhere. Farming equipment laying piled up at the corner of the fence as we made our way through it. Children's toys laid against the wall of the house.

We pulled up to the door and just as I was lifting my hand up to knock on it, Sarah pulled me back, I turned to look into her face. She looked straight at me with a look I haven't seen on her face in a long time. She was visibly scared. She didn't say anything, she just looked at me. I tried to be strong and give her some confidence, make her feel safe at my side. So I nodded, relaying the fact that I was aware of what she was trying to say.

I turned around and knocked lightly on the door. We took a step back and waited to see if there was an answer. We both kept staring at the house, at the windows, at the edges around the bend from the walls that delimited the property. After a few moments of not getting any response, I stepped to the door and knocked again, harder this time. As I was about to hit it the third time, the door opened, which prompted us to jump back, but there was no one behind the door. It just swung open a little bit, screeching as it did, and stopped mid-way.

We could see inside the house, there didn't seem to be any movement at all. So I got close and pushed the door wide open. The screeching the door made, filled up the inside as an echo increased the sound tenfold.

"Hello! Hola!" I shouted in English and Spanish, hoping for an answer.

Everything seemed to be in its place, there was a thick film of dust covering it all. Sarah was stuck to my back, so close I could feel her breath on the back of my neck. She was breathing deeply and constantly, I could feel her frailty sleek through her whole being and into mine.

We walked around the house, to the kitchen and the rooms, that were behind the fireplace.

"Anybody home?" I kept yelling, in case someone was there.

The bedrooms were set up as neatly as the living room was. The beds were still made and there were still items on top of the shelves and on the desks, the side tables, the wardrobes. There were dolls and toys in the kids bedrooms, clothes hanging neatly on the closets and even towels hanging on the bathroom walls, but no sign of anyone around.

It seemed as though they had vanished on thin air. As if though they had just disappeared one day. So we went back to the living room and sat for a moment. We looked around at the pictures on the wall, at the little details that decorated every single space inside the house. Photographs hanging on the walls, memories of what used to be a normal, happy life.

There was a bookshelf at the side of the fireplace, filled with books of different sizes and colours. I stood up and got close to it, so I could read the titles. They were all in Spanish, but I could recognise a few of them, a few of the authors that were displayed on the spines.

"Gabriel Garcia Marquez", "Octavio Paz", "Miguel de Cervantes"…I pulled out that one and looked at the cover. "Don Quixote de La Mancha".

"I read this book a while ago, it's one of the classic books from the seventeen century," I said to Sarah as I turned around to show her.

Sarah was sitting down on the couch, she was fixated on a frame she was holding in her hands. She was infatuated by what was in that frame. She didn't even heard me, so I put the book down and walked over where she was, sat next to her and looked at the photograph she was looking at inside that frame.

It was a family portrait. The Mother and the Father with six children, three daughters and three sons. The parents were sitting down and their six children were standing right over them. They were all smiling, the Father had a portentous grin, you could tell he was proud of the family he had and the Mother was static, happy as can be. It was a beautiful photo.

"Are you ok?" I asked Sarah as I caressed her hand, that was steady holding the frame.

She turned to look at me.

"They look so happy!" she said.

I just smiled and nodded. Sarah turned to look at the photograph and placed her hand over the image, caressing it with her fingers. As she did the image rose from the frame. It was a 3D image that rose from the surface. Sarah held the frame flat up so we could see the image that began moving as we did. The family was setting up their places and preparing for the still shot. They were all smiling and hugging each other while they took their places and as soon as they did and were completely still, the sequence began again.

"It must have been wonderful to have a family like that. To have brothers and sisters, loving parents. You can tell they loved each other," she said.

I knew where she was coming from, we never had that. We were conceived and raised in a lab, out of a test tube and some genetic material, manufactured for a purpose. The only family we ever knew, growing up, was the warmth, loving care that Gloria provided. So, this idea of a happy family, was just a beautiful fantasy we had in our minds. The need for a loving touch would always be a fleeting hope we had in our childhood.

I understood what this simple image had sparked in Sarah's heart, I felt the exact same way. It was something we would never experience. We had each other and that would have to be enough.

We stayed there for a while, feeding off the sentiment that place had cherished through all the memories it kept. Sarah wanted to keep that photo, so we took the frame and she placed it in her backpack. She didn't know this family, but it represented a dream she had, since childhood, when we filled our days with fantasies, ideas we got from all those books we read and that was enough.

We walked through the village, we stepped into every single house. We saw all the memories each one held dear. It was a lesson in history. Every single house had a different tale to tell, but at the end it was the same basic one told over and over again. This was the backbone of humanity, the one thing we cherished the most.

This interaction between us, the countless experiences we shared, but mostly, our ability to reminisce.

Most creatures in nature follow the same behavioural patterns, they will gather in units to fulfil certain requirements of support, some instinct that needs to be cradled. Humans though, we recognise the need to be together, the value of family and the joy that comes out of sharing. That is what makes us unique, what separates us from the rest of the species. That we have the capacity to process those needs, to project them with sentiment, to assign feelings to those interactions with our own pierce. We are the only species who can choose to love, or hate, who can decide on the basis of judgement and not because its instinctively bias. We are a unique species.

The more I thought about this, the sadder I became.

Sarah noticed that, she could sense what I was feeling, even before it manifested on me. She saw a single runaway tear that popped out of my eye, unwillingly, pushed out by the sadness I was mustering inside.

"Are you ok?" she asked concerned.

"I'm good, I was just thinking."

She brought her hand up to my cheek and caressed it with her thumb, wiping off the tear that had escaped my eye.

"You don't have to pretend with me. I know you feel it too. It's ok to be sad," Sarah said.

"I know, I just don't want to feed on it. You know?"

"Feed on it? What do you mean?" she asked.

"I want to be strong for you. One of us has to be."

Sarah smiled at me, she looked into my eyes and kissed me.

"You are my rock! You've always been. I don't know what would be of me, without you by my side, but that doesn't mean that you can't feel."

I smiled at her, it felt good to be recognised. To know that what you do, has an impact, to know that she cares about me as much as I care about her.

"I know!"

We embraced for a while, I needed to feel her warmth invading me. That was the only cure for my pain, the only comfort I could ever wish for.

I wanted to cry, I needed to unload everything I was bottling inside, but it just wouldn't come out. I just felt this calm take over and I was at peace. It was her presence, the fact that she was next to me, gave me the strength to face anything.

We got to the last house on the town, we wanted to go in and meet this last family, but as soon as we got close we saw what was beyond. At the edge of town, scattered around a huge old tree and nestled under its shadow, laid a cemetery. From the distance we could see the stones that delimited the graves at their feet and on top, a cross from each and every one of them.

There seemed to be hundreds of them. There was not a single stone repeated, all of them were of different sizes and shapes, representing the people that laid under them. Each and every one unique in their own way.

We were drawn to it, like insects attracted by the light, we dismissed everything in our minds. We got close to the graves, but something stopped us in our tracks, right before the first one, right next to the entrance to the graveyard that was marked by a portal, crowned by a single cross on top of it, just over a sign that said.

"Cementerio de San Carlos."

Sarah and I looked at each other, hoping to get the strength we needed to go in. She grabbed my hand and together we crossed the threshold under the portal and stepped inside. We got close to the first grave, Sarah crouched to get closer to the stone that marked the grave and the epitaph written on it.

"Aquí llace el cuerpo de Annelle Garcia Sanchez. Madre, hija, hermana, esposa y amiga. Sus virtudes excedieron por mucho a sus defectos e inspiró a muchos a seguir sus metas. Educadora incansable y mártir de las letras. Nunca se detuvo, ni en sueños dejo de promulgar sus doctrinas que hicieron de las vidas de todo el mundo a su alrededor un viaje ambivalente. Descanse en paz."

"What does it say?" Sarah asked.

"Here lies the body of Annelle Garcia Sanchez. Mother, daughter, sister, wife and friend. Her virtues exceeded her defects by far and inspired many to follow their dreams. Tireless educator and martyr of the written word. Never held back, not even in dreams did she stop enacting her doctrines that made everyone's life around her, an ambivalent journey. Rest In Peace."

"That is beautiful!" Sarah said as she watched the stone it was written on.

"It is! She most have been a great person," I said.

Sarah extended her arm and caressed the stone. At that moment it represented much more than just a headstone. It was the whole journey of a soul, buried under it, described in a few words for anyone to read.

Sarah got up and looked around us, there were hundreds of graves.

"These are the people that lived in this town. This was their home," she said.

I just nodded as I looked around at the hundreds of graves that filled this patch of earth, their last resting place.

Sarah grabbed my hand and pulled me to the next grave. She crouched again.

"Read this one to me. Please!"

She was holding my hand still, so I pulled it up to my mouth and kissed it. Then I focused on the engraving on the stone. I moved a few branches aside that were covering it and began reading.

"Here lies Rodrigo Bárcenas Lopez. Father, son, husband, brother and friend. Last survivor of a brave cast of warriors that fought tirelessly for freedom and equality. Lieutenant in the Mayan liberation front. Representative in the house of Deputies. Founding member and proud citizen of the town of "San Carlos". Soldier in permanent fight for the rights of the oppressed and the least fortunate. His soul will always live on, in the breath of those who claim injustice, in those who search for a better tomorrow. Rest In Peace."

"Wow! He was a famous person," Sarah said.

"Yes, I believe he was. He was a politician of sorts, an activist."

Sarah turned and looked at the rest of the graves around us.

"They each have a story, they each live life their own way. They all deserve a page in a book," she said.

"I guess so, but there wouldn't be enough paper to print them all," I said.

We spent hours going from grave to grave, reading about the lives of the inhabitants of this small town, stories of their achievements in life, of the details that made each one unique. Written posthumous so that whoever read it, would know who they were.

"I somehow feel that I've met them, that I knew them," Sarah said while we stood at the edge of the cemetery.

I grabbed her hand and nodded.

The day was coming to an end and the sun was dimming in the background. Slowly falling behind the mountains in the distance, painting everything with a bright light, giving it life before the darkness prevailed. The shadows were lingering, growing poignant, foreshadowing the coming of the night.

We decided to take advantage of the towns hospitality and spend the night in one of the houses, re live what would have used to be, being part of this community. So we picked out a house at random and went in. We felt like strangers at first, but as we saw the pictures on the wall, the frames filled with their stories laid out through the whole house, on top of the mantles that cradled the tables, on the wear and tear of the pots hanging out from the kitchen's ceiling, on the bumps and tears decorating the sofa, on the little trinkets that described their craze and in every corner of their lives laid out randomly from wall to wall, we felt home.

There were three bedrooms in the house. The first one, to the right of the entrance, was the boys room. There were two bunk beds placed against opposite walls, with a chest in the middle. The beds were still tidy, as if someone would be sleeping in them that night. The second bedroom had two small beds in it and you could tell, right away, it was a girls room. The walls were painted in light pink and the beds had beautiful organza fabric bed covers on them. There were dolls and plush toys on top of them and a desk on the side of the room. That was Sarah's favourite, she went in and spent hours looking at everything in there. There were tons of photographs and memories laid all over the room.

Sarah sat on the desk and discovered some make up inside the drawers.

"I remember seeing these in magazines that I looked through in the library. I always wondered about them," she said as she picked through them.

"Well! Put some on," I said.

Sarah looked back at me with her eyes wide open and a smile on her face, a smile I've never seen before, one more I could add to the list. She looked so young, her face was lighted up, you could sense the excitement in her eyes. It was as if she was 10 years old again, playing with her Mom's make up.

"You think I could?" she asked me doubting.

"Of course! There is no one here but us."

She turned around and picked up something that looked like a pencil, from inside the drawer and outlined her eye lids, when she was done, she picked up a little box filled with colour squares and picked one of them, with a small brush she tinted her eye lids gently, as she looked at herself in the mirror.

I had never seen her like that, so concentrated in something, lost in herself. It was like looking at a rebirth of sorts, when you discover a completely new you, you uncover the possibilities that lay inside of you, the ones you never thought of before, the ones you didn't realise you had.

She played with them for hours, I stayed there watching her, feeding of her smile that kept sneaking out between her teeth, glowing every time she looked at something new on her, something the colours brought on her face. It was mesmerising, to see her so happy. After a while she turned to look at me with a huge smile on her face.

"Well? How do I look?"

I looked at her closely, she looked different, even her traits had changed a bit. There was colours that weren't there before, her cheeks had this tantalising redness on them, her eyes were bordered in blue that sparked the colour of her eyes, that seemed to light up from behind, as if her soul was gleaming through them, her lips were sticking out of her face, jumping at me, seducing me, they were rouged in passion, soft and sensual and her skin seemed perfectly toned, evenly delicate, porcelaneous like.

"You look beautiful!" I said astonished.

She smiled, happy to hear what I had to say about her new image, about her playfulness. She stood up and walked to where I was. I knew she intended to kiss me.

"Wait, I'm gonna ruin you make up. It looks so perfect."

She smiled, placed her arms around my neck and got so close I could breathe through her nose.

"That's what it is for, its meant to end up all over your face."

She kissed me with so much candour, I could feel excited in places I didn't knew I could. She pushed me back on the bed and climbed on top of me. I could taste the colours of the make-up mixing up with the taste I was so familiar with, with the one I was in love with, seasoning her beauty.

She stood up abruptly and pulled my hand, I got up to chase her into the master bedroom. She threw herself on the bed, I followed her. Our clothes flew and our bodies melted. The night was ours.

The next morning I woke up entangled in the sea of sheets that wrapped us both. Sarah was lying on my chest, with her arms around me. I could see her face resting on my bosom, covered with her hair, so I pulled back what I could from it, so I could watch her sleeping. I could see half of her face reflecting the tenuous light that sneaked in through the curtains. Her skin was still shimmering, reflecting the light in all those tiny specs of dust that she was covered in. The colours had faded and were running a bit around the edges, smudged against my whole body. Her lips were splattered with rouge colour, far beyond the lines that she had marked on them last night and all the black lines around her eyes were blurred beyond recognition, but she still looked beautiful underneath all that. It was her under there.

I sighted with a deep breath, that made her whole head raise and then fall back into place. She was still out, dreaming a pleasant dream. She looked peaceful and happy.

I looked around the room from my vantage point, I could see all the memories that still hanged on the walls, that were laid out all around us. Memories of what used to be the life they shared in this house. In that moment, all I could think about was our own. Our house and the things we gathered to entice our world, to make it our own. The little pieces that built our personality, our own unique taste.

This was theirs, we were in their own space, surrounded by what they put in here to make their lives their own. While I was thinking about all that, Sarah showed signs of life. She wasn't ready yet to wake up, but she sensed I was and murmured.

"Hey! What are you up to?"

Her eyes were still shut, but she could still see me wondering around the room with mine.

"Nothing, just looking around. It's interesting to see all the things they had. You learn a lot about people by the trinkets they hoard."

"Go back to sleep!" she said with a deep voice.

It just made me laugh.

"Hahaha, you can go back to sleep. I need to use the restroom," I said while I struggled to get up from the bed. I needed to get out from under her.

She moaned and complained about it, as I tried to move her head from my chest. So I grabbed a pillow and placed it under it.

"Here, use this instead."

She grabbed the pillow, with both her hands, turned the other way and went back to sleep.

I was finally able to get out of bed and went into the bathroom. I was stretching as I was relieving myself on the toilet. When I was finished, I stood there wondering if it would flush. I didn't think about it before, if there was water running to flush it out. So I tried and it did, I could hear the water filling the reservoir again and suddenly I got this urge, as I looked beside me. There was a shower in there. So, I walked a couple of paces and I opened it up, turned the knobs and water came out of the shower head. It was dirty and cold at the beginning, but water non the less, as it flowed more, it cleared up, inviting me, so I jumped in, to take a shower. The pressure was low, but it still brought me back to the waterfall and the feeling it gives you to sense all that water running down your body, hitting you in the head and the shoulders, massaging your tired muscles and that sense of peace it gives you.

I was lost in those thoughts when the door to the shower opened, I heard it, my eyes were closed, lost in that feeling I had. I felt Sarah embrace me from behind and turned my head around.

"I thought you might like some company!" she said.

I turned around and opened up my eyes, I saw this beautiful face staring at me, her eyes were partially opened, small droops of water were hitting them, there was still a lot of make up on them, covering all of her face, so I turned around looking for something she could use to wipe that off her face. There was a couple of bottles of soap on a shelf and handed her one. She squeezed it onto her hand and then scrubbed her face with the soap for a while, rinsed her face on the water and asked.

"Is it all off?"

I looked at her face, it was a work of art. Her skin glowed with the small droplets running down on it, cleansing her face, hydrating every single part of it, so I couldn't resist and I kissed her. I loved to feel her lips drenched as water ran down on them and into her mouth.

She kissed me back, but then she pushed me off, hard.

"Is it off?" she asked concerned.

I laughed at her reaction and looked at her face.

"Not quite, you need to scrub some more."

"Where? My eyes?"

"Yeah, all over really. Here use some more."

I took the soap bottle and squeezed it on her hand. She took the soap and scrubbed her face some more, then she rinsed it out with water and asked again.

"How about now?"

"Almost there, that black stuff, around your eyes, is still there."

"Ashhh, I'm never gonna put on make-up again!"

She said as she took the soap and tried it again. She squeezed it and handed it over to me. I took some of it and washed my hair while she scrubbed hard. I rinsed the sap off under the shower and when I opened up my eyes, she was still scrubbing her face.

It took her hands with mine and stopped them, I didn't wanted her to obsess about it, maybe even do some damage to her skin.

"That's enough!" I said.

She rinsed her face with water and turned to look at me.

"Is it all off?" she asked.

I looked at her, she looked desperate, I've never seen her like that.

"Yes, it's all good, it's all gone."

She smiled at me, relieved. And embraced me. I didn't understand what had taken over her at that moment, later I realised that she got scared when it wouldn't come off, thinking that maybe she would end up looking like that, like when she woke up and saw herself in the mirror.

"Here, I'll wash your hair."

I turned her around, grabbed the soap bottle, took a little soap and placed it on her hair. I gently massaged it and I could tell she calmed down. I massaged it for a while and then rinsed it under the flow of water that cleansed it.

"There! Much better."

She looked at me and smiled, I did too, I was glad that I could make her feel safe, that I could give her that peace that she lacked sometimes. I felt the same way about her. She had the exact same effect on me. I guess that is one of the most important things we crave from each other. That sense of belonging, the need to feel cared for, the urge to touch, to ground ourselves, to know that we are not alone, even if we were, but we had each other and that cancelled the feeling of loneliness we were destined to have.

"Thanks Baby, I don't know what I would do without you," she said as she cuddled in my arms.

"And I don't know what would I do without you."

We stood there for a while, under the drop of water that somehow washed our worries away. After a while, I pulled up my hand and looked at it. I could feel it wrinkling.

"Come on, let's get out of here!" I said while I turned off the water.

I opened up the door and stepped out of the shower, grabbed a towel and offered it to Sarah. Grabbed another one and placed it around her shoulders and then grabbed one for me and dried myself up with it.

We got dressed, made the bed and gather our things. Went down to the kitchen, filled our bellies with some canned food we found lying around and filled our canteens with water. When everything was left the way we found it, we set on our way. We said thank you to our hosts, watching us from somewhere, through their photographs, said our goodbyes and walked out of the house. It was almost noon and the sun was high above in the sky.

We walked down the path that lead us out of the village, that twined down the valley and up the mountains ahead. The sights were spectacular, the jungle was thick and green all over, shooting up at the sky, competing to reach out for some rays of sun. We saw some monkeys roaming the tree tops, curiously looking at us, wondering what we were and what were we doing there.

By nightfall we decided to make camp near a river we had been following downstream, hoping to find another settlement on its bank, but night caught us before we could reach anything other than a soft plateau surrounded by tall trees, right next to the river bed.

We set up our tent and started a fire, spent a while looking up at the stars in each other's arms. We were tired from walking, we had covered a few miles that day and our bodies quickly shut down embraced by the millions of lights that covered the void above. Sarah dozed out first, so I carried her in my arms and placed it inside our tent. I laid there beside her, looking at her face and the calm she was in, her face was glowing and even thought she was out, she was still smiling coveted by my eyes that couldn't stop staring.

After a few moments I was out too. We needed the rest.

Chapter 12
Crumbling Will

The next morning, I woke up to the light of the sun sneaking in, intermittent, through the air vents flapping in the wind, allowing a glimpse of what the day looked like outside.

Sarah was still sleeping, so I thought I might go outside and prepare some of that coffee she enjoyed so much. I sneaked out of the tent, as quietly as I could, trying my best not to wake her up. I started the fire again, grabbed some fresh water from the river and placed the coffee pot over the fire.

A cold breeze was blowing across the valley that morning, I could feel it in my bones that purposely shivered, sending a chill down my spine. I stood there wondering what it was, this premonition I had. I kept looking around, trying to spot something different in the atmosphere, something that might be out of place, but there was nothing odd around.

I thought it might just be my imagination, playing tricks on me. Struggling to make a common morning, something more interesting. So, I dismissed it and focused on getting that coffee ready for Sarah. I waited a few minutes, concentrated on the fire, the flames that danced with the wind, that slowly fed their thirst, making them rise up and heat up the bottom of the pot. After a few moments the whistling of the pot gave nuance, so I picked it up and poured the coffee into Sarah's mug.

Walked back inside the tent and sat next to her. She was still sleeping and I was hoping that the smell of the coffee, piping hot inside the mug, will wake her up as it did every morning. I even got the mug closer to her, in hopes that she would open her eyes after the smell would incite her senses, but it wasn't working.

She just stood there, in mobile.

"Sarah! Good morning honey!" I whispered sweetly in her ear as I kissed her cheek.

As I did, I sensed something was wrong. She felt hot, hot beyond the warmth the covers provided, so I placed my hand on her forehead and I felt her hair moist around her face. She was sweating profusely and her skin was burning up.

"Sarah! Sarah!" I called her name, hoping to wake her up, but there was no response.

"Sarah! Honey?"

I moved her a little, back and forth but she stood still.

My heart began racing and I felt like suffocating. I raised my arms above my head and placed my hands on my head, instinctively, while I looked at her laying there. I got close and picked her up and laid her on my legs. I got close to her face to feel her breathing, she looked so pale. She was breathing shallow, her lips had lost her colour and her whole face was dull, she was missing that glow that was always on it.

My mind was running scared, wondering, trying to find information about what was happening, while my whole body was entering a panic mode. I didn't know what to do, I couldn't understand what was going on. I just held her while I rocked back and forth, hoping that she would just wake up and everything would be fine.

I jacked off the blanket that covered her and pulled her up, closer to me, while I got invaded by this horrible thought of losing her. I was about to freak out when I saw it…

It crawled away as soon as I picked her up, it went directly towards the edge of the tent, trying to escape. My reaction was to try to stop it, it was responsible for whatever was happening to Sarah and I had to hold it responsible, I needed to know what it was and what had it done to her. So I put Sarah down gently and stood up, as quickly as I could, I jumped to where it was crawling to and try to stop it.

I fell down to the ground and almost caught it with my hand, but it managed to slip away through the crevices on the fabric. I saw it slip away, I stood up and rushed outside trying to catch it. I saw it as it crawled away from the tent and into the bushes outside.

It was a centipede, almost a foot long, thick and slimy. It had a red head and a long pointy tail that looked like a claw with two spiky fingers. I lashed into the bushes, sure that I will find it there and kill it, I guess, that was all I had on my mind, punish it for what it had done to Sarah. It was more of a survival instinct that anything else. I wasn't going to let this stand, it would have to pay, I needed to know what it had done to her. I pushed the brushes out of my way with my hands, hoping to spot it right away, but it wasn't there.

"It couldn't had gone far!" I thought.

I searched through the bushes, I looked all around, picked up a few rocks, but it was nowhere to be found.

I was desperately looking for it, frustrated, when I suddenly had a moment of clarity.

"Sarah!" I yelled.

I went back into the tent, she was still laying on the floor, she hadn't moved at all. I got close and picked her up. I felt her breathing, I tried to find her pulse and finally I did, very faint under her pale skin. Her heart was struggling to beat and her lungs hindering to find the air to fill them up. Her hair was almost all wet from the excessive sweating and her head was burning up.

"The river!" I thought.

I had to get her temperature down, I knew that much. So I picked her up and carried her to the river, I stepped inside and I slowly placed her in, holding her up, so her face wouldn't go under. Made sure her whole body was in the water, just her face was over the surface, so she could breathe.

She didn't move, or made any sound when she hit the cold water. She was in a trance of some sort, but her body struggled to breath and keep her functions going. I held on like that for a while, as I stared at her face.

I was frustrated trying to find something in my mind, something I might have read, or seen somewhere, maybe a glance of a medical journal, or a story in a book that could give me some sort of guide as to what to do next. How to get her off this curse, how to heal her and get her to wake up.

I placed my cheek on her forehead, to feel her temperature, it had gone down. I couldn't feel that burning sensation she had before. I took her out of the river and placed her inside the tent. I looked around the floor, just to make sure there were no more of those things that bit her.

I took her wet clothes off and while I was doing that, I was also looking for the spot where she was bitten. I needed to see what had happened to her. I finally found it, on the back of her right calf. They were two punctures, small incisions side by side. They had dark red circles around them and the circles were protruding a bit, but I could see blood in the middle. I didn't wanted to touch them at first. I wouldn't want to cause her more pain than the one she was in, but I thought that I might be able to suck out the venom or whatever that creature left inside of them.

The problem is that I had no idea of how long she had been like this, how long it had been since she got bitten. I knew it had been a while, maybe it was during the night, when she was asleep, or maybe when I left the tent to make coffee. I felt responsible for it happening, for not being alert and avoiding it all together.

I was thinking the worst, but I knew I couldn't let myself go down that path. It wouldn't help her at all, if I was to save her from this. So, I did all I could do, at that point. I placed my lips on her leg, just over the bite and I tried sucking something out of them, but they were to small and nothing came out. So I took out a knife and cut them open a little bit, I didn't wanted to hurt her. I saw blood coming out of them and so I sucked some more. This time I could feel her blood coming out from them. I sucked as much as I could and spit it out, then sucked some more and repeated that several times.

I had some antibacterial gel in my pouch, I put some on top of the wounds and covered them up. I felt her forehead hoping that she was not getting hotter again, but outside the water she felt hot to my touch again, so I took a pot and went for some water. I don't remember what the day was like, I couldn't concentrate on anything else but her, I don't know if the sun was shining up above, or if it was raining, if it was day or night. I just went into the river, got some water and came back into the tent. Took a small rag, plunged it into the water, squeezed the excess and placed it on her forehead. I fixed the pillow under her head with my other hand while I held the rag on her forehead. I looked at her laying there, I just couldn't believe what was happening.

I wanted her to feel comfortable, I pulled a blanket over her and then thought that would make her hot, so I pulled it off, I placed her hands over her and just roamed her with my eyes. I didn't know what else to do. I felt so helpless, so useless. I just wished we were back at home, I knew that was what she would have wanted, to be in her own bed, in her own home.

I began to think of all the possibilities, on how would I be able to bring her home. We were at least 25 miles or more from there. I began to go over every place that we had been through in the past few days, the path we took and how long would it take me to get her back home. What if the trip would make her worst? What if she would wake up in the middle of the trip? Maybe it would be best to stay put until she woke up, but what if she didn't? What if there was something I could do back home?

There were a lot of things to consider and no one to weight on it, it was only me. I needed to make a decision for her well-being, to save her life.

I was thinking of all the scenarios of what could happen. while I was concentrated on changing the rag on her forehead to keep the temperature down. That was my main concern.

After a while, her temperature stabilised and I could feel her body ease. Her eyes were still closed and her breathing had also flatten, it was steady, slow but steady. She had stopped sweating profusely. I tried to wake her up, but she was non responsive. Her pulse was also steady and within range, it was on the low side of 70 per minute, but she was hanging on.

So, I calmed down for a moment, sat down and began structuring my plan to get her home. It wouldn't be easy, we were about thirty miles from home, according to my calculations and the information on my GPS.

I would have to build a stretcher or find a way to carry her all the way home. She was light but I wasn't as strong to believe I could carry her all the way. So the idea of a stretcher that I could pull made more sense.

So I gathered all the wood I could find and began building the stretcher. It took me a few hours, but I was certain it would do the job once I'd finished it.

I set up my rout on the GPS, carefully placed Sarah in the stretcher, picked up the rest of our stuff and began the journey back home. I wanted to be certain that she was as comfortable as possible. She was the most important part of my life and I concentrated on the task ahead. Getting her safely home. I wasn't thinking of the rest, I couldn't do that. I knew that if I did, I would plunge in desperation because I had no idea what to do to make her better and no hope of curing her.

It was morning when we started and by the evening we had walked a third of the way. I couldn't stop, I didn't wanted to, I didn't wanted to rest. The adrenaline in my body kept me going but by eight o'clock it was pitch black and I couldn't see the way. I had to stop. I put up the tent and placed Sarah inside. I made sure that she was breathing steady and that her pulse was hanging on. She was still sweating but nothing compared to what I had seen before. I kept moistening her lips with water. That's all I could do for her, that and hope that she would wake up, that she would be ok.

I kept pacing around the campfire I had built, thinking of all the possibilities, of how I would get home faster. I would have to begin at the break of dawn, as soon as the first light guided my way. There would be no rest for me until we got home and I was sure she was safe. So I paced and I paced, until I saw the first light sneak from behind the mountains. As soon as I could see beyond the darkness, I placed Sarah back in her stretcher, gathered our stuff and began walking.

I knew I had to speed up the pace and double my efforts from the day before, if I wanted to get home that day. So, I began to choose a little rougher paths, in hope that they would be in a straighter line and that would save me time. In all this passing I didn't hear her moan or complain about any of it. It was as though she was in a deep sleep, nothing would disturb her slumber. I stopped, for a few seconds at a time, to moisten her lips and check on her vitals. They were steady and, somehow, she looked content, in peace.

There was no expression on her face, but her tone was pale. I couldn't stop thinking about it, I tried to think about something else. About our path and where should I go from there, about the things that we had lived, all the memories that filled my head, happy memories with her, the love we shared and every little detail of her face, the warmth of her body and the immense joy her smile sparked on me. I had to keep the bad thoughts away, at any cost. I couldn't falter on my mission to get her home safe.

I made good strides by the end of the second day, we were just a few miles away from home. I could recognise a lot of the markers that I'd seen so many times before. My heart was pumping faster, knowing that I would be home soon, that I would get her home and somehow, everything would be fine.

I couldn't feel my feet and my legs were numb but my pace would not falter. I was running on will, the muscles had stopped working a while ago, but I could see the finish line, it was in our grasp and I couldn't stop now. The light was fading and the whole scene got splashed with red and gold tones that died in the arms of the blackness that surrounded us. It was pitch black again, but my GPS kept pushing me forward. Counting down the distance that separated us from our home, from that sense of security we needed, from the hope that she would be alright once we were there.

So, I just kept going, through the darkness. Guided only by the love I felt exploding in my chest, the love that gave me strength and the power to surpass this.

We were thrown by the darkness into a patch of thick brush that made it harder to go through, I had to push with everything I had left to open up a path and walk through it, but as soon as we were on the other side I saw our goal, on the other side of the plain that held our ground, there it was, our home.

I shouted excited, hoping that she would hear me and wake up.

"Look! Sarah! We are home! We are home!"

I turned to look at her as I kept on moving forward, but she was still asleep.

"Sarah! Sarah! Look, we're home!"

I turned around and faced our destination, a few moments after, we were home. I put the stretcher down and, without resting, I took her out of it, carry her inside and placed her on her bed. Tears were running down my face, I had fulfilled my promise and gotten her home. Now, I expected her to fulfil hers and wake up.

I moistened her lips again, checked her pulse and her breathing. She was stable, but her eyes wouldn't open. I kissed her, but she didn't kiss me back.

I began to feel reality kicking in, my legs faltered and I felt to the ground, right beside our bed, next to her and I passed out.

I was in total darkness, there was no sound, I was alone and it felt cold. I remember trying to concentrate on my thoughts. I was trying to think of Sarah, but I couldn't see an image of her. My eyes were wide open but I wasn't able to see. I thought it was the end, that I had died and this void, was the place where you ended up after you passed. It would be ironic, all those souls searching for heaven, for something beyond their lives, the misery they wanted to run from and you end up here, in the void, with nothing to show up for.

Maybe this is peace, the absence of everything. We accumulate experiences throughout our lives, good and bad and the memories, the scars that they leave on us, linger on. Maybe, at the end, you are detached from all that, from the baggage we all carry, from the things we accumulate and that, that is peaceful. To go back to a clean slate.

I accepted that as my destiny and with acceptance came peace, I didn't feel anything, I was just…numb!

Every speck of my being accepted that, except my heart. It kept on beating, pounding stronger as time went by, it wouldn't falter, it wouldn't give up, there was still life left on it, there was still something that pushed it to beat. I could feel it bumping in my chest, pumping blood through my veins, feeding my brain and every inch of my body.

It surged slowly, a tenuous light motivated by the heartbeats, it flickered as it resonated in the void. A faint sound that began to rise as the light got brighter and brighter with each pump, with each beat of my heart, and within the light images began to reveal. Like flashes that surrounded me, stronger, brighter as they materialise in front of me, and all around. Her face taking centre stage, glowing like a star, her smile breaking the darkness I was in, overtaking everything, imposing its will on me. She was calling me from somewhere else, tempting me to reach out for her, pushing me to break out from this dream I was in. I felt the warmth of her touch and my heart burst out of my chest, discharging life into every corner of my being.

My eyes opened, literally, and light invaded them, flooded my brain and filled my lungs with her scent. I sat up, extended my hand to grab the bed next to me and turned my head to see her. She was laying there, on top of the bed, she was still sleeping but I could see her chest moving, breathing. I pulled myself closer to her and caressed her head with my hand and kissed her cheek.

It was almost dark outside, which meant I had been out for a while. I was still tired but glad that we were home, that I had endured enough to get her here.

I stood up slowly, my legs were reluctant to function, they were in pain, I could feel them pulsating, but I insisted, I had to take care of Sarah. I got some water and moistened her lips and cleaned her face with the wet rag. Felt her heart beating steady and her breathing shallow.

I fell down to the ground, releasing the weight of my legs and sat down next to the bed. I had to let them rest some more. I tried massaging them with my hands, but even the lightest touch sent them off screaming in pain. So, I just let them be.

I didn't wanted to go back to sleep, go back to that void I was in, I didn't wanted to forget Sarah, forget all the things I cared about. So I kept my mind busy, thinking about the ways I could bring her back, the reason why she was unresponsive and the damage that creature could have done to her.

I knew it wasn't fatal, she would have died then and there, but I was worried it could be permanent, that she would never wake up. Her vitals were steady, which meant that her body wasn't fighting it anymore, whatever that creature poured into her was not making her worse. So, why wasn't she waking up?

There was not much I could do, I would have to find all the information I could, find out what kind of creature was the one that bit her and know its nature, the damage it had inflict on Sarah. Maybe a treatment for it, something I could do to make her better, to have her wake up.

I spent hours going around and around in my head. Looking at the archives we had in the vehicle's computer. Looking for something that looked like the creature I saw that day, but I couldn't find anything similar.

Medically she looked fine, the assessment form the computer was that her physical state was good, her heartbeat was steady at a normal pace, her blood pressure was normal and her breathing was constant and strong but she wasn't waking up and nothing this machine would tell me could explain it.

So, all I could do was sit beside her, try to keep her comfortable, keep her hydrated as best as I could and wait. So I sat next to her and looked at her face and dream of all the moments we've had together. I actually began to talk to her, or at her, better to say, because I was doing all the talking. I would tell her about things we lived through, times we've shared and she would just listened, or I hoped she did.

When the night fell and covered everything with calm, I would dread the thought of going to sleep, taking my eyes off her, fearing something wrong could happen if I took my attention away from her.

"What if she wakes up and needs something and I'm asleep?" I thought.

I couldn't allow my eyes to close, but my body was still recuperating from the effort I put in while getting home. My legs were still pulsating, I could feel them tremble sometimes and my whole body needed rest. After a while of fighting with it, my eyes just wouldn't submit to my will and I faded away.

I woke up scared, panicking, after I realised I had fallen asleep, sitting right next to Sarah. So I startled myself as I woke up and looked at Sarah, her eyes were still closed. I got close to feel her breath and placed my fingers on her neck to feel her pulse, everything seemed normal. So I kissed her gently in the mouth and said softly.

"Good morning my love! I hope you slept well during the night. I've been right here, next to you, in case you needed anything."

I placed my cheek against her, just to feel her warmth for a moment, feel her skin caressing mine. I took her hand and raised it up against my face. I missed her so much!

It had been two days since we got back and there was still no signs of her regaining her sense, but at least, there hadn't been any issues with her vitals, she was steady. I kept changing her gauss, several times a day and I didn't see any sing of infection on the wound. It was beginning to heal.

I tried to avoid going into this dark places with my thoughts, it was just natural to think about the worst case scenarios, of what would I do if she never woke up, but I couldn't stand the thought of it. Every time they began to creep up on me, I just shut them down. I began to remember things that we shared. I focused on the good, mostly her laugh and the way it always filled my soul, it was a catalyst of joy. The sweetest sound that tickled my ears, I longed to hear it again.

I spent the day and night by her side, re-living every single moment we had together, that was the only way I could get through this without going crazy. I would pace back and forth inside our bedroom, going around the bed, it helped me concentrate on what I needed to do to stay positive.

Think about her and every single thing I loved about her. That was what kept me sane.

I tried to stay awake as long as I could, but my body was tired and the night took over, my eyes closed again and I fell asleep.

Even my dreams were about her, there was nothing else in my mind and no room for anything else. She was all I cared for.

I remember seeing her face looking at me, smiling, with one of those million smiles she had. Feeling her love embrace me, I was in a safe place with her. It felt so real that when I finally opened my eyes and actually saw her looking at me from the bed, I thought I was still sleeping.

She was laying on her side, resting her head against her arm, watching me sleep on the couch. I slowly opened up my eyes and saw her there. I could feel her eyes roaming every part of my being, I could feel the love that she had for me, reflected on the one I had for her and that made my heart beat, my whole body respond to her warmth, even without touching.

"Good morning sleepyhead!" she said almost whispering.

I smiled and looked at her, it was so real.

"Wow! You look so beautiful, I missed you so much! Am I still dreaming?"

"No dummy! Come on, help me get up. I'm starving!" she said as she was trying to get up from the bed.

I couldn't believe it! She was actually awake and I was too?

"Are you…am I awake?"

"Of course you are!" she said while she frowned.

I stood up quickly and helped her to sit down on the bed. I couldn't help it and I embraced her tightly, felt her body next to mine, smelled her neck that intoxicated my senses. She was awake, she was ok.

"Thank you, thank you!" I said, over and over again.

"Wow! Why am I so weak?" she asked me while I crumbled in her arms.

I couldn't contain the feelings that took over, all that tension, all the worry that kept me at bay for hours on end, the endless bad thoughts I ignored, the terrible pressure on my chest just vanished and out came this rush of emotions. I couldn't stop crying, my eyes just flooded with tears of joy.

"What's wrong? It's ok!" Sarah said, while she tightened her embrace as hard as she could.

She lift up her hand and caressed my head.

"It's ok! Was it a bad dream?" she asked.

I couldn't hold it, a loud laugh just broke out, it filtered through the wailing that wouldn't stop.

"Ha-ha. It was, but I'm glad it's over," I said.

I lifted up my head to look at her face. I grabbed it with my hand and spread my fingers down her cheek, feeling her lightness. She looked straight at my eyes and wiped my tears with hers.

We looked at each other for a few moments and I kissed her, and I felt how she kissed me back. I missed her so much, I dreaded the thought of losing her and now I could put it away.

She pulled back and looked at my face, she knew there was something more in my mind than just a simple nightmare.

"What is it? You are scaring me."

"I'm sorry, I'm just so glad to see you. For a moment there, I thought you wouldn't wake up."

She thought about it and looked around us.

"Last thing I remember, we were together in our tent, I fell asleep and then I woke up here. What happened?"

I smiled and stared at her, I was so glad she was out of it, whatever it was.

"Come, let me make you something to eat and I'll tell you about it."

I stood up and helped her to get up from the bed, Her legs were numb and I had to pull her up and help her stand, she felt a little druggie, she was week from a few days of fasting.

"Wow! It's like I've been asleep for days!"

I just laughed, she had no idea of what she had been through.

It took a moment but she got on her feet, I helped her walk to the kitchen and sat her on a chair at the table.

I squeezed some oranges and served her the juice and sat it in front of her. She took it right away and was about to seep it.

"Slow, take little sips, just take it slow."

So, she did.

"It feels strange, this is orange juice, right?"

"Yes, it is. You were just…well, you were asleep for a while."

Sarah turned to look at me baffled.

"What do you mean, a while?"

"Maybe it's a good thing that you don't remember, after you went to sleep in the tent, something bit you and you were sick for a while."

"Something bit me? Where?"

"On your calf!"

She extended her hand and reached out to try and touch it. She felt the gauss I had placed over the injury right away.

"Auch! What was it?" she asked as she felt the wound.

"I wish I knew, I saw it crawl from under you, it left the tent and I tried to catch it, but it crawled away and I couldn't find it."

"What did it look like? Was it a bug?"

"It looked like a centipede of some sort, it was big though, at least a foot long and it had this…prod!"

"What? It stung me with that?"

"I don't know if it did sting you or bit you, but you have the mark there. I was worried sick, you wouldn't wake up and you had a fever, chills and you were sweating a lot."

Sarah was beside herself, she couldn't believe that all that had happened to her and she had no idea, she couldn't remember a thing.

"How did you bring me here? We were far away."

"I built a stretcher and I pulled you home."

She looked at me amazed and concerned about what had happened. She extended her hand to me and I grabbed it. She pulled me close and had me sat next to her.

"Is that why I feel so weak?"

"Yes, you were out for a few days."

229

She looked at me, I could tell she felt mortified.

"I can't even imagine what you went through, I'm so sorry!"

"Don't be, it wasn't your fault. I was just worried sick not knowing what to do to make you better. I had no idea of what would happen then, all I knew is that I had to get you home."

She lift up her hand and caressed my face.

"What would I do without you?" she said.

"I asked myself the exact same thing a thousand times this past few days, but how are you feeling, besides being weak, does anything hurt?"

Sarah thought about it for a moment as she tried to move a little. She could barely lift up her legs and her arms, even talking was a daunting task.

"My back hursts a little and I seem to have no strength at all, but besides that, I feel ok."

"Your back probably hurts because you were laying on it for so long, it's still healing and the heaviness is the lack of food and your body still recuperating, eliminating whatever that "thing" put in you. But it's obvious, your winning that battle!"

Sarah smiled and took another sip of the juice.

"I'm so lucky to have you watching over me."

I smiled and stood up, walked to the stove and grabbed a pot.

"I will make you some soup, that will make you feel a lot better."

Sarah closed her eyes for a moment, she was still tired and weak, she needed to rest a lot to be able to go back to normal, but first she needed to eat something.

"I know you want to go back to sleep, but you need to eat first. Hold on, it will just be a few minutes. I'm making your favourite."

She opened her eyes and smiled as she looked at me.

"I'm starving!" she said as she moved her head around, trying to shake the stagger that stood over her.

After a few minutes, I picked up a plate and served her the soup. I placed it in front of her. She tried to grab the spoon next to her, but she even had trouble closing her hand and lifting it up, so I grabbed the spoon and feed her some soup.

"Here, I'll do it."

I picked up a bit of soup and blew on it.

"Careful, it's hot!"

I pulled up the spoon, she opened up her mouth and I poured it in. She savoured it for a moment before she passed it.

"It's not too hot?"

"No, it's delicious, just right."

So, I took some more, blew on it and placed it in her mouth. She slowly ate it, but I could tell it was making her feel better already. The warmth of the soup and its contents were making her whole body come alive. It was as if I was caressing her insights, comforting her with my care. I was happy and glad to see her eat.

I sat there and fed her the whole bowl and even served some more. After she was finished, I helped her up and laid her back on the bed. I made sure she was comfortable, I checked the bandage on her leg and sat in front of her.

She looked at me with a big smile on her face.

"I don't want to go to sleep, I want to be with you."

"I know, I don't want you to go to sleep either. I'm afraid," I said while my voice trembled a little.

She extended her hand and I grabbed it.

"I won't leave you alone, I promise!"

Her eyes were closing, she was very tired. She needed the rest, so slowly she went back to sleep. I wanted to stop her, I was dreading the thought of her not coming back, not waking up, like before, but I couldn't hold her back.

I just stood up and pulled a blanket over her, covered her up, got close and kissed her on her cheek and on her forehead as I caressed her hair and I sat back on the couch in front of her.

I sat there for as long as I could, just looking at her, making sure she was breathing, watching over her sleep until clam took over and I dozed off as well.

Chapter 13
The Poignant Refrain

I slowly opened up my eyes, I was surprised by the fact that I was lying in bed, next to Sarah. I couldn't remember when I switched from the couch to the bed. I must have been so tired, I didn't even register that. I could feel her body next to mine. I turned to face her, she was laying on her back, her eyes were still closed and her chest was moving softly up and down, which made me ease.

I still had this unrest, this part of me that dreaded to see her sleeping, wondering if she would wake up, so I just watched her sleep. She looked so beautiful, her face glowing with the subtle light that sneaked into the bedroom. That glimpse of heaven I could see reflected on her skin.

I don't know how long I stood there, just watching her dreaming, wondering what would be inside her head. After a while, she began twitching, moving slowly, changing positions until she turned and laid on her side, looking straight at me. Our faces were so close I could inhale her breathing, I could taste the gale in her mouth, that enticed me. I could see her eyes roaming under her eyelids, looking for something in there until finally they opened and saw me looking at her. She smiled.

"Good morning! What are you doing?"

"Just admiring you!"

"Creep!" she said, which sprung a giggle on me.

"Yeah! I'm creepy, I've been watching you for a while."

She smiled while she looked back at me.

"I was afraid that you wouldn't wake up."

She lift up her hand and caressed my face softly with it. She switched her wonderful smile for a serious look.

"I'm ok, I will never leave you!"

She got closer and kissed me. It tasted like heaven.

"How do you feel?"

"I feel a lot better, I don't feel as weak as I did. That soup was really good."

"It was a love infusion!"

She smiled again, I was proud of the fact that I could make her smile still, after all this time.

"Is there more?" she asked.

"Oh, there's a lot more where that came from."

"I would love to see that!" she said as she pulled me close and kissed me again.

I was just so happy that all of that had passed and that she was back to normal. I just wished that whatever was left inside of her, wouldn't come back again and hunt her in the future. That she had gotten over it and there was no aftermath. I wanted her to be healthy and happy.

"I can make you some more."

"I would love that. Thank you!"

"Do you want to sit outside on the porch? Breath some fresh air, see the sun go up, while I cook your soup?" I asked.

"Yes, that sounds lovely."

I got up, rushed to the other side of the bed to help her out. She turned and placed her feet down on the ground, grabbed my hand and pulled herself up as I helped her stand. She stood there for a minute, holding her balance. She looked at me and smiled, nodding, so I helped her to walk out the bedroom, through the living room and out to the porch. I sat her down on the couch outside and lifted her feet up and placed a footstool under them.

"Comfortable?"

"Yes Baby, very. This is beautiful!" she said as she looked at the scene in front of our house.

The sun was coming up on the horizon, the waterfall was right in front and everything around us was coming to life. The chirping of the birds in the trees all around and the sound of the water crashing down on the rocks below completed the scene.

"It will be ready in just a moment!" I said.

Sarah smiled at me and nodded.

I went back inside and fixed her some soup. This time I put a little bit of spice in there, just to tingle her senses. I brought it outside when I was done. I placed it in a table just beside the couch, she sat up and dug right in.

"This is delicious! What did you put in it?"

"A little spice, thought you might like it this way."

"I love it! Thank you Baby!"

I watched her eat, it was always a treat. She was gentle but determined, she enjoyed it so much, it was contagious. So, I went in and served myself a bowl of soup and brought it outside. We shared the dawn and each other's company…and a bowl of soup.

A few days passed and she got her strength back, she was full of life again, as she always was. What happened, became just a fleeting memory and we put that whole incident behind us. Little by little my sudden bursts of anguish that woke me up in the middle of the night, worried about her not waking up, passed and I could rest next to her.

Everything was back to normal, our normal, waking up in each other's arms, making love in the morning as the sun snuck in through the curtains and I got possessed by her scent, her closeness, then off to the waterfall, get soaked in its wonderful bliss and swim naked in the lake chasing each other down.

It was our piece of heaven, our own little hideaway.

Every day, when we sat down to watch the sunset, I wonder about humanity, about the destiny that faith had bestowed upon it. We had not seen a human for years now, no transmissions of any kind. Our only contact with the outside world was our vehicle, the batteries were supposed to last for ever, but it was still, rotting away and it was harder for the computer to launch each time I turned it on.

We were distanced from technology, we didn't need it to go about our days, there was no contact with anyone, so it lost meaning and purpose. It became useless and dull. I just kept it going, anytime I could, so it wouldn't die, there was always a glimpse of hope, a chance that we were not alone in this world. That some humans had survived, like us, hiding away from the threat of annihilation, like we had, but as time went by it became less and less viable.

A few times a week I used to go out and hunt for food, I had gotten pretty good with the bow and arrow and even made my own from scratch, following schematics I found on the archives. I had several traps set up all over, hoping to get whatever became curious enough to step in one. We had some farm animals that also supplied us with food.

Sarah was always waiting for me to come back and bring something she could cook, she was amazing at it, she could cook anything and made it taste heavenly. We had our own orchard where we cultivated all kinds of spices and vegetables, we gathered berries and roots in the forest and had even set up our fish farm in the pond.

We managed to sustain ourselves and made our lives as rich as we could. We missed Gloria every day, we prayed before every meal, like she taught us to do, we needed to give thanks for the life we had, for surviving, to whomever was in charge.

"Thank you for what we are about to receive. For the bounty we have, the peace that surrounds us and for the love we share. We are grateful for one more sunrise, for one more dawn, for the moon and the starts and the joy of life that we share in your grace. Amen."

We refrain from going in another journey, after what we went through it didn't sound appealing, but we still wondered on what could be out there. We talked about the places that we've seen and the experiences we had, the marvel and beauty of it all, but somehow we never talked about what happened to her, it wasn't a memory that we wanted to keep alive.

We had everything we could want in each other, we kept ourselves busy every day and most of all we enjoyed each other's company.

Life was good, we ate, when we were hungry, we made love, whenever we felt like it, we bathe in the lake, under the waterfall, whenever we craved and still we had time left to enjoy the marvel of nature that bloomed all over us.

I use to go out and check on my traps, from time to time, hunt for something we could eat while Sarah was doing her own thing in the house. That day, in particular, I was eager to go out and make my runs, check on my traps and maybe shoot some arrows and bring home something good that Sarah could prepare.

"I'm going out Babe! I need to check on my traps and see what I can get for dinner," I said to her.

She looked at me, but somehow she seemed sad to me, the way she looked at me said more than words.

"What? What's wrong?" I asked.

"Nothing! I was just looking at you," she said.

"But you seem sad!" I said.

"No, not at all. I was just remembering, when we were young. When we first met and I used to look at you when you weren't noticing."

"You use to do that?" I asked.

"Yeah! Of course. I had a lot of questions about you. I use to ask Gloria and she would tell me stories about you two. She would tell me a lot about you, she really cared."

"I use to ask her about you too."

"I guess she always wanted us to be together," she said while she smiled.

I nodded and smiled back, thoughts of Gloria invaded my mind. I missed her a lot!

"I'll be back soon!" I said while I gathered my things.

I got close to Sarah and I kissed her. She placed her hand on my cheek and pulled me back and she kissed me properly. Then she looked into my eyes.

"Have a great day, don't come back to late!"

"I won't, I'll see you soon. I love you!"

"And I love you!"

I smiled, she was my world. I was so grateful to have her by my side.

I walked out the door and headed into the woods, I was hoping to get that special something to bring back home. I got to the first trap after a few minutes. It was empty, I checked on the trap, to make sure it was working and kept on my journey. The second trap I had set up was empty too, but I could tell it had been triggered. I couldn't figure how, but it seemed as though they had figured out a way to do that without getting caught in it. I thought I could be dealing with a very intelligent creature or a very lucky one.

I reset the trap and covered it with some loose leaves, this time I wanted to make sure it was hidden. I had to outsmart them, that was the only way.

I walked away, enough so they wouldn't spot me and I took a vantage point from where I could see the trap. I thought maybe they were around. I knew they had to have studied the trap in order to beat it, so I wanted to see if they were some locals. I was curious of what it was that had become so smart.

It was a beautiful day, the sky was light blue, no clouds in it. I lay down on the grass and looked up at the sky for a moment. I could see the tree tops swaying with the breeze, the wind moving them briskly on the tops and the leaves whistling as they did. It was so peaceful.

That's when I sensed it. It was watching me, stalking me from a far. Hiding in the woods, between the foliage, using it to camouflage itself, but I was able to see it from where I was. The eyes gave it away. They were like two flashlights shining out.

It was a jaguar, the largest one I've had ever seen. It was a hunter, just like I was, but in this case I had become the prey. I was sure it had been following me for a while, but this was its territory. It was the one who had triggered the trap and figure out how it ticked. I knew they were extremely intelligent animals and after the war they had probably evolved even more.

My adrenaline levels kept me focused, I had to protect myself and outsmart it. I only had my bow and arrow to defend myself with and my boning knife, in case it came to that. I knew I needed to get up high, somewhere it couldn't reach me or at least be able to have the advantage, see it when it got near.

So I looked around for a tree I could climb, that was strong enough to hold me and keep me safe. The best option I could see, was like fifty feet away and I made a run for it. I knew that it will be watching me, waiting for the perfect moment to attack, when I was the most vulnerable.

As soon as I began running towards the tree, I could hear it running behind me. There was a short field in front of where the tree was, an open space where I would be exposed and easy to grab, so I ran as fast as I could. I could feel it running after me, but I couldn't look back, it would slow me down, so I ran until I reached the tree and began climbing it right away. At first I was jumping from one branch to the other, but as I got higher it became harder. The branches became smaller and more twirled. It was just behind me and I could see it climbing too. Jumping from one branch to the other, right on my back.

I stood on a big branch, twenty feet above the ground and I turned back to see where it was, right when it jumped towards me, while I heard a loud roar speeding my way. I was able to lift my leg and throw a kick and hit it right in the face while it was flying towards me. I took it by surprise and it fell down the tree, but not before one of its paws swung towards my leg and scrape my calf as it went down.

I fell down on the branch and was able to embrace it and stay put. The jaguar fell down all the way to the ground with a loud bang as it hit it. It took a moment for it to get back up and growl at me from under the tree. I could tell it was hurt because it didn't try to get back up right away. It just paced around the bottom of the tree looking at me, growling!

After a few seconds my mind got the information from my leg and the pain took over my head. I sat on the branch and looked at my calf. There was blood dripping from it. I gently pulled up my pant leg, but the pain was too much, I stopped half way and I was able to see three large gashes on my calf. I could see them underneath my pants, that were torn off too, there was blood soaking them and I could barely move me leg without a pulsating pain raking up. So I, very slowly, lifted up my leg on the branch and laid myself back against the trunk, so I could rest for a moment and get my heart rate back down.

I could see the blood dripping from my wound. I knew I would have to, at least, stop the bleeding, but I was frozen for the moment. I needed to calm myself down and think this over.

I could see it pacing down around the tree, looking up at me, it knew I was hurt, just waiting for the right moment, figuring out how to get up here and take its prize. It could smell the blood pouring out of my leg and could almost taste me. It's tongue kept moistening its mouth, savouring the kill.

For the first time in my life I felt afraid for my life. I had been afraid before, afraid of losing Sarah when she was sick, afraid in my dreams, I had been aware of the danger before, but this was so real and so close that it triggered and entirely new self-defence mechanism. For the first time, my life was in danger and I needed to figure out how to get out of it alive.

First I thought that it would get tired, or bored, or simply give up and leave, but it was determined to get what it had come for. It had all the time in the world and it would wait until I gave up.

I had to stop the bleeding first, I was beginning to feel light headed, sign that I had lost a lot of blood already. So I ripped a piece of fabric from my pants, from where it was already torn, which hurt like hell. Even it looked up at me and paused when I screamed. I tied it around my leg, just under my knee and I tighten it as hard as I could while I screamed again from the pain. All this while balancing myself on the branch, careful not to fall.

I placed my leg on top of another branch just above the one I was sitting on, so that my leg would be up and the blood would run towards my body, instead of out of it. I rested my head against the tree trunk and I took a breath. I wanted so bad to close my eyes, but I knew that if I closed them, I could lose my balance and fall from the tree, hit the ground and I would be an easy pray for it...wait a minute!

Suddenly I had this idea in my head. I looked down at it, still pacing around the tree. It wasn't concentrated on looking up anymore, it was just waiting for something to happen, but what if I could fall on it. I didn't have any weapons that I could defend myself with, no way of getting a message to Sarah, and even then I would just put her in danger with this jaguar pacing about, but I could catch him distracted and fall on it. The hit could put it out, hurt it somehow. It was my only hope. The drop might also hurt me, but it was a chance I would have to take if I wanted to get out alive.

I would need to wait a bit, until it was tired or bored of pacing around and got distracted enough for me to throw myself at it. So, I waited, I was watching it, while it was watching me. I kept struggling with staying focused, staying awake.

My leg had stopped dripping blood but the pain was not subsiding. It was constant and poignant. It took a while for it to stop pacing and come to a stop a few feet from under me. I could tell that it was also plotting something. It kept looking around, growling, thinking of ways to reach me.

I kept struggling with my eyes that wanted to close, my eyelids felt so heavy, I could barely keep them open, but I knew that I had to. I couldn't just close them and rest, I wasn't sure If I would wake up afterwards. I needed to stay focused on the task at hand, I needed to get back home to Sarah. I kept thinking that she would be mortified when she saw me, that was my biggest fear. Not that I would probably get eaten by a jaguar, or that I could pass away and bleed out, fall from the tree and get mauled; it actually was: what would Sarah feel when she saw me? The grief I would cause her and the terrible anguish she would feel. That was my biggest fear!

I kept staring down at it, it was just standing there, breathing, waiting.

While I was up there, my mind began wondering, so I needed something to distract me with, something to focus on besides the problem at hand. So, I went to that happy place I always went to when I needed comfort, recapping every single happy memory I had lived through.

Most of them included Sarah and some of them Gloria, the two most important people in my life. Those memories had kept me alive many times before, kept me focused on my journey and now I called up on them to keep me safe and awake. I wanted, so bad, to get through this and see Sarah again.

It kept looking up at me, wondering what was I thinking, what would be my next move. I could see its tongue roaming around its mouth, savouring the feast to come. I could tell, patience, was one of its virtues and it was obvious that this will be a long duel.

I would have to stay put for a long time and my wound could start to get infected If I didn't treat it properly, I needed to clean it and make sure it wasn't infected already, but every time I tried to move my leg and look at it closely, I began to wobble on the tree branch and felt I could lose my balance. So I stayed put, trying to keep still.

I tried to concentrate on the very limited options I had, to get out of this, but the pain from my wound began to creep up my leg and it was unbearable, I couldn't dismiss it anymore. The bleeding had stopped with the tourniquet I had applied, but the blood was coagulating and making everything around it very sticky. I needed to clean it soon.

After a few hours and several scares, after almost dozing off and falling down, I finally saw the cat loosen up a little. It wasn't going away, but at least it was settling and it laid down under the tree. I could see it licking its paws, maybe savouring the little amount of my blood that was wedged inside its claws, or maybe just cleaning them up before dinner.

Right then, I began to plot. What it I would let myself go, silently, just drop down form the branch and land on top of it? It was laying right under me, I would have to calculate my fall precisely, so that I would land on it. That would surely do some damage, but It could also mess me up real bad.

If I landed on top of it, like I planned, its body would ease the fall and absorb most of the blow, but If I missed, by only a few inches, I would give myself up entirely. I might as well just serve myself in a platter.

I didn't see any other way, there was no help coming and I was running out of options. It wasn't going away anytime soon and I began to think that maybe it was waiting for some help itself. What if more of them showed up?

I needed to act soon and this seemed like the time to do so. I needed it to go to sleep or something that would distract it for a moment. Just enough to get its attention away from me, to give me a brief window to act.

I kept looking down at it, trying to measure the distance between us. How far was he from the branch I was in, how my body needed to be positioned, when I fell on it? Every time I looked down, it seemed that I was higher and higher. I needed to concentrate on what I was doing, eradicate this fear I had of falling down.

It had to be silent, precise, quick and definite. I slowly pulled up my legs, trying to keep my balance, minimising any sound, so that it wouldn't be aware of what I was planning to do, just waiting for the perfect moment. I figured that the best position I could be in, to inflict the greater damage on it, was a foetal position, with my legs crawled up in my chest, concentrating all my weight on a smaller area and hit it with my knees and all my weight behind them, while I was falling down.

So, I did so slowly. I brought my legs up to my chest as much as I could, ignoring the excruciating pain I was felling because of my wound, as slowly as I could, keeping my balance on the tree branch. Keeping my back aligned against the tree trunk, to centre my weight. I grabbed my knees with my hands, pulling them as close to my chest as I could, getting ready for the moment.

It remained in the same position, licking its paws, calm and posed. It was just under me, a few feet away from the trunk of the tree. I saw it pull a sudden move with its head towards the back of its body. It felt something creeping up on its legs, maybe some ants, curious, looking for food, going up its back paw.

It felt uncomfortable, so it began prying on its paw, trying to get them off.

This was the moment! This was it! The window I had been waiting for. It was distracted, lost concentration on me, it had lost its focus. I had to act!

I closed my eyes for a second, gathering strength and courage from inside. I looked down on it, calculated my fall and let go, falling on my side, holding my knees tight against my chest, facing them forward. I didn't make any noise while I fell from the branch.

In my mind, it felt like an eternity. The fall lasted a lifetime of anguish, my life flashed before my eyes in that time, but the memory that dominated everything, was Sarah's smile. So, I hanged on to that, gave myself up to the hope of seeing it again.

Outside my mind, the fall lasted only a second or less, by the time it reacted to its instinct, it was too late. I hit it dead centre on its back with my knees and all my weight behind them. My hands instinctively separated from them, just as I was about to hit down and sprung forward, trying to ease the fall.

I hit it hard, its head was looking up when I plunged on it. My whole body smashed on its back, like one big sledgehammer. I heard a loud crack and I could feel my knees smashing through its body. After that, I bounced off and landed on my side. I must have hit my head too, against something, because I lost conscience for a moment. I ended up rolling on the side of it and it took me a few minutes to open up my eyes again.

I was laying on my back, with my arms and my legs wide open, my head was pulsating and I was hurting all over. My first thought made me react and I turned my head to my right, to where it was supposed to be.

It was just lying there, immobile. I could see its chest moving very slowly and faint. There were no other noises, which to me, indicated it was out.

I began to move my arms and legs, slowly, to make sure they weren't broken. The pain was unbearable, it was all over. My head, my legs, my arms, my back. I slowly began to feel my arms and legs react, I could move them, so first I tried to roll on my side. Every effort to move came at a huge price. It felt as if a thousand daggers were being pronged onto me. Once I was on my side and I could place my hand on the ground, I tried to get up. First I tried to pull my legs up, which hurt like hell, my head was facing it and I remember smelling the dirt under the side of my face. The dust that was still settling down again, after our bodies smashed against the ground and triggered a cloud to rise up around us.

Slowly I pulled myself up, first on my knees and hands. I could feel my knees reacting, to the weight of my body, they were bruised from the fall and the weight made them more prone to the pain they were already in. So I pulled up my good leg and stomped it on the ground, pushed myself up with my hands and assisted with my other leg so to achieve being vertical.

I was still dizzy, but I was able to stand up straight, sort off, waggling. I kept my sight on it though, making sure it wasn't getting up too, but it remained in mobile. I got close to make sure it was down for good. There was blood coming out of its mouth, that was open, but I could tell it was still breathing, with a lot of difficulty. I could hear the sound of the air being dragged into its lungs, struggling.

I felt sad for it. It wasn't my intention to kill it, but I had to protect myself from it. It was me or it.

I could tell it was in pain, it was suffering. My fall must have caused internal damage and that sound it made while trying to breath, was an indication that it would end up suffocating eventually. I couldn't leave it like that, but I couldn't take care of it either. I needed to take care of myself, clean that wound and go back home to Sarah.

I was in pain too, but I was able to walk, limping with my bad leg, so I left it there, to its fate and went on my way. Limping home, as fast as I could. I had lost a lot of blood and I could feel it affecting my whole body. I was weak and I had a lot of trouble concentrating and keeping my eyes open.

I kept looking backwards, afraid that the jaguar would, somehow, come back from it and come after me, angrier than it was before, or maybe some other predator would pick up my scent. That some other animal might sense that I was hurt, an easy pray and come after me.

Paranoia was settling, fuelled by the lack of blood to my brain and my sense of survival. I was also trying to concentrate on navigating through the forest. It was already dark out and that made it harder for me to see my points of reference, the signals that would guide me back home.

I could feel my mind slip away, I was tired, diminished and the pain was too much to bear. I tripped on a rock and fell to the ground face first. I think I lost consciousness for a moment. I just remember dreaming about Sarah, she was smiling at me, calling me, asking me to come back home. The dream kept repeating over and over again.

I was really struggling, I wanted to get up and go home to her, but my body was shutting down slowly. There was no force left in it to comply with what my head was asking it to do. I needed to rest, to gather my strength, but I knew that if I relaxed and let myself go, I would probably never wake up.

I kept telling my eye lids, to open up, my arms to push up and my whole body to react to my commands. I kept hearing Sarah's voice in my head, calling me, pushing me to go.

I took a hard long breath, filled my lungs with air and pushed myself up with everything I had left. Brought my knees up and raised my body up. I was on my knees and know I needed to stand up, so I took another deep breath and brought my good leg up on its foot and pushed upward as strong as I was able to. I placed my hands on the ground to push myself up and I was able to finally stand up, wobbling, struggling to keep my balance, but I was able to.

Once I could plant both feet on the ground and stay straight, I began moving forward. Slowly, breathing as steady as I could, focusing on the road ahead, on putting one foot in front of the other one. I thought I recognised some trees, lining on the opposite side of the plain. I was sure I had seen them before but couldn't recall where I was, my mind was rambling, but I saw it as a good sign. At least I recognised the place.

I kept concentrating on pushing my feet forward and keeping my balance, I instinctively headed towards the line of trees I found so familiar, my heart was pumping whatever was left of blood in my body a little bit harder, fooled by my head into thinking that I was close to home. That I had made it back and I would see Sarah again.

I finally arrived to the spot, right next to the line of trees that looked so familiar to me. I kept going past the line they formed and into the forest behind them. I kept looking up at them, I was sure this was a familiar place, but my mind kept struggling with its thoughts, my heart was racing fast, I was confused as to why. I couldn't see home anywhere near, so why was my heart in such a rush? I kept walking forward, using my hands to push myself between the trees.

I stepped on some branches on the floor, they crackled as I did, breaking as I stepped on them. It was strange that they would be all loose like that, I was roaming through thought, memories that struggled to come out. I had heard that crackling before, I knew I've stepped on something and then it came to me… just a second too late.

I froze, knowing exactly what would happen next. As if I had envisioned it. It just happened so fast.

The hoof that I have attached to the end of the pole, that swung suddenly from behind the bushes, that sprung quickly from the mechanism, that was triggered precisely by a pedal, that was hidden consciously between the twigs on the ground, that I stepped on; thrusted with surgeon like precision into the centre of my stomach, driving through it like knife on butter, penetrating inside of me and thrusting out the other side, sticking out from my back.

I felt it hitting my body, like a hard punch on my stomach. It must had been less than a second and I was pinned to it.

I looked down instinctively, I knew exactly what had happened, but I needed to see it anyway, blood hadn't even began flowing. I could just see the end of the hoof penetrating my body. Everything around me went silent while my brain had this out of body sentiment.

I couldn't believe what had just happened. The hunter had been fooled by one of his own creations. I was still shocked, processing my foolish fallacy, when the pain took over like a slap in the face, sudden, precise, definite.

I was clipped to it, hanging from the end of the pole that held me upright. My legs were unresponsive, I couldn't actually feel them. The pain was radiating up from my stomach, directly to my brain that was overwhelmed with signals, dominated by the deafening sound of silence. As if everything around me had paused to see me, to watch the jester bamboozled over its own creation.

Then, I began hearing it, dripping, one by one, slowly, with a sombre cadence that only grew stronger and faster as I looked down again. Blood was flowing from the edges of the hoof, from around my flesh that embraced it unwillingly.

I could move my arms, so my first reaction was to grab the pole and try to push myself back, away from it. To try and free myself from its grasp. It took all my strength to do so, but I did. The weight of my body helped and it sucked me down to the ground. My body lashed on to it, while a sudden, unmistakable rumble broke the silence that clasped everything around me.

I remember opening up my eyes, looking at the sky above me, listening to the subtle whispering of the wind that roamed the tree tops above, swaying them about, contrasting with the steady brilliance of the stars that punctured the blue void beyond. It was a calming tune, an adagio that played in the background while I steadily bled out on the field.

I knew I was done, hope abandoned me, dripping away with every ounce of blood that left my body. I couldn't feel it. As the blood abandoned my veins and flooded briskly out, so did the life that I had left. Blood rushed up to my mouth and flooded my lungs, which made it impossible to breath. I coughed instinctively, spraying blood into the wind, covering everything around me with the colour of despair.

I was done, I knew I just had a few seconds left in this world and so I would fill them up with the happiest thoughts I could muster. My head got filled with images of Sarah, of her beautiful face, of the smiles that fuelled my happiness, of the taste of her mouth that fed my days and incited my nights, of her smell that elicit heaven in her presence, of her touch that ignited my passion, of her voice that was calling me into a better place.

My eyes filled up with tears, thinking about her. I had failed her, I was leaving her all alone in this world. I was invaded by sadness and sorrow. I would never see her again. My only comfort was that she would be the last image in my mind, the last breath I took, the last beating of my heart.

And so it was, my heart stopped beating, my lungs ceased breathing and even though my eyes were still open darkness took over…death came to pass.

Chapter 14
The Vigil

Darkness invaded everything, I was lost and the vastness that surrounded me was infinite, outright, blunt.

There was no pain, no suffering, no grief. I felt nothing, as if everything was taken away from me, as if I had been emptied, stricken of everything I was. Just an empty vessel roaming in this dark void.

It began after a while, it was faint at first, distant, like an itch you can't pinpoint, that grows slowly, becomes more evident, but it was undeniable. It was there, present, and it kept building up.

I couldn't quite unmask it, couldn't determine what it was, but as it grew, it also disturbed the darkness I was in. Flashes of light began to puncture the void, like stars on a mantle. It grew stronger and more present, surrounding me everywhere, until there was nothing but light, until an image appeared in front of me, clear as day.

I was suspended, looking down at the ground. I could see my body lying on top of the brush, covered in blood, lifeless, my skin was pale white, absent of the fluid that gave it entity. My eyes were still wide open, but they were vapid, not even reflecting the light that shined upon them.

It was sorrow that invaded me, that somehow brought me back to that place. There was something undone, there was an incomplete task that needed to be fulfilled so I could rest In peace. So my soul could travel beyond this patch of earth I was stuck in.

I could feel that affliction taunting me, but didn't understand what it wanted me to do, what the purpose of it was.

You see, for a soul to move forward it has to be detached from everything that bind it to this world. It has to be cleansed of all the memories, good and bad. Renewed, so it can attach itself to a new purpose, to a new life.

When there is an unfinished task, something that prevents it from release. The soul lingers on in this world until the task is fulfilled, until it can be free of attachments. It happens seldomly, but when it does, the whole structure of the life cycle is interrupted, paused for an indefinite period of time, until the task is done.

For this to happen, the event has to be unparalleled. The sentiment has to be so strong that it can't be denied, it can't be ignored and doing so might bring a cataclysm.

I remained suspended, over my body, looking at what was left of myself when something caught my attention, it pulled me like a magnet and in an instant, in the blink of an eye, I was inside the place I use to call home. I was floating over the living room.

I could recognise the room and the things that filled it, but there was no memories of any of it. There was no recollection of the life that brought them here.

Life happens day by day, moment by moment and it is the recollection of everything our minds and our hearts experience that make it entity. We collect things that represent those experiences, to remind us of what we've been through. We surround ourselves with the things that reflect our own personality, that materialise our essence. To gather how transcendent our lives have been, but I had been abolished from recognising any of it. There were no memories left to taunt me.

So, why was I here? What was the reason I was stuck in this earth? Why was I given this task, without any means of completing it?

To me, everything in that room were just…things!

And then I saw her walk in. Hysterical, completely out of her mind. Ranting desperate at the wind.

"Where are you? Why are you doing this to me?"

Pacing back and forth, she would go out of the room and then back in. There was no solace in her intent, just an overwhelming fright that was driving her mad.

"Something bad has happened! I can feel it! Why are you doing this to me?"

She kept ranting on, but it wasn't anger that drove her, it was desperation that piloted her mania. She was worried sick about something…or someone.

I got close to her, so close I could feel her shaking, vibrating in waves across the room. Her eyes were closed while she nodded, breathing heavily, trembling uncontrollably. I stood there wondering what had her so upset, when she opened up her eyes and looked straight at me.

It began as a ripple in her eye, a flake in her iris, that turned into a stain in her cornea and it grew and grew, like ink diluting, it spread around everything, tainting it all with a premonition.

I knew her! Right then, when I looked into her eyes and they saw through me. I felt something, something that brought back memories from when I was still alive. They flooded my head, hundreds of images of her, of that smile that warmed my heart. I began feeling her pain, her desperation took over my calm and I could understand what she was going through.

She was worried sick for someone, something bad was in her mind. She knew this was something terrible, but she was trapped in here. Not knowing what to do, where to go. Not knowing what had happened to her loved one. I could tell her mind was running around, trying to figure out what to do next as time kept passing and her desperation grew stronger while the minutes rushed by. It invaded her, like a disease ramping through her.

She broke contact and pulled back, she felt something too when we locked sight, but she was too confused to recognise it. To desperate to make sense of it. We had made a connection and I had no idea how that could happen. I was just a spirit caught in between worlds, lingering in a space within the living and the dead, but she saw me. Somehow she did.

It somehow made sense, I was the one she was worried for, I knew that much. I mean, my body, or what was left of it. I had seen it laying there, mangled, broken, dead.

Her mind was filled with images of me, of us and it was just logical that she would have dismissed, what we just had, this impossible connection, this link between two opposite dimensions, as one more image of us, in her mind.

I saw her roaming the house, not knowing what to do next. She had been at it since the day before, when I didn't come back from the hunt, as I always did, right before the sun went down. I knew that! Why did I knew that? Those memories were supposed to had been erased, discarded like everything else in my brain, but they were there. I saw an image, a memory of her standing at the door, smiling, running to greet me, embracing me, I could feel her arms around me, holding me and her smell…that intoxicating scent.

How was this possible? I was dead, deprived of everything human. I wasn't supposed to feel or even remember anything, but she was the only thing in my mind. I felt compelled to ease her pain, to give her the peace she needed, but then, the images of my body hit me like a right hook to the face. I couldn't allow her to see me like that. That would break her heart. That wouldn't help her at all.

So, what to do? What could I do? I mean, I was a spirit with no power over this world, no way of talking to her, of letting her know what had happened to me. Or no way of easing her pain. Was I here just to be witness of it, of her discovering what had happened to me? Was this punishment? Punishment for what? For loving her?

There were no answers and no way of knowing the solution to this riddle. I was just stuck looking at her mania arise, without the possibility of easing anything.

She finally sat on the couch, sobbing, defeated. I got close, my instinct was to hold her in my arms, to let her feel me beside her, but? How could I? I just sat next to her. I saw her hand was on top of her knee, it was shaking uncontrollably and something in me reacted. I lifted my hand and placed it on top of hers and the shaking subsided.

She turned to look at her hand, she felt something grasping it, but she couldn't see anything on top. At first she let herself be nurtured by the feeling that gave her calm, that eased her pain, but then, paranoia kicked in.

Why was she feeling something on her hand, why was she sensing something that wasn't there. A presence she couldn't see?

She jumped off the couch, fear took over! She was looking all around, wondering what was happening.

She was disconcerted, scared out of her mind.

"What's happening? Who's there?" she asked over and over again, moving her eyes briskly through the room.

She cornered herself at the end of the room instinctively, pushing herself against the walls, limiting the space between her and whatever was in the room, invading her sanity.

I felt impotence, anger that arose from the fact that I was just a ghost in her world, in her presence. There was nothing I could do to let her know it was me, I was the one she was suffering for. I was only making things worst. How could I make her understand?

I didn't even knew, if I could, what to tell her, how to tell her what had happened, how to make it better. There was no way for me to do that, she would be devastated, left alone in this world. I knew what she would want to do. I knew in my heart that she wouldn't want to go on without me, she wouldn't want to be alone. The pain, the sorrow, the loneliness would be too much to bare.

I couldn't let her do that! I felt frustration take over, I felt powerless and mad. I became increasingly angry as I dwelled on it. The unfairness of it all. I felt it brewing up inside, like a soda pop fizzing inside a bottle. It kept boiling until it couldn't hold it no more and it just blew out. It just exploded in a loud scream.

She couldn't heart it, to her it was just a subtle breeze that blew through the room and nestled in her hair, but as it did it pushed one of the frames on the table, beside the wall and it fell down, it landed on the floor, right next to her. She saw it fall down, without any apparent reason why. It landed face down on the rug.

She stood still for a moment, looking at the frame, scanning the room, making sure there was no one there. Curiosity made her stretch out and grab the frame. She knew which one it was, just by looking at it, but she picked it up anyway and looked at the photo on it. It was a photo of me, smiling, taken way back, at the lab, by Gloria. A souvenir she kept and passed on to me years ago.

She calmed down, looking at it. She was still struggling with her thoughts, she couldn't understand what was going on, but looking at the photo gave her solace and that was exactly what she needed. I could tell that her mind was going over all the possibilities, every scenario that could fill in the blanks, that could explain what was going on, that would reveal my faith to her.

I roamed across the room and sat next to her. I placed my hand on hers, she was still holding the frame, but as she felt this tingling on her hand, she raised it and turned it around, exposing her palm up. I placed my hand on hers, placed my fingers between hers. I knew that she could feel my presence, she could feel a force clinging on to her hand, interlacing her fingers. She closed her eyes and images of me flooded her mind.

When she opened up her eyes, I was looking right into them, as close as I could. Her eyes were roaming around, trying to see beyond her plain, allowing her mind to wonder into the impossible, clinging herself to a radical thought, to a fantasy that exuded love and hope, that defied logic.

"What happened to you? What is this?" she asked almost whispering.

She could sense I was close, close enough to listen to her voice, faint, filled with hurt and sorrow.

She was about to ask something else, but the mere thought of what that meant, made her retract. She closed her eyes back up and sighted as tears rolled down her cheeks. She began breathing heavily, trying to control herself, to calm down.

When she was ready, she opened up her eyes again, slowly.

"Are you dead? Is that what this is?"

She could barely ask the question, barely grasp the thought. She closed her eyes again and took a deep breath. I placed my other hand on top of hers. I wanted to hold her, embrace her. I needed to give her solace, something I was unable to, or I didn't know how.

It was frustrating not being able to master my new condition, to understand how to relate to reality, to make my voice be heard, whispering in her ears, my urge to succour her pain, be felt by her.

I just sat next to her, holding her hand.

"I don't know if I can go on!"

Her mind was running, she was looking for answers, for hope.

"What if you need me? What if you are in some kind of danger? Is that it? You need me to go and look for you, bring you home?" she asked excited.

I was terrified of the thought. If she found my body, what was left of it. By know It could be half eaten by vultures or worst. I was terrified of what she would feel, of what that would do to her.

"No, no! Don't!" I thought, but how would I stop her?

Her eyes were everywhere, she was constructing a possibility, a plan in her mind, a way to find me, to get me home, to keep me alive in her head. Hope had taken over and there was no stopping it.

She stood up, set on her plan. She had decided, in that moment, that she would go and look for me, that she would bring me home. In her head, I was alive, I was in trouble and needed her help. That is what hope does to you, it limits the scope of possibilities and only allows you to see the positive outcome. It narrows your view, but I couldn't allow that to happen. I knew what that would do to her, seeing me like that.

She gathered a few things, she thought she might need and headed for the door. I had to stop her, but how? I was just a ghost in her world, unable to physically act. Just then, I remembered how I was able to push that photo frame, somehow.

I rushed to the door, while I packed all the frustration I felt inside, the worry, the fear I felt of her suffering and I tried to push the door closed with everything I had. I belted a loud scream as I lashed upon the door.

The door slammed shut, just as Sarah was about to walk out through it. She stood still, frozen, paralysed at what had just happened. Only her eyes were moving around, roaming the door and everything around it. Trying to figure it out.

First thing on her mind was that a strong current blew in the room and pushed the door shut, so she looked around at the windows in the room, but they were all closed. There was no air flowing into the room, so that was not a possibility.

She swallowed nervous a couple of times, while a very real chill ran up and down her spine. The thought of me being somehow present around her, the hope that I was in her mind talking to her, the idea that I was standing next to her, became real!

I knew that she was freaking out, that her mind was running around all this terrible thoughts. I could see the terror in her eyes. It was not just the thought of my imminent demise, the idea that I could be dead, but the thought that something might be haunting her, that there could be a presence with her, in that room.

The frame falling over could have been anything, the wind blowing, a small tremor, gravity, but this? The door slamming in front of her like that was no feat. There was a warning behind it, there was something there with her, in her house, telling her something, but what exactly?

Sarah fell down on her knees, she was afraid of what could be, but she didn't feel threatened, there was no evil in her prowess. There was a certain warmth she could feel surrounding her, subtly caressing her skin, warming against her cheek bones. There was something familiar about what she felt.

It wasn't a stranger in her presence, it felt so much closer to home.

"Patrick?" she whispered softly.

"Is that you?" she asked, afraid of the answer.

I kneeled down in front of her, as close to her as the trickle that arouses your hair, that incites your skin to crawl and I kissed her lips with mine. I couldn't resist! It just happened unexpectedly. A force that pulled me close, that incited my desire to melt with her.

She closed her eyes, when she felt a force pressed against her lips. This gentle pressure that folded the verges of her mouth. It was a feeling she couldn't deny. A familiar one that she could recognise.

For a moment I was back with her, while her eyes were closed, she could see me in her mind, she could feel me pressing against her.

But then she opened up her eyes and I was gone. It might have been wishful thinking, it might have been the urge she had to be with me, but I felt it too. Even beyond this threshold, we were meant for each other.

I was invaded by this powerful feeling, by this uncontrollable sadness that maunder my condition. I would never see her again, at least not with my own eyes. I would never love her the way we used to, the way we fused into each other when we made love. It would all evanesce into memory. It would be no more, but most of all, I was deeply saddened by her desolation. I had abandoned her and I had no idea of what that would do to her.

I wanted her to live. I wanted her to go on, she deserved happiness. She deserved to gather light every time she opened up her eyes, to breath the scents of morning with every rest she took in, she deserved it all and I couldn't give it to her anymore.

We weren't afraid of being alone, of the thought of becoming extinct, but that was because we had each other. We didn't need anyone else, as long as we were together, nothing else mattered, but now, she was all alone in this world and I couldn't even imagine how that would feel, what that would do to her.

So, I sat there for days and watched her skip from one stage of grief, to the another. Watched her cry, sleep, wonder. Time just skewed away as she threw herself into depression, into a dark place, but I stood by her side, holding her hand, sharing her pain so the load would lighten.

After a few days, she had overcome every stage and she finally reached acceptance. She had made her peace with the fact that I was not coming back, that something terrible had happened to me and that she would have to face the future on her own.

There was still sadness in her intent, but I could sense peace in her heart.

She still had one last thing to do, before it was all set and done. She needed to find my body, figure out what had happened to me and give it a proper burial, a last goodbye. That was something she needed to do for herself.

She was ready for it, she had accepted my faith but, she needed to know the whole story.

So, she gathered a few things and waited until the sun was up in the sky. She headed for the door, she paused before opening it up, like asking for permission, she knew I was still there, lingering next to her. She pulled the door open and walked through.

Chapter 15
The Toughest Road

I needed to guide her to where my body was. She could have looked for years and never found me. So, I needed to help her. I knew she had to have closure.

It was hard at first to communicate with her. There was just so much I could do to relate where she needed to go, but she was so smart and began noticing the subtle signs I could give her. A branch moving with no apparent reason, a rock that fell on its own, a noise ringing out of place.

She tried to concentrate on them, although her mind was busy with all the memories that flooded her sanity. She couldn't stop thinking about me, about us, about all the things we lived, about all the love we shared. She just lost everything that formed her world, because that was all we had, each other.

So, I had to keep her focused, if we were going to get there and back, before dark. We couldn't waste a lot of time in reminisce. There would be lots of time for that later.

I knew it was the hardest thing she had ever done, I could see the weight of the world on her shoulders. The struggle just to put one foot in front of the other, it was too much of a burden for her to carry and then there was the anticipation that held her back. This was something she knew she had to go through, she had to know, but that didn't take away the fear of realising the facts, of finding my body, of that dreadful truth materialising in front of her.

I had to keep her focused, have her concentrate on the task at hand, just to keep her from going down a hole I knew she wouldn't be able to pull out of.

It was too much burden to ask anyone, she had every right to lose her mind. It would have been the easy way out. Just to let herself get lost in her memories, pretend that none of this was happening.

I couldn't allow that to happen, she deserved to live life and not to inhabit an empty vessel filled with images of the past, stuck in time, re living the same moments again and again without any sense of present and future. I didn't want that for her, it wasn't right, somehow I knew that much. I knew that was the reason I was held back, the reason I was put in here. That was what I needed to do, to be able to move on.

To guide her through the darkness and made sure she was able to move on, to live. She had a bigger task at hand. She was the last human alive in this world.

It was a lot to put on her shoulders, a lot of responsibility for anyone to bare, but this was the hand she was dealt and I was responsible for that. It was never something I wanted, It just happened, but I was responsible just the same. That was my task, to see her pull through.

So, we walked through the woods, as I guided her towards my body.

I was fearful of what she would find, once we got there. My body had been exposed for a few days now and it was very likely that it had been consumed by all types of creatures. It was just nature doing its beading.

I just knew this would be shocking for her, it would be for anyone that saw a gruesome scene like the one we would find, but for her, seeing the one she loved like that, would be even harder. I just hoped that wouldn't haunt her.

It was almost noon when we reached the plain where my body was at, right under the line of trees in the far end. I signalled the way and she walked through the field towards the place where my body laid. She paused several times before reaching the line of trees beyond the plain. She was afraid of what she would find. She needed to prepare herself for it, she needed to gather her strength.

We got to the place where she could see my silhouette from the distance. My body was laying over some brush, right next to a group of trees that towered above it. She stood there for a while confronting her fears.

"I don't think I can do this! I can't!" she said to herself, time and time again.

Her breathing was erratic, her heart was jumping out of her chest and her whole body was trembling uncontrollably. She felt this terrible anguish taking over. She couldn't stand, her legs gave up and she plummeted to the ground. She fell down on her knees until she lost consciousness and her whole body dropped to the ground.

I rushed to where she was just to see her fall. I couldn't hold her to ease her fall, I just watched her as she fell down.

She had been so brave, coming this far. This wouldn't be easy.

She was in and out of consciousness for a few minutes. Mumbling non coherent words. All I could understand was my name, repeated over and over again. I could tell that she was thinking about me, rambling on, trying to erase what was actually happening and replacing it with a happier thought.

She finally opened up her eyes and slowly regain consciousness, she pushed herself up and sat down for a moment. Her sight bolted to the ground, she was reluctant to look up and see what she dreaded. She tried to control her breathing, she didn't want to have another episode. So she took long breaths, trying to control her heart beat from going over. Slowly, she raised her sight to look at where my body was.

I had fallen back on a shrub that nestled my body, so all she could see from where she was, was the shape of it, moulded into the brush and the blood, dried up, tarnishing the soil under it, all around, a big blood stain that marked the spot.

At that moment, she realised her worst nightmare was true. There was no way I was alive after that, after so much blood evaded my body. She knew she was looking at en empty shell, a lifeless piece of me laying there.

It came like a flood, it just burst out of her eyes, this unstoppable river of grief that poured out of her body, that moaned repeatedly out of her being, a moan that turned into a scream that exploded loudly, a scream that echoed around the world, a pronouncement so poignant that it shamed the sun, that dimmed abashed at her sorrow.

She cried and cried until her eyes were dry, until the shivers scattered and her breathing eased down to a pulp. There was no calm in her heart, it was just resignation that took over. She stood up slowly and pace by pace she got close. She got as close as she could.

I had fallen down on some deciduous shrubs that surrounded my trap, thorn filled bushes that detoured the predators away from their pray and in my case, kept the vermin from eating on my flesh, so my body was in better condition that I expected.

She saw it from the edge of the brush, the thorns were picking her feet and her legs but she didn't seem to notice, her body couldn't feel anything other than the pain of loss, the sadness that took over her whole world.

She roamed my body and saw the mangled flesh that was left. The hole in my abdomen and the shreds my leg was in. She turned to look at the contraption I had created and that had ultimately cost me my life. She nodded with her head because she knew, at that moment, what had happened.

My eyes were closed and my face was pale, absent of any sign of life. The ground beneath me was soiled with my blood, that had abandoned my body down to the last drop. She got close to me and caressed my face with the same tenderness she always had. Her eyes were flooded with tears she couldn't control, they ran down her cheeks and plunged from her face down to the ground.

I could see the thorns picking her flesh on her arms and her legs, but she didn't mind. It was as though she couldn't feel them thrusting in on her.

She grabbed my head and lifted it up, grabbed my arm and placed hers under it, embracing my body. She pulled me out of the shrubs and laid me on the ground next to them.

She looked at my body, sobbing quietly. The pain she felt was gaping, it was coming directly from her chest that could barely contain her heart's beating. One after another it pounded on it, like a wounded critter begging for mercy. The blood travelled through every corner of her body, pushed by her heart, smiting every part of it, pulsating relentlessly on every ambit.

Her hands quivered as she caressed my face. She couldn't process what was going on entirely. It felt like a nightmare and she couldn't wake up. My body was laying lifeless next to her. She could scarcely see my mangled corpse in between the blood soaked garments that covered it, her eyes were too watery to focus properly, but she couldn't take them off.

She sat there for a long time, keeping me company. Hoping to wake up, but she never did. She just sat there dwelling on her thoughts, her happy memories of us.

Eventually the weight of reality kicked in and she began processing what had happened. She was all alone!

Her heart slowed down and a numbing cold possessed her heart and her body. She began shivering, proof that she was still alive. Her senses awoken from the catharsis they were in and in a rush of feelings, her whole body ached.

She felt each and every poke of the thorns that penetrated her skin, the terrible heart ache that incited her and the awful hangover that the bolt of adrenaline, that flushed through her system, left behind.

At that moment, her only thought, her only wish, was to die. She was hoping, with all of her heart, that her life would end. Right there, where mine did. She had lost all the will to survive.

"What is the point?" she kept asking herself.

"I don't want to go on without you!" she said.

She lift up her hand and stroke her chest several times. She wanted to hit the one thing that kept her alive, shock it out of existence. She was hoping her heart would stop and allow her to just fade away into the same place I was in. She wanted to follow me, even in death, but her heart wouldn't stop. It kept beating relentlessly, without skipping a beat. It wouldn't concede to her wishes. It wouldn't violate her destiny that forced here to stay in this world.

She was disappointed. Morbid thoughts invaded her head. She thought of a hundred ways she could end her life right there. She was tired, exhausted and torn.

Terrible plans brewed up in her brain. None of them included logic, none of them saw her moving forward. It wasn't even a possibility that she conceded. She wanted to die, she wanted to leave this place and go with me to wherever it was I was going.

I couldn't allow her to do that, she needed to live for as long as she could. Death wasn't the answer, I knew that much, it was just another step and she wasn't ready for it. This world needed to keep her around a little bit longer.

She took another look at me, at my body lying there. She couldn't believe what was happening, that I was dead. It wouldn't settle in her heart, there were too many memories that superimposed over this one. This wouldn't be the last image of me in her head, nestled in her heart. Her mind had decided so, it would block this one out, it would leave it lurking in her worst nightmare.

She sat there for a long time, trying to grasp sanity, to come back to a reality she despised, a reality she neglected. She was torn between her morbid thoughts and the fact that she was alive, that her heart wouldn't stop beating, the fact that she needed to go on.

Eventually she began to think about what she needed to do. She couldn't stay there any longer, soon night would take over and she would be exposed in the darkness all by herself and her instinct wouldn't allow her to go that way. Hunted by predators.

So, she began devising ways to get me back home. She couldn't carry me back and she couldn't leave me there, or she wouldn't. She had no tools to try and build something to carry me with.

She made several attempts at moving my body. She tried carrying me on her back, but even thought my body was drained of all the blood, it was still too heavy for her to carry on her own. She tried dragging me by my feet, but it was an impossible task, my body kept tangling on anything on the way.

So, she knew it would be impossible. She would have to bury me there, next to the place where I had passed. It was the only logical thing to do. She didn't wanted my body to be eaten, butchered by animals and vermin and she couldn't get me home, and even if she could, it would be only to bury me there.

She turned to look at the valley she was in, the sun was high up in the sky, the void above was painted in a beautiful blue, just sparkled with a few white clouds that extended from one edge to the other. The line of trees in the distance gave way to the mountains in the backdrop and the green pastures that waved towards them seemed like an ocean, moving evenly with the blow of the wind. There was peace about it, a peace that settle her heart. There was something heavenly about it.

She turned around and saw a clearing on the valley, just beside a small formation of rocks that stood proud in the middle of that ocean of green. The clearing was a patch of earth that remained virgin. Somehow the soil there resisted to allow the green mantle to take over.

"That is the perfect place. You would love it, it's the only space that has your name written all over it," Sarah said as she smiled.

She dragged me there and placed my body on the side of the clearing. She began digging a hole with her hands, the soil was loose enough that she was able to dig it deep enough for my body to fit. Then she placed it inside and sat down just beside and stared at it for a while.

She was conflicted about what she needed to do. It was a simple task, to cover me with dirt, bury my body in that place, but it turned out to be much harder than it sounds. She was having trouble with letting go, with the thought of disposing of it.

It's that thought that lingers in our brain, the possibility of some alternate reality where life goes on as it was before. That paradox of life and death, where death is definite and life so fleeting, That is the one that sometimes becomes hard to accept. We clinch on the memories of life, just to be forgotten eventually, dissolved in the timeless quarry of death.

That is what held her down, she was reluctant to let go. She didn't want to forget, to bury my body and have me forgotten. She just sat there, defeated, tired, depleted. Her heart was broken in a million pieces and her body was exhausted.

All she could do was stare and hope, hope that I would somehow wake up from my slumber and everything would be left in the past, all the pain would end and life would go on with me by her side. That was the wish she was longing for, the fantasy she was yearning.

The sun was going down on the horizon, the day was coming to an end and she had a few hours left of light. I was beginning to worry, because she had a long way to get back home. She couldn't stay out here by herself, but maybe that was exactly what she wanted, to stay there and wait for her faith to take her.

I needed to incite her to move, to finish what she started and get back home. So I tried to move some of the sod that was laid next to the hole where my body was in, push it inside to fill the hole, cover my body with it, but I just managed to push a little that stumbled over the edge and fell over, it wasn't much but it was enough to get her attention.

She looked at it falling into the hole and wondered why, she looked around curious, so I pushed some more, I pushed as hard as I could. That effort vibrated, like ripples on water, and the sod began to fall in, as if it was its will to fill back the hole she had made, as if my body wanted to be buried.

She knew I was still there and understood what I wanted her to do. She stood up and pushed the rest of it inside, covering my body. She grabbed some stones from the outcrop next to her and covered the hole until it was done.

She fell down on her knees in front of my grave, she closed her eyes and rested for a moment. It had been the longest day of her life, an endless affair that had stolen everything from her. She was drained physically and emotionally, but she needed to get back home. She knew that this wasn't a place she could stay, but her body was shutting down.

I got close to her, try grabbing her hands and pulling her up. She could feel my presence, so she leaned on me, got up on her feet and began walking back. As she did, she turned to look at the grave, one last time. Her head just dropped in shame, in sorrow as she stumbled away.

I held her hand as she walked and finally crawled back home. It was already dark when she got there. She was filthy, broken and depleted as she made it through the door, she just fell on the floor and passed out. I looked back at the door, it was opened and I gathered all my strength and pushed it close.

I stayed there, watching over her as she slept. A day went by and she didn't move an inch, her body was spread out on the floor the same way it did when she dropped on it over a day ago. Her chest was moving steadily, so I knew she was breathing, at least I was certain that she was ok.

I spent the time looking at her, looking at this creature that was the source of my biding in this world. Her whole body was filled with reminisce of what just happened. Her hair was sodded with dirt and sweat, her fingernails clogged with the dirt that filled my grave, broken and beaten; her clothes soaked and ripped; her knees and hands scrapped and bleeding and her face drenched with the sod that now buried my body and smeared with a thousand tears that never stopped flowing.

I felt this uncontrollable urge to hold her, to help ease her pain but I couldn't. It was not in my nature anymore, I was just a fleeting presence in her world. I was a ghost haunting her.

I couldn't do anything but wait, let time go by and hope that she would awake from it. That she would open up her eyes and realise, she was home.

It took another day for her body to recover and, after two days, she finally opened up her eyes. She tried to move but her whole body was aching like it never did before. She could only moan as pain distracted her from anything else. She just rolled over on her back as her eyes were struggling to stay open and her mind tried to recoup the memories that roamed her head. She was confused, I could tell by the way her head was twisting, blunted by all the signals invading it, sharp thrusts of pain that rushed to her brain as she tried to move her arms, her legs, her torso that was glued to the floor, unable to progress.

Her senses began to function again slowly, she first tasted, whatever seized her mouth, it was a foul taste that she rejected, spitting out as she roamed her mouth with her tongue, trying to clear her palate. She turned abruptly to her side to spit some more, as her arm supported her body, but the pain made her go back down. Her mouth was dry and bitter as she coughed a few times. The pain was unbearable as her chest was struggling to comply with her will to breath. Everything was hurting, every inch of her being was sending signals to her brain, freaking out.

She pulled up her arms as far as she could and saw them filled with dirt, filthy and she shrugged and closed her eyes back again. She needed a bath urgently, but the thought of her walking all the way to the waterfall was just too much.

She laid there for a while longer, until her sense of self was stronger than the pain that controlled her will. She tumbled around, got on her knees and finally pushed her way up on her feet. She stood there wobbling, trying to catch her bearings, feeling a little bit dizzy as she opened up her eyes.

She looked around, she was home and a sense of relief filled her lungs. She took a deep breath and as she was releasing the air, she felt a chill roam her body. Everything in there reminded her of us, of me. She bowed her head as her heartbeat accelerated slowly. She wanted to control it, so she took a few deep breaths to try and calm herself down.

It wouldn't be productive to dwell on the facts that she already knew, she had to try to move on little by little. There'll be a lot more crying, she would always miss my presence around her, but she knew that I would like her to go on. To live, whatever time she had left in this place.

Hunger was the last thing on her mind, her stomach didn't agree with it though, it began to rumble as soon as she got on her feet, but she felt this urge to clean herself up first, so she slowly walked outside the house and headed for the waterfall. She grabbed some new clothes on her way out the house and painfully made her way around the lake.

Every step was like a bolt of lightning down her spine, but with every one she learned to live with it and it gave her the strength she needed to move forward. She reached the waterfall, took her dirty clothes off and threw them a side, slowly got into the waterfall.

At first it was all pain as the water hit her body, cleansing it from all the filth that embalmed her, but as her muscles got pounded the feeling became more bearable. She took the bar of soap and began to scrub her arms, her legs, her hair, her whole body until the last trace of dirt was off.

She laid against the rocks under the waterfall and enjoyed the feeling for a while, she deserved that after all that she had been through. Memories of us still commanded her thoughts, they would never go away. How could they? She kept thinking that those memories could drive her mad, but they could also be the source of her happiness moving on, if she could just get passed this terrible pain she felt that had a hold of her heart and didn't want to let go.

She finished washing off and her nose filled up with the smell of lavender from the soap, she loved that smell. She looked down on the bar of soap, the one that I had made for her. She knew then that I would be present around her all the time, in the little things I did for her, in the little details that formed her world. The stuff I did for her, and the things she did for me too. The love between us would never go away and she didn't wanted it too.

She would have to miss having me around, but I would never leave her side. I would always be present.

She was smiling as she dressed back up and walked back to the house. Our home, that placed that we built up with our own hands, it looked somehow different then, she noticed things that had blended into habit, but now they were sticking out again, as they had done at the beginning when they had prominence.

The beams of wood that formed the structure, the bindings that held them together, the carvings just beside the entrance door, the rambling of the wood on the floor that screeched as she walked on, the way the light sneaked in through openings on the ceiling. It was our place and it will be there to keep her company through it all.

She laid on the bed and sighted, she felt a lot better, the healing process had begun. She felt peace take over, calm embraced her. Her body was still tired, sore and fragile.

She moved around on the bed until she found a comfortable position and she fell asleep again.

I embraced her while she was laying there, she looked so beautiful. I wanted to remember her, keep her tattooed in my mind.

Chapter 16
The Last Epitaph

I stayed for as long as I was able too, which wasn't much. I had fulfilled my mission, the one thing I had to do and now it was time to move on. I could feel it pulling me, dragging me from her side.

It was inevitable, it was the way and there was nothing I could do to avoid it. I just felt attached to her, I was having trouble leaving, partly because I knew she would be left all alone in this world and part because I wanted to hang on to her. I knew I would forget about her. Those memories would be erased so that I could move on.

It's just the way it has to be; if you were able to hang on to those feelings, to those memories, you would never truly leave this earth. There would always be a part of you stuck in here, clinging to reminisce.

Sarah was trying to move on from losing me, from the thought of being all alone, but all she hoped for was for the nights to last longer, for the days to end so she could plunged into her dreams where she could see me, where she could hang on to happiness, as she knew it.

She barely ate, she was just struggling and I couldn't blame her. Time was all she had to bend to her will, it was all she could control. Her eyelids were heavy all the time and the bed became her shrine. Depression took over, it was like a heavy blanket that she wore all the time.

She had no one to answer to and no one to tell her otherwise, hope had left her body and there was nothing to hang on to.

So, leaving was hard for me. It was the hardest thing I've ever had to do. The guilt began to consume me and that was exactly why I couldn't stay. I was between worlds, still hanging on to this one, the one I wasn't part of anymore. My body was dead and buried and I was just a spectre lingering.

I had to say goodbye, so I got close, as close as I could, one afternoon while she was laying on the bed, hoping that her eyes would close and darkness would take over. She was thinking of nothing, trying to avoid the reasoning, hoping to dismiss thinking about the present and the future, clinging to the past, to her memories of us.

She looked pale and thin, but her beauty persisted over everything else. Her hair was dangling over her face, restricting the light that wanted to reveal her grace. I could only see her right eye shining through, reflecting the beams of light that plunged upon her face and the point of her nose that stuck out, like a periscope, feeding her air.

I wanted to see her, one last time. So I pushed her hair off her face as I struck my finger across her forehead. She reacted to it, not scared, but surprised to know I was still there, biding around her.

"Patrick?" she asked in a subtle voice.

So I waved my fingers on her forehead again. She closed her eyes imagining my hand caressing her face.

"I'm afraid! What will happen to me?" she asked, as if I knew the answer.

I knew in my heart that she would be ok, she was strong and I knew life would give her a chance. She was the last one of our kind, hanging on to a dream that began thousands of years ago and now, it seemed, was on the twilight, near the end, but not yet.

I got close and pressed my lips against hers. Her eyes were still closed and I could feel her lips on mine and I knew she felt mine on hers too.

I had no answer to her question, she would have to find that on her own, all I had was love for her.

I left that evening, she was asleep, deep in her dreams, where I knew she would be safe.

The sun would rise again for her the next morning and life would go on for as long as destiny wanted her to stick around. Days and nights got confused inside her head for a while, her eye lids remained shut so light wouldn't disturb her grief, but eventually, the other parts of her being that didn't answer to her will pushed her out of bed.

It made her realise that she wouldn't be able to stay hidden forever, that life was still happening, even without her participating and that even the worst of things pass.

So, she stood up unwillingly and kept living. She ate, she went to the waterfall and cleansed herself, she made the bed and went out to get food and she thought a lot, mostly about nothing. It was just one sombre thought after another one. She looked at the sun rising up in the morning, she listened to the birds chirping at dawn, announcing the break of a new day, she would feel the water falling over her body, massaging her weakened figure, but nothing made her smile.

There was no reason for her to. Happiness was nowhere to be found inside her gloom. Everything was pale in her sight, absent of colour, of the sparkle that makes it all brighter. It would take her a while to overcome this affliction that had a grip on her.

And her smile, that beautiful manifestation of hope, of love, of happiness, that prowess of beauty that adorned her whole self would have to languish, as her memories would, in a safe place within her heart.

One day she was cleaning when she came across a piece of paper I had written for her. She had asked me to translate some of the epitaphs we saw at the cemetery, the one where we had found Gloria's family buried.

She grabbed the paper and read it, her eyes filled up with tears as she did. Memories of that day invaded her senses and sorrow flowed like a river from her eyes. She remembered it so vividly that she was transported for a moment in time, back to that precise instant. She could see me writing the translation down, she could see me smiling as I did, it made me happy to do anything she asked me, to fulfil her most insignificant desire and as I did, smile in her memory, she couldn't help it but obliged and there it was.

After so much sorrow, amongst so many tears, even through so much pain, her smile shined. It was in response to mine, but isn't that what a smile is? A reaction to a feeling deep inside, a simple gesture that beholds so much it can't be contained and it shows naturally, without us having to command it, it shows out of nowhere. So it did, after all this time, being hidden, tucked away somewhere in her heart.

It faded away slowly, as if she would be ashamed of smiling, but it remained in her mind, it sparked a thought, a task she had devised. Something she wanted to do for me and that gave her purpose, gave her a glimpse of hope in the future, the near future, but it was a step forward and everything she needed to move ahead, was a first step.

She wanted to do an epitaph for me, to lay some words about me, a promulgation of sorts, so that I never turned into an empty grave, just a pile of rocks covering a car case, guarding a desolate hole, so that my life could be told, so that anyone, if any, who stumbled upon my grave knew who lied there. A few words to define my character, my passing in this world. A reminder of who I was and the mark I left on the people I loved.

It became her purpose, a reason to persist, to write those vocables, to resume everything I meant to her in a few words. It might seem like an easy task, but words are zealous, they require honesty, fervour, passion, clarity and, most of all, bravery. They can express everything you hold inside, every little burst of emotion that fills your soul, or they can say nothing, be blunt. They are instruments for communicating our thoughts, for transmitting our feelings and they can be the most effective way, if you know how to use them.

So, Sarah set off on her task. She wanted to write my epitaph, she wanted to express what I was for her, so that it would remain there for anyone to see, to read and by doing so, they would know who I was and what legacy I left in this world. It didn't matter that no one would actually read it but her, she was thinking of the possibility, it was a wish for the future, a hope that she wouldn't be the last, that somehow our race could survive, could persist and move on.

She first had to find the words to say, so she sat down every day to write, to try to convey what was on her heart, on her mind, inside her memories of me, of us and that made her feelings burst. She laughed, she cried, she even got mad at me, time and time again, but through it all words flowed, they were ripped from the memories, like grapes from a vine, she had to picked them out, squeeze them into a paragraph that expressed the way she felt about me.

It was a labour of love and it didn't come out in one day, it took her a while to finish it, to polish it as you would do with a gem, with the most precious thing you possess.

When she was done, certain of what she had put down into words, she searched for the perfect vessel to cast it in. Something that would withstand the test of time, that would hold, what she had written, jealously and would keep it for ever.

She searched around our place, hoping to find the right thing, it took her a while to find it. She wasn't sure what she was looking for, but somehow she knew she would know when she found it. Something inside her would let her know.

It was a Saturday night, during a storm, she was just lying down on the couch in the living room when she saw a flash of light illuminate her space. She was startled by the sudden light and then she heard a loud bang. Louder than anything she had heard before. She reached up and covered her ears with her hands. The strenuous noise was followed by a serious of deafening sounds.

She was afraid for a moment, thinking that it was a cataclysmic event, but after a few seconds, the noise subsided and only the sound of the rain pouring down remained. She got up and walked to the door, stepped outside, but stayed under the porch by the entrance to the house.

Just a few feet away, she could see the rubble that was left. One of the biggest and most beautiful trees that had stood proud and strong in front of our home had been struck by lightning. It had been split in half and the mighty foliage that adorned its top was scattered all over. It seemed that it had exploded into a million pieces.

There were even some leaves still attached to portions of twigs that were thrown away in the process, all over the porch, at her feet, covering the floor she was stepping on. Sarah reached down and grabbed one, brought it up into the light to see it up close. It seemed to be untouched, like it was just ripped out of the branch it was hanging on to and thrown across the field and on to the floor.

It was an oak tree that stood there for a thousand years, born in the wild, attracted by the beauty of the waterfall that provided constant irrigation to its roots. Surrounded by a grove of different types of trees that formed a line that surrounded the field in front of our home.

She stood there looking at it, fallen, as if it were a lost soldier that stood its ground until it was time to pass. She took the branch inside and placed it on the table, next to our bed.

That night it would sleep under her protection, tomorrow would be a new day.

The following morning the sun sneaked through the crevices illuminating the room, kissing her cheeks with its warming touch. As soon as Sarah opened up her eyes, she went outside to oversee the damage that was left out in the night.

The trunk was split open, right in the middle, as if it had been cut intentionally by a sharp object. She made her way through the debris that got thicker as she got closer. When she finally got to where the trunk was, she saw a perfectly cut surface on the inside of the trunk, slightly burned, but flawlessly finished.

In her mind, she pictured a section of it and the words she had written appeared right in front of her eyes, carved into this piece of wood. It was a sign; she was sure this would be the one. She devised a way to cut that piece and carve the words into it. It took her a lot of effort and time, but she had them both; her will to see this to the end gave her the persistence she needed to get it done.

She cleaned up the debris until everything was cleared up. She cut down part of the trunk and left the rest standing as a reminder of what had happened and after a few weeks of work, the epitaph was finally done.

She had carved the words she'd written on to the wood with so much love, with so much patience. Every day she would work on it, carve another letter, another word, until it was all done. The memories of our time together flowed as she carved each one, it became a catharsis of sorts, each letter carved became an emblem. She had collected all her memories and cast them onto the wood.

She walked to the site where she had buried my body over a month ago; it wasn't an easy task. She had not been there in all this time. She had avoided going, trying to ignore it, the pain it would bring, but she needed to give me this gift. This gesture that sealed our story, that gave her closure and allowed me to rest in peace.

She nailed the epitaph on to a large stake, big enough to hold it in place. So that it will remain there until time would embrace it.

She placed the epitaph at the head of my grave and sat there for a long time, just keeping me company, remembering every single memory she had of our time together, those feelings that she kept in her heart and that would flow through her veins until the day she died and finally join me again.

She placed flowers beside it, moistened the soil that covered my body with tears and kissed me goodbye.

She would come every Sunday to see me, she would bring me flowers, it was her way of letting me know that I was still alive in her memory, inside her heart.

Loneliness was the hardest thing that she would have to endure, she tried to fill the void with the memories, the images she kept alive in her mind. She kept busy making sure everything in the house was kept neat, tidy and clean. It was a coping mechanism not to go in sane.

She had these long conversations with me, words that just slipped out of her mouth. She went on and on, telling me about her day and the little details that she kept for me. In her mind, I never left, I was right there beside her.

A few years had gone by and her constant visits were the only thing that remained unfettered. The one thing that filled her time with hope, the thought of feeling close to me. It was her way of hanging on to the love that kept her alive.

She had this constant that guided her through the darkness, that signalled to her North Star, that gave her peace when she needed comfort. She would sit next to my grave and read my epitaph, the one that she had written, those words that poured from the very deep of her soul.

It was her way of honouring my memory and keeping me alive in her heart.

That day everything around her was in harmony, the sun was hanging on low in the horizon, prolonging the moment for her. The wind was blowing softly across the plain and the trees would bow in harmony to the gusts that commanded them. The world was in harmony with nature, embracing her with the beauty of colour, of warmth.

She kneeled gently and placed her hand on top of the pile of rocks that sealed my grave. She lifted up her eyes to see my epitaph and, as she had done so many times, she read the words carved on the piece of wood, the words she had written, the ones that flowed from her soul, as if they were new, as if this would be the first time she did.

"Here lies the last human being.

The last soul in search of paradise.

He defined what a Man should be:

Kind, loving, caring, strong, gentle, compassionate.

He made this a better world.

He will be missed, remembered and cherished.

There is good to be found in human character.

He was proof of that, he was the essence of it.

Beloved man, partner, friend, husband and father."

Her eyes filled up with tears every time she read it again and again. Her heart would never stop bleeding for me, for us.

It was hard to get up, the grief was too heavy and diminished her will to go on. You could see it in her face, pulling her down, squeezing every ounce of sadness from her heart that yearned the past, the one thing she couldn't have.

Her eyes were fixated on my grave, on the words written on my epitaph, as they concentrated on the last one, "Father", that always filled her soul with hope. That word represented everything we were conceived to be. It finally became real, after all the excruciating pain, the loss. Our love had made it possible. Or maybe, being too close to dying had switched something in her. The Universe giving humanity a last chance, a new hope of making it right this time.

A small hand came into view, offering itself; she looked at it and raised her hand to meet it. Another one showed up on the other side; as she turned to see it, she grabbed it with her other hand. She stood up and saw the most beautiful sight. Her twins, product of her love for me, product of her will to live, to persist. They will be the beginning of a new dawn. The start of a new chapter for humanity. She would never be alone…

"And God said, go and multiply…"

THE END

Printed in the USA
CPSIA information can be obtained
at www.ICGtesting.com
LVHW010821260124
769834LV00001B/50